Common
Lives
By: Jae

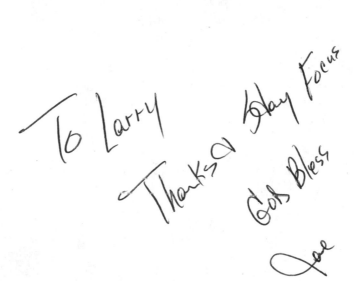

To Larry
Thanks Stay Focus
God Bless

Jae

Published by: Jae
Cover Art by: Alvin D. Pettit Jr.
Cover Design by: Ty Goode & Triflava
Publishing Consultant: Marlene Ricketts

ISBN: 978-0-9769335-4-0

First printing

All Thanks to God...

How Great is our God

Sing with me

How Great is our God

And all we'll see

Is how Great is our God...

Dedication...

To my daddy Jerome McCardell

My mother Rosie and especially my Bunny (Blair)

Acknowledgements...

Although it's been a long time coming, Common Lives would not have been possible without the support from Hayden and Ovetta Moore. The many pre-readers and my father (Jerome), God bless you for the time spent. And to all of my dear friends for their love, lasting patience, which gave my life meaning and endurance.

Thank You!

Preface

Perhaps the saying is true... "You really do reap what you sow." But, how does that work in friendship? It is suggested to "do unto others as you would have them do unto you." But, I dare you... just this once. Remove that halo from your head and recall the time when you did the unthinkable to the very one you loved. Was it so easily forgiven or did they ever discover you were the true culprit of the wrong doing. More than that, did they ever realize that a "wrong" had even occurred? humm... something to think about...

Now – before we begin, let's go back in time approximately 17 years ago when four young girls, somewhat fresh in college pledged to be friends until the end. My question is... the end of what? Well, it was the night before Spring break was to begin, April 17, 1987. Now since their friendship was in its infancy stage, Meagan, Waverly, Sidney and Dominique decided to venture out to do something different by not spending the Spring break with their families. Instead, they journeyed to Meagan's parent's summer home in "Cape Cod."

Waverly, who was the oldest of the four, was up to her neck with a toddler, a new husband of six months and final exams to pass to ensure graduation. Meagan and Dominique were nearing the end of their junior year, both dreading moving on to senior year... While Sidney was simply loving life as a freshman would – doing who and whatever she pleased. So, with efforts to try and ease the frustrations of life, Meagan suggested to her new friends that they spend the Spring break together. Something about getting to know each other better... And with very little money available, driving there was imperative. Little did they know, it would pour down raining for most of the drive up as well as the entire week spent. Reluctant to turn back, they decided to stay and make the most of it.

From scrabble to charades, from ghosts stories to what was thought to be their life stories, these girls exchanged intimate tales until ultimately Sidney suggested that they take their friendship a step further and become "blood" sisters. I believe the thought occurred to Sidney after she'd drowned her third "Lowenbrau" which repeatedly forced her to the bathroom. On one of her trips, being the "oh so nosey" Sidney Sharpe, she was snooping in the medicine cabinet and noticed a straight razor glistening as the light from the swinging ceiling lamp moved slightly back and forth.

This is perfect, she thought while cutting her forefinger, frowning at the blood as it trickled down her finger into the palm of the hand. But, by the time the pain caught up to her brain, she was moaning loud enough for the others to hear her. They reasonably assumed she was on the commode and figured her stomach was a bit upset from all of the pizza and beer she devoured. So, they all just looked at each other, shaking their heads in total agreement and continued on with their conversation. Needless to say, they were quite surprised when Sidney returned to the room bleeding and smirking simultaneously...

Meagan was the first to comment by asking Sidney, "What in the devil have you done to yourself?" Sidney, trying hard to contain her laughter, went on to explain that she thought it was time they moved their friendship to the next level by becoming blood sisters and that the devil had nothing to do with it. She went on to say that every girl should have a blood sister and how lucky they were to have three. Disagreeing, Waverly added that perhaps every girl should have a blood sister, but Sidney was not going to be hers... Now of course Dominique was all for it and somehow quickly persuaded Meagan to go along. But, by the time they looked to Waverly, she needed a few more beers and a cigarette to get up the nerve to have her finger sliced.

*Well, **that** I suppose was the beginning of not only an unusual getaway retreat for four, but also the beginning of unconditional love and friendship among them. Well – there was ONE condition... They all had to commit to support each other NO MATTER WHAT! And that is precisely how these girls lived the next decade and then some... together. "All for one and one for all." Now I am not suggesting that the years were hardly easy. But, somehow always remembering their commitment to believe in one another, using all of the time spent as a foundation, it made their individual problems seem more like lessons than trauma. So – where do we begin?... "In the Middle"*

Chapter One

In the Middle

"Okay, take a deep breath. Now – slowly blow it out. Good Girl. Now breathe. Okay, okay, now tell yourself – you can do this. You've been here before. Okay, maybe too many times. But that first day back is always humiliating. And what if I really don't want to be here," *Sidney said to herself as she closed her eyes then pressed the fast forward button in her head.*

"The room was crowded and yes, overly lit. As I entered, always – always from the rear door, I tried opening it slowly hoping this time it would not squeak. Somehow though, it never failed – the door made that irritating sound causing the few who were not really focused on the Speaker to notice that I was not only late, but realized it's been a while since they'd seen me. And, if that wasn't enough, it almost seemed as if one could call this a "Smoking Cessation" meeting instead of an "Alcoholics Anonymous" meeting. Two out of three were exhaling tobacco while the other third fanned the clouds of smoke. Then we must not forget about the so-called flavored watered down coffee. How does one ruin instant coffee? Last, but certainly not least, they really expect me to tell a room full of strangers exactly what's bothering me most – my innermost darkest secrets. Personally, I would rather watch Lifetime."

So, Sidney opened her eyes, blew off those preconceived thoughts of why she wasn't thrilled about the idea of returning to the group and said,

"I know... I'm running out of bright ideas. I have to change my stinking thinking. My justifications for my behavior and my reactions to what I believe are *my* reality – it's not sitting well with me anymore. I'm running out of time. I can't be late. Let me get this last puff in. Look at me. There was a time when I never smoked in my car. Fuck it! What time is it anyway? Quarter till eight. Shit! – you *would* ring now. Well I'll just turn you off. And where are you – Mr. Pager? You'll have to get turned off too. No time for conversation. I'll have to check my messages later. That's why we have machines. Besides, I've got to go."

Sidney then rushed off to the dreaded meeting.

Meanwhile, on the other side of town, the clock still ticks...

"Oh God!" shouts Meagan. "I've been in this same position for eight hours. Can't you give me something to speed up this process?"

"Mrs. Tyler, we've been over this part already. It's just not good for you or the babies," answered Dr. Stone.

"Well I've changed my mind. Just take 'em! All this pain can't possibly be good for us either! Dra – do something!"

"Baby, calm down. We can do this."

"*We* aren't doing anything! I'm the only one having two babies in this room. And where is Sid?" Meagan said as she scanned the labor room, utterly confused.

"Beats me – I tried calling her earlier. No answer – so I left a message on her home phone and on her cell," Waverly said.

"Maybe the twins are waiting for their aunt Sidney to arrive," Dominique said – chuckling to herself.

"Diamond, that's not funny—well, maybe it is funny," laughs Waverly.

Next thing you know, everyone was laughing. And, for the first time that day, Meagan put down her shoulders. I mean she actually let go of the idea of controlling the situation. Somehow, little miss perfect had in the back of her mind what childbirth was going to be like, but was disillusioned when reality struck. First, all – not two of her best friends were going to be by her bedside. Her loving husband would remember everything from Lamaze class. Meagan's Mother would be in the labor room with her – not in the hall doing who knows what. And, her not so young body would be able to spit those babies out like an old man spitting out the juice from chewing tobacco. Plus, I believe Meagan's labor room was much smaller than her money had paid for – something to do with another patient staying longer than the hospital had expected. So, I would imagine the joke was on her.

"You girls are crazy. I'll be right back. I need a smoke," Drake said – laughing as he moved away from Meagan's bedside.

"I thought someone quit smoking," Waverly whispered, with a touch of sarcasm in her voice.

"The moment the twins are born, Dra promises to smoke his last cigar. Right Honey?" Meagan said, reminding her husband of his promise to her.

"Yes Dear."

Drake then left the room. On his way down the hall, he noticed his mother-in-law sitting in the hall looking strangely puzzled.

"Hey Kat, ya doing Okay? You're not worried about Meagan? She's done well this whole pregnancy. Dr. Stone doesn't see any problems at this point – Kat!" Drake said as he looked at Katherine while waiting patiently for an answer.

"No Baby, I'm just sitting here remembering every time Meagan has made me proud to say that I'm her mother. You know, they say you only get one mother. I don't believe that. You get as many as you need," Katherine said in a very soft voice.

"What are you talking about Kat?" Drake said as he stood there with his mouth opened.

"Remember when the two of you met?"

"We practically ran each other over."

"That was the way it was set up from the beginning for you guys to meet Dra. You couldn't have met any other way. You came into Meagan's life – not when she wanted you, it was when she needed you. It's hard to explain destiny. It's something like aging. It can be done gracefully with a proper diet and exercise – or – well you know what I mean. Every individual has his own path and they sometimes alter. Nevertheless, we end up right where we are supposed to be. I don't believe in chance. Things are as they should be."

"Well Kat, on that note, I know it's time for a tobacco break," Drake said as he continued down the hall.

Katherine sat there looking even more puzzled from the outside than before. But, one can never define a person's inner thoughts. Of course Drake was far too busy to notice anyone else's reality. He was about to become a Father. Blessed with not one child, but two. This man wasn't sure whether to stick his chest out or run for the boarder. For the last eight hours of labor, Mr. Tyler was in and out of the delivery room smoking his imported cigars.

Mind you, Katherine sat in what appeared to be in the same chair for almost the same amount of time. So now as the day grows shorter, Katherine realizes that her time too – is running out. So, she closed her eyes and began thinking to herself,

I have to tell her. I have to. What if I died tomorrow? Meagan would never know the truth. And it's not so bad. Huh! Well if it's not that bad, why has it taken me almost twenty years to convince myself? Today, tonight, Okay – now! What am I so afraid of? God knows I am afraid, but I have to tell her soon…As soon as my grandbabies are born. I know we promised to tell our daughter everything when she became a teenager. But, the timing was just never right. Now you're gone Theo, and I'm left to do this alone. What if she hates me when this is all over? Meagan and Drake are all I have now. I can't lose them. Will someone please help me? Send me a sign or something Lord . . .

Katherine then opened her eyes and stood to her feet. Suddenly, Dominique bursts out of the doors of the labor room, shouting…

"It's time, it's time!"

Her voice rolled down the hall so loud, it startled the devil out of Katherine. Trembling, she whispered, "That's too fast!"

"Mother Kat, your Baby is ready to have her own babies! I have to find Dra," Dominique said as she hurried down the hall.

Katherine continued to stand there frozen from fear and utter excitement. Next thing you know, Drake and Dominique flew past her before she was able to make up her mind whether to go into the labor room or just wait until the babies were born.

Well, before Drake and Dominique could clear the doorway, Waverly was screaming to the top of her lungs,

"Nia's here Dra! Nia's here and healthy!"

"Hey! What do you mean Nia's here? Baby, you were supposed to wait for me," Drake said – confused.

"Tell that to your daughter!" cried Meagan.

"I was gone for only a few minutes. What happened to – you know," Drake said.

Everyone laughed.

"He's so stupid Dr. Stone. Please excuse my husband. Dra thinks that childbirth really cares about time," Meagan said as she laid there – legs uncomfortably in the air awaiting her next arrival.

"Oh God, this really hurts," Meagan cried. "Where's my Mother? Katherine!"

At that very moment, Katherine stuck her head into the labor room and said ...

"Mother's here Me-Me. Don't cry, this will all be over soon. Then, there will be plenty of time to cry."

"That's not funny Mother," Meagan said in a very soft voice.

"Okay, this next contraction should do it. Get ready Meagan," Dr. Stone said.

For the next few seconds, the room was frozen. No one moved a muscle. Meagan was sweating bullets. Drake was at the end of the bed, with the video camera attempting to catch a Kodak moment. Dominique was biting her fingernails. Mother Kat was gazing at the first newborn, remembering Meagan as a baby. While Waverly – can you believe it? – had tears in her eyes. Then the final moment arrived. Meagan began to moan as she pushed as hard as she could.

"This feels like constipation in slow motion," Meagan said.

"You're doing well," Dr. Stone said as she sat at the end of Meagan's bed like a catcher behind homeplate waiting for another pitch.

"I see her! Come on Nyle, Dad's ready this time," Drake said in his manly voice.

"This is too much for me. I think I need a smoke now!" Dominique said as she walked towards the door.

"Diamond – come back here! You don't smoke!" shouted Meagan.

"Good try" Waverly said, with a crooked smile on her face.

"Hush your mouth Waverly Corrine. Look at you – you're not doing any better cry baby," Dominique replied, trying not to laugh.

Finally after several screams, Meagan gave birth to her second daughter, Nyle. Everyone else exhaled as well as if they had just given birth too. Remarkably, the next sound that filled the room was of the twin daughters, Nia and Nyle. Their tones were very soft. It even seemed as if they were talking to each other instead of crying.

"This is so unbelievable. I have to call Vincent," Waverly said, as she looked for her purse.

"Are both babies okay Doctor?" Meagan asked.

"Everything is looking terrific," replied Dr. Stone.

"I can surely see all fingers and toes," Dominique said with a big smile on her face.

"I'm so very proud of you Me-Me! This has been a long time coming – and you did it! They are both beautiful girls," Katherine said as she rubbed Meagan's head.

"Hey Baby, we did it! I love you so much," Drake added.

"Sure about that Dra? From over here, it looked as if you were playing "smile you're on candid camera," Dominique said, laughing with joy.

"Let me see my daughters. Mother can you believe this? Both girls are alright," Meagan said with a voice of relief.

"Well, of course they are," Katherine whispered.

"Okay folks, now it's time to clear the room so that we can get Mrs. Tyler and her twins settled," Dr. Stone said as she directed everyone out of the room.

"This means you too Dad!"

"Okay Doc, we can take a hint. Baby, would you like me to bring you something when I return?"

"No Silly! Well maybe a Nanny and a cow. I'm so tired, I just want to sleep for a day," Meagan whispered, as she closed her eyes and finally began breathing normally.

●●●●

R *ing…. Ring…. Ring…. Ring…. Ring…. Ring…. Ring….*

"Is that Vincent?" Dominique asked smiling from ear to ear.

"Wait…Hey Baby, the…" Waverly said.

But before Waverly could get her words out, the answering machine clicked on.

"Where's a good man when you need him? I don't believe this!" Waverly said, as she called their other line to the house.

"Simmons residence – may I help you?" Maria, the housekeeper, said.

"Maria – Hi. Is my husband around?"

"No Madam, I have not seen him all day. But, Master Victor is here," Maria replied.

"Let me talk to Victor."

"Master Victor! Your mother's on the phone," yelled Maria, calling him from the bottom of the staircase.

"I have it! Mother what's up? Did Auntie Meagan have the babies yet?"

"Hey Beasley – Yes, your Auntie gave birth to two healthy girls, Nia and Nyle. Where is your Father? I told him I would call so he could come to the hospital when Meagan had the girls. Have you heard from him?"

"Not since this morning. He said he was going to be at the hospital all day doing rounds. Would you like me to call there mother?"

"No, I'll call. But while you are on the phone, say hello to your Auntie Meagan before she falls asleep Beasley."

"Congratulations Auntie Meagan! How does it feel to finally be a mother?"

"Wonderful, unbelievably wonderful," Meagan said as she fell off to sleep.

"Okay Beasley, your Auntie is a little tired...unavailable. I'll be home soon. But if your Father calls, tell him to call me. Love you! Good Bye," Waverly said as she smiled at Meagan, wondering to herself. *Where is he?*

"Mother Kat, would you like to get something to drink while the nurses get Meagan and the twins together?" Dominique said.

"Okay Sweetie," Katherine replied. Katherine then kissed Meagan and said, "I'll look in on you before I leave Me-Me."

Waverly and Dominique both kissed Meagan good-bye and left the labor room. Next, the nurses took the twins down the hall so they could be fed and cared for. Finally, the air had settled and Meagan got just what she requested. Some rest.

"Waverly, are you going to join us for some coffee before you go?" Dominique said.

"No, I'm tired. I'll just check on Meagan tomorrow. It's been a long day. If I don't see Drake on my way out, give him my love. It's always a pleasure to see you Mother Kat. Hugs and Kisses Diamond," Waverly said as she left the hospital.

On her way home, Waverly tried to reach Vincent again.

"You have no messages!"

"Hey, I guess you're busy right now. When you get this message, please call me. Meagan had the babies about an hour ago. I tried calling you. It's a quarter after nine. I'll be home in thirty minutes," Waverly said as she ended the call. Then she thought... *All right Dr. Vincent Simmons, since you won't answer your cell phone, I know you have your pager on.*

Beep... Beep... Beep...Beep... Beep... Beep... Beep...Beep...

Why is it that a woman's intuition is always correct? Waverly may not have known her husband's whereabouts, but Girl did know that the pager's never off. But who could hear it over that old jam, "Lets' Get It On" by Marvin Gaye playing in the background. Not to mention all of the moaning going on.

The room was barely lit by a few candles on the nightstand and someone must still be in love with the idea of burning incense because the smell was strong. Was its purpose to intensify the moment or hid the aroma? Anyway, it was difficult to tell who was doing who...

● ● ● ●

"O h, Vincent, Oh. This feels so good Dr. – Work it!! Are you like this with all of your patients? Oh... Do it again," cried Payton.

"Payton...Payton...Oh...Wait a minute – did you hear something? Oh... Payton... stop. That's my pager. It might be the hospital," Vincent said, looking for his pants. "Awe shit!!!"

"Who is it?" Payton asked as she rubbed the top of her double D-cup breasts, trying to tempt the Good Doctor.

Smiling, Vincent answered, "It's my wife. I probably should be leaving now. But before I do, let me just say this has been another wonderful afternoon."

"It's evening Vincent! And if our time together is always so wonderful, why are you so quick to leave when she calls? Why don't you just leave her!"

"Yeah right! Make sure you clean up and lock up before you leave. And don't forget to change the sheets. In fact, take them with you. I'll get them from you later," Vincent said as he was leaving.

"See you next time Doc."

"Don't forget to change the sheets Payton... as if I'm your maid to order. One thing's for sure, I'm no fool and you are a messy mess Dr. Simmons," Payton said to herself as she played with the pillows on the bed.

••••

*M*eanwhile, back, at the hospital, Dominique and Katherine were just returning from the Café when they saw Drake in the hallway.

"Hey girls, where's Waverly?" he asked.

"You know sleeping beauty. She left a little while ago. In fact, I have an early day tomorrow myself. So I really need to be on my way as well. How about you Mother Katherine? Will you be staying much longer?"

"Not too much longer. It has been a long day for all of us. But, before I go I think I'll peek back in on Me-Me," Katherine said as she kissed Dominique good-bye.

"Let me see you to your car Dominique, it's getting late," Drake said as he checked his watch.

"Okay tough guy," giggled Dominique.

Dominique and Drake soon there after left the hospital while Katherine stood there, looking in the opposite direction of the hallway contemplating her quest. But then something crazy happened. The corridor that was a moment ago short, seemingly stretched three times in length causing Katherine to second guess her motives. Finally she started taking baby steps towards Meagan's room....

I'm just going to go in there and tell her that she's not mine. I mean she is my daughter, but I didn't give birth to her. Come on, this happens all of the time. She's not the first little girl to be adopted. Boy, it's getting warm in here, Katherine thought as she stood at Meagan's door, pushing herself to open it.

She opened the door and saw that Meagan was still asleep. Katherine then gave a sigh of relief and whispered, "I guess I'll have to wait until tomorrow."

"Mother, what will you wait until tomorrow for? Is everything all right? Meagan said as she sat up in the bed.

Katherine began crying uncontrollably.

"Mother, Mother Kat, what's all this for? Granted, it's been a very long day,"

"No, it's not that Meagan…"

"And when have you ever called me Meagan? Tell me what's wrong *right now!*"

"I'm trying to tell you! It's just harder than I ever imagined. Even now I can't get it out without hurting!"

"What do you mean hurting? Who is this going to hurt? This cannot be about the twins Mother!"

"No, it's not the girls. It's us!"

Katherine then paused for several seconds, holding her head down in utter shame. For she knew, the time had finally come. And it didn't matter how she nor Meagan was going to feel about this. She had no other choice. Meagan began to cry.

"Meagan, I always wanted to be honest with you. Ever since you were a baby. But Theo kept telling me, 'Honey it's not that important. Wait!' Now look, he's not even here… Yet, I'm still struggling for the right time."

"There you go calling me Meagan again! I'm your Me-Me! Me-Me! Mother! And what in the hell is wrong with us? One moment you're saying how proud of me you are and now you want me to just believe something is wrong with our relationship? You're losing me Mother!"

Next, one of the nurses rushed into Meagan's room to see if she was all right. Believing Katherine was the cause for the tension in the air, she asked Meagan if she would prefer her Mother to leave now?

For a few minutes – nothing, I mean nothing at all was said. Tears continued to roll down both Meagan and Katherine's faces, while their hearts raced like never before. It was almost as if they were in the midst of a fight, which both of them were losing. Yet, neither was ready to stop… Again, the nurse repeated, "Mrs. Tyler, would you like your Mother to leave at this time?"

"No – Not yet! Leave us alone for now," Meagan said, as she reached for her robe.

Feeling her daughter's anguish, Katherine tried helping Meagan with her robe, referring to her as Me-Me again as she did it.

"Don't! Don't! Now you remember my name! And what is so important that you feel the need to share with me now? For a second...No, well okay – I had a nasty thought that you were going to tell me that my life has been all lies – that I'm really *not* your daughter or maybe, you're my stepmom. Maybe my mother died giving birth to me. Worst, you found me on your doorstep. Mother, you're turning red on me!" Meagan yelled, as she looked straight into Katherine's eyes.

The room was dim and cool. The only sound that was heard appeared to be the fan. Katherine looked around the room, hesitated and shook her head. The words, she felt, were far too ugly to say.

"You're crazy!" Meagan shouted.

"Me-Me!"

"You're crazy!"

"But Me-Me, I love you."

"This is not happening. Not to me! I have it all! The big house! The perfect husband, two point five kids. Okay, maybe they're just babies now. Eventually they'll grow. I am a "best selling" author, a young white female with, what use to be, great curves, fair skin, beautiful hair and a Colgate smile. Do I have to continue? Yes – you're crazy. Say I'm wrong mother. Say it! Say something!" Meagan shouted at the top of her lungs.

"This is not going to well," Katherine mumbled.

"No shit! And I really think you should be going. I mean you can't talk or won't. Whatever! You don't even have enough sense to deny this bull," Meagan said, as she began wiggling her way to the edge of the bed.

"Stop it Meagan! It wasn't like that!"

"Well, how on God's earth was it? What was it? Who are you really? And why now!"

"All right! Okay... I'll tell you! I did not give birth to you! Now, there it is! All cards are on the table. So – now what?"

"Oh no you didn't just say that! Lies! You're telling one. It's something else," *Meagan said, as she closed her eyes and remembered the first time she played in the snow with her mother and father. Flashbacks…Suddenly Meagan opened her eyes, which were filled with salty water and whispered,*

"Let's try this whole thing again – Mother. What the hell is wrong with us?"

At that moment, Meagan simply forgot the minor detail of having just given birth to two babies. She was still very heavily sedated. So, of course when she attempted to get out of the bed, Meagan fell to the floor.

"Nurse! Nurse!" Meagan cried out, as she reached for anything to pull herself up.

"Me-Me, look at yourself. Let me help you up,"

"Don't! Don't put your hands on me!"

Her face was now flush. She then began counting. I would assume that she was attempting to calm herself down. Finally, Nurse Nancy came bursting in and shouted – "Mrs. Tyler, are you all right?"

"I need you to get her *out of my sight.* I would also like you to make sure she won't be able to return while I'm here. Is that understood?" Meagan said, as the nurse was helping her up.

"Of course," replied Nancy.

"Me-Me, now you're going too far with this."

"I'm sorry Ma'am, but I have to insist that you leave now."

"Me-Me we should talk about this," Katherine said, with a look of fear in her eyes.

Meagan just looked up at Katherine as if she never knew her. Her tears stopped in the middle of her face. Her hair was messy and her gown was soaked from all of the excitement. Then the nurse finally got Meagan to her feet. At that time, Nancy noticed Meagan was bleeding.

"Oh my God, is that blood!" Katherine yelled.

"Will you please leave? We will take care of your daughter. Let's get you back in bed Mrs. Tyler. Can you feel anything?"

Exhausted, Meagan simply shook her head "no"... But knowing that it was a good chance Meagan's body was in shock; Nancy immediately got her into the bed and paged Dr. Stone.

As for Katherine, Girl did not want to believe how this was all playing out. What she feared most – seemingly had become real. So emotionally distraught, she wandered over to the Nursery, peaked through the glass window and silently began praying. Tears rolled down her face and she hurried away. Wow! Talk about mother/daughter drama!

●●●●

Well, back at the parking lot, Drake and Dominique were laughing at one of Drake's bad jokes.

"I thought the tradition was – you're supposed to give out your cigars Dra," Dominique said.

"You hate traditions."

"I know, but I'd still like one. Maybe I'll take it to work with me tomorrow. Oh! And give me one for Waverly," Dominique said, as she opened her car door.

Drake then threw his arms around Dominique and said, "Give me some love crazy lady."

"Good night brother-in-law! Tell Meagan, I'll call her later tonight."

Pausing, Drake asked, "Hey what do you think happened to Sidney?"

"You know Sidney, she'll make up something bizarre," Dominique giggled as she pulled off.

Chapter Two

Changes

*D*on't blink. You blinked!"
    "So, how does it make you feel? Sidney –
    Sidney, would you like me to repeat the
question?" Lane said.

"Of course not! I heard you. I would like to say, I don't know. But! Don't say it!"

Before Sidney could finish her statement, the group shouted, "I don't know is not an answer!"

"I know, I know! – but how do you think it makes me feel? Like shit! I can't keep doing this. Back and forth – in and out of this comatose cycle. I'm not even sure of *who* I am some days. On one hand, I'm not only successful and smart; I'm a perfect 10 – Five foot seven, light brown hair. So, what if it's not natural. The bedroom eyes are mine. Smooth tanned skin and a perfect size six. Now on the other hand, I can't seem to get through one day without running to something or someone to pull me outside of myself." She paused to take a breath before continuing

"It's like having poison ivy; however, it's on the inside of my skin. It irritates the hell out of me and I'm the only one who knows this. No one else notices. On the surface, I'm perfect. I'm at the peak of my career. I also believe I'm at the top of America's most wanted singles list. I know, it's funny but to be very honest, I feel as if I'm missing something very significant in my life and it hurts some kinda awful. This is really driving me crazy. And, let's talk about driving for a moment. Yes, I'm going to buy another car. Why? Quite frankly – because I can. It's my second addiction. My list of runaway ideas are endless." Sidney continued as she began to cry softly. "I always – always end up back in a dark corner, high... I'm done."

Then all together, the Group said, "Thanks for sharing..."

"Well, we are out of time again. Let us gather up front for a moment of silence, followed by a silent prayer," Lane added.

The room was still for several minutes. Finally, everyone was on one accord and with certainty, said Amen! As the group started to disburse, Lane noticed Sidney trying to hurry away and said,

"Sidney, can I see you for a second?"

"What's up Lane?"

"Do you have a few minutes?"

"Not really, you know I hate this place," she replied while looking everywhere but at Lane.

"I just wanted to know if you're okay. I haven't seen you for a while. I've tried calling, but I guess you didn't want to be bothered."

"I didn't and I'm fine! It's not you Lane. I really like you. I'm just not ready for a relationship – especially not in these rooms. You do understand, don't you? I really have to go but I promise to keep in touch. Be good to yourself Lane," Sidney said, as she walked away.

Shaking his head feeling used, Lane thought to himself, *how can a woman be so cold and beautiful at the same time? What a waste!*

Poor fellow...You see – Lane is just your average hater. He was upset when Sidney didn't fall for him after one afternoon of great sex. Now Sidney may have problems with filling that unidentified hole at the bottom of her stomach, but enticing men to do just what she wants, "on any given Sunday"... well that wasn't an issue. Sorry, where was I – Oh, after Sidney left the meeting, she ran into Kelly on the way to her car. Now Kelly was supposed to be Sidney's active sponsor. However, Sidney took to the idea of sponsorship just as she did with her relationship with the opposite sex... meaningless!

"Well if it isn't the devil herself. Sidney Sharpe how are you treating life? Let me guess. The hospital is still in denial about your ability to administer drugs. And, of course your family and friends remain in the dark. Oh, and let us not forget, the dogs of the whole Washington/Baltimore area are still sniffing at your front porch. Say nothing if I'm wrong!"

"All right Kelly Girl, I missed you too. It's so good to see you. And yes, you were right. I can't do this alone. And I don't know anything about staying clean forever," Sidney said, as she reached for Kelly's hand.

"Where are you parked?" Kelly asked.

"Right beside you."

"Okay, you've been gone for less than ninety days and you really needed a new car. Yeah – Right! And, did I hear you correctly, sharing something about buying another car? *Child!* Outside of the fact that you refuse to stay sober, for more than ninety days at a time – you're still my nigger."

"Okay Kelly, stop joking. I know I have a car fetish."

"And a man fetish, a clothes fetish, and let's not forget how much you love fine cuisine."

"You see, that's why I didn't want to get close to you people. But, seriously Kelly, you appear to have your life back under control. You look great. Tell me honestly, why do you still come here? I know you hate it just as much as I do. So why?"

"You just said the magic word."

"Which is?" Sidney responded.

"*Appeared* my friend. Nothing, I mean absolutely nothing is as it *appears*. We're just people. All of who are on the edge of sanity and insanity Sidney. Besides, life is far too complex to believe that we've solved its mystery just by staying clean. So, that's why we say one day at a time. Give me a hug and call me every day this time Miss Sharpe. I mean it!" Kelly said, as she gave Sidney a warm hug and kissed her forehead. "Don't say it."

But wanting to thank her again for the umpteenth time, all she could muster up when she looked her dead in the eyes was, "Good night Kelly Girl."

●●●●

*N**ow isn't it funny how the mind can play horrible tricks on us at the blink of an eye. Listening to Kelly had her convinced for the moment, that maybe, just maybe, this time... But, as soon as she was alone in her car, a burst of fear ran up Girl's spine. So just as many people do when they're alone and full of fear, she began to reason with herself...*

"All right, get a grip on yourself. Remember, it's just a feeling that will probably pass before you can repeat "The Lord's Prayer" ten times."

Sidney then loosened her collar, ran he fingers through her hair and took a deep breath. As she blew it out, she noticed the silence in the car and said,

"No wonder I'm tripping, I haven't returned to the real world yet. What time is it anyway? Ten minutes till ten. That's why I hate going to those NA/AA...whatever you call those meetings. They take up entirely too much of my precious time. And, I bet I'll have to go in early tomorrow. Oh no! I forgot to turn my pager and beeper back on," *she whispered as she rumbled through her bag. Then as she briefly scanned the caller I.D. she thought,*

Okay, now... who is this? Waverly Corrine, the car dealer, oh and my sister Sherian. I'll call her when I get home. I'm sure she's just acting like my mother again. Let's see what Waverly Corrine wants.

Ring.....Ring......Ring......Ring.......Ring.....Ring.....Ring....

"The Simmons residence, may I help you?" said Maria.

"Hi Maria, is Waverly Corrine still awake?"

"Hello Miss Sidney, I believe she's still awake. Hold on for a second. I'll see for you."

Maria then put Sidney on hold and pressed the intercom to the Master Bedroom.

"Excuse me, Madam. Madam Waverly are you resting now?"

Thinking it was her husband on the phone; she quickly set her book down and asked if it was him. Maria answered politely, "No Madam, it's Miss Sidney."

Eager to talk to Sidney as well, Waverly grabbed the receiver and yelled, "I'll take it. Thanks Maria. Miss Sharpe, where in the @#%!!.. I sure as hell hope you have a plausible excuse this time for making us all worry... You know Meagan went into labor this afternoon. Where were you! I called and paged you. So, were you doing one of your disappearing acts again, or did you simply say to hell with us?"

"No Waverly. I did not say to hell with anyone. I got a little caught up at lunch so I decided to go to one of my support groups."

"I cannot believe you. We were all supposed to be there Miss Sharpe. I know you couldn't have possibly forgotten!"

"Okay, I can tell you are not listening to me... so I'll only ask once! Waverly Corrine did Meagan have the twins or not? I cannot do this with you right now. I've already had a very long day."

"Well, don't blame me for your choices in life. Yes, Meagan had two beautiful angels, Nia and Nyle. And you will be able to see at least one of the births."

Puzzled, Sidney replied "What in the world are you talking about?"

"Girl, that darn Drake missed the first delivery   out taking a smoke."

"You're kidding!"

"I wish I were...."

"Damn, it sounds like you guys had a wonderful time. I can't believe I missed it. Look, I'm going to get off this phone and go visit my nieces. Sweet dreams," Sidney said, as she blew Waverly a kiss.

"Sidney – now you know it's too late to be visiting Meagan."

"Not for me!"

"Sid wait!! Are you *really* alright? I mean, no one knew where you were... We were worried shitless..."

"I'll tell you all about it when I see you in the morning. We are scheduled to go running, right?"

"Okay, be safe. I love you Miss Sharpe."

"And I you."

Smiling, both girls ended the call exactly at the same time. You would think they were looking at a two-sided mirror. Sidney and Waverly shook their heads at the same time and in the same manner. Then gave a nod of assurance as if they were both relieved they had finally connected that day... Women!

Sidney, with little time to spare, immediately made a u-turn in the middle of the intersection. She was determined to see Meagan before she did anything else. And for the next few minutes, she could think of nothing but how awesome it was that her oldest and dearest friend, Meagan, finally had her prayers answered. Overwhelmed with joy, she screamed...

"Yes, yes Lord! If you did it for Meagan, I guess I have no other choice but to believe it for myself. I know I'm a complete mess. I know I keep asking for the same things, as if you haven't heard me the first hundred times. So, I won't ask again. Just keep me until I can keep myself. Yes, Lord, that's our deal! Yeah, Okay!" *But, I wonder how Meagan's feeling right now*, Sidney thought to herself.

●●●●

P aging Dr. Stone. Dr. Stone. Paging Dr. Stone..."

"Hi, this is Dr. Erica Stone. How may I help you?"

"Dr. Stone, it's Mrs. Tyler. She's bleeding very heavy," Nancy said.

"Okay, Nancy, get her comfortable. I'll be right there," said Dr. Stone as she glanced at her watch.

"All right, let's clean you up a bit. While we are doing that, I'll check your temperature just to make certain it's not too high. How do you feel Mrs. Tyler?" Nancy said as she removed the first pad and replaced it with a clean one.

"My heart feels like – like it's running a race and my head's been placed on a merry-go-round. Not too good huh," Meagan replied as the tears rolled down her face.

"There, there, my child, whatever's worrying your heart, he'll fix it. And Dr. Stone is on her way," Nurse Nancy said.

Meagan just cried even more. At that moment, Drake walked into the room.

"Sweetie, what happened? What's wrong? We've just had the babies. Don't you think you're moving kind of fast – with the baby blues stuff?" Drake said as he stood there not knowing if he wanted to move closer or leave the room.

Meagan just looked at Drake with confirmation.

"Yeah, I have the blues."

Then she gave Nancy a look suggesting to her not to say anything about Katherine. Nancy knew what Meagan wanted and nodded her head.

Drake walked over to the bed, held her hand, and said, "Where's your mother? I don't think she left without saying good-bye. Would you like me to find her for you baby?"

Meagan looked at Drake. Of course she didn't want her mother there, but before she could respond, Dr. Stone entered the room.

"All right young lady, let's see what's causing this bleeding," Dr. Stone said, as she moved towards Meagan's bedside.

"Bleeding! No one said anything to me about bleeding!" shouted Drake.

"Slow down Mr. Tyler – let's find out what the problem is for certain. In the meantime, why don't you go and look in on your two daughters. I'll take care of your wife, and meet with you soon after," Dr. Stone said.

Drake kissed Meagan's wet lips for several seconds, rubbed her forehead and said, "I love you Mrs. Tyler."

Meagan then looked at Drake until she could not longer see him. She closed her eyes and started praying to herself. After Drake left Meagan's room, just that fast, he had forgotten what he was supposed to be doing. All he could think about was Meagan.

"Oh God, I know we've had this conversation before. It's just that we've waited, well maybe not always patiently – but we still waited for our blessings. Now that they are finally here, Meagan…Meagan has to be all right. She has to stay to help me raise them. No! I'm not accepting this. I'm just overreacting to this whole blood issue thing. Right!" said Drake as he paced the hall – back and forth.

Finally, after twenty minutes passed, Drake realized he had been up for at least twelve hours. Functioning without food and very little water, he was simply exhausted. So, he decided to sit for a moment and try to rest his mind. Poor thing, he fell fast asleep.

"Mr. Tyler, Mr. Tyler, wake up…"

Drake rubbed his head, open his eyes and noticed Dr. Stone was standing over him. "How long have I been out?"

"About thirty minutes Mr. Tyler."

Drake stood to his feet, taking a deep breath, and tried to focus. He noticed the hall looked a little cloudy. He shook his head and said, "How's my wife?"

"I think you'd better sit down."

"What do you mean?" shouted Drake.

"I'm sorry, she didn't make it," Dr. Stone whispered reluctantly.

"No!...No!...No!...God   No!   God
No!....No!....No!....No!....

●●●●

OOPS....

Mr. Tyler, Mr. Tyler, wake up," Dr. Stone said, as she padded Drake on his shoulder. "You must be having a crazy dream. Wake up."

Drake rubbed his head, opened his eyes and noticed Dr. Stone was again standing over him. He closed his eyes for a second, opened them and said, "Let's try this again. How long have I been out? And how is my wife?"

Dr. Stone smiled and said, "Maybe about thirty minutes and Meagan is fine. Actually, she's nursing your daughters as we speak."

"Thank you Lord!" shouted Drake. "I could kiss you Dr. Stone. I was so afraid, well never mind! What was wrong with her?"

"Meagan had something called uterine atony. It's a girl thing. But, we fixed it. Why don't you go on in and see her. I believe she's waiting for you," said Dr. Stone, as she walked Drake to Meagan's room.

Knock... Knock... Knock...

"Come in. Oh it's you," Meagan said with a half smile on her face.

"Hey Baby," said Drake with his brows raised.

"Daddy's here girls. Come on over here big guy and peek at your daughters before they fall off again. Bet you don't know who's who," said Meagan chuckling.

"Let's see. Well this one with the over sized head must be Nia," said Drake as he held the child close to him.

"Stop it Dra. Don't start making fun of our daughters. Besides that's Nyle your holding," said Meagan as she tried to hit Drake.

"Okay Baby, maybe we should leave the name tags on for a little while. Just until their looks change enough for us to tell them apart," Drake said smiling.

"You're funny Mr. Tyler. You mean until you can tell them apart. I know our daughters thank you very much," Meagan said, as she turned her lips upside down.

"This has been a very long day Honey. I did mention to you how proud I am to be your husband and your babies Daddy," Drake said as he looked straight into Meagan's eyes.

Meagan put her hand directly on Drake's lips and said, "Hush, don't say another word. I know. I'm with you too Dra. You've never let a single day past without honoring me as your wife – so, I already know and believe this is real. Besides, you've been here all day and I know you're tired. Why don't you go home, get your sexy self into our Jacuzzi, smoke your last imported cigar and relax. Eat already! I'll call you in the middle of the night for some phone sex okay?" said Meagan as she winked her eye at him.

Drake just exhaled then smiled, shook his head and laid baby Nyle down. Nothing else was said. All that was heard were the cooing sounds from the twins. Drake kissed Meagan good-bye and left the room. Baby Nyle was lying in the basinet. While Nia was still nursing off and on in Meagan's arms, Meagan drifted off to sleep.

What a sight! Huh, one thing was for sure – the love Drake and Meagan shared. And I do believe everyone knew it. I even think there could have been a slight sense of envy from Waverly because among the four friends, only she and Meagan were married. Now isn't it ironic how one could think they want some part of someone else's life, not even knowing or caring about the other's past and present sacrifices, just believing that some how the grass was greener. You and I both know that some are artificial. But, that's another book. Well, back to Common Lives.

As Drake was leaving the hospital, he ran into Sidney as she was coming in.

"There you are! I knew you wouldn't let us down!" said Drake as he kissed Sidney and handed her a cigar.

"One day I promise to be on time. I'm so sorry Dra," Sidney said.

"Now you know better than that. We're family. Besides, Waverly and Dominique did just fine. You're here now and that's all that matters," Drake said.

"You're right. So tell me, who do they look like?" Sidney said as she smiled.

Drake answered, "I don't know, like babies! You'll have to see them for yourself. Oh, and Sidney she's registered as Meagan Tyler not Meagan Simone.

"Okay, like no one knows who she really is. You famous people are too much. Good night brother-in-law," said Sidney as she hurried into the hospital.

But, just as Sidney was approaching the elevator, it dawned on her that she was going to see Meagan empty handed. So, she turned around and went racing to the gift shop. Of course, it had been closed for at least an hour. So Sidney peeked through the glass door and noticed the clerk was still there. Immediately, she began banging on the door.

"Please, please let me in!" shouted Sidney.

The clerk came to the door and said, what else, "We're closed!" Sidney went on to explain that she had to buy something for her so-called sister, who had been trying to have a baby for the last five years. And, she even threw in the fact that Meagan already had experienced four miscarriages. I forgot to mention that Sidney had a way of getting just what she wanted. Needless to say, the clerk opened the door. Sidney gave the woman a big hug and quickly selected some flowers. As she started towards the cash register, she noticed a book entitled "Stop Pouting, Get It Back Together."

"Mmm," she said, "This is perfect. I'll take this also."

The clerk nodded her head, smiled and said, "Good choice. I'm sure she'll be pleased."

Sidney thanked the clerk again, and then hurried off to see Meagan. I did mention earlier that visiting hours were probably over. By the time she arrived at the last gate, I mean desk, the nurses on duty looked at her as if to say, "You must be lost."

"May I help you?" she said.

"I'm here to see Meagan Simone – I mean Tyler. Meagan Tyler."

"Mrs. Tyler is resting now and visiting hours ended some time ago," said Nurse Marjorie.

"Marje is it. I don't think you understand. I missed the delivery earlier today, and I'm not leaving until I see my sister," Sidney said in a very sharp tone.

"Your sister. Really! Meagan Tyler is white," replied the Nurse.

"What difference does that make? So was our Father. I'd get him for you, but he's dead! Would you like a sample of my blood as proof!" yelled Sidney.

"What's going on over here?" said Nurse Nancy.

"I told this young woman that visiting hours were over, but she insists on seeing Mrs. Tyler. And, she says she's her sister," Nurse Marjorie said with utter doubt in her voice.

Nancy looked at Sidney first, then at Marjorie, shook her head and said, "Why don't you take your break now. I'll take care of…"

"Miss Sharpe! Sidney Sharpe! Yes, why don't you take something – maybe a Valium? Oh! sorry, she wasn't trying to work with me. I just want to see my best friend before the day ends. You understand, don't you," said Sidney, attempting to look sad.

"Of course I do. Mrs. Tyler has had a very long day. I'm sure she would be happy to see you Miss Sharpe," Nancy said. "She's at the end of the hall, last room on the right."

"I owe you one. Thanks lady," said Sidney as she hurried down the hall.

●●●●

*O*nce she reached the door, Sidney smiled, closed her eyes and took a deep breath. She opened her eyes and slowly opened the door. Meagan was still asleep. Baby Nia's eyes were wide open a she nursed in Meagan's arms.

Meagan, on the other hand, exhausted from her day, wasn't quite holding Nia correctly. Poor Nia was barely hanging on. Sidney laughed and picked up Baby Nia.

"You are so beautiful. Look at you – you little person. Let Auntie Sidney give you a big kiss," Sidney kissed the baby's forehead and said, "Look at those eyes – you must be Nia. And is that your sister over there?" As she looked into the basinet, Sidney noticed that the babies were identical. "Wow," she whispered. "This is incredible. Same eyes, same color hair, little oval heads. You two are going to run your parents ragged. Well, if you're Nia, then you must be Nyle."

As Sidney held Nia close, she leaned over and kissed Baby Nyle. Nyle looked up at Sidney and gave her a big smile.

"Aren't you something!" At that moment, Meagan woke up. Still heavily sedated, she rubbed her eyes and saw that Sidney was holding one of her babies and smiling at the other.

"Sid, I was so worried about you."

Sidney then turned towards Meagan saying, "They are so beautiful. And you – you are simply fabulous. Perfect in fact. You did it girl."

"I love you too. But really – I know better than that. It happened again, didn't it Sid," said Meagan as she reached for Sidney's hand. A tear rolled down Sidney's face. Both girls just looked at each other and smiled gently.

"I did want to be here for you Meagan. But, after I woke up in another strange place, the only thing I could think of was to find one of those meetings to go to."

"Well then, you did the right thing. Didn't those people say that you have to put yourself first or something like that? Recovery, that's what it was – right?"

"Yeah, that's what they say," laughed Sidney. "I'm tired of the whole thing, but I'm not here for all of that. I'm here to see my girl. How are you holding up?"

"I'm not so sure. Everything went just fine. But, when it was all over – you know, just as things were settling down, my mother... my mother said – well she tried telling me. Never mind!" Meagan said as she shook her head.

Sidney put baby Nia in her basinet, sat down next to Meagan, looked her right into her eyes and asked, "Is there something you need to tell me?"

Meagan just closed her eyes and shook her head – no. "I can't, not now. I'm not even sure if I'm believing all this. And, to top that, I started bleeding again."

"Bleeding!"

"Yes, but Dr. Stone said it was nothing. Some uterine atony stuff. My uterus didn't close properly. She fixed it. The bleeding stopped and I'm fine."

"All right, well we both know that's anything but true. Maybe after you get some rest, you'll be ready to talk about it."

The phone rang and Sidney answered it.

"Good evening – it's the nursery," Sidney said, as she handed the phone to Meagan.

"Hi. Yes you may come and get them. Okay, see you in a few minutes. They need to check out the twins again."

"Are they okay?"

"Oh sure, every so often the doctors monitor them – just to be safe. I think they do that with all newborns. Then, they'll bring them back to me."

"They are beautiful Meagan."

"Do you think they look like me?"

"Well, if that's what you want to believe. Yeah, I think I can see it," Sidney said, as she nodded her head.

"Yes, I see it too."

Sidney and Meagan both started laughing.

"You are one silly lady Meagan Simone. It's a shame your readers don't know this side of you. Maybe one day," said Sidney as she kissed Meagan's forehead. "I really need to be on my way home."

"I wish you didn't have to go. Are you going running tomorrow with Waverly and Diamond?"

"Of course and yes I'll stop by before I go to work. What would you like for breakfast?"

"Any and everything you'd like to bring me."

"One thing for sure, whatever is on your mind – it's not interfering with your appetite. I'll see you in the morning big girl," Sidney said, as she walked towards the door.

"Hey Sid, thanks for my Gift Shop flowers. They're very nice. But, isn't it a little late for them to still be opened," said Meagan with a big grin on her face.

"You're welcome. And yes, they were closed. As a matter of fact, I stole them along with that other gift for you smarty-pants! Bye," she replied laughing as she walked out the door.

"That's my girl! Now what else did she so-called steal for me. A book! "Stop Pouting, Get It Back Together." How appropriate. Okay Sid, two points for you," said Meagan with a funny look on her face.

Just then, Sidney poked her head back into the room and added, "One question! How did you know about the flowers?"

"Next time be sure to remove the tag, dah!"

"Oh, good night."

"Night."

•••••

*T*hese girls are too much. Meagan, on the one hand, was just relieved in knowing that Sidney was okay. It really didn't matter to her that Sidney wasn't there when she gave birth to the twins. What mattered most was that she was trying to take care of herself. Now Sidney, as you can see, does what she wants – when she wants. She knows that she can never play back this moment, so instead of lying to her best friend, she jacks! She's totally honest with Meagan and tries to reassure her by telling her how much she really wanted to be there. Priceless! Well back to Sidney.

On her way home, Sidney played back her entire day, then fast forwarded it. Suddenly, it occurred to her that she hadn't spoken to Dominique all day. On top of that, her head was beginning to hurt from the lack of food. So softly she said,.

"Breath. I know I have a Motrin in here somewhere. Oh good, there you are. Damn, out of water. Well too bad. You're not the first pill I've swallowed without water. Let me call Diamond."

Ring...Ring...Ring...Ring...Ring...Ring...Ring... Ring...Ring...

"Sorry, I can't come to the phone now. But, you know what to do – so do it!"

"Diamond, it's me – Sidney. Just calling to be calling. I saw Meagan and the babies. Yes, I've talked to mother Waverly too. See you in the morning. I will be there! Night!" *Then she tossed her phone on the passenger seat.*

"Maybe I can catch Houston's before they close their kitchen. *But just as she pulled up across the street from the restaurant, Sidney noticed a familiar face. She continued looking for a few seconds, just to be certain then thought,* "Vincent! Why in the hell are you sitting there this time of night, running your mouth on the phone?"

Sidney thought about it for a few minutes more and decided that she really didn't want him in her space that night.

I'll just find something at home, she thought while pulling off.

••••

Dex, pick up! Dexter pick up the damn phone man!" said Vincent as he rubbed his head.

"Vincent – hey Bones what's going on? I see you've been burning my phone up for the last half hour. You must be in one of your sticky situations," Dexter said, laughing just a little.

"All right Dex, maybe just a little," replied Vincent.

"Talk to me Bones."

"Well, it's a little warm on my side of town, so naturally I need some shade," said Vincent, with a half smile on his face.

"Now would that be with number one or talented number two? And what exactly are or were we supposed to be doing?"

"Man, it's with number one again, but tell her we were at meetings all day in Rockville. Remember that Pfizer CE Program?"

"You mean the one that ended last week. The same one you kept pushing me to attend alone?"

"Yeah Man! But don't get too carried away with the timing. Just make something up, and be sure to ask her to remind me that the last session will end tomorrow. Tell her to make sure that I bring my documents from the very first review. Oh and give me about twenty minutes before you call her. Cool!" Vincent said, as he glanced at the clock in the car.

"You're a wild Man. I know what to say. Twenty minutes – don't forget the documents. Yeah, I got it," Dexter replied, shaking his head.

"Good! Good! What are you doing anyway? Isn't it past your own curfew?"

"Let's not be confused now! I'm on my way back from New York. I was attending a real conference – thank you. Besides, my lovely Vanessa knows exactly where I am. She's in fact, waiting up for me as we speak. Let's see, in about two hours, I'll be soaking in my hot tub – in which I'm sure she'll have the temperature just right. Followed by a light meal, I'd say, Vanessa will do more fruit than veggies. Then the main dish shall be a back rub and of course, her specialty," Dexter said very convincingly.

"Specialty – you're a trip. Would that be a head message Doctor?" Vincent said, as he cleared his throat.

"That's why I'm on my way home and in sixty seconds, I will be clearing my line. So now, will there be need for anything else?"

"No, I think you've said a mouth full. I'll see you in the morning. Thanks Man." Vincent then ended his call to Dexter while contemplating which lie to tell his wife, Waverly.

Ring....Ring....Ring....Ring....
Ring....Ring....Ring....Ring....

●●●●

Y   eah, it's about time – a quarter till twelve. I shouldn't answer," Waverly whispered to herself. "Well good morning, I mean good evening Dr. Simmons."

"Hey beautiful! I see you've been missing me. But, before you get out the knives, put your shoulders down. My phone's been on the blink and I was stuck at a conference all day. So . . . . What have you been doing with yourself all day?"

"I don't wish to tell you right now, I'd rather kick you in the butt . . . ."

"Well, I could think of a few better things to do. Like, right now I'm at Houston's – your favorite. How about I bring home something sweet for you?"

"I don't really care. I'm tired and I'll probably be asleep by the time you actually get here."

"You'll just make it that much harder on yourself. You know I cannot go to sleep without touching your warm skin. So, I've got about five minutes to twelve. I should be home by twelve-thirty and let's just say that "no" won't be an option. Until then," Vincent said, as he ended their call.

"I hate when he does that to me – until then. Who ends a call without saying good-bye?" *Waverly said as she got out of her bed and headed for the bathroom. But then the phone rang again.*

"What now?" She said while making a U-turn back towards the phone." Let's see – you forgot to tell me how much you love me, followed by a good-bye."

"Good evening Judge, who told you that I'm secretly in love with you anyway?" Dexter said.

"Dr. Cummings, I'm sorry I thought you were my husband," Waverly said.

"Well I do apologize for calling so late, but I wanted to remind Bones that the last Pfizer meeting ends tomorrow at the University and please tell him not to forget the ledgers from the very first review."

"Your apology is not necessary and of course I'll make sure Vincent knows about the last meeting and the ledgers. Is that everything?"

"I believe so. Maybe we can all have dinner soon."

"How is Vanessa?"

"Wonderful! I'll tell her that you asked about her, but I'm serious, dinner soon."

"Okay Doctor, have a nice morning."

"Good night Judge, see you soon," Dexter said as he ended their call while thinking. *That damn Bones is something else!*

•••

ones!... Now who would want to be labeled Bones? Do you think Dexter gave him that nickname because he tries to poke every woman he meets? But, all jokes aside, Dr. Vincent Simmons is one smooth operator. Sorry, I did say all jokes aside. Well it's about time, day one has finally come to an end. It is now midnight. Take one guess. Who gets up almost ever night at this time just to pitter-patter around the house and catch up on things... Good try, Dominique Blake. But, instead of an alarm clock, Dominique programmed her stereo to play – what else, Luther's greatest hits... "Superman can fly high way up in the sky... Cause we believe he can. And what we choose to believe can always work out fine. It's all in the mind."

"Cat naps are definitely not what they used to be," Dominique said as she rolled out of her bed.

Dominique first headed for the bathroom to start her usual hot bath. Then she looked into an oversized mirror, just over the double

sink and said to herself, "Today is going to be the best day ever
– challenging, but good."

*She then took a long look at her teeth. Why do people do that
anyway? Sorry, I thought I'd ask. Next, she walked into the kitchen
to get a glass of water and noticed her answering machine was
blinking.*

"You have two messages…first message – "Diamond, it's
me Sidney. Just calling to be calling. I saw Meagan and the
babies. Yes, I've talked to mother Waverly too. See you in
the morning. I will be there! Night."

Next message… "Hey baby, it's me. I've been thinking
about us all day. I can't wait to see you again, smell you,
touch you, kiss you… Did I say taste you too? I hope while
you're napping tonight, you're dreaming about us. Love you
Girl. I'll call you tomorrow…"

"I love you too," said Dominique as she picked up the
phone immediately trying to return the call.

Ring…Ring…Ring…Ring…Ring…Ring…Ring…
Ring…Ring…

"Hey, I know it's late, but when you wake up, I want my
voice to be the first one you hear. And yes, I was dreaming
about us. You know I miss you as well. Besides, we don't
have that much time left before we can be together forever. I
did have a wonderful day. Meagan had the twins. Nia and …
Nia and Nyle. They're fabulous too. I can't wait for you to
meet them. Maybe we'll start with just one. I do love you
too. Call me at work tomorrow. Hugs and kisses,"
Dominique said as she hung up the phone.

*Dominique then took a deep breath. But, before she could blow it
out, her phone rang. Needless to say, she did not let it ring twice – nor
did she check her caller-id.*

"Well *hello* there," said Dominique whispered believing it
was her lover.

"Oh no bitch, you've got it bad. Wrong one," Franklin
said, laughing.

"Frankie isn't it past your bedtime?"

"Maybe, but I was waiting for you to get back up."

"You know I thought you were someone else."

"I know who you *thought* I was. How are you guys doing anyway?"

"Thanks for asking and we're doing just fine. It's just one thing I'm a little nervous about."

"Don't tell me, you're still worried about the meeting with your so-called friends. That's exactly why I don't have people in my space that I need to dress up for."

"Just stop it Frankie! I am going to tell them," Dominique said with a smart tone in her voice.

Franklin started to laugh and said, "And exactly how long did you say all of you were friends? Really, close friends. Was that fifteen years or better? Yet, you've never said a word... deception is so nasty!"

"Okay, I'm done talking to you. Maybe I'll see you at work later today."

"Wait a second Diamond, I wasn't trying to make it worse for you. All I'm saying is – if you are *really* close to them, none of this will matter girl."

Next thing you know, the line went dead.

• • • •

ominique's a mess. You know she hung up on him. Women! Speaking of women, let's catch up with Sidney before she goes to bed. I think I hear some water running. Do you hear it? Oh, that's Miss Sharpe in her bathroom, standing in front of the mirror, rinsing her face. Do all women talk to themselves when they are alone ....

"You look a little tired," Sidney said to herself as she turned her head from side to side. "Cute, but tired. Damn, this has been a long day. But, where did it go? First, you had lunch with Drew – next, you were drinking again. I can't figure this shit out!"

Next, she placed her hands over her face and said a silent prayer. In fact, the same one the group repeats after every meeting. Then, Sidney sat down on the side of her hot tub and began rubbing baby oil on her damp body. Again, she started talking to herself.

"I'm better than this. Same story, different day. Yeah, that's it! Everyday, I'll go to one of those meetings, stay away from men for just a little while... Especially that damn

Vincent," whispered Sidney as she turned off the lights before going to bed.

Now it's too dark in here!

●●●●

Chapter Three
False Pretenses

Oh, that's better. *Will you look at this. He's good! I told you. I'm sorry – I would do him. They say for better or worse. I guess in this particular case, it would be truth or dare, to tell the truth – the whole truth and nothing but the truth, so help me somebody!*

"What are you doing Vincent?" said Waverly.

"You know I can't lie next to you without tasting you."

"But I don't want to do this right now."

"That's okay Baby. Count to twenty, then think real hard and tell me what you want," said Vincent as he continued licking Waverly's breast.

Poor Waverly, she just kept on breathing in and out. Trying so hard to resist her six foot two, two hundred and twenty-five pound, simply gorgeous, hunk of a husband. Could you? I would have just given in. And Vincent he's not the type to accept "no" or anything close to it as an answer. So, he kept right on tasting her, moving from her breast to her perfectly toned thighs. I could tell he was enjoying every minute of it – being in absolute total control. Waverly just kept breathing harder and harder. I don't think I recall hearing her count to anything. Vincent then looked up at her for a second. Once he made eye contact with Waverly – need I say more? That dog went straight for the kill. Mmm – nasty – aint no hope here.

••••

Several hours later, Meagan was at the end of what I would call a nightmare. She tossed and turned for a minute, then finally woke up. Her heart was beating fast. Her hands were shaking and her forehead was drenched. She sat up in the bed and looked around the room to recall where she was. The sounds Meagan heard were muffled at first, but then she realized the phone next to her bed rang several times before she could focus her mind to tell her hand to pick it up. I'll give you one guess to tell me who you think it is....Good try!

"Me-Me," said Katherine.

Meagan shivered for a moment, but said nothing. It was almost as it she'd pushed the pause button on the recorder of her mind.

"Me-Me", I know you're there. I know you're confused. We have to talk about this."

Instinctively, Meagan slammed the phone down. She started running her hands through her long dark brown hair, rubbing her neck and taking slow deep breaths.

"Not again… Not again," Meagan whispered to herself.

But then it happened again. The phone started ringing. It rang again and again. I thought someone turned up the ringer volume. That damn thing started getting on my nerves. Well, the little bit I have. Okay, that's enough. Pick it up Meagan! What am I saying? The girl can't hear me! Thank you Lord!

● ● ● ●

*T*here was a knock on the door, followed by a familiar visitor who was not in a comatose state.

"Excuse me. Would this be the room of Meagan Simone? The same lady who just, yesterday, gave birth to my two beautiful nieces? Meagan! I'll answer the phone," Waverly said, as she moved closer to her.

"Don't!!" shouted Meagan.

Now Waverly seldom listened to anyone so she immediately picked up the phone.

"Good morning, Meagan Tyler's room," said Waverly.

"Waverly, what are you doing there this early?" Dominique asked.

"Who is it?" said Meagan, looking a bit distressed.

Waverly then put her index finger up to suggest that Meagan wait one moment.

"I thought I was here checking on my friend before beginning my day. And how are you today?" Waverly asked.

"On schedule Miss Lady. Please be on time. My job's not like yours, they can start without me. Anyway, I didn't call for you. Let me speak to Meagan."

"Who is it Waverly Corrine?" said Meagan, this time with her brows raised.

"Hold on to your horses!" she replied.

"Excuse me!"

"Not you – Meagan. She's acting kind of strange this morning," Waverly said.

"Kind of? Well you must be rubbing off on her," said Dominique, laughing.

"That's okay, you'll need another favor again," said Waverly as she handed Meagan the phone.

"Hello," she said looking puzzled, not really sure of who was on the other end.

"Good morning pumpkin. And how was your first night of being a new Mommy?"

Meagan gave a sigh of relief, pleased it was not Katherine on the phone and said, "I'm okay."

Dominique and Waverly both, although on opposite sides of town, were confused. Waverly, on the one hand had just walked into what I would consider a maze, while Dominique felt as if Meagan's answer did not fit the question. There was no doubt in their minds – something was not right with Meagan. Like I said before, these girls are good.

"All right," said Dominique. "I'll be stopping by later. Would you like something good to eat?"

"Huh, I'm sorry Sid. What did you say?" Meagan said.

"I'm Diamond. I'll tell you what – how about, later on, I'll bring you a few good things to eat. Then we can play catch up, okay? I'm going to hang up now. Love you girl," said Dominique, as she ended their call.

Meagan just sat there holding the phone mumbling, "okay, okay." Then, the dial tone came and Waverly looked at Meagan first, then gently removed the receiver from her ear.

"Okay Meagan Simone, why don't you lie down and rest your mind. Have you fed the twins yet?"

"What time does that chart say?" Meagan asked.

"Let's see. Last feeding was at five-thirty a.m. Looks like the next one's not until seven-thirty. Good, you have about forty-five minutes before they return. I'm going to leave now, but I'll call you later," Waverly said as she kissed Meagan's forehead.

Meagan just looked up at Waverly like a lost child – sorry, I mean a lost puppy.

"Call me later," Meagan said as she watched Waverly leave the room.

You see – true friendship is sometimes funny. Granting one his or her own space to fall short – not quite meet the mark or even being emotionally unavailable. Now – we're not suggesting that they be

allowed to never be held accountable. Just every now and then,
without holding it against them or even worse, throwing it up in their
faces whenever it's convenient for us...

●●●●

4 4 3 – 5 5 5 – 9 6 9 7...ring...ring...ring...ring "Pick up
Sidney Sharpe...pick up," Waverly said, as she checked her
eye, thinking one of her lashes must have fallen into her eye.

"Good morning, Sidney Sharpe. How may I help you?"

"Miss Sharpe, are we running behind this morning?"
asked Waverly.

"Well hello Mommy Dearest. I'm not sure how you're
running, but Miss Sharpe's on point," Sidney replied as she
fixed her hair, while waiting for the light to change.

"Okay now – cause between last night and this morning, I
really need to be balanced."

"Waverly Corrine – would you care to explain that
comment to me? You know it's too early to be speaking in
"tongues.""

"You're not funny Sidney. I'm serious! My husband –
let's just say he's definitely not his usual self. Beyond that, I
saw Meagan this morning and either her Doctor has her on
some serious drugs or I'm afraid she's losing it. Did you get
a chance to see her last night?"

"Yes, I saw our girlfriend. I do know that something's
troubling her. She wanted to tell me, but I don't think she
was quite ready. I believe it has something to do with her
mother Katherine. That's all I could figure out. Look, I'm
here at the hospital now."

"You're at the hospital! Now! How in the world are you
going to be able to meet us at the park in twenty minutes if
you're with Meagan playing doctor?" Waverly asked as she
shook her head.

"Calm down Judge Judy. I am taking our friend some
breakfast and then I'll be headed your way. Capiece!"

"Sidney Sharpe!"

"I'm losing you...I think we're breaking up. Waverly
Corrine, I can't hear you," said Sidney as she pressed the end
button on her phone.

Waverly wasn't shocked at all by Sidney's way of ending their call. All she could do was smile and shake her head. Sidney – on the other hand had bags in one hand and a fruit shake in the other, glanced at her watch and headed towards the elevator. Just as she raised her head, the elevator doors opened. Now Sidney, with one thing on her mind, immediately stepped into the elevator. But, you know when one person is entering a particular space and another is attempting to exit that same space, a collision is bound to happen unless a more patient person allows the other to go first. Well, guess who was getting off of the elevator... Crazy huh – Nurse Marjorie, accompanied by another co-worker, Assistant Nurse Danise.

"Okay, why don't you go first," said Nurse Marjorie as she stepped aside.

Sidney, remembering Marjorie from the previous night, just turned her lips up and gave her a stupid look.

"Good morning Dr. Sharpe. Nice to see you again," said Assistant Nurse Danise.

"Oh – Hi Danise! So this is where you disappeared to," Sidney replied.

Danise smiled as the elevator doors closed and said, "That is one brilliant Doctor."

"Did you just say Doctor? Do you know that woman?" asked Nurse Marjorie, as she stood frozen in her place.

"Along with most of the medical field. Dr. Sharpe's one of the top Anesthesiologist in the Country.   Beauty and brains," said Assistant Nurse Danise.

"Well, I'll be damn," replied Nurse Marjorie with her mouth wide opened.

"Come on girl, let's go home. And close your mouth," Danise said as she grabbed Marjorie's arm, pulling her down the hall.

I guess the correct phrase would be "Cat's got your tongue!" Well just as Sidney entered Meagan's room, her pager started beeping.

Beep... Beep... Beep... Beep... Beep... Beep... Beep... Beep...

●●●●

*ow there aren't many things that catch Sidney by
surprise. But, when she observed Meagan on her knees
praying, Sidney Sharpe was totally thrown. She
instinctively emptied her hands and put her pager in off
mode. Next, (can you believe it) she fell to her knees
beside Meagan and joined her in prayer. After giving
thanks for several minutes, Meagan exhaled and stood to her feet. She
had a gentle smile on her face. It was as if she'd received confirmation
of what to do. Then she noticed Sidney was still on her knees in
prayer. Meagan rubbed Sidney's head softly. Sidney then raised her
head and stood to her feet as well. These women are so unpredictable.
Sidney had tears in her eyes.*

"Now what's all this for?" Meagan asked as she wiped Sidney's face.

"I was just thinking of all the things we've been through together. Remember when Waverly had finals and Victor was sick?"

"Yes! You, Diamond and I took turns sitting with him until his fever got too high," replied Meagan.

"I know – then, Diamond called Waverly on our only cell phone. Remember – she yelled at us and told us to take her son to the hospital."

"We were so young. We didn't know how to care for a child then," Meagan said.

"Did you hear yourself? We were young and maybe we didn't know much then. But, look at us now. Diamond's a partner at one of the best law firms in D.C., Waverly's the youngest black female sitting judge, and you my friend – well let's just say that stores can't seem to keep your books on the shelves," Sidney said in total amazement.

"Aren't you forgetting something?"

"What?"

"Last I heard, you were the best at what you do as well. Speaking of that, don't you have somewhere to be?"

"I know! I mustn't keep Inspector Gadget and Mommy Dearest waiting. Are you really okay?"

"Yes, I'm better. I'm going to take a shower and get ready for the twins' feeding."

"Well okay girl, if I don't talk with you later, you'll know why."

"Oh yeah! your meetings. That's good Sid. I want you to take care of yourself. By the way, is that car in yet?"

"I think so. The dealership left me a message yesterday. I need to check all my calls anyway. Let me get out of here. See you later Meagan Simone," Sidney said as she kissed Meagan almost directly on her lips.

"Bye Sidney Sharpe," Meagan said as she watched her leave the room. Then, she turned to the mirror and said, "As for you, what did that book say – Stop Pouting, Get It Back Together!"

Meagan looked at herself for several seconds, turning her head from side to side and said, in a not so convincing voice, "I'll try." Then she went to the bathroom, closing the door behind her.

●●●●

*M*eanwhile, at *Rock Creek Park*, *Dominique* was in the middle of stretching just as *Waverly* walked up to meet her.

"I see that someone has little or no energy this morning," Dominique said.

"I have good reasons to be moving slow Miss Blake. My sleep was broken last night. On top of that, I got up extra early to check on our girlfriend okay?"

"No need to state your case. I'm just being observant. Have you had anything to drink besides your fruit juices?" asked Dominique.

"Sometimes I hate being so close to you and your girlfriends. Where is it, you little health addict?"

"In the backseat of the truck Miss Lady. And could you hurry it up, I'm just about stretched out," Dominique said as she was bending over placing her head between her legs.

Well as Waverly climbed into the back of Dominique's Range Rover, girlfriend accidentally bumped her finger on the briefcase, which was in front of the cooler.

"Damn it!" she yelled checking to see if she had broken a nail.

At that very moment, Sidney approached the truck with a big grin on her face. Of course, she noticed her clumsy girlfriend hurting herself. Now Waverly Corrine, as they refer to her most of the time, is one smart cookie. But, I don't think I mentioned that she's also – how can I put this nicely? –a little off-balanced. Two left feet, accident prone, always bumping into something or worse, someone. You kind of get the picture. Well, anyway, Sidney just stood there shaking her head and smiling at Waverly.

"My...my...my...such language for a district court Judge. And while you're in there, will you pass me a bottle of water?"

Waverly turned her head knowing it was Sidney and replied, "Mind your business Miss Sharpe. This manicure is only two days old. Besides, are you not here for something else?"

"All I said was your choice of words are a bit harsh for a lady Judge."

"Here girl," said Waverly as she handed Sidney the bottle of water.

"Let's get started, I'm sure our instructor awaits."
Both girls walked off.

"Waverly, would you like me to look at that?" Sidney asked as she reached for Waverly's hand.

Waverly first attempted to show Sidney her finger, but then looked at it and quickly pulled it away.

"You're not funny Sidney," laughed Waverly.

"What is so funny?" asked Dominique.

"Mommy dearest got a boo-boo and I only asked if she'd like me to take a look at it," answered Sidney.

"Oh Lord, the day is still young. Ladies it's almost seven-thirty, can we get started. I would like to get to work before lunch time," Dominique replied as she began running up their usual path.

Waverly and Sidney glanced at each other then followed. After about twenty minutes, Waverly stopped as usual and asked, "Can we pause for a second?"

"You can't be tired already," Dominique said.

"You know girl's getting old," Sidney said as she continued running in place.

"Both of you can go straight to hell. I need a minute."

"You probably need more than that. You did say your sleep was disturbed last night."

"Oh really! What about last night? Are you saying that Daddy's acting right again?" asked Sidney.

"I didn't say that. In fact, he was *too* generous if you know what I mean."

"Do tell!" Dominique said as she checked her watch and sat on the ground.

"Damn girl, this isn't the Love Connection. Calm down, we understand that it has been quite a long time for you," Sidney said.

"Hush your mouth Sidney Sharpe!" said Dominique as she placed her hand up in the air.

"May I please continue my story? Anyway, you know he was M.I.A. all day yesterday."

"*M.I.A.?*"

"Missing in action Gomer," replied Sidney.

"Anyway, by the time he returned home. Vincent was just *too* nice. Normally my loving husband wants me to service him."

"Service him! Did I miss something?" asked Dominique.

"Head! You know that pleasurable thing women do to men. However, there are some men who do it too," Sidney said laughing.

"Anyway. Boyfriend started from the top of my head and did not end at the bottom of my feet. Before he was done, I was flat on my belly – ass all up in the air. It was as if he had taken lessons. By the time he was finished with me, I was furious. Unfortunately, I was too tired to say a word. But, that's not all – he never penetrated me. You figure it out," said Waverly with a funny look on her face.

"He never penetrated you?"

"Fucked her Dominique!" yelled Sidney.

"I don't need you to spell it out for me Sidney. I got that part. Damn, he's good."

"I know, irresistible too," said Waverly as she continued running.

"Come on my green little straight laced friend," said
Sidney as she stretched her hand out to help Dominique to
her feet.

"You don't know me. You think you know me – I'm not
green," Dominique said as she rolled her eyes at Sidney and
jogged off.

Sidney stood there with her eyebrows raised, giggling to herself.
Next, her pager beeped.

"Who is this? Oh – Sherian – this is your second call. I
am fine sister dear. What could she possibly want?" Sidney
said to herself as she erased the number.

Sidney then checked her watch and ran up the hill to catch
up with Waverly and Dominique.

"That was good! I'll catch up with you ladies later. Hugs
and kisses," said Dominique as she pulled off.

"Do you have a busy day Sid?" asked Waverly.

"My first appointment's not until 12:45 p.m. I'm going to
call in anyway as soon as I leave here. Are you going to be
okay? Don't let that man trip you up."

"I will be fine. I have special plans for my beloved
husband."

"That's what I'm talking about. You know the rule of
thumb when it comes to a female's intuition."

Can you believe those two women eagerly shouted...

"First and foremost, our first intuition is always, always
correct. And last, but not least, we're never wrong!!"

Then they began laughing and giving each other high fives.

"Love you girl," Waverly said as she blew Sidney a kiss
while opening her car door.

Sidney simply returned the kiss and replied, "And I you."

● ● ● ●

*N**ot a minute later, Sidney's cell phone rang again.*
Waverly waved good-bye and pulled off. Sidney nodded
her head then instinctively checked the caller I.D before
answering.

"Good morning Sherian. Before you start
with me, I did get your message last night. But,
it was really late when I arrived home."

"Look Sid, I understand that you are a little busy. And maybe you're not trying to totally disregard my calls. Believe it or not, I'm not checking up on you. Right now, I'm trying to pretend that I really don't care what you're doing."

"Yeah all right my darling sister. Would you care to tell me what's on your mind?" Sidney asked as she dropped her car key.

Sherian shook her head and said, "You really think this is about you? Do you recall a dear sweet lady named Phyllis Maple?"

"Would that be the same woman who gave birth to us?"

"Yes, and she is requesting that we meet her at 3:45 p.m. in her doctor's office today."

"3:45, 3:45," Sidney mumbled as she picked up her car key.

"Don't you even say that's going to be a problem. You normally find time to do whatever you please. Mommy seldom asks anything of you. You're so selfish! I can't believe you Sidney!" Sherian said in a very harsh tone.

"You're the one tripping. I was simply trying to recall my schedule for today. I am expected at the hospital this afternoon," Sidney replied.

"Then it will work out just fine. The doctor's office is less than a three minute stroll from your office."

"I know where it is," laughed Sidney.

"I don't get it. What is so funny?"

"Nothing! Nothing at all. I just find it very interesting how you always manage to put demands on my time, almost as if… Never mind, forget it. I'll see what I can do about this afternoon."

"Unless you're in the middle of surgery, be there!"

Next, there was a long pause in the two sisters conversation. Sidney then closed her eyes, took a deep breath, shook her head and said, "Look, if there's nothing else you want of me, I'm going to hang up now."

"Why do you always do that?"

"Do what?"

"Take things the wrong way."

"I'll see you later, okay. And I will try to be there," Sidney said just before she hung up the phone.

After the line went dead, Sherian looked at the phone and shook her head. Now it would be safe to say that Sherian and Sidney are definitely sisters. I would even go as far to assume that they are probably just alike. However, I believe that the friction comes from the two being fifteen years apart. Maybe Sherian knows something that we don't. Just maybe, she's desperately trying to save her younger sister from some of the same mistakes she made. Well anyway, back at the Law Offices of Sherman, Blake, Edmonds, and Wright. Dominique has just stepped off the elevator.

●●●●

Good morning Miss Blake," said Barbara, one of the office receptionists.

"Well good morning Barbara. Did Lauri come in yet?" asked Dominique.

"You're not that lucky. But, you did receive two calls this morning. One from a Mrs. Davis and the other was a Miss Nelson. Hey, I made some vanilla roast coffee. Would you like me to bring you a cup? Two sugars – no cream?" Barbara said with a smile.

"That would be great," Dominique replied as she walked down the hall towards her office.

Just before entering her office, Dominique glanced at her watch and looked over at her Secretary's desk. Unfortunately, all she could do was shake her head and move forward with her day.

"Let's see. Urgent. Okay, 410-555-3712. Come on, pick up. Good morning, may I speak with a Mrs. Davis? My name is Dominique Blake. I'm returning her call from the Law Offices of Sherman, Blake, Edmonds and Wright," Dominique said as she tapped her pencil on the edge of the desk.

"Oh – Hi Miss Blake! I'm Mrs. Davis! Thank you so much for getting back with me so quickly. I was referred to you by one of my colleagues. What I need to talk with you about is simply unimaginable. In fact, it's not appropriate for the telephone. Can you see me right now?"

"Well my first appointment isn't due for at least an hour," Dominique said as she glanced at the schedule on her computer.

"I know it's really no notice, but if there's anyway at all possible?"

"Where are you now Ma'am?"

"I am right across the street at the coffee shop Miss Blake. I was hoping that – well, if you had a moment. There is one other thing I need to mention; there is another family involved. In fact, we thought it would be better if your office represented us both. Her name is Miss Nelson," explained Mrs. Davis.

"I'll tell you what – let's take one step back to review your case. How does that sound?" Dominique said as she politely interrupted Mrs. Davis.

"I'm sorry! I know I'm racing! It's just that my boy's still in intensive care. And right now, I'm just not so sure of my next thoughts," Mrs. Davis replied.

Suddenly, there was a soft knock on Dominique's office door. One second later, Laurie peeked her head through the door and said, "Excuse me. Good morning Miss Blake. You have a Miss Nelson on line four."

Dominique smiled at Laurie, then placed her hand over the receiver and said, "Thank you! Oh and good morning to you Laurie. Okay Mrs. Davis, I have Miss Nelson on the line. Why don't you come to my office now, while I take this call."

"God bless you. I'll be right over," *Mrs. Davis said as she closed her eyes and shook her head. But just before Dominique could answer the other call, Laurie returned. This time with a hot cup of vanilla roast.*

"Two sugars, no cream," she said placing the hot mug on Dominique's desk.

"That's perfect! Now any minute a Mrs. Davis should be here. When she arrives, escort her to one of the conference rooms. Thanks for holding. Dominique Blake speaking, how may I help you?"

"Good morning Miss Blake. A Mrs. Davis gave me your name. We met at the hospital when it was brought to our attention that the same snake abused our boys. Now, I'm not quite sure of Charlie's age, but my grandson Scottie's only sixteen. I would have never allowed him to work at that shop if I thought this could happen. I know Scottie's almost a man, but to me he's still just a boy," said Miss Nelson in a very concerned voice.

"Miss Nelson – right now I'm not at all familiar with this case. However, I would like to see you later this afternoon if that's possible," Dominique said as she turned herself around in her chair.

"Well right now, I'm on my way to pick Scottie up from the hospital. They're going to discharge him this morning. This whole thing seems like a nightmare. I haven't had a good night's rest in three days," Miss Nelson said as she blew her nose. "I'm sorry! Don't pay me no mind."

"Well then, it's settled. We'll meet at 3:00 p.m. today at my office. That should work out just fine because by that time, I will have already spoken with Mrs. Davis. If necessary, we can all meet again later tonight or first thing in the morning. Now – since this matter definitely involves your grandson, I'll need to speak with him as soon as possible. Will Scottie be able to accompany you today?"

"This has been so very hard for him to accept. And, I'm not really sure of what actually happened. How can people be so cruel to children?" Miss Nelson said as she shook her head.

"Now it's going to be imperative that we all meet. And as soon as he knows this – the easier its' going to be on him to accept this whole ordeal. I really don't know what else I can tell you."

"Very well, Miss Blake. My boy and I will see you at 3:00 p.m. But, as God is my witness if what my grandson's saying is true, hell will seem like *heaven* to that bastard once Annie Nelson's through with him! Good day Ma'am," said Miss Nelson as she ended their call.

●●●●

*N*ow *that was funny! Grandma's not playing. I sure as hell would hate to be on the other end of that stick. That last comment even caught Dominique by surprise. All girl could do was, look at the receiver and shout in utter amazement, "Damn!"*

At that moment, Laurie opened the door and said, "Mr. and Mrs. Davis are in Conference Room 4. The snack bar is set up and there's fresh water on the table. I'll grab my laptop and meet you in two minutes."

"Thanks," replied Dominique as she smiled and shook her head.

"Is everything all right Miss Blake?"

"Yes, but I have a feeling this meeting's going to be a mouthful. I'll probably need another cup of that tasty blend. Will you be so kind? I'll just be one minute behind you."

"Sure lady," Laurie replied, as she closed Dominique's office door.

Dominique then went into her private powder room and immediately, as always, began a silent prayer asking only for fairness, insight and the ability to wait patiently for an answer. Oh and of course, favor. I'm sure by now you're convinced that Dominique Blake is profoundly smart. However, even Dominique knows where her power comes from. The girl always prays before formally meeting a new client. Once she was done, Dominique glanced at her oversized mirror, and made a funny face at herself. She then left her office and headed for the conference room. Upon entering the room, Dominique noticed a confused sense of silence. She walked over to the huge oval shaped redwood table, held her hand out and said with a smile,

"Hi, I'm Dominique Blake. It's a pleasure to meet you both."

Now can you believe that absolutely nothing was said – I mean the Davis family gave no response. Mr. Davis sat back in the chair with his hands folded and his head hung low. While Mrs. Davis rocked back and forth, holding her bible tightly pressed against her breast. Dominique took a deep breath, exhaled, and looked over to Laurie and then back to the Davis'. Her eyes moved upward in the direction of the grandfather clock on the wall. Then she thought to herself,

I have about forty-five minutes before my next client arrives. And Mrs. Morris' is always – always in a hurry. Okay, think Dominique.

Dominique sat down at the end of the table, which placed her to the left side of Mrs. Davis. At that point, Mrs. Davis turned her head toward Dominique and looked right into Dominique's eyes as tears rolled down her cheeks and her lips began to quiver. Ironically, words did not follow. Dominique looked at Mrs. Davis and said,

"We will fix this."

"I can't possibly begin to... Our son Charlie's in really bad shape," Mrs. Davis said as she wiped her tears.

"Can you tell us what happened?"

"I really don't know... Three days ago, Charlie didn't come home from school. Then, he called me around 5:30, wanting to know if he could meet his friend Scott at the Mall. Charles rambled on and on about how they were going to grab something to eat at the Mall. Of course, I said yes, thinking that – okay, he should be home no later than 9:30 or 10:00. We had a late dinner. That was around 7:00. Afterwards, my husband went into his study to work on a project and I had a glass of cognac. I believe that I dozed off and a little after that... The last thing I recall were those horrible sounds. I couldn't figure out exactly where they were coming from. Then, it dawned on me that it was the doorbell and someone was banging on the door – non-stop," Mrs. Davis said as she looked over at her husband.

"And where were you Mr. Davis?" asked Dominique.

"Just a few minutes before the doorbell rang, I stopped working for a moment to go to take a leak. My first thought was, Charles must have forgotten his keys again. So I was in no hurry to get the door. But, then Daisy started swearing and screaming. I knew right then that something had happened to Charles," explained Mr. Davis.

"It was horrible! The police officer told me that my son Charlie had been sodomized and drugged. And if that wasn't enough, by the time we got to Howard University Hospital, we found our Charlie in a coma," Mrs. Davis said trying so hard not to cry.

"Wow! I can see why you couldn't possibly talk about this over the phone. Is Charles still unconscious?" Dominique asked.

"We saw Charles earlier today and yes he's still out of it. But, that boy Scott is going to be released this afternoon. I don't trust him! Never did!" Mr. Davis said in a very harsh tone.

"Stop that right now Ethan! Scottie's not the blame for this. He and Charlie's been friends for a very long time. I won't believe anything else. And, you shouldn't either Ethan Davis," Mrs. Davis retorted.

"Why do you think Scott is at fault Mr. Davis?" asked Dominique.

Mr. Davis first looked at his wife – then at Dominique and answered, "My son has been in a coma for three days. Scott Griffin, granted was shaken up for the most part, walked away from this unexplained episode with a few bumps and scrapes. I believe the only reason the hospital kept him under observation was because, for two days, that coward refused to talk about it. I knew right then, Scott was familiar with the culprit. But no, he remained silent. Fortunately for us, his grandmother scared some sense into him. Those doctors tested that boy for everything. They even talked about placing him in a mental ward," laughed Mr. Davis. "You know that little sissy sounded off then."

"That's when the police picked up Scottie's boss. They're charging him with statutory rape, assault in the first degree and attempted murder in the first degree. Some how, I still don't think that's enough considering the shape he left our boy in," explained Mrs. Davis.

"Let's go back for one moment. You said the police are charging Scott's boss for this. Who exactly does Scott work for and how did the two boys end up in this man's company?" Dominique inquired.

"Scott works at a well-known hair salon called Colours and Cutz," Mr. Davis explained.

"I know the place. Remember when you asked me about a month ago, who colored my hair Miss Blake?" interrupted Laurie.

"Yes, I remember. Good! You're already familiar with the place. Have you rescheduled another color appointment yet?" asked Dominique.

"I wasn't quite due. I mean, I probably could use a few more highlights," said Laurie as she continued typing notes on her computer.

"This is still so very incomplete. Without having spoken directly with Scott and Charles and not to mention the fact that I haven't reviewed the doctor's findings... Then there's the police report. Unless you're leaving something out, I believe we have enough to get started. I just need you to sign some documents acknowledging our firm as your Attorney. Excuse me for one minute," said Dominique, just before she left the conference room.

"May I have a glass of water?" asked Mrs. Davis.

"Of course," answered Laurie.

After giving Mrs. Davis a glass of water, Laurie began passing Mr. Davis several documents.

"You mean to tell me you need all of these signed before you can see Charles?!" Mr. Davis asked shaking his head.

"I'm afraid so sir. This will ensure the protection of Charles, as well as our firm. It's just a formality," explained Laurie.

At that moment, Dominique returned with Franklin and said "Mr. and Mrs. Davis, this is Franklin Lewis. He will be assisting us with this case."

"Please to meet you both," Franklin said as he nodded his head.

"Laurie, do you have all the signatures needed?" asked Dominique.

"Just about."

"Good, we'll get started with this. I'll call you later after my meeting with Miss Nelson and Scott this afternoon. Do either of you have anymore questions?"

"No."

"Me neither. I just want to know what happened to my son," replied Mr. Davis.

"That's a very good question. I should have some answers for you later," Dominique said as she walked the Davis' to the elevator.

"Thank you so much Miss Blake," said Mrs. Davis as she gave Dominique a very tight hug.

The elevator doors opened and Mr. and Mrs. Davis stepped in. As the doors began to close, Dominique looked Mrs. Davis right in the eyes and said,

"You're very welcome."

As she turned around to go back to her office, Franklin was standing directly behind her shaking his head.

"Don't say one word! I know exactly what you're thinking. Let's at least wait until we talk to Scott," Dominique said as she grabbed Franklin by the arm pulling him down the hall.

After entering her office, Franklin closed the door behind them. Dominique and Franklin looked at each other, and then Franklin said,

"You know, this whole thing sounds a little fishy. How does two teenagers get drugged and sodomized at the same time? I'll bet they were willing participants. Not only that – it sounds like, from what you told me, the father's in deep denial about his son's sexuality. Many many holes."

"Maybe so Frankie, but they were still very much under age... After my next appointment, I'm going to visit the hospital. Why don't you make a few calls to get the status on our salon owner. Call me as soon as you know something," Dominique said as she rubbed her chin.

At that moment, Laurie buzzed Dominique on the intercom.

"Yes Laurie," said Dominique as she waved good-bye to Franklin.

"Your 10:00 o'clock appointment has arrived," Laurie replied.

"Good. Give me five minutes and send her in," Dominique said as she glanced at her watch.

Next, Dominique picked up her phone and immediately called Waverly.

Ring...Ring...Ring...Ring...Ring...Ring...Ring... Ring... Ring...

●●●●

Good morning. Judge Simmons' office. Grace speaking. How may I help you?" asked Grace.

"Hi Grace, is the Colonel available at this time?"

Grace giggled and answered, "Always for you Miss Blake. Hold one moment while I buzz her for you. Excuse me Judge Simmons; Miss Blake's on line two."

"Thanks Gracie... Miss Blake, isn't it a bit early for lunch?" Waverly asked as she skimmed through her reviews.

"I think you should keep your day time job because your jokes really suck. I was just calling to see who would be accompanying Meagan tomorrow when she's released from the hospital? You know I'm always eager for new clients, but I'll be damned if the most unlikely folks haven't crossed my path this morning. They left such a bitter taste in my mouth that I've forgotten which blend of coffee I had this morning," explained Dominique.

"Well I have no doubt you'll be sharing in one, two..." Waverly mumbled.

"Waverly Corrine – two teenaged boys were, and I quote, sodomized and drugged at the same time. Can you believe it? Supposedly, the employer of one of the boys carried out the crime. But, what's more bizarre – now get this, the employer is an owner of the one and only 'Colours and Cutz!!'. Now what would a salon owner be doing with two under age children. I don't get it! First you shampoo hair and then clean up the place. Okay, but then your reward is, I give you some drugs then force myself on you," Dominique said as she shook her head.

"Well that would be a bit bizarre. Mmm, you and your clients."

Laurie buzzed Dominique again. This time reminding her that Mrs. Morris, who's always – always in a hurry, was on her way in. Dominique's red flag immediately rose. So of course, Girl ended her call.

●●●●

Waverly on the other hand, found herself caught up in what I might describe as a Deja vu moment... You know, the thing you people do when you're dreaming, yet you're wide awake. Or would that be considered daydreaming. Well, you get the picture. Anyway, Waverly Corrine was having a moment. Can you believe the Girl's thinking back to when she was but a girl – perhaps sixteen or maybe a little older?

Now that wouldn't be suds, possibly shampoo. No she did not work at a head shop. Did girlfriend have her very own little shop of horrors? No, no, no, don't snap out of it now! Dag! Just when it was getting good. And now it looks as if she has the shakes. Oh Miss Thing, one might believe you have something or someone up your judicial robe. I mean sleeve. And I know that's not perspiration on your forehead. I think I smell something fishy in Judge Simmons' Chambers as well.

Anyway, Girl took a very long deep breath – then blew it out slowly as she closed her eyes, trying desperately to erase those unforgettable thoughts from her mind. She opened her eyes and continued breathing in and out slowly until she was able to calm herself down. I guess it would be safe to say that Waverly Corrine just experienced a panic attack. But, why is it that when we're on the edge of sanity versus insanity, they're far and few souls we feel close to. I mean she just got off the phone with Dominique. Meagan is having drama of her own. While Sidney, well you know Sidney. The only other person who might somewhat be available is none other than Dr. Vincent Simmons – Waverly's other half. So what else is a girl to do? Call her man for some comfort.

Ring...Ring...Ring...Ring...Ring...Ring...Ring...Ring ... Ring...

●●●●

H oward University Hospital, how may I direct your call?" said the operator.

"Good morning. I'm trying to reach Dr. Vincent Simmons, but was directed to you. Can you transfer the call to his office for me?" Waverly asked.

"Of course Ma'am. Who may I say is calling?"

"His wife, Judge Simmons."

"Good morning Judge Simmons. Hold one moment please while I connect you... I'm sorry he's not picking up."

"That's strange. Vincent said he would be at the hospital today – something about a meeting with that Pfizer group. Is that making any sense to you?"

"Can you hold for one more minute? I'm going to check with someone else. It will only take a second," explained the operator.

The operator then placed Waverly on hold. However, that one minute turned into three minutes and fifteen seconds. Poor Waverly – not really being her razor sharp self was truly ready to hang up. Reluctantly, her need to know exactly what the hospital operator was going to come back and tell her was far greater. Finally, that irritating elevator music paused again and the operator returned.

"Judge Simmons – sorry it took so long. I checked with Dr. Simmons' office. First, there was a conference, but that ended over a week ago. Second, Dr. Simmons is on call today. Maybe you misunderstood him. You might want to check the sports club. I know a lot of our physicians go there when they are in between shifts," explained the operator.

Waverly's forehead wrinkled and she immediately reflected back to the conversation she had with Dr. Cummings the night prior. She rubbed her forehead and exhaled, forcing herself to relax and not react. Girl's good. A little off balanced from time to time, but she's definitely a thinker. Some people just feel and react accordingly. Not Waverly! She has the patience to play the entire album. Before she could respond to the operator's findings, her mind was already made up to fully uncover her beloved husband's blatant lies.

"I'm sorry. I'm sitting here looking at my calendar and it's on the wrong date," she said with a slight giggle in her voice.

"That's quite all right. I sometimes do that myself. May I help you with anything else?"

"No, I think you've helped enough today! Thank you for your time," Waverly said as she ended their call.

Waverly shook her head and rolled her eyes simultaneously as she rested her back in her beautiful antique captain's chair. Girl thought to herself for a moment and then buzzed her Secretary.

●●●●

Gracie, would you get Judge Michael on the phone for me please?"

"Right away Judge Simmons."

Waverly stood to her feet, stretching her tensed body, while glancing in her tall oval mirror noticing just how attractive she really is. Girl turned her head from side to side and said,

"If you really think you're going to get away with this shit again…"

But, before she could complete her thought, Grace buzzed her back.

"Judge Michaels is on line one."

Waverly Corrine wasted no time getting to the phone.

"Don, how's my favorite colleague?" Waverly asked in her most charming voice.

"Much, much better now, after hearing your sweet melody," answered Judge Michael.

"You're too much. Anyway, I wish I was just calling for a friendly chat, but that's not the case Don."

"Then why don't you tell a friend what's on your mind."

Waverly placed her hand on her forehead and said, "Now Don, before you go on telling me to think of my position, consider my family, or think very hard about what I'm about to share with you, the answers are yes! yes! and of course! Right now Don, I believe I'm just fed up and tired of being made a fool of. You've always told me to trust my very first intuition. And, I can truly say that my head is clear."

"Waverly, are you talking about your marriage?"

"I'm afraid so. I don't hate him. We've been through too much. I just can't accept his duel lifestyle. And, the funny thing about Vincent is, I really believe he thinks there's nothing wrong with it. I know he's seeing someone else. I just know it. When I confirm this information for the um-teenth time, I'm asking him for a divorce. We've raised our son. What other reasons are there for us to continue on this way? Convenience!"

"How about love? You mentioned that you guys have been through hell and back. Could these feelings you have so strongly be related to some of your unresolved issues from the last time this happened?"

"I've thought about that too and the answer is no. I have healthy relationships all around me. I know the difference. When you're constantly questioning how you feel about someone else's behavior... There you go! Grounds for suspicion. Besides, I'm in a place in my life where there's no time for unfulfilled days. There was a time when Vincent was all the man I needed and wanted. But now, you know I don't need that anyone. Especially a self-centered, Mr. "know everything" like him. Sometimes I think he wants to be the woman in this relationship," Waverly said with her lips upside down.

"Come on Waverly Corrine. How so?"

"He just does! For starters, he owns more beauty products than I do. And do you know my darling Vincent visits the salon twice a week. He probably screwed his hairdresser too. But, that's not my problem with him. I don't trust him anymore. So really, what's left?"

"Now I know this is going to sound elementary, but have you guys considered counseling?"

"Year right! Judge W.C. Simmons and her well-known husband, Dr. Vincent Simmons sitting in front of a shrink. You've *got* to be kidding! I was thinking more so about hiring a P.I."

"That's nasty! You know one could find all sorts of things when you go looking. Do you really want to dig up a bunch of old waste?"

"Whatever it's going to take to get my point across. Remember last summer when you had that situation with Marla? That never went public and your daughter was returned home safely. That's the same kind of discretion I need. And, money's no object. So what do you say? Are you going to help a girl out or what?" Waverly asked.

"Of course I'm going to help you. But..." Judge Michaels said just before Waverly interrupted him.

"No buts Don! My mind is made up. Someone once told me, never write a check that your ass can't cash. So if my husband's willing to live on the edge, then he must also be ready to suffer the consequences. Life's a bitch and then you die; or worst, you turn into one."

"Okay, okay already! But, remember you've been warned. Let's see. Where is it? Okay... here we are. The name of the company is Sheppard Investigations. When you call them, be sure to ask for Keith. Oh and one more thing... Please listen to Keith before you make anymore decisions. He's a very bright young man," explained Judge Michaels.

"Young man! How old exactly is this boy?"

"Waverly Corrine, do you want the number or not?" Judge Michaels replied.

"Of course I want the number . . . ."

"You're something else lady. The number is 202-555-0555. Now, is there anything else I can assist you with?"

"No Donald... But you do know how much I truly adore you."

"That's what you keep telling me!"

"Good day Judge Michaels," Waverly said with a big smile on her face.

"Good day to you Judge Simmons," Judge Michaels replied as he smiled just before hanging up the phone.

Waverly, mind you couldn't help but think to herself... In the past it's been several times she needed and wanted her husband's support. Needless to say, Dr. Simmons somehow managed to be totally physically and/or emotionally unavailable. Who could blame her at this point? So, girlfriend adjusted her Gucci frames, took a sip of the herbal tea that was still sizzling hot and immediately called Sheppard Investigations.

•••

*U*mm... *202-555-0555..." The telephone rang three times. Waverly, being angst and somewhat fearful too, held the receiver firmly. Girl checked her nails and glanced at her watch twice before someone finally picked up.*

"Sheppard Investigations... Good morning, Sheppard Investigations... Is anyone there? Hello...." said the Secretary.

Now this is real special. Girlfriend goes through all of that and just when it's time to put your money where your mouth is – she's speechless! All that talk and no action. Didn't she just tell Donald, "as soon as I confirm this for the um-teenth time, I'm asking for a divorce." And now, you're hanging up! You do need help girl. So what now?"

"202-555-0555. Okay, you can do this," Waverly mumbled to herself.

Ring...Ring...Ring...   Ring...Ring...Ring... Ring...Ring...Ring...

"Good morning, Sheppard Investigations. How may I help you?" said the Secretary once again.

Ironically, before Waverly could respond, Grace buzzed her with an urgent call. Waverly placed her hand over the receiver and said, "What is it Grace?"

"You have a call on line two," she replied.

Waverly shook her head, removed her hand from the receiver and said, "Good morning. I'm sorry. Will you hold for a moment?"

The Secretary exhaled and said, "Sure."

Waverly quickly placed the Secretary on hold, while she answered the other call.

"Judge Simmons."

"Hey beautiful! How's your day going?" Vincent asked with an inviting tone.

Waverly's brows rose instinctively as she hesitated with her answer.

"My day is going! Where are you?"

"Well that's the reason I'm calling. Your Prince Charming is going to be stuck at this conference for the rest of the day. I thought I'd touch base now so you wouldn't be worried or miss me. They're supposed to serve us dinner afterwards. So, I'm figuring I should be home no later than eight or nine. Will you wait up for me?"

"Wait up for you. I believe it's a little premature to say exactly what I will or will not do later. Look, I was right in the middle of something when you called . . . ."

"Are you blowing me off Mrs. Simmons?"

"Of course not, but I do need to get back to work. Call me later if you get a minute," Waverly said with a frown on her face.

"That's a winner. Until then," Vincent said as he ended their call.

Waverly simply closed her eyes and shook her head. Almost forgetting about the other call until she noticed the light was still flashing.

"Hello! Are you still there?" Waverly asked.

"Sure am. May I help you at this time?" the Secretary replied.

"I hope so. I'm not quite sure how this whole thing works. I was told to ask for a man named Keith. Is he available?"

"Well right now he's with a client. May I take your name and a number where you can be reached?"

"No! I mean, my name is Corrine and right now I'm at work. I can't get calls here. I mean, I can, but I don't think I want him calling me at work. I was thinking maybe he could meet me somewhere public," Waverly said tensely.

"Can you hold for one minute? Let me see what I can do," said the Secretary just before she placed Waverly on hold.

Funny... Can you believe that same irritating elevator music came on? Waverly just shook her head and whispered to herself, "Not this again."

Fortunately for her, the Secretary only took a minute.

"Hi Miss Corrine. Thanks for holding. Keith asked if you could meet him at Houston's around five?"

"Five – I guess if that's the only time he can see me. I was hoping he could fit me in closer to lunch time."

"Sorry, Keith is really booked up for the next month or so."

"Well five it shall be."

"Good! The reservations will be under the name Sheppard. Oh, one other thing. I need a number where we can reach you – only in case of emergency. We are very discreet," explained the Secretary.

Waverly hesitated and said, "This is what I'll do. I will be at Houston's at a quarter till five. If for some reason Keith cannot be there, have him call the Restaurant."

"I think that can be arranged. However, if you decide to use our services, there's a thousand dollar deposit required along with a photograph of the person you wish to have investigated. And no personal checks."

"Wow! You think you've covered everything," Waverly said as she sat up in her chair.

"Its just procedure Miss Corrine. I have to go over this with all of our new clients. One thing's for sure! We guarantee results on all jobs taken," replied the Secretary.

"Well then, I look forward to doing business with your company. Thank you and good day."

"The pleasure's mine. Have a fantastic day Miss Corrine," said the Secretary just before she ended their call.

Waverly, however, being predetermined to restore wholeness to her life was still very undecided of her next move, concerning her uncommitted spouse. And what would one do in a space such as this? Same boo-boo, different day. Okay, you choose not telling your friends until you've convinced yourself that there's no turning back – especially if you've been down this road before. You try not to contaminate your children in hopes that they won't end up on drugs or in therapy. But, then there's work. Who can be productive when you're emotionally unavailable? Although most people are either off balanced and/or emotionally unavailable... Girl surely stated earlier that therapy wasn't even a minute option.

From a surface view, Judge W.C. Simmons has all of her ducks in a row. She's the youngest black female judge in her field, I believe she's a perfect size eight, long healthy light reddish blonde hair – although it's always, always pinned up. Flawless skin! An inviting smile, more muscles than one of those appetizers at Houston's, and a somewhat off sense of humor. Did I mention that Missy has great curves? Her son's a straight "A" student in his second year of college and we cannot overlook the fact that her husband is, outside of being in the class of cheaters, a prominent physician.

So I would imagine she has to be very precise with regards to her character and which decision to make. It will have a direct affect on the rest of her life. I once heard someone say, if it doesn't affect you directly – well, it doesn't affect you... I think you missed that. How about the phrase, hitting home? So before you sit there and assume what you believe Waverly's next move should be, ask yourself, "what would I do?" And, take a risk and not kid yourself about it. You know some are quite content in their make believe world. Tricky, tricky...

So *Waverly Corrine, being the big Girl that she really is, sat back* in *her beautiful antique captain's chair and removed her designer frames. She blinked her green/gray eyes, just a few times to regain her sense of direction. Funny, just as I said before, Girl somehow redirected her mind to automatically switch to work mode. You could say it's like riding a bike. Once you know, you never forget. Whether it's sunshine or rain. If you feel happy or sad, a girl's gotta do, what a girl's gotta do! So, Girl pulled herself up to the desk and continued working. Of course, she checked her watch first to see how much time remained before her meeting with Keith.*

●●●●

Chapter Four

What if

A few hours later...

"First of all, I would like to apologize for failing to take that additional step forward when Meagan's blood level remained so low during most of her pregnancy. There are many – many instances where women are anemic during pregnancy. Which was your case Meagan, " Dr. Stone said as she tried explaining her reasonings for being simply careless.

"I'm not sure I'm following you Dr. Stone. Where – where are you going with all of this? We are totally aware of the miscarriages we've suffered before the birth of our girls. You said yourself, my health may have been poor due to a terrible diet and lack of rest," Meagan said as she stared into her Doctor's eyes trying not to associate her Mother's conversation with the one she was having now.

Drake, who's always, always the optimist, just sat there. You know, not really sitting up right – more hunched over with his arms resting upon his thighs. But, can we freeze this screen for a moment.

My guess is, as crazy as all this seems, neither one of them would be here if they'd stopped at miscarriage number four. Drake kept pushing the issue of the need for them, him, whatever you wish to call it – to have a complete quote/unquote, family. He had Meagan, whose body had been broken down, convinced that the Priest told him they would have children some day. All Meagan wanted was to please her husband. Now I have no idea what you're thinking, but I can tell you that Dr. Erica Stone is truly baffled.

Let me just say that Dr. Stone is a highly intelligent African American doctor. The Tyler's admire her solely on the basis that she is the best in her field. Granted, I'm no Einstein, but all babies are routinely tested at birth for everything under the Sun. Now something's not adding up! Dr. Stone is simply trying to pass on some prudent information to the Tyler's. Are you still with me? Good, then hit your pause button.

"Meagan. Mr. Tyler, today most of your daughter's test results were received. Now some of them will have to be run again, just for certainty. But, as I was examining your daughter Nia, while reviewing the test results and knowing you as the parents of this child, it dawned on me how something like this slipped through the cracks." Dr. Stone said as she placed her hands in her side pockets.

Drake and Meagan first just looked at each other, then back at Dr. Stone. Drake reached over and grabbed Meagan's hand as he pressed his teeth tightly together still waiting for Lords knows what. And can you believe in the back of his mind, he was hopelessly thinking that this too might well be a dream. Maybe...

Dr. Stone took a deep breath and said, "Nia has the 'Sickle Cell Trait.' I know this can't possibly make sense to you. It didn't make much sense to me either. But, regardless of what I want to believe, blood tests, especially a series of them, are never wrong."

Meagan stood to her feet, raised her right hand in the air and began shouting, "All of this is simply outrageous! Not only is it unlikely, it's damn right unacceptable! Nothing fits. And no offense to you, you're out of order for bringing this to us. Are you color blind? I might not be a doctor, but the last time I checked, that shit happens to black people. People like you!"

Typical white girl... Drake just pulled Meagan down close to him – trying so hard to give his wife comfort, when it suddenly hit him that there was without a doubt, absolutely nothing he could do. The two just sat on the edge of that tiny uncomfortable hospital bed and cried softly. Dr. Stone, being truly a woman of God was not annoyed at all by Meagan's reaction. If anything, I believe she too felt their pain.

"I'll leave so you two can be alone for a little while," *Dr. Stone said as she stepped backwards slowly until her back was flush against the wall. She reached for the doorknob while turning her head back towards Meagan and Drake. At that moment, Dr. Stone thought to herself, This is the part I truly hate. I understand that I'm just their doctor and it would be easier to accept that things happen, but this is unusual. There has to be more to this.*

I hope so – because last I looked, that disease is found primarily in African Americans. Now either there's a little bit of black in Meagan or Drake, or someone is going to have to come up with a pretty good reason for all of this. Even still, I'll bet Meagan is really blown away by this...

"Dra, why is this happening to us?"

"I don't know. But, we're definitely getting to the bottom of this mess. Something's very wrong and someone's not telling us everything," Drake said as he wiped Meagan's tears.

"Well, don't look at me!" Meagan said as she pulled away.

Drake chuckled and said, "I'm not talking about you silly."

••••

M *eanwhile, over at Howard University Hospital, Scott Griffin was preparing to leave. But, you know just as Franklin thought, somehow something wasn't quite right. And, you know Dominique had that same feeling. My guess is – there's no doubt that someone's holding back. Is that water I hear again? Oh, that's Scott taking a leak. I wonder what's in the back of his mind. Maybe he'll feel like sharing with us...*

"Ah shit!" Scott said as he felt his rear end, trying to count just how many stitches he had. "Damn! it never fails, you tell folks a little and as always, they take as much as they want. Ooh! as bad as my tail hurts, it'll be weeks before I can do anything," Scott laughed to himself. "Damn! my boy Charlie's weak. I don't know why I believed him when he told me that he did this before. One thing's for sure, that punk better not say one word. At least not until I collect my money. Huh, the next time, I'm going solo... What time is it? I don't believe this! They took my watch! I still had two payments left. I'd better hurry! My Grandmother will be here any minute. And, I'd better check in on Charlie before I leave," Scott said as he tried to move quickly.

This little kid is not right. Anyway, once he approached Charles' door, Scott hung his head down, took a deep breath and slowly pushed the door open. I believe he was checking to see if anyone else was in the room...

"Damn Man, you look kinda crazy lying there like that. If I'd known you were going to fall out boy, I would have left your ass home. But I know exactly what you're doing and it's not working. You want me to feel responsible for this.

Well, I don't!! And, you'd better keep your mouth shut until I collect my coins. You here me Charlie! I know you do. Cause if you don't, we're both screwed! No money and no more work for me. I'm serous Man! Won't you just wake up so that everyone can see that you're okay? Then maybe this can all be over. Charlie if you can hear me, there is one thing you should know – my Grandmother and your crazy folks were talking about getting a lawyer. If that happens, there's no way we're ever getting out of this. You're really messing it up for both of us. I gotta go before my Grandmother gets here. She's a hand full all by herself," Scott said as he was leaving the room.

Ironically, just around the same time Scott was exiting Charles' room, the devil herself was stepping off the elevator. Scott, on the other hand, was on the look out for his Grandmother – so as he glanced down the hallway, at first he was startled. But, then he displayed a sneaky smile. Without a doubt, he was elated to see her. Can you imagine? It was just like in the movies. You know how everything is moving – but in slow motion. That tramp just tossed her very defined, asymmetrical bob back and forth. With her perfect curves making a statement all by themselves, her low cut blouse and very short skirt, one might confuse this visitor with a street walker were it not for that big square white I.D badge swinging from her long neck. Who wears "come get me pumps" before six? And I thought fish net stockings were played out or are they thigh highs. Whichever the case, Mrs. Gina Hernandez looked stank.

"Why Scottie, it's good to see dat you're all right. I was a little concerned about you and your friend Charles. But, dat's not why I'm here," Gina said as she placed her hand on Scott's shoulder, walking him back to his room.

Gina closed the door behind them, locking it to ensure there were no disturbances. Scott just raised his brows and sat down softly on the edge of the bed. Gina walked over to the windows and closed the draperies for only who knows why. I trust that Scott was accustomed to her behavior because he didn't appear to be concerned.

"So tell me, what sort of bonus can I look forward to Gina? I know it's worth more than our usual payment. And then there's a watch in question that I know I possessed when I last saw you and your hubby. Apparently it's missing in action now. And I'm sure by now you really want to know exactly what I told the police regarding the matter at hand. It's a funny thing what the mind remembers or remembers to forget," Scott said as he shook his head.

Gina took a deep breath, moved very close to Scott bending over to be eye level with him. Girlfriend then rolled her tongue around her dry mouth with a frown on her face. I would imagine that she was attempting to intimidate him. Scott being unsure of her next move, sort of leaned back just a little. He promptly raised his brows and said, "What?"

"Let me just let you in on a little secret you cheap, good-for-nothing wanna be girl! If my husband Tony is not released soon, I will make the remaining time you have here on earth – Hell! I could care less what you said to the policey, but you'd better fix it now! *Den*, maybe I'll consider *dis* bonus you're babblin on about – comprendé?" yelled Gina as she poked Scott in the chest with her finger.

Scott simply laughed at Gina first and then moaned a bit as his stitches throbbed from being so fresh.

"You are truly a work of art. And I have no problem playing this game with you – but let me just share one thing with you Princess Grace. We had an agreement. And as nasty as this whole thing is playing out, you *will* take responsibility for the part you've played or suffer the consequences one way or another. So while we are all waiting patiently, let's try keeping it professional. No more girl jokes. I, in return, will remember that you're my boss and not that old "-*itch*" that came in here sniffing herself then accusing me of being a sell out. Besides, we really should work together on this."

"Oh really! And why is *dat*?"

"Let's just say I know something you don't."

"And what makes you think I don't know everything there is to know about you Mr. Griffin?"

"That's my point! It's not about me," Scott laughed.

"You're just stalling. Hoping for a miracle you little shit!" yelled Gina.

"What's all the name calling for? I believe we both want some of the same things – so why don't you crawl back into your dry little hole and wait for my call Mrs. Hernandez.

Once I see where Charlie is with all of this, we'll let you know exactly how much you'll need at the appropriate time. So, comprendé to you!" Scott said with a devilish look on his face.

Gina immediately started shaking her head and patting her foot with both hands resting on those hourglass hips. I, myself, was waiting for some steam to rise off the back of her neck or perhaps a bell to ring. You know, like in the arena at a boxing match. Only in this particular case, Gina Hernandez and Scott Griffin had no use for gloves. Their tongues were lethal enough. Nevertheless, Gina, at this point, was simply furious with Scott's mood. Seniorita began speaking in tongues. Or at least that's what her native language sounded like to Scott.

"Okay Keisha, it's time for you to disappear. If I've told you once, I've told you a thousand times too many – you can't be talking that Españòl shit around me. I never got past learning "my name is" and counting from one to ten that semester. So remove yourself quickly before I get angry with you," Scott said as he pointed towards the door.

Gina, with not much else to say, just turned around, hesitated and mumbled to herself as she exited the room, "I don't believe *dis*! I told Tony to wait! Not now, he said! Next time – Next time he said!"

"And good bye to you too, Cheeta!" Scott yelled as he laid back in the bed.

Mmm, somebody's feathers are truly ruffled. But, you know what, timing's priceless. Just as one set of elevator doors shut, the other set opened. Gina missed Miss Nelson by a hair of a second.

I once heard a wise fellow say, "never let a female pooch and an old alley cat cross paths while they're both in heat." Or was that an old wives tale. Whichever the case, these two women need not occupy the same space without a chaperone. Well, I would imagine by now you too are sensing that maybe someone scorched some day old fish. Yeah, this is definitely one of those fishy situations. Fortunately for me, I've had a mouth's full. How about you? What time is it anyway? I was just thinking the same thing. We are already here. I wonder if she even remembers...

●●●●

*N*ow, *which one of these rooms are you in.* "How is Mr. Kimble's pressure?" Dr. Cummings asked.

"He's doing just fine Doctor," answered the nurse.

"Dr. Sharpe – He's ready for you," Dr. Cummings said softly.

Sidney's a mess. Girl stood there thinking to herself, It's about time... If he weren't so over weight, he'd be under in seconds. No chance... This, I'm afraid is going to take a little longer. It's 3:15... Okay fat boy, go to sleep my baby.

"Did you say something Dr. Sharp?" asked one of the surgical nurses.

"No, I was just thinking out loud. Vital signs are looking good. Okay Dr. Cummings, your Mr. Kimble is now dreaming. Nurse – will you hit the CD player. That seems to help the time go by," Sidney said as she watched the monitors carefully.

"You can say that again..." Dr. Cummings said with a chuckle is his voice.

The assistant nurse giggled as she reached up to turn on some classical jazz. And it was true indeed. One hour passed by as if it was ten, fifteen minutes tops. Mr. Kimble was awake again, feeling refreshed. And Sidney was signing his chart preparing to make her fast escape.

"You did well Mr. Kimble," Sidney said just before she left the O.R.

It's funny though, when dogs are in heat – they will do almost anything to capture their prey. I mean your attention. So, as Sidney was pulling off her scrubs, getting ready to wash her hands, Dr. Dexter Cummings stood there – somewhat dazed. His mouth was slightly opened and he was out right drooling.

"Is something on your mind Doctor?" Sidney asked.

Of course he wasn't expecting her to say anything – so naturally Sidney's words went right over Dexter's head.

"Are you all right?" Sidney said as she moved very close to him.

"Yeah...sure...I'm fine. I was just admiring your... your work. You are *really* good at what you do. Are you married?"

"Excuse me! I really don't think my personal life involves you."

"Hold on! I didn't mean to imply anything. Certainly not to offend you at all! I was just..." Dr. Cummings mumbled just before Sidney interrupted him.

"You were just what? Hoping maybe – wondering – if by chance... wishing perhaps?" Sidney said as she looked directly into his eyes, waiting for him to lie.

Dr. Cummings just smiled and shook his head.

"Yeah, sure you're right! Just as I thought," Sidney said as she moved Dexter out of her way so that she could wash her hands before leaving.

Dexter turned around and started to remove his surgical gloves so that he could join her. Sidney, being a tad preoccupied, splashed water everywhere.

"You know, you Doctors are all the same. Always – always trying to push up on a sister. And what if I am attached. Like that would make a significant difference – probably not. Must have jungle fever. I'll tell you what, if I ever forget who I am, you know get desperately desperate; I'll shoot myself first before considering calling you! How about that! Have a great life, Doctor," Sidney said as she shook water in Dexter's face on her way out.

Sidney laughed to herself on the way down the hall then mumbled, "Men, boys... who can tell the difference."

●●●●

*U*nfortunately for Miss Sharpe, it was now twenty-five minutes after four. That's not good. Remember the old saying "fashionably late." Well Sidney at one time did live up to her name – Sharpe – precisely on time, every time. But, during the last year, Girlfriend has been anything **but** prompt. This could be why her sister Sherian made it an issue for her to show up on time. But, do you want to hear something funny? Sherian is a very smart woman. She knew her tardy sibling would be racing the clock – so Sherian told Sidney 3:45, but the real time was 4:45. Tricky, but pretty damn clever. So,* *while Sidney was racing, just trying to get there, she was actually going to be arriving about fifteen minutes early.*

Finally, as she stood directly outside of her Mom's Doctor's office, Sidney noticed that her body was still, but her heart was beating rapidly. She tried counting backwards only attempting to calm herself down before entering the office. Soon, Sidney exhaled then gently opened the door.

"Hey, glad to see you made it," Sherian said softly.

Sidney quickly looked around. The office had only one other patient visual, standing to the left of her at the receptionist desk. She glanced up at the clock as she walked over toward her sister. Sherian stood to her feet, reached for Sidney's hand and kissed her on the forehead. Sidney knew then that everything was all right. All their lives, Sherian always – always kissed Sidney's forehead to reassure her that God was still God. And that she was still his daughter.

"Calm down little girl, you're actually right on time," Sherian said with a smile.

"Is that so!" laughed Sidney "You are always – always playing games. One day you're going to cry wolf and no one's going to believe you Miss Sharpe. You're a trip!"

"And I feel the same way about you too little girl."

Both girls laughed.

"Where's Mama?"

"She's in with Dr. Frankenstein. He said something about wanting to meet with Mama before he sat down with all of us," Sherian said as she shook her head.

"You're not funny Sis. I just hope it's nothing serious. I can't imagine being left here with just you and "Miss Bootsie.""

"There you go jumping to conclusions. Mama is as healthy as they come. She's not leaving either one of us. And stop talking about my cat. You know you love her just as much as I do. Besides, why are you always thinking the worst in situations? Just because it's associated with your line of work? I know there are a great number of people that get cared for. Everybody doesn't die Sidney Sharpe," Sherian said, as she looked her right in the eyes.

"True... But, all this coming down here to meet with Dr. Who, it's not making a lot of sense."

"Maybe...But, I'm sure Mama has good reasons for wanting us here. So come on! Stop trying to predict someone else's future. This is no séance and you're not one of those witches from Eastwick," Sherian replied as she gave Sidney a silly look.

"That was good. I'll give you two points for that one. But I wish they would hurry up. I can't stand waiting like this."

"Well, isn't that the pot calling the kettle black. There's still only one true comedian in this family," laughed Sherian.

Both girls just giggled a little. Sidney pushed Sherian's head gently then reached down to pick up one of those Women's magazines. Sherian just pretended not to be a bit bothered by Sidney's response, then laughed even more. A few minutes passed by and then the receptionist told them both that Dr. Caplan was ready to see them.

"Second room to the right," she said.

Sidney always – always being the eager beaver that she is, of course, entered the room first.

"There's my Girl... Give me some sugar," Miss Phyllis said as she extended her cheek out to Sidney.

"Hey Mama!" Sidney replied.

"Come on over here Cher. These are my two jewels, Sherian and Sidney Sharpe. And, this is my good friend and Doctor, Kylin Caplan," Phyllis said as she placed one arm around Sherian and held Sidney's hand.

"Pleased to meet you both. Why don't we all be seated," he replied.

At that very moment, the room enclosed a still silence. You know like wanting to know something so bad, that the anxiety reaches its peak. Your stomach begins to flutter. And you dare not think, for your own thoughts may confuse what you're about to hear. You know – sitting there looking somewhat stupefied. So, with that in mind, Mama Phyllis just sat there, knowing exactly what the issues were. Sherian being the optimist, refused to allow herself to feel the slightest bit of discomfort. While, Sidney Sharpe held a look of... I know there's more to this and it'll all probably end in more confusion.

"Your Mother wanted you both here when her test results were returned. I'm not even sure if you know what your Mom was being tested for," Dr. Caplan said.

"I knew something was wrong when Sherian insisted that we be here," Sidney said as she shook her head.

"Wait a minute Sid. It's not all that bad. I'll be in and out of the hospital in less than two days," Phyllis tried to explain.

"No one mentioned anything to me about Mother having to stay in the hospital overnight!" Sherian yelled.

"Excited now Big Sister, because you weren't fully informed," Sidney said as she looked over at Sherian.

Sherian looked at Sidney, then back at Dr. Caplan. It was quite obvious that she was not only taken by surprise, Sherian Sharpe was heated. She stood to her feet so fast, the chair she was occupying sort of flipped over, hitting her Mom on the leg.

"I'm not listening to anymore of this!" she shouted just before leaving the room.

"Ouch damn it!... Cher don't... come sit down baby," Phyllis said as she rubbed her leg.

The door slammed. Phyllis took a long deep breath and exhaled slowly. Sidney just chuckled a little shaking her head.

"Now Dr. Caplan, after witnessing that stunt, can you really believe some would think that I'm the ugly duckling? My older sister, well, to put it mildly – there aren't many words to describe her. Although she only has me by a few months shy of fifteen years, Sherian acts more like my Mother than my Mother does. I tried telling Missy that there was more to this, but she couldn't hear me. I'm really not trying to hear this myself, but there are a whole lot of days when I prefer being absent – so get on with it," Sidney said as she sat back in the chair.

"Your Mother has a small tumor located just above her neck on the left side of her head. Now, we believe that we can go in quickly and remove this before it's able to do anymore damage," Dr. Caplan explained.

Sidney's head dropped.

"Sid...Sid... I know what you're thinking, but everybody doesn't die. You somehow just got too close to her. I'm gonna be just fine. Look at me lil lady. We are a family and family don't lie to one another. So come on! I need you to be strong for me. And, Cher's gonna need your courage," Phyllis said as she rubbed Sidney's hand gently.

Sidney took a deep breath and raised her head and said, "Okay, that's Dr. Kylin Caplan – is it? One thing you need to know, I will hold you personally responsible for my Mother's well being. Meaning, if for any reason, something irreversible happens to Phyllis Maple, you need not return to work. Okay? Are we together on that?" *Sidney said, as she seemingly looked right through him.*

Dr. Caplan smiled and replied, "Nothing will happen to your Mother. It's a simple procedure. I'm sure you're familiar with it. In fact, her room should be just about ready. What time is it anyway? Ten after five. They're expecting us at six o'clock – so now would be a good time to go on over and get settled in."

"You guys surely don't waste any time putting people under the knife. When is this scheduled?"

"I'm sorry you've been in the dark about this whole thing. But, I informed Miss Maple days ago that if her results returned positive, we would go in immediately. She's on the book for 6:30 a.m. tomorrow. You can stay with her tonight if you'd like Miss Sharpe. Although it's really not necessary," replied Dr. Caplan.

"Mmm, Mmm, Mmm, this was much more than I anticipated. Mama, how *could* you keep this from us? Go through this all alone? We are your daughters. How would you feel if Sherian or myself hid something like this from you?"

"Worried .. But I'm sure you two would have waited until you knew for certain what was what," *Phyllis explained.*

Well, I suppose that old wives tale's true. "Apples don't fall far from their trees." Or was it a wise man that quoted that. But anyhow, I'm sure you get the picture. Wait a minute! How about "like mothers, like daughters" or was that "like fathers and sons." Never mind. Moving on...

Sidney checked her Mom in and then tried to reach Sherian. Funny, this time sister dear was M.I.A. – missing in action! Get it?...

"Mama, I have to make a run, but I promise you – I'll find your daughter and return before you can say "The Lord's

Prayer" ten times," Sidney said softly just before kissing her Mom on the lips.

"I'm fine baby girl. But, please take it easy on your Sister. Cher's not like you. She'll be all right. Just give her time."

Sidney glanced at the clock above and replied, "Time is one thing we're running short on..."

●●●●

*M*eanwhile, back at the Law Office of Sherman, Blake, Edmonds and Wright, Franklin Lewis had just returned from his Easter Egg Hunt.

"Is she with someone Laurie?" Franklin asked.

"No, but she's on the..." Laurie said as Franklin strolled past her desk, letting himself in Dominique's office.

As he opened the door slowly, Franklin heard Dominique giggling. He noticed her not so long toned calves were showing just a bit as she appeared to be lounging back in the chair behind her art-deco glass top desk. Unsure if Dominique was on or off the phone, Franklin quietly snuck up on her and walked his fingers up her legs. Dominique jumped! Removed her legs from the bay window and turned herself around in the chair, now facing the desk. She gave him a look to suggest that she was indeed engaged in an important personal conversation with someone special. Franklin twitched his mouth while thinking to himself, I bet I know who that is... Dominique continued smiling, as her ear remained glued to the phone.

"I can't wait to see you too... Hugs and kisses... And I you," Dominique whispered just before ending her call.

"Oh Miss Thing, you do have it bad. That was the mystery piece was it not?" Franklin asked.

Dominique just sat there slowly rubbing the top of her b-cupped breast while remembering the scent of her new lover's perfume. It was quite obvious that Girlfriend was in a daze. You know la-la-land. At this point, Franklin Lewis was most definitely sure that the party on the other end was without a doubt – THE ONE!

"Earth to Diamond – Earth to Diamond! Are you there?" Franklin said as he attempted to tap on Dominique's head.

Dominique looked up at Franklin and burst into laughter. She shook her head and said, "You're just too young to

understand. This – my dear friend is *true love*. Granted there
is a great deal of lust in the air, but for the most part, she is
THE ONE!"

"Now Diamond, let me take a moment and share
something with you. Never ever judge a book by its cover.
This may be a young black stallion that stands before you,
but I too have been around the block quite a few times
myself. Besides, I'll bet I could trade a couple of tricks, I
mean secrets with you too. Plus I'll be thirty in, okay, eleven
months", Franklin said as he plucked a lint-ball off his
designer sweater.

"Frankie, you're crazy."

"I believe you are confused. I'm not the one with a Mack
truck parked up my nose after screwing some Asian chick for
less than six months. And not only are you going to Wed
Miss Szechwan, you've convinced yourself that you are
ready to raise a rug-rat with her. Need I say more," Franklin
said as he leaned on Dominique's desk.

"If you don't get off my desk! And stop hating on me
because your last quest with that Dr. Dolittle didn't go as
planned. Besides, I have more important issues on my brain
right now. Hannah won't be able to get away in time for our
initial visit with that social worker. I don't know what I'm
gong to do Franklin. I don't want to go alone," Dominique
said, as she looked up at Franklin.

"Well, don't look at me! I've had bad experiences with
those types of people. They assume they have all the
answers. But, most of their incestuous lives are quite
dysfunctional. You need to just make one of your good-good
girlfriends go with you, " Franklin said with a chuckle in his
voice.

"You think everything's a game!" Dominique said as she
shook her head.

"Wake up and sniff the roses Mary! It is!"

"Just forget it! You're never much help anyway. Speaking
of help – did you find something on our Mr. Hernandez?"
Dominique asked.

"I'm glad you asked! Diamond... I told you before – I
smelled fish. Now it took me a few calls and unfortunately

cost you several dollars! But word has it on the strip, that Tony and Gina Hernandez are without a doubt into ... how do you say... dirty movies, child pornography, S and M and a few other tricks. If you know what I mean... And get this! Take a ridiculous guess as to how long these Spanish-flies have been in existence."

Dominique, being completely thrown, just sat there with her arched brows raised and her bottom slightly lined with chestnut nearly touching the desk. "You're telling one," she whispered.

"Now I may be a lot of things Diamond, but this fairy's no story teller! Tis all true! Let's just say when I was entering grade school, our Hernandez's founded sex, lies and then some. Oh, and check this! T.G.H and Associates, who's really their alias, also own real estate in the middle of downtown Baltimore, a title company in Georgetown, Brooke's Antique shop in Fells Point, a Laundromat slash cleaning service in Southeast D.C., a fleet of dump trucks, plus these jokers own a small dealership. And wait a minute! Under construction as we speak is ... you're not going to believe this... Do you recall some advertising last month on that new dance studio?" Franklin asked.

"Not Tender Touch on L Street," replied Dominique.

"Yes Tender Touch Dance Studio, Where everyone's a star. Or at least get touched," Franklin laughed.

"That's amazing... But, I can't say I'm totally shocked. Most high rollers have washed their coins one way or another – but by-pass all that. How do you know for sure about the sex scams?" Dominique asked.

"Who else Miss Blake? The underground Hags! I refuse to believe you're so green sometimes," laughed Franklin.

"You are the second person who called me green today. Just for the record, I'm as down as they come. Some things I just pick-up on later. Besides, I have an image to uphold."

"And a false one at that. Speaking of false people, what happened with your 3:00 client?"

"She called around 3:30 to move her appointment to a later time. I'm hoping they'll be able to keep this next one. There are still many many pieces to this puzzle. But, from the looks of things, I'm ruling out sodomized. We'll have a much better case, if we go with pedophilia," Dominique explained.

Next, Laurie buzzed Dominique and said, "Miss Blake, your six-thirty's here."

"Thanks Laurie show her to the conference room. I'll be there in five... Franklin – I want you to find out, in exact figures, just how much are the Hernandez's worth. That's insurances, stocks, bonds, and even any IOU's. I even want to know if they have piggy banks in their closets. My guess is we'll probably never see the inside of a courtroom. You follow me!" Dominique said firmly.

"I'm on it Miss Blake. Consider it done," Franklin said as he left Dominique's office.

●●●●

*W*ho is she calling now? Oh, Miss Sharpe....

"Hey girl... are your hands full?" Dominique asked.

"I'm a tad preoccupied, but no. What do you need Miss lady?" Sidney replied.

"I was thinking if you're free tomorrow morning after running and our good-good girlfriend accompanies Meagan Simone home, then maybe – just maybe..." Dominique said in a very soft tone just before Sidney interrupted her.

"We're not in court Miss Blake! Just tell me what you need me to do." Sidney said.

"I have an appointment in the morning with a straight-nosed social worker," explained Dominique.

"*And...*"

"My friend won't be able to go. So, will you go with me? It's very informal. It shouldn't take that long. But, it's very important to me. It's about alternative methods of conception."

"Of course I'll go! But back that thing up... Did you just say – my friend won't be able to go? As in your boyfriend? Like maybe he's coming to town soon? Like maybe we'll be breaking bread with him shortly?" Sidney asked with a big grin on her face.

"Yeah, yeah, yeah – something like that. What are you doing anyway?"

"I just left the hospital. I had to register my Mom. She's having surgery at the crack of dawn. And right now, I'm going to find one of those dreadful meetings to attend. Damn... I almost forgot!" Sidney shouted.

"What! What's wrong."

"Nothing, I need to give my Mother's doctor a call."

"Okay, it sounds like maybe your hands are full. I would much rather have you taking care of your Mom and definitely yourself. What's with all the surgery? Is it serious? Do you need me to be there with you?"

"Well Dr. Kylin Caplan doesn't seem to think so. But *maybe*... Maybe I could use your support. Then we can explore these options of yours."

"Wait a minute! Don't hang up! Sidney you mentioned you were looking for one of those NA meetings. Did you relapse again? Because if you did, there's no need in dwelling over spoiled milk. We'll just have to keep on trying until we succeed. You've done greater things before. Plus, I need you far too much for you to simply give up now . . . ."

Sidney took a deep breath and said, "I think I get the picture. Yes I slipped. But, I only had a glass of white wine with Drew. I know it's not him. I don't know...it seemed to make sense at the time. I suppose my body can't handle much of anything. My head felt light and I became nervous. It's funny though, I excused myself from the table as if I had to tinkle. Drew Carmichael never saw me again. So, I ran to one of those meetings. It all happened so fast. But I was through with myself when I found out Meagan had the twins. So, naturally going to one of those groups everyday this go round, kinda makes sense."

"You are a mess. I can't believe you left Drew at the table without saying good-bye. Are you sure you're okay?"

"Yeah, I'm fine. But, I can't call him just yet because I made a vow to myself after living the same insanity."

"What on earth this time?"

"Don't you dare laugh! I've made a promise to myself to keep men out of my schedule for a little while."

"You are really reaching now. I'm going to hang up on that note so you won't hear me laughing Sidney Sharpe. Bye girl. I love you!"

"And I you!"

As they ended their call, both Sidney and Dominique were giggling. In fact Dominique tried very hard to straighten her face before meeting Miss Nelson. Needless to say, the Girl just giggled even more while exiting her office. Now Sidney on the other hand, tried just as hard to shake off that funny feeling. Girl knew in the past exactly how many times she had taken men out of her diet and then put them back. I guess it was funny. She even peeked in the rear view mirror for what I would call – some confirmation. Not! Then it hit her that she was supposed to be calling her Mom's doctor.

●●●●

I hope you're still there," Sidney whispered to herself.

"Dr. Kylin Caplan, how may I help you?" he said.

"Dr. Caplan, it's Dr. Sharpe – Phyllis Maple's daughter. Do you have a minute?"

"Of course Dr. Sharpe, what can I do for you?"

"Now, I'm almost certain that you've gone over this with my mom, but I'm not at all satisfied. And, I didn't want to mention this in front of my mom."

"What's on your mind Dr. Sharpe?"

"It's this whole thing! One minute she's healthy, then the next you tell us without warning, she has to have surgery. I was a family practitioner for a few years before I switched to anesthesiology and I know how these things can occur. But I didn't quite hear your mention what kind of tumor my Mom has. I'm hoping an explanation will help me to accept this a little better."

"My apologies for not telling you earlier, but it's called Glioma. It's a small tumor found in the lining of the brain. I'm almost certain it will be a simple procedure with a good prognosis," explained Dr. Caplan.

"I'm very familiar with Glioma, and you'd want to make sure it will be a very simple procedure. That's all I wanted to know. I will see you in the morning Doctor."

"Well I hope you'll be able to rest a little easier tonight Dr. Sharpe now that you're informed."

"No! I'd prefer you to tell me that you've made a terrible mistake and, in fact, my Mother's the wrong patient. But since there's not a chance in hell of that, I'll just see you in the morning," Sidney said before ending their call.

Dr. Caplan just looked at the phone and said, "My she's short!" If he only knew – how short. Hopefully, he will never know...

Chapter Five

Puzzled

*W*ell, my curious reader, I imagine by now you too might be a bit puzzled yourself. Unless you are an elephant by chance...probably not. However, you have to admit, Common Lives has a lot of stuff with it. Where must I begin? First, there's Meagan who's just given birth to two much wanted baby girls. But then at the same time, her mother Katherine nearly swears that she's not Meagan's biological parent. Who does that?

And if that isn't enough drama, her own Doctor tells her and her loving husband that their newborn baby girl, Nia has the sickle cell trait. Coincidence! I don't think so.

Second, we have Judge Waverly Corrine Simmons who not only suspects her unfaithful husband of maybe cheating on her, but Waverly states (and I quote), " When I confirm this information for the um-teenth time, I'm asking him for a divorce!" Is the word um-teenth really found in the dictionary? Whatever... Anyway, I guess, "seeing is believing" because Girlfriend is about to hire an investigator. And on top of that, she's also having daymares. Or would that be considered daydreams. But, I thought daydreams were primarily pleasant. I don't believe you would break out in a sweat if you were thinking good thoughts. Anyhow, Waverly knows something that she's not willing to share with us.

But then there's Dominique Alisa Blake who appears, and I emphasize the word appears, to have it all together. But at the same time, she's caught in the middle of a sex scandal with two teenaged storytellers. And she's secretly hiding the fact that she's a girl watcher from her best friends. And, her lover Girl's not even of the black persuasion. How phony can you be?

Last but certainly not least, Sidney Sharpe – definitely my favorite. She's not only real, Girlfriend has flaws. She's a perfect ten and I'm not referring to her dress size. She's smart, not afraid of much (besides maybe her own shadow) and don't sit there and claim that you've never been frightened by your own shadow. Anyhow, Sidney Sharpe is how do you say, the kind of girl most women would die to be like. But, at the same time, hate on... Why? I'm glad you asked. Girl has everything, on the surface. Beauty, brains, money, men, security and favor... what a combination. Now, you may be wondering why I mentioned favor. Well, Sidney somehow manages to find herself in the most unlikely spaces. Yet, she always – always comes out with minimal damage. At least publicly anyway. My guess is that she's trying to fill a bottomless pit. Oh and by now you might even be

*asking yourself – how in the devil I could have so much dirt on these
girls? Again, I'm so glad you finally asked.*

*Let me take a moment of your time to introduce yours truly before
we move forward. My name is Roman Dakota. And yes, my friends
call me Roman Dakota. Okay, who is Roman Dakota? Have you ever
heard the expression, "If I could only be a fly on the wall." Well my
friend it's not just an expression. I am, how would you say, a fly on
the wall. I thought you'd find that amusing. So now, that's all out of
the way, why don't we continue with Common Lives...*

●●●●

"I guess I wasn't quite what you expected," Keith said as
he sipped his iced tea.

Waverly just sat there not in a daze, but more so
thinking to herself, *No you're not... I thought you'd be
nerdy and actually you're simply gorgeous! Tall and
handsome. He looks like he works out too. Beautiful skin
tone, pearly white teeth...Mmm...I bet you could put a
hurting on a sister. And your shoes are even expensive. Wait
a second! Snap out of it girl! What are you thinking? He
reminds you of your no good husband – only ten years
earlier. Haven't you been hurt enough?*

Keith's brows rose slightly then he repeated, "I suppose
I'm not what you expected. I totally understand if you're a
little uncomfortable."

"I'm sorry," Waverly whispered as she rubbed her
forehead then exhaled. "I was just thinking too much again."

Keith smiled and replied, "I know exactly what you mean,
I do that often myself. But, before I can move forward with
your case, I need to know one more thing."

"Anything... I already feel naked."

"Corrine, are you one hundred percent sure that you want
to go through with this? And before you answer too quickly,
you need to understand that many people (both men and
women) say they want to know these things. But, when it's
staring them directly in the face, it's a horse of a different
color. Some are even murdered when the shit hits the fan.
And, let me just say I'm not only a private investigator, I also
offer protection for my clients," Keith explained.

"That may be so in some cases, but Vincent likes to fuck not fight! Excuse me, did I just say that?" Waverly said as she placed her hand over her mouth.

Waverly and Keith looked at each other then started laughing. Waverly shook her head and said, "Will you pretend you didn't hear that? I am so – so close to being ticked off, sometimes I forget who I am. Your answer's yes! He's not getting away with this again. And if it takes exposing the good doctor's infidelities, then so be it! You know to be totally honest I would, just for once, like to know how it feels to have a man who's primary mission is to love only me. Do you think I'm being foolish for wanting such a thing?"

"I wouldn't call it foolish. Maybe now you know what you want. I don't see anything wrong with that. I think sometimes we men get caught up in society's perception of us. It's the same as being tempted. You know you shouldn't, but at the same time, you hear this crazy voice telling you to just do it. Now I'm not suggesting it's the right thing to do, but that's how it usually goes down," Keith said as he shrugged his broad shoulders.

"So are you supposed to be the Devil's Advocate now?"

Keith smiled and replied, "No! I was just trying to help you understand that nine times our of ten, it's never personal."

"Well let me just say, by the time I'm done with Dr. Vincent Simmons, he'll know just how personal it really is... So tell me – how long do you think it'll take?"

"Now that will depend on your husband. However, there is another way...but, you may not want to do that."

"You just don't know how desperate I am... What else can we do!"

"Okay, okay, calm down. I will need access to your house. And for you to write down your husband's schedule. Plus, try to remember every place he's ever taken you. But leave out the spots you've taken him. Most men won't frequent the places their wives have taken them. Did you bring the photo?" Keith asked as he flipped through his roller-dex.

Waverly looked up at Keith and said, "Yes I did and here's the deposit. You must be very good at what you do. I don't even want to know why you need to get into my home...I guess I could have that information you need in the morning."

"I'd rather you do it now, if you can. And while you're doing that, let me see your house keys so I can make a copy real quick," Keith said as he reached into his Hugo Boss suit jacket and pulled out what appeared to be a small piece of hard clay enclosed in a plastic case.

"What on earth are you doing?" Waverly asked.

"This is an old trick I learned from my father years ago when he allowed me to tag along on what ever case he was working on. Most people thought of my father as being strangely unique. I saw him as a very wise man. Simply put – brilliant. Unfortunately or fortunately depending upon your point of view, his death made me want to work that much harder. So I moved down from Canada not too far from here and started my own business, Sheppard Investigations," Keith explained as he handed Waverly her keys back.

"Are you saying you're Keith Sheppard? I just assumed that I was meeting with one of the employees. Please accept my apologies!" Waverly said as she scratched her head.

Keith looked at Waverly sort of puzzled and said, "What – What's wrong?"

"Nothing, nothing at all... I guess you can say that I feel a little "in-bare-ass" as my good friend Sidney would put it."

Keith smiled and replied, "Don't' be embarrassed on my account. I've seen far worse. And that's the first time I've heard it put like that. You must have some unusual friends."

Waverly put on a phony face while thinking to herself, *If you only knew how unusual.*

It's funny though, how your own thoughts and words can trip you up. Literally holding one's self hostage. Unfortunately for Waverly Corrine, it was time for her to put her money where her mouth is. Besides, didn't she just say not only a few hours earlier, never write a check that you're a** can't cash. So knowing now what needed to be done, Waverly began writing down everything about her loving husband she could possibly think of – which included the good, bad and the ugly. Sixty minutes passed by and yes, Waverly Corrine was still writing...

"That's quite a list…" Keith said in a soft voice.

"I'm almost done… You did say to remember every place… I'd forgotten just how many places we've been together. I guess that's what kept me blinded for so long," Waverly whispered as she began to reminisce while holding her bottom lip between her teeth.

Then, she looked up at Keith and for the first time Waverly's eyes watered. Now I can't say for certain if it was from remembering their history or perhaps coming to terms with her reality. But then, we already know that underneath that judicial robe, Waverly Corrine is without a doubt a real softy. So who knows for sure? It may be that soft music in the background playing mixed up with her hormones. Women do tend to trip when it's that time of the month… Anyway, Keith reached for Waverly's left hand and rubbed it gently. He displayed one of these reassuring smiles and said,

"It's okay to keep some of those good times… You know what I think?"

"What do you think Mr. Sheppard?"

Keith took a deep breath and said, "It's not all true…"

"What!"

"That rule of thumb!"

"The rule of what – wait a second! Is this one of those make me feel better moments?"

"Maybe… I just thought you should know that all men are not dogs. And even dogs have favorite bones. I would even bet my last dollar that Vincent still loves you very much," Keith said just before Waverly snatched her hand away.

"To hell with Vincent! Let's get this ball rolling!" Waverly shouted as she handed Keith the notes….

●●●●

Meanwhile, back at Prince George's County Hospital, the air was still a bit salty. The test results were in and now it was clear who carried the "Sickle Cell Trait." Drake left the hospital about an hour ago. He said he needed to clear his head. My guess is Drake must have slipped into a deep sense of denial. With no one else to call, he turned to his dear sweet Mother-in-Law, who with her nervous self, stood directly outside of Meagan's room praying for the right words to convey.

As she opened the door slowly, she noticed that the room was empty. But then Katherine heard water running and it appeared to be coming from the bathroom. As she moved closer to the bathroom, Katharine saw Meagan rinsing her face. At first she thought that Meagan might have been cleaning herself up, but then she realized Meagan was in tears. Exhausted from everything, I imagine after rinsing her face and swearing relentlessly, Meagan looked up in the mirror and saw her Mother standing there with tears in her eyes as well.

"Mother! Oh, Mother!" Meagan yelled as she turned around practically falling into her Mother's arms.

"There-there my precious daughter, Mother's here. We'll fix this Me-Me – I promise you," Katherine whispered as she stroked Meagan's hair, holding her tightly.

Katherine put Meagan back into bed. Simply spell-bound by the Doctor's findings, Katherine began pacing the floor.

"Mother, I don't understand. I tried! Nothing's making any sense! The Doctor says it's me!" Meagan yelled as she cried even harder.

"I can't help but to think that somehow this is all my fault! If only I'd pushed your Father just a little more, maybe then we'd have a better sense of direction," Katherine said as she placed both hands over her face, covering it.

Meagan looked over at Katherine and said with confusion in her voice, "What exactly are you trying not to tell me Mother? I mean, now would be the perfect time to confess whatever sins you may have left. Do you understand what I'm saying to you Mother?"

"Yes, of course I do… Just remember, what I'm about to share with you Sweetheart, was done solely out of love. When your Father and I found you," Katherine said just before Meagan interrupted.

"Found me! What in God's name are you saying?" yelled Meagan.

"Me-Me just let me finish! We truly saw you as a gift from God. It didn't matter one bit how you came to us. I had not so long ago found out I was unable to bare a child of my own. So finding you was perfect. Simply priceless! It wasn't until later that I learned you carried the Sickle Cell Trait. By then, we were unchangeably in love with you. Besides, it was treatable. And chances of you passing it on were very slim. I figured that we'd cross that valley when we got there, if ever. A few years passed, you became stronger and Theo convinced me that it didn't matter who your real parents were," Katherine said as she began to weep.

"Are you saying that you have no idea where I came from?"

"Oh God! I'm afraid so Me-Me... you've got to believe me when I tell you no harm was intended. You cannot imagine how many times I've tried to tell you this in the past and now Satan himself has finally found a way to have a snake rise up out of the ground to bite me. But, you can rest assured of one thing; I'd rather burn in hell before I consider this as being over. We will bring to the light everything there is to know about you my little angel," Katherine said with reassurance.

This is not looking too good. Meagan just sat up in the bed breathing irregularly. It was obvious she was trying to catch her breath. In that moment, none of this seemed real. It kind of reminded me of a novel I once heard about. Where the daughter learns that her parents really aren't her parents and she sort of looses it. Or was that a movie? Yeah! What was that called? You know, the Exorcist! Where the girl's lying in bed crazy out of her mind and her head begins to spin. That was good! I'm sorry, where were we? Anyway, Meagan closed her eyes and ran her fingers through her hair. She then looked at Katherine and said, "Where do we go from here?"

"Back to the very beginning my dear. I may not have some of the answers you requested, but I sure in hell know who does! Your Mother has an another call to make," Katherine said as she picked up the phone to place a call.

"Who are you calling now Mother?" Meagan whispered.

"Shh...." Katherine whispered a she placed her index finger in the air. "This will only take a minute, Hi!... is Father Murphy still around by chance? Yes, this is Sister Kat. Yes, I'll hold... Father, my apologies for calling you so late, But I really need to see you as soon as possible... Yes.... Well, I can be there in thirty minutes. Thank you so much,

God Bless you Father," Katherine said just before hanging the phone.

Meagan sat there in utter amazement. Curious to know exactly what part Father Murphy played in all this. I mean, Meagan and her family have been members of that parish for years. In fact, all of her life – it was the very same place where she found her true love, Drake Tyler. So yes, curious may even be an understatement.

Katherine rubbed her head and said, "Okay, let me just think for a moment. Me-Me, besides Dra, have you told anyone else about this?"

Meagan shook her head and answered, "Oh no! Who would I tell? I'm not even sure if I believe this myself! No! No! Tell anyone! I think I'd rather have a root canal without the drugs!"

The room went silent for several seconds. Meagan placed her hands over her mouth and said, "Mother, what if Drake tells someone? I don't think I'm ready for everyone to know!"

"Calm down Me-Me! We will just have to make certain that they don't! And what are friends for anyway? Besides, you are scheduled to leave in the morning right? Just don't say a word until we talk again... What time is it! I've got to meet with Father Murphy before it gets too late. Are you going to be all right?"

Meagan took a deep breath and said, "I'm so tired...I didn't sleep well last night. I kept having this strange dream about Daddy. He was alive Mother and he told me that you were dead! I just started running and running! But then, I'd run into Daddy and it would start over!"

"Me-Me! Look at me! That was just a dream. This is real! We just need some answers and you need some rest. Would you like me to get the nurse to give you something to help you sleep?" Katherine said as she touched Meagan's forehead, checking to see if it was warm.

"Yes, but it's almost time for the twins' feeding. Maybe after that..." Meagan whispered as she was lying back in the bed.

"That's better... I'm going to leave now, but remember, not one word! I'll see you in the morning," Katherine said as she kissed Meagan good-bye.

Meagan immediately closed her eyes and began counting backwards. But, can you believe the Girl started with the number fifty. Meagan's something! But at least at this point, she was really trying to make an effort to calm her over-active self down. Soon, she saw pleasant visions of raising her two beautiful daughters in her head. Meagan always – always believed in family and friends and shared everything with them. That's why I found it strange when she said absolutely nothing to Sidney, Waverly or Dominique! Now yet another burden to bare. And I bet you Mother Kat has not placed all of her cards on the table either! No, there's more to this! Yeah, there is much more to this! But we can revisit this later? You're so kind... I wonder how Miss Blake's handling her under-age storyteller... Is that Dominique scratching her head?

● ● ● ●

"Now I'm not going to try and make this sound good. I can't even begin to paint you a realistic picture without first saying, this puzzles me! I also know that a lot of things can happen. Maybe even get fabricated a bit. Possibly blown totally out of context. Scott, we all know that something did happen to you and your friend Charles Davis. But, lets not waste everyone's time. Just cut to the chase. You boys may have been drugged, but drugged *and* ?" Dominique said as she shook her head.

"Now wait a damn minute! Whose side are you on Miss Lawyer?" yelled Miss Nelson.

Scott just sat there allowing his grandmother to once again fight his battle...

"Yours of course Miss Nelson! But, let us stop and think clearly for a moment. We have two healthy teen-aged boys. Scott's at least five-foot-seven and one hundred and thirty pounds maybe. And the Doctor's report says – wait a minute! Here we are! Charles Davis, five-foot-five and weighing one hundred and twenty-seven pounds. Now—first we would have to convince a jury that these two strong, healthy teenaged boys were helpless. Then—assumingly one man,

Tony Hernandez, at six-foot-one and one hundred ninety pounds persuaded both boys to drink spiked Pepsi. Then— when they were both unconscious, he literally sodomized them! That is what you're saying happened?" Dominique asked sarcastically.

This was sounding a little too unbelievable to Scott now. He sat there knowing Dominique was not going to be easy pray, so he pondered his thoughts for a moment then blurted out, "Yeah, that's exactly what I said! But you need to understand; first of all, it was late. We were exhausted and famished! Tony told us that he was going to order Chinese, so we waited around a while laughing and joking, thinking we were going to get a free meal. Charles became thirsty first. So, Tony offered us something to drink. Next thing you know, Charles stared throwing up most of his intestines. I don't remember too much more after that. I know I was cold and I think I was lying in something wet," Scott said as he shrugged his shoulders.

"You were both found in the park near the edge of the wishing pond. I believe someone put you there so it could look as if you guys had overdosed on drugs!" Dominique said as she scribbled something down on her notepad.

"Yeah, yeah, that's exactly what happened!" shouted Scott.

"Okay then, how would you explain the alcohol and marijuana found in your systems?"

"I don't know... I mean you explain it! You're my lawyer! I mean maybe we had a brew and smoked a little earlier that day. Yeah, it's all coming back to me now. Around lunchtime is when it happened. We were in the locker room and they were passing it around. Yeah, they were passing it around..." Scott said with a sneaky look on his face.

"Okay I think I get the picture. Then we'll just have to wait until Charles wakes up to hear his version of the story. How does that sound to you Miss Nelson?" Dominique said as she looked over at Scott's Grandmother.

"If that's what my Grandson says happened, then that's what happened!"

"All right then. I will call you tomorrow. Let's hope that Charles is conscious by morning," Dominique said as she showed Scott and Miss Nelson to the door.

Miss Nelson shook Dominique's hand before leaving. Scott, being the devil in disguise, turned his lips upside down and sort of rolled his eyes at Dominique. After they were long gone, Dominique replayed their visit in her mind and thought to herself, No that little boy-boy didn't roll his beady eyes at me! She chuckled for a moment and then placed a call to Waverly. "Pick up the phone Waverly Corrine! I know you hear it!"

●●●●

*W*averly's a trip. Of course she heard it. She has one of those speakerphones in her car that interrupts music when there is an incoming call. I think she was just thinking too much again.

"How may I help you Miss Blake?"

"And a good evening to you Judge Simmons! Two things – One, I was hoping you could accompany Meagan home tomorrow. I wanted Sidney to do something with me tomorrow morning and two – we need to meet extra early tomorrow if we're going running. Sidney's Mom is having surgery first thing and I didn't want her to be alone," Dominique explained.

"Surgery! Why! What's wrong with Miss Phyllis?" Waverly shouted.

"I'm not even certain. But I have to admit; it's not making much sense. This is the first I've heard of Miss Phyllis being ill."

"You are too much Miss Blake!"

"What are you talking about girl?"

"What's the expression—you can take the lady out of the courtroom, but you can't take the courtroom out of the lady!"

"You are crazy! Just be at the park an hour earlier."

"Diamond, what ever happed with those boys today?"

"Girl, you wouldn't believe it if I told you! For one, these are not little boys we're referring to. My guess is, Charles, who is still in a coma had too many drugs and perhaps gotten over excited. While Scott, is truly in a class of unique storytellers all by his lonesome. It's definitely a fact that the two of them were engaged in some sexual activities. Whether or not it was willing is a horse of a different color. It's funny though because after hearing Scott Griffin's version of what he said happened, I almost wanted to believe him myself," explained Dominique.

"Since when did you start believing your clients?" laughed Waverly.

"Around the same time you stopped taking bribes Judge Judy," Dominique replied.

The two women laughed even more.

"I've got to go now. I promised Meagan I'd bring her something good to eat. Be good to yourself Waverly Corrine. I will see you in the morning," Dominique said.

Waverly kept giggling and said, "Yeah, I'll see you in the morning."

Life's sometimes tricky. Isn't it simply amazing how your true friends can pull you outside of your reality? Causing one to see just how humorous their so-called rigid life really is. Laughing at Dominique's bad joke made Waverly forget just that fast what was really going on with her. But, as the old saying goes, "easy come – easy go." Or was that a wise man that said it. Never mind, I'm sure you get the picture. Anyhow, as Waverly pulled up in her garage, Dominique Blake was still very much fresh on her mind. So, she couldn't help wonder to herself, once again about that not so bizarre scandalous situation with those boys. It's crazy though, I think it even excited Missy a bit. Needless to say, Waverly Corrine slipped back into that trance she was in earlier that day. Luckily for me, girlfriend picked up precisely where she had left off. Now who's voice might that be in your head Judge Simmons...

•••

"Corrine, are you almost done with Miss White?"

"Yes, this is her last rinse. When I'm done, may I take a break?"

"Sure hun. But, let me speak to you for a sec first..."

"Yes, Miss G."

"Did you think about what I asked you earlier? You really could make a lot of money! You really could make a lot of money!... A Lot of money!..."

Oh no, not again! Can't you see she's tripping? I mean busy right now! Kids today... they're so persistent!

"Mother! Mother! Are you all right? I thought I heard you down here," Victor said as he tapped on Waverly's car window.

Waverly unfortunately snapped out of her maze, smiled at her son and said, "Hey Beasley!"

Now you know neither of them could hear what the other was saying. So, Victor waited until his Mom opened the car door to see if she was all right and if she needed help with the box of files she sat on the front seat.

"Hey baby! How is my favorite man?" Waverly asked as she touched Victor's face.

"Fine Mother! I thought I heard you pulling up. Need some help?" asked Victor as he kissed his Mom.

"Sure, your Mother's tired! It's been a very unusual day... " Waverly replied as she grabbed her purse and reached for her briefcase.

Victor then walked around to the other side of Waverly's car to get the box of files. Waverly just stood still for a moment in their three-car garage trying not to think about her unfaithful husband. I think it was difficult though; considering Vincent's red Porsche was parked right beside Waverly's silver BMW. Yet, Waverly displayed a look on her face suggesting that maybe, just maybe she was tired from her long day and not at all pissed by her husband's series of lies. But! – Did I mention that Waverly Corrine has one of those dry senses of humors? As she stood there patiently, Girl actually pondered the idea of keying their wedding date on the hood of Vincent's car or maybe even punching small holes in all four of his tires.

No, she thought. *I would be revealing my feelings prematurely to that two faced devil.*

●●●●

o after Waverly was truly unable to go with her first instincts, she decided to enjoy what was left of her preoccupied evening. So Girl accompanied her son that stood a few inches taller than her into their almost five thousand square foot home. Waverly always, always, dreamed of becoming a princess some day. So, building her very own palace was as close as she could get. And a palace is exactly what it was.

Waverly designed this tri-level mansion when she first laid eyes on one of those ball player's homes on the television show, Cribs. She had just been appointed to her judgeship that very same weekend. Mr. and Mrs. Simmons was celebrating her victory over a bottle of Chardonnay and Cuban cigars when it hit her that their condo overlooking the water was not going to properly represent the youngest black female judge in Washington D.C. So, Girl took the first check from her new job and most of their savings, then hired one of the best architects from California to bring to life the home she's always dreamed of as a child.

It set on a hill at least two hundred feet behind tall evergreen trees that lined the main road from the south entrance of a gated community. And yes, there was a security guard keeping a watchful eye twenty-four seven. There was a cobblestone circular driveway in the front of the house and a hot tub leading to the heated pool in the back of the house. If you entered from the right side of the home where the three-car garage is located, you'll notice that you're coming in on the bottom level of this estate, which by the way, had an oversized storage area in the rear and family area, filling most of the space with a fire place sitting directly in the middle of the room. Also on this level was a small kitchen area with an espresso bar and another master suite with a customized shower for two. Leading to the second level, a spiral staircase placed you in the main hall right between the Main Kitchen and the Study. This conventional home also has three Sunrooms. One off the Main Kitchen, one off the Living Room, and one off the Master Bedroom on the third level. And with three other bedrooms on the third level, a Garden Bath in the Master Suite and an oversized old fashion Hall Bath. There was always a place to run and hide. Mr. and Mrs. Simmons' sunken Great Room (as they called it) was approximately twenty feet by twenty-six feet. It's located to the left of the curved staircase as you enter the front entrance through those tall stained glass double doors. Simply breathe taking! And, last *but certainly not least, their formal dining room set on an octagon platform surrounded by beautiful marble columns that Waverly found in Italy on one of Vincent's last minute "I love only you" trips.*

And if that wasn't enough, W.C. Simmons was about to embark on another birthday. And let's just be truthful and say that most women dread turning forty at least five years prior. So you can be certain that Waverly Corrine had tons of different creams and ointments for everything under the sun to help maintain her youthful appearance. And yes, proper rest was at the top of her list. So off to bed is where she went.

•••

nd time – let's just say that time waits for no one. It was now five a.m. Rock Creek Park was cool and unbelievably quiet. The only clear sounds were the birds singing and you could vaguely hear the other runner's sneakers hitting the pavement. Dominique Blake and Sidney Sharpe were already there, both anxious to begin their day. Waverly on the other hand just pulled up. Rested, but moving somewhat like a turtle. As she walked over to the girls, she couldn't help but think, Is this as good as it gets?

Dominique noticed their slow girlfriend first and yelled, "Sleeping Beauty has finally arrived!"

Waverly picked up her pace just a little and replied, "It's a new day Miss Blake. Let's not spoil it with your juvenile remarks!" *Sidney giggled because she knew one should never joke with Waverly Corrine before she's had her morning coffee. Waverly's not a morning person. Dominique could care less.*

"Are you ready?" Dominique said as she began running in place.

"Give me a minute to warm up!" Waverly replied as she began to stretch her tense body.

Sidney glanced at her watch, checking to see just how much time she had to spare before her Mother's operation was to begin. Trying to keep a positive outlook on the situation, she immediately prayed to herself, "God just keep me until I'm able to keep myself. And wherever my sister may be, please let her see that her place is with our Mother." Then she took a deep breath exhaled, then shouted," Time's up!"

So naturally, Sidney and Dominique started up their usual path first. Then of course Waverly Corrine followed. And again, twenty minutes into their run, as usual, Miss Waverly stopped to breathe. Dominique and Sidney both noticed after a few seconds passed that their good-good girlfriend had run out of gas once again. The two glanced at each other first then decided to go back for their hopeless friend. At first, nothing was said. Dominique continued jogging in place and shaking her head at Waverly while thinking to herself, I can't believe you! Strong as hell in your black robe, but as "weak as a punk in Boys' Town" *in your Donna Karen sweats.*

Sidney simply found it amusing. And, since Waverly decided to take a break, Sidney thought it would be rude not to join her. By this time, the park was beginning to get a little busy. So before the girls could address their issue and move forward, two older gentlemen jogged by them. One nearly broke his neck when he failed to see a stone in his path. It was obvious that the old man was drooling. Sidney immediately looked over to Waverly and said, "Looks like someone has a secret admirer! You'd better tell that old goat you're happily married!"

Dominique cringed then replied, "He's probably just a dirty old man looking for a young concubine or worst, wanting nothing more than a Virgin Mary, to raise up!"

"Damn girl, that's kind of low isn't' it! Pops might just want a little excitement! I hope you don't feel that way about all men, cause last I heard – aint' nothing wrong with a little bump and grind! Tell her Waverly! You haven't been married all this time for nothing!" Sidney said as she placed both hands on her curvaceous hips.

Waverly snickered and said, "Maybe I have..."

"See, that's what I'm talking about! Wait a minute, rewind that last statement!" Sidney shouted.

"I'm afraid you heard me correctly. Vincent's fucking and it's not with me! And what makes it even worst, he looks at me right in the face and lies through his pearly white teeth," Waverly replied.

Dominique stopped jogging and asked Waverly, "Does he blink, looks to the left or right, maybe even stutter over most of his words? Or another way you can be sure, if a dog's – I mean a man's telling one is if he raises his tone then tries turn the tables!"

"Well, I can see why you over charge your clients Miss Blake," Sidney laughed.

"Why do men lie? I mean they lie about everything. Case in point – take my beloved husband. We've been together on and off since college. Maybe I did want to get married first because I didn't want to be labeled as the lawyer with the baby's daddy sneaking on campus. And yes, I did adore Vincent for years. But then he started contradicting himself when asked about his whereabouts. That lead to more unexplained trips away from home until I just decided to either deal with it for the sake of saving face, or direct all of my energy to my son and work. I have no idea how so many years passed by. It was almost like sleeping with the enemy. He was oh so good when I pretended not to know what was really going on. But, when I was forced in a position to confront that bastard, he'd somehow convince me that I was imagining things. After a while, I managed to detach myself from the notion of ever being loved the way a man truly loves his woman," Waverly explained in very sad tone.

"That does not sound like the Waverly Corrine we know and love. Girl, how could you keep all this from us? Pretend I'm five years old and explain this shit!" Sidney said.

Dominique just stood there with her mouth hung opened waiting for an answer and thinking to herself, That's why I can't stand them, don't trust them and the thought of a prick crawling up on top of me! Well, the idea simply makes me want to vomit. Dominique batted her beautiful chestnut eyes and shouted, "Well, spit it out!"

"You see, this is why I chose to keep it to myself. And besides, how do you tell your girls that your fairytale marriage of less than two years tops is now causing you to wonder. Not to mention that your child's still in pampers. I don't think so! But, my two beautiful, black, bold, priceless friends, the joke is over! As we speak, Dr. Vincent Simmons slash butt hole..." Waverly said just before Dominique interrupted her.

"Don't you mean ass hole!"

Waverly chuckled then replied, "Whatever! Anyway, he's about to be caught red-handed."

"Ooh… no you didn't!" Sidney yelled.

"You hired a Dick, I mean a Private I!" Dominique blurted out just before she started laughing.

But before Waverly could try to answer, she and Sidney both started laughing as well. And from up here, it even sounded like the birds in the trees had joined in. But, that was a good thing. Waverly needed a break in the conversation. I believe girlfriend was indeed broken-up by this whole whatever you wish to call it. She may have been able to fool her friends, but I wasn't buying it, not one bit!

"Tell me lies, tell me sweet little lies… tell me lies," murmured Sidney as she made a silly faced then started to dance.

At that moment, all three girls glanced at each other, giving the signal that it was truly time to bond in song. Displaying all talents, the three formed a soul train line and began to dance rather seductively while singing one of those old pop rock songs.

"Tell me lies, tell me sweet little lies. Tell me lies. Oh no you can't despise – when you tell me lies."

Sidney was doing the Snake, Dominique was doing the Moonwalk, and Waverly – well, I guess she was doing the Robot.

"Okay, okay, it's time for Q and A. Most men lie about their what?" Sidney said as she looked at Dominique.

The size of their penis, Dominique thought to herself. But then she replied, "How much money they make!"

"That's a good one Diamond! But, how about if they're happy at home after you peep the fact that they are married. And why do they lie about being attached anyway?" Waverly said as she related her comment solely to her husband.

"I have no idea Girl, but do us all a favor and figure that one out before you decide to marry the next prince charming."

"Okay, all right, my turn! Men lie most about their name! Always going under an alias! What's up with that?" Sidney said as she shook her head.

Now of course it was Dominique's turn again, so as she stood there, not thinking very hard at all, Girlfriend decided to share one of her own life's experiences.

"I have both of you beat! How about the fool that's caught between Clark Kent and Superman?" Dominique said as she raised her brows and turned her lips upside down.

Waverly and Sidney both looked at each other then back at Dominique. Fortunately for them, they both knew that their good-good Girlfriend, Diamond, usually stays left in most cases. And sometimes, can go left or right based on what's working for her at the time. This wasn't one of those times. Neither Waverly nor Sidney had a clue. I couldn't even see, with my big eyes, which direction Miss Blake was headed.

"You know the one, not really certain if he wants to be with a woman or perhaps deep down inside Mr. Wonderful secretly desires a man. Because I hear it all the time at work, that there's a little bitch in all men," explained Dominique.

Waverly and Sidney just stood there in awe. This was not coming out of Dominique's mouth. Okay, so what if Miss Blake's always – always kept her love life to herself. I'm sure you too have that one special friend who chooses not to kiss and tell. Come on, I know you can't possibly think that your closest comrade tells you everything. That's what I thought!

"I hope you're not suggesting that all this time, we've been sleeping with little girls! Because that would explain why I haven't been able to find a good man!"

"There aren't any," laughed Sidney.

"You're stupid Sidney Sharpe. I don't think that's what Diamond's trying to say. And while we're on the subject, let's not forget that we lie too. I'm serious – since the begging of time. The very first lie a woman told was... I'm a virgin and you will be my first!" Waverly said with a big grin on her face.

"That's cold!" Dominique whispered.

Sidney looked at Waverly and thought to herself, *That one worked for me during the first two years of college.* Then she replied, "Okay maybe I've lied in the past about how many lovers I've had..."

"I bet you have!" Dominique said under her breath.

"All right you little health attic, what lies have you told?" asked Waverly as she looked over to Dominique.

"You mean to you?" replied Dominique.

"That's not funny and you are a professional storyteller Miss Attorney at Law…" Waverly said.

By this time Dominique had begun her cooling down exercises. And no, she wasn't about to tell her two best friends that she's lied all of this time about her sexuality.

No – this is not the right time. It's too early in the day. I can't even suggest to them to sleep on it. Take a nap! No! Dominique thought to herself then finally replied, "I don't lie! I simply tell them to let me get back to you on that one. Or, I say absolutely nothing."

"That figures! I have one! How about how good the sex was?" laughed Sidney.

Then Waverly blurted out laughing and said, "What about when we have them thinking that we had an orgasm! Because sometimes I'm just not feeling it. I just want him to get the hell up off me!"

"No Boo! I'm not feeling you on that one I'm not faking an orgasm! I'll show a nigger first – what to do before that lady sings. And if all else fails, he'll just have to take notes while I take matters into my own hands," Sidney explained as she adjusted her clothes and patted her hair.

"That was too much information. It's getting late, I think we should be headed out of here," Dominique said as she continued up the path.

Sidney and Waverly soon followed, laughing and cracking jokes on Dominique.

"Do you think our friend is still a virgin?" Waverly asked.

Sidney giggled and said, "No, I don't think so. But Gay – that's questionable!"

"I hope you both grow hair on your chest for talking about me behind my back. You know I have perfect hearing ugly girls," Dominique replied.

●●●●

*M*eanwhile, *over at Howard University Hospital, Sidney's Mom was waiting impatiently for her scheduled surgery. Miss Phyllis had on two pair of socks and three of those thin hospital gowns because all morning long, she was complaining about her room being terribly cold. Her oldest daughter Sherian had arrived at three* *a.m. that morning just around the same time she started fussing about the temperature in her room. So, Sherian tried to be supportive by granting her Mother's request and going home to get her some socks, warm pajamas, her Bible and a little old antique box that she had since the girls were little.*

Now Miss Phyllis Maple may have been somewhat unreasonable but she was indeed up there in age. In other words, just like her daughters, this old lady was fearless. Raising two little girls alone without the financial or physical support of a father for either of them. She still somehow managed. Always knowing exactly what to do. And when all else failed, Miss Phyllis would go off by herself to pray with her little old antique box and her Bible that was even older than the box. But something didn't quite fit with Miss Phyllis that morning. Outside of being very cold, Miss Phyllis was feeling weaker than she's ever felt in the past. And that scared her the most. So not wanting to alarm her daughters, she decided to stay in prayer and keep her feelings to herself. Unfortunately, they were revealing themselves in other ways. Miss Phyllis kept checking the time nervously and forcing her daughter Sherian to get the nurse to adjust the temperature in her room every half hour. Then she began singing old church hymns. That even appeared normal until Sherian noticed her Mom talking to herself while fumbling through that old box of hers.

Miss Phyllis thought that Sherian was still asleep, but it was easy to tell that Sherian was concerned by the way she sat there with her eyes cracked opened, saying absolutely nothing while at the same time, playing possum. Then, Miss Phyllis began writing something in a little black book – the same book Sherian remembered seeing in the past.

I know as old as she is, Momma's not keeping a diary! I know I should have peeked into that box on the way over here. It's not like I haven't picked locks before. Besides, I don't think it's the same as breaking and entering. Maybe it's more like reading someone else's mail... I wonder where you keep that key? Wait a second, I'm getting entirely too old for this shit! Sherian thought to herself as she made a gesture letting her Mother know for certain that she was waking up.

Miss Phyllis noticed her immediately so she closed the book quickly then practically threw it back into the old box, which laid at the end of her tiny little hospital bed. She cleared her throat attempting to direct any attention elsewhere and whispered,

"Cher are you awake baby?"

Sherian played along just as she had done many other times in the past and replied,

"I'm not sure, what time is it?"

Exactly thirty-five minutes before these over anxious quacks experiment on my mind, Miss Phyllis thought to herself.

At that moment, Miss Phyllis felt a really sharp pain on the lower left side of her head.

"Oh my God!" *she yelled as she placed her left hand directly on the area where she felt the pain. Then, seconds later, Miss Phyllis's head began to throb. It looked as if she was trying to shake it off because she started shaking her head and batting her eyes. And even in the mist of her pain, Phyllis Maple was simply astonishing. Yes, she was indeed self-willed and her determination was unbelievable. Yet, with her naturally straight silver stranded hair, and those hazelnut eyes, Phyllis Maple had the ability to charm the most hardened heart. Always giving her last without question. And when she smiled, how do you humans put it? Throw in the towel; raise the white flag because this battle was over. Basically, there was no point in fighting with her because you would surely lose. So yes, Miss Phyllis just sat there bothered by her ailments and the thought of those doctors taking what was left of her sense of who she was. She continued moaning…*

"Momma, are you all right? Because I can get your doctor. They should have been in here by now. I know it's almost time for your procedure. Momma, where is your watch?" Sherian asked as she started looking in the nightstand drawer beside her Mother's bed.

Miss Phyllis then reached under her pillow and pulled out an exquisite old grandfathers watch. This particular piece of jewelry was over fifty years old and had been given to her as a present by her former employer many many years ago. You could tell it was restored by the way it gleamed like new. It also hung from a brand new white gold chain. Sherian often wondered growing up, "Why would a woman want a man's watch?" But then again, Sherian never knew the history behind this irreplaceable piece or it's true value.

The original owner died over fifty years ago. So, that left Miss Phyllis and the person who gave her this watch the only two who knew what it was really worth. I believe Sherian wanted to have the

*watch appraised so that she could auction it off at one of their yearly
sales at the antique shop she and her Mom owned. Nevertheless, the
piece of jewelry was simply breath taking. It was yellow-gold with
white-gold trim and it had rose buds embedded in it. And, what made
this piece even more unique was the rare canary three-carrot diamond
that sat smack dab in the center of it. Yes, this watch was rare. But,
it was also priceless to Miss Phyllis Maple. And like American
Express, she never ever left home without it. So as she handed her
daughter the watch, Miss Phyllis whispered,* "Here – you can see
what time it is. This medication has my eyes hurting when I
keep looking at it."

*Sherian took the watch, glanced at it while thinking to herself, I
really don't think it's the medication, old lady. It's probably
your age.*

"It's a quarter after six Momma. The nurse said earlier
that you were scheduled at 6:45, which gives Sidney only
fifteen minutes to get her un-Godly late self here. I tell you
Momma, if anything ever happens to you, I have no idea
what I'm going to do with that one…" Sherian said as she
fixed her Mom's pillow.

*Miss Phyllis looked up at Sherian, reached over and grabbed her by
her wrist and said firmly,*

"I don't ever want to hear you talk like that again!
Whether or not I'm in the land of the living or is as dead as a
rattlesnake, dried up in the Sahara Dessert! You've had it
easy your entire life! You know exactly what you're going to
do with Sid. TELL HER! I've done my part! And when I'm
dead and gone, you will be all she has. With the store and
what I've tucked away, you two will have more than enough
to bid me farewell and get by for several seasons. That's all
that matters to me. So you look me right in the eyes Cher and
promise me now that you'll do right by Sid! Promise me!"

Sherian exhaled, nodded her head and answered, "Of course I'll
do right by her. You don't think I've tried in the past? Sidney
has a mind of her own."

"Just like you… You two are more alike than you care to
believe. Yet, there's something about Sid that forces her to be
courageous and press on in spite of how things appear. And,
you my overzealous one, are quick to respond. Although

she'll need you, you'll need her as well. We're family and despite what you may have heard in the past, family is all we have. The same blood runs through all our veins. Do you understand what I'm saying to you Cher?" explained Miss Phyllis.

But, before Sherian could acknowledge what her Mom was saying to her, Sidney and Dominique walked in. Sidney first rubbed Sherian on her back then leaned over to kiss her Mother good morning. Dominique followed, smiling at Sherian then hugging Miss Phyllis and kissing her on the cheek.

"It's good to see you again Miss Phyllis. And how are you doing Sherian?" Dominique inquired.

"Just fine Dominique. How are things with you?" Sherian replied.

"Good, good!"

Sidney glanced at her watch and said, "It's about that time Momma. We should get you ready now. The nurse will be in here any minute to get you."

"I've changed my mind! I've lived with it this long, I don't really think I want those quacks messing with my mind!" Miss Phyllis said with her lips poked out.

Dominique placed her hand over her mouth and smiled. Sherian just shook her head while Sidney gave her Mom one of those reassuring looks and said, "Momma, Dr. Caplan is not a quack and you do need this procedure. Dr. Caplan assured me that this would be a simple procedure with good prognosis but without it... Momma, your health might be in danger... You are the biggest girl I know, you can do this. You really can."

There was silence for a few minutes while the women waited. Then it dawned on Miss Phyllis that she almost forgot to do something very important. She reached for her old antique box, rubbed it and handed it to her daughter Sherian.

"Can you keep this for me while I'm in surgery?" she said

Sherian smiled at her Mother and nodded her head – yes.

Miss Phyllis then cleared her throat and asked Sherian, "What did you do with my watch?"

Sherian pulled the old grandfather's watch out of her jacket pocket and handed to her Mother. Miss Phyllis then turned towards Sidney and asked her to hold out her hand. Slowly, she placed the old antique watch in Sidney's hand then said in a very soft tone, "Will you hold this for me?"

Sidney's eyes watered then she answered, "Sure Momma"

Just then two nurses, one male nurse and the other a female nurse came to get Miss Phyllis. As they rolled her out of the room, those tears that watered in Sidney's eyes came rolling down her face. Dominique noticed that Sidney was scared so she walked up behind her and held her tightly. Sherian just looked at both of them almost as if she was slightly jealous because no one was there to comfort her. Or, maybe she wanted to be the one to hold her sister at a time such as this. But, as her Mother said earlier, always – always being quick to react, Sherian frowned her face and walked out of the room with the antique box tucked underneath her arm. After the door closed behind her, Sidney began to dry her face with the end of the sweatshirt she had on.

"It's understandable... I would imagine I'd feel the same. But, I never knew my Mother. She died when I was very young. My Father took me away when I was less than two years old. I remember him always trying to turn me against her by telling me how she was crazy and that she never really wanted me. He said I was his only love. My Father was a very sick individual," whispered Dominique as she looked away.

And in that blink of an eye, Dominique Blake experienced a flashback. It was during a time in her life when she first started to develop into a young teenager. She could vaguely see her Father standing over her while she was taking a bath trying to clean herself up because earlier that day in school, Dominique's menstrual cycle began. At the time, she remembered being very uncomfortable by the way he watched her scrub the blood off her inner thighs. And as she looked up at him with tears in her eyes wanting desperately for him to leave the bathroom, all he kept repeating was . . . . .

"Well Dominique Alisa, you're a woman now... You're a woman now... A woman!"

"Diamond are you all right? It looked like you stepped out for a minute. One minute you were telling me how sick your Father was and then – poof! Your eyes glazed over and you looked as though you were wondering. You sought of faded out on me. I had no idea that your Dad's health was bad. You never really mentioned your parents before. Outside of the fact that they both died when you were young," Sidney said as she looked at her friend mysteriously.

"Yeah – but that was a whole other life. One that I'd rather not disclose. And totally different from the one I'm living now. Besides, that's the ugly part of my story. It's not yours! I mean I know that you never knew your Father, as I never knew my Mother. But, you have a sister, no matter how overprotective, who loves you very much. And a fantastic Mother, who I can't see God taking away from you right now. You said yourself that the procedure is simple. So let's just both put down our shoulders, go have a cup of mocha and wait until this is over. What do you say?" Dominique said as she smiled at Sidney.

Sidney took a deep breath, looked around the room then answered, "Okay Girl, come on!" *On the way down the hall they passed by Sherian who was on the pay phone. Sidney asked her sister if she would like a cup of coffee from the Café. But, Sherian still being a little ticked, quickly nodded – no. Sidney simply smiled back at her older sister and continued down the hall with Dominique.*

● ● ● ●

And speaking of being ticked off. . . .

I*'ll give you one guess as to who, at this precise moment, is confessing her sins to the Priest. But, first let me tell you that not only did she drive all the way over there the night before just for someone else at the Parrish to tell Girl that he had an emergency and would be unable to keep their appointment. Missy thought that somehow he would return soon. Therefore, she proceeded to wait for him in the sanctuary. But what she anticipated would take maybe an hour or two, actually took all night. The Priest did not return until 7:00 a.m. this morning. And, feeling sorry for having to leave so abruptly before their originally scheduled appointment, he saw Katherine immediately. Time's up!*

"So as you can see Father, there are many unanswered questions for me and my daughter, Meagan. When my husband and I came to you over thirty-six years ago, we asked you to help us with the decisions we were facing then. You assured us that first – the birth mother had no intention of every coming for Meagan and second – it was God's will for us to raise this child as our own. But, with all the years between then and now, let me just say – if there was a chance to meet Meagan's birth mother, that chance is long gone. And, I have no clue where to even begin looking Father. Telling my daughter that I am not her birth mother isn't going to be enough information for her. Her baby Nia has the Sickle Cell Trait as well. Now, maybe I could somehow manage to keep this "tainted" secret from my little girl all these years," Katherine said as she began to cry.

"But how do you convince yourself that it's perfectly okay to allow your daughter (that you lied to all of her life) to now lie to her daughter as well. The child is going to know that something's not right with her. And just like my Meagan, if Nia has a child of her own some day, she could pass the trait on to her little one," explained Katherine.

"There, there my child. God has reasons for all of our existence. I'm sure if we search our hearts, we will find the answers," replied Father Murphy.

"I'm sure God has many reasons for what he does and please excuse me for being so forward, but to be very honest with you Father, it is not God who I have questions for, it's you. I've been in prayer for a very long time about my daughter. And, the one answer that has been extremely clear to me is that you hold the key to her identity. I'm aware of the oath you've taken Father. But, this is different. We must know! Meagan's whole future is at stake!" Katherine shouted.

"I see. But, for now I must ask you to go home to your daughter and comfort her in her time of need. I will call you when I find the answers you seek . . . . And Katherine, I'd like you to remember one very important thing – things are just as they should be. The only chances in the world, my child, are given by God when there's yet but the same lesson to be learned. You didn't just happen here Sister Katherine. There is more to be learned then the identity of your daughter. I believe that God is trying to tell you something as well," explained Father Murphy.

Now with Katherine feeling even more frustrated than before and trying very hard not to "Kirk-Out" on the Priest, there was nothing more for her to do at this time but join him in prayer. After that, she followed Father Murphy's instructions and for the record, can I just say that this is getting crazy even for me!

Now what? Still no answers... At least not for Katherine to convey to her daughter. Speaking of mothers and daughters, our newest Mommy, Meagan Simone Tyler is preparing to return home with her two beautiful daughters. Do you smell that? Oh my Lord! Guess what's in pamper number one or would that be pamper number two. What are the chances of two babies having an accident at the same time? Pew! That smells worst than anything that I've landed on in the past. This Mommy definitely has her hands full. Let's go back to the other hospital and see how Miss Phyllis is doing.

"Paging Dr. Cummings. Paging Dr. Cummings, you're needed at Nurse Station Five."

"That little hound's probably wanted at the police station as well," Sidney said with her lips turned upside down.

Dominique looked at Sidney sort of confused and asked, "What are you talking about?"

"Nothing Girl!"

"Come on Sidney Sharpe, out with it!"

"All right, all right already! I just believe in my own opinion, Dr. Dexter Cummings is nothing more than a common criminal," Sidney said as she blinked her eyes at Dominique.

Dominique just looked at Sidney in utter amazement and replied, "You are tripping!"

"No, I am very serious. You tell me – how can a man as fine as he is and as married as he is, be pushing up on me while we're both in the middle of surgery. And to add insult to injury, how likely is it that he's also good friends with that lying ass Vincent. So, as I stated, he's guilty in the first degree for attempting to cheat on his wife with me. And guilty in the second degree for conspiring with a known felon, Dr. Vincent Simmons, who I hope burns in hell for what he's done to Waverly or worse, rots away in a tiny little cell off on Rikers Island," explained Sidney just before she took her last sip of Mocha.

Dominique had absolutely no response to that. True, there was some validity to Sidney's assessment. But, as Dominique sat there across from her friend of more than fifteen years, Girl knew exactly how she had gotten to the point of distrusting men. So, that would also include Vincent. Now as for Sidney, that remains to be seen.

"Let's get out of here Girl and go check on your Mom," Dominique said as she stood to her feet.

Sidney just looked up at Dominique and replied, "Cat's got your tongue. I told you! Boys will be boys and there are only a few good men!"

Both girls giggled all the way out of the Café. In fact, these two comedians were still giggling as they stepped out of the elevator. I don't know, I guess that was sort of okay considering no one really wanted to be feeling down and out. That tends to make matters worse. But, as they walked down the corridor, both swaying and pausing, the air appeared to be a little tight. You know, somewhat stuffy, yet not noticeable. It was so quiet but at the same time, you could almost hear the heartbeats of the few people, including Sidney's and Dominique's, who were in the operating room waiting area. Sherian was engrossed in a conversation on the hospital's courtesy phone with her employee about the store. While one woman was passed out on the sectional as, her nine year old played beside her with a crossword puzzle.

One gentleman was talking on his cell phone to his daughter, while another man sat there with his head almost between his legs. As the girls approached the doors, which lead to the short hall just before the operation area where Miss Phyllis was, somehow Sidney thought she imagined hearing the monitors, she usually checks when she's working, going off.

This couldn't be! she thought. Then the sounds were seemingly getting louder. It was almost as if she could hear the conversations on the other side of the doors as well. She first looked at Dominique and asked her if she heard anything. Dominique shook her head — no. Sidney being very uncomfortable at this point proceeded to enter into the first set of operating doors. Sherian noticed her impatient sibling, but continued with her phone call. Hesitantly, Sidney moved close enough to the oversized double doors, which allowed her to peak in through the square fiberglass windows to see precisely what was going on. She scanned the room quickly and then focused in on the monitor to make certain her Mother's health was indeed just fine. Lord and behold, and I do not use the phrase loosely, the line was flat. Sidney's eyes bubbled up with tears as she turned her head – counter clockwise. This is not happening.

"Momma!" she whispered.

Remotely considering the notion that her eyes were playing tricks on her, she shook her head and blinked them trying to regain a clear vision. Sidney then started wiping her eyes trusting this time that her mind wouldn't be playing tricks on her. At that moment, the tunnel vision she was experiencing was no more thanks to one of the nurses that noticed her in a restricted area.

"Dr. Sharpe, you know you're supposed to be wearing your hat and booties back here," she said as she tapped Sidney on the shoulders.

Just then, Sidney realized that she was not seeing things and from the looks of it, Momma Phyllis had gone on to be with the angels and the Lord. Simply taken by her newfound reality, Sidney looked into the nurses eyes and as her lips began to quiver, she whispered,

"My Momma…Momma…Momma's gone…"

First, the nurse didn't understand what she was trying to say. But, then as she looked around and noticed all the activity going on in the operating room, which stood directly in front of them, it became painfully clear to the nurse, knowing that Sidney's Mother was in surgery, that something must have gone wrong. The next sounds that filled the room were the screams from Sidney's weeping voice as she pushed opened the double doors, which stood between her and her dead Mother, Phyllis Maple.

"Can someone please get Dr. Sharpe out of here!" shouted Dr. Kaplan when he noticed Sidney had forced her way into the O.R.

Sidney just continued screaming and swearing resembling behaviors of a crazy woman on a rampage. Forbidding anyone or anything to stand in her way, Girl, just pushed down two technicians and the cart holding most of the implements just to be by her Mother's side. Naturally, other staff members were running into the operating room at this time attempting to help control the situation. But, all that was heard was Sidney Sharpe screaming to the top of her lungs, "No! No! Momma…No!"

Out in the waiting area, everyone began looking around. Tears rolled down Dominique's eyes as she looked over at Sherian. Sherian's eyes opened widely as she tried to stand to her feet, falling to the floor first as she heard her younger sister's cries. For a split second, Dominique was undecided as to whether to help Sherian to her feet or find her best friend whose cries she heard as well. Shaking her head and looking back and forth, Dominique ran as fast as she could to Sidney.

"Damn it!" Sherian yelled. She had not noticed the wastebasket near the phone and it cause her to trip and fall. So, after she managed to get to her feet, Sherian rushed off to be with her family leaving Jamie, the store Manger, on the phone wondering what in the world had happened.

Chapter Six

Tripping

wo floors up on the other side of the hospital, as the nurse was examining Charles Davis, she noticed that his charts had changed in the last half hour. Charles, who had arrived at Howard University Hospital four days prior, slipped into a coma during surgery. The doctors thought the coma might have been due to a stroke from an alcohol and cocaine overdose. When Charles was brought into the hospital, it was obvious that drugs were in his system. But, when the emergency room doctors examined him, they found bruises on his hands and buttocks. And, because of the massive bleeding from his rectum, surgery was performed. At that time, it was confirmed that Charles Davis had been sodomized and drugged. The semen found in Charles' rectum was a ninety percent match with the sample taken from Mr. Tony Hernandez. Yet, the authorities had no known suspects until Scott Griffin came clean about who they had been with. I believe he sounded off only to keep those doctors from running more tests on him. Nevertheless, from the looks of things, Charles Davis was no longer comatose.

"Charlie, my name is Rebecca. Do you know where you are?" asked the nurse.

Charles continued to look straight ahead while thinking to himself, *Well, chances that I've died and gone to heaven are out. And I don't feel any restraints on my arms or legs so that rules out a mental ward. Either I'm in a hospital or my parents redecorated my room. Whichever the case, I think I'll play stupid for a little while.*

The nurse then leaned over to get a better look at Charles' eyes and said, "How do you feel? You've been in a coma for four days. We've been very worried about you. I'm going to get your doctor. I'll be right back all right Charlie? Don't be afraid. You're safe here."

The nurse rubbed Charles' forehead and left the room. After Charles was certain the nurse was gone, he sat straight up in the bed and looked around quickly as he tried to remember what he might have done four days ago to end up this way.

"A coma! Feel Safe! I know that the right side of my body feels heavier than the left. And what in the hell is she talking about?" Charles said to himself.

Next, Charles realized that he had to go to the bathroom. As he attempted to get out of that tiny little hospital bed, Charles felt his bladder being release without his control. "Ah damn!" *he shouted as he peeked under the sheet only to notice there was a tube running from his penis into a small bag hanging on the side of the bed.*

"I'm totally fucked," *he whispered as he started feeling on his other body parts to make sure there was nothing attached to them. Then it hit him! Charles suddenly remembered sniffing cocaine and pouring vodka on Scott's chest while laughing at a sexual gesture that was being made to him by a woman he had just met named Gina.*

Charles began to shake his head while thinking to himself, I'd better play stupid. Yeah, play real stupid. That's right, I'll have a slight case of amnesia. How would you say? Selective memory. At least until I talk to that damn Scottie, who got me caught up in all this mess in the first place.

Charles then decided to call Scott to inform him that he was awake and tell him they should talk as soon as possible. Scott's answering service clicked on.

"What message would you like to send Sir?" said the operator.

Charles through his frustration and embarrassment blurted out, "Yeah, I have a message. Tell him just like this – Boy, the joke is over. I'm up now and you should get here before I decide to remember everything that happened at that whore, Gina's house. Oh and bring me a smoke. You got that lady?" Charles said as he kept looking at the door to keep watch for the nurse's return.

"Yes, but that's a long message," replied the operator.

"Well, do the best you can Lady!" Charles said just before hanging up the phone.

Not knowing what to do next, Charles simply laid back in the bed and re-adjusted the sheets to look as if he never moved. Then he waited nervously for the nurse and doctor to return. A few seconds later, his doctor entered the room. Pleased to see Charles out of the coma, the doctor smiled as he walked over to Charles' bedside.

"Well good morning young man, it's good to have you back. I've already called your parents and gave them the good news. How do you feel? Do you know where you are?" asked Dr. Stevens.

*Here we go again – another jerk asking stupid questions
as if I was slow or retarded. Do you know where* **you** *are Dr.
Butt-hole?* Charles thought to himself. But, then he replied
rudely, "I guess it's safe to say that I'm in a hospital. But,
how did I get here and why does my right side feel so
heavy?"

"The police found you and your friend Scott in the park
passed out and near death four days ago. So you were both
brought here and treated. You slipped into a coma during an
emergency procedure and now you're back thank God. Why
don't you relax and wait until your parents arrive – then we
can talk more. Would you like something to eat or drink?"
asked Dr. Stevens.

"Why not Doc. It doesn't' seem like I'm going to get
much else," Charles replied as he shook his head.

*Dr. Stevens then took a closer look at Charles, examining his eyes
first to see if there was anything abnormal about them. Second, he
checked his heart and pulse rates just to be certain that they were okay
too. Last, before leaving Charles' room, Dr. Stevens looked over the
current readings from the charts so he could compare them with the
one's from the day before. Charles, just sat there fumbling with the
bed sheet a little and scratching his forehead while thinking to
himself, My Father's going to kill me... That wouldn't be too far
fetched considering Charles' Father is one of the top news anchors at
Washington, D.C.'s own WBAB News, "Where we tell the whole
story" is their tag line.*

*But, I believe they specialize in gossip. In fact, as we speak, one of
the reporters, Peter Van Adams, is in the break room carrying on
about a very wealthy Spanish man being arrested two days ago for
having something to do with a couple of teenagers found in a near by
park in pretty bad shape. At least that's how he put it. And of course,
Ethan Davis pretended to know absolutely nothing about it since one
of the teenagers was whom he wanted to be his pride and joy, Charles
Ethan Davis, III – his namesake.*

*But, when Charles Ethan Davis, II became famous with very high
ratings, the station promoted him. That's when he dropped his first
name because Ethan Davis sounded better to the head executives on
the top floor. Mmm, I suppose with a reputation like that, I too might
not want all of D.C. knowing that my only son was found sodomized,*

drugged, and left for dead with or without knowing the whole story. This was bad – very bad.

● ● ● ●

So Ethan, what do you think of that?" Peter said as he looked over at Ethan.

Ethan looked Peter dead in the eyes wanting nothing more but to be invisible and said, "That's not my field. I just announce what you guys find. I don't believe you'll be interested at all in what I think."

"Ooooh!" whispered one of the staff members.

Then there was chuckling by two other staff members and before Ethan could make his great escape, an announcement sounded over the intercom informing him that he had a call on line four. First, Ethan stared at the phone not wanting to answer the call in front of his colleagues for he knew in his heart of hearts that this call was about his son, Charles.

"Are you going to get that?" Peter asked as he looked at Ethan being somewhat confused.

Ethan thought for a moment, and then replied, "It's probably your old lady. I think I'd better take it in my office. You know, to avoid any embarrassment."

Eyebrows rose as Ethan made a fast get-away towards his office. And sure enough, he was correct. On the other end of the line was Daisy, excited about Charlie coming out of his coma.

"Ethan Davis," *he said as he answered the call hoping this time the voice on the other end would have better news. Anxious to share the good news, Daisy Davis, with a big smile on her face, blurted out,* "Our son is awake Ethan!"

Then for a moment, Daisy thought the line was dead because of the overwhelming silence. But, there was nothing wrong with the phone. Ethan was not only tongue-tied, he had closed his eyes and began thanking God for allowing his only son to see another day. And before he could tell his brain to tell his mouth to speak, Daisy repeated, "Ethan, our son is awake! Did you here what I just said? ETHAN! Say something!"

"When? Is he all right?" Ethan said as his heart raced. Then he took a deep breath and said calmly, "What I mean is, does all of his physical and mental components function properly?"

Daisy exhaled then replied, "Well, the doctor said that his CAT-scans are good, but..."

"But what Daisy!" Ethan shouted.

Daisy hesitated first and then answered, "He said that some of the charts when compared with the cat-scans... well, there may be some paralysis on Charlie's right side."

"Oh no! Oh God, why is all this happening now? What could I have done so bad to deserve this shit!" Ethan yelled as he hit himself in the head with the end of the palm of his hand.

Totally upset by her husband's comment, Daisy decided to remind him that the world does not revolve around his comings or goings. In other words, Ethan had allowed his new promotion at the news station to inflate his ego. Therefore taking no responsibility for the image of the station controlling his personal life. That issue caused most of their marital problems. If I were Ethan, I would have kept that last comment to myself.

"Ethan, this isn't about you! This is about our son Charles! I refuse to believe that at a time like this, all you can think about is your bull-headed self! This is about the station isn't it? I swear, if I didn't promise before God, my family and half a church of your prejudiced so called friends... I'd march right on into WBAB News station and tell those fooled souls just who they're dealing with! You're unbelievable! Do you even care?" Daisy whispered as she began to cry.

Ethan's head dropped because he was definitely feeling mixed emotions about his son and his new position at the T.V. Station.

What am I going to do if this scandal leaks out, Ethan thought to himself. Then he replied, "Of course I care Daisy? What kind of man do you think I am? I just can't help but think if I'd been around more instead of chasing my career... Maybe then I could have kept that damned Scott Griffin away from my boy!"

"You know we can't pick Charlie's friends. He's going to have to learn just as we did. I don't recall your parents having much luck in telling you whom you could or could not befriend. Why must you persist in thinking it will be different for Charlie? He is your son? And like it or not,

Charlie's more like you than you'd care to admit," Daisy responded with disappointment in her voice.

Ethan just stood there in his office that was no bigger than a small study, shaking his head. And truly deep down inside, he wanted nothing more than for his only son to be all right. We could even stretch it a bit and say that Ethan Davis wanted his heir to be the spitting image of himself – strong, fearless, knowing exactly what one wants and taking it. But, most of all, Ethan Davis did not want his son, who was not far from becoming a man, to be Gay.

I mean really, do you know of any sane person who wished for a Gay child. But, then that would be better than a Jeffrey Dahmer. Nevertheless, I'm sure you too could understand. In his mind, for Ethan Davis, the stakes were extremely high. So after about two minutes of uncomfortable silence and with Daisy waiting patiently for her husband's response as she'd always done in the past, Ethan decided just for right now, not to hold himself hostage for believing somewhere – somehow the choices he made in raising Charles must have been tail backwards. Therefore, leaving him, as this boy's father, solely responsible. Confused? How about believing that our teenaged children are extensions of ourselves. In other words, believing who we are through their behavior. You got it now!

So, with that in mind, Ethan Davis took a deep breath, exhaled, and then asked in a sincere manner, "So when are we meeting with Dr. Stevens?"

"Well, I told him that you would be getting another break around 2:00 o'clock this afternoon. I'm headed over there now. I'm just glad that at least this part is over," Daisy said with a slight smile on her face.

Ethan smiled as well and said, "Me too! Now what about that lady lawyer? Shouldn't she be meeting you over there?"

"I was thinking the same thing. But, I tried calling both of the numbers that she gave us. Of course, her office is not open this early. And, the other number rings the answering service so I left a message," Daisy said as she exhaled.

"Okay dear, I'll just meet you at the hospital around two... Oh and Daisy, tell Charles... tell him... just give him a hug for me and tell him that I'm on my way. Okay?" Ethan said.

Ethan then lowered the phone placing it against his broad chest while thinking aloud to himself, "I know – I know. There's nothing more I can do right now. But thank you all the more for showing a stubborn man like me that there's more to this life than money, prestige and approval from a bunch of folks who I know could care less if I were hit by a fast moving car or shot and left for dead in a dark alley. I must be crazy. But if you could, please don't let this crazy mess hit the media." *Poor Ethan. Just when you think you have it all figured out...*

● ● ● ●

*S**peaking of men who dare to think life's full of peaches and cream. If you ask me, all this joker has and I stress the term joker – is hard times and bubble gum! And at this time, I believe he's fresh out of bubble gum. As we speak, Dr. Vincent Simmons sleep is being interrupted by an annoying sound coming from their new state-of-the-art doorbell. Not to mention a new upgraded system installed against his wishes. Maybe Vincent wasn't enthused about it because the system speaks when someone is ringing the doorbell announcing, "You have a visitor." Vincent first tried the intercom to see who was disturbing him. But, not only did the system malfunction, the person on the other side of his front door continued ringing the bell. And now the visitor had begun to bang on the glass doors. Vincent was heated at this point, not even stopping to put on his house robe. Vincent, with his tall and sexy body answered the door in his fitted boxes.*

Squenching his eyes as he looked through the closed glass doors he said, "May I help you?" *The gentleman on the other side of the double glass doors answered,*

"Good morning Sir, are you Dr. Simmons? Your wife mentioned that you might still be home. My name is Keith – I'm here to clean your carpet and refinish your hardwood floors."

Vincent cracked the door just a bit then said, " My wife...what?"

"I'm sorry she didn't tell you."

"My wife does this to me all the time – makes appointments, plans trips, then at the last hour enlightens me! Women, cant' live with them and it gets a little chilly without them."

"If you want, my crew and I can wait out here while you get yourself together," Keith said as he took off his hat and wiped his baldhead with a soft cotton towel.

Vincent thought for a second remembering he had planned a prior engagement with Payton for lunch. Besides, there really wasn't any reason for him to hang around the house anyway especially since his sleep was already broken, he thought.

"What the hell!" He shook his head "no" and said, "It will be cool! You boys can just start down here while I get myself together."

Vincent opened the door wide enough to let Keith know that he was welcome to enter his home. But, just to be certain Keith was indeed who he said he was, Vincent asked to see his identification. Keith being two steps ahead of Vincent reached into his inside jacket pocket and pulled out a work badge with a photograph of himself professionally displayed on the badge. The badge indicated that Keith was the owner and manager of Picky People Cleaning Service – commercial and residential. Vincent peeped it quickly then looked over Keith's shoulder at the white van advertising the cleaning service as well parked directly behind his brand new Silver S Class Mercedes Benz which he preferred to leave in his circular driveway. Vincent is such a show off!

So being satisfied he replied, "Catchy name!" He then turned around and headed for the staircase. Keith just observed him while thinking to himself, *I got you boy! And if you're not careful, I'll have your woman too!*

Suddenly, Vincent turned around as Keith was entering the Foyer and said, "Tell me. Has Waverly's already paid you guys for your services?"

Keith smiled and replied, "No, she said something about leaving a check here or..."

Vincent chucked and responded, "That's just like her. My wife has this antiquated belief system that the man's suppose to pay for everything. You'd think a well-paid district judge would be partial sometimes."

"I can bill you if you're a little short today," Keith said.

"No, I'm cool! How much?" Vincent asked.

Keith flipped through his invoices then answered, "First visit on a house this size will run you about $1,050. You

know – if it will help, we take MasterCard, Visa, Checks...
whichever is easiest."

*Vincent just looked at Keith, shook his head again and chuckled a
bit as he walked up the stairs. Keith knowing he had no time to spare
and surely none to waste brought five guys along to expedite the
process sufficiently. Three of the five were actually going to clean and
buff the floors, then shampoo the carpet while the other two
strategically placed tiny "bugs" in most of Dr. Simmons' belongings.*

*Mr. Keith Sheppard along with his female assistant Heather,
would spend the rest of the morning and most of their afternoon
tailing the no-good, I mean "good" Doctor. Conveniently, Heather
was parked two houses down in a black Ford Expedition setting up
the surveillance equipment, awaiting Keith's call. With much more
work to be done, this was going to be a very interesting day.*

*But with the clock still ticking, forty-five minutes passed and Dr.
Simmons was standing at the foot of his staircase with his brows
raised and his gym bag slung over his shoulder, thinking to himself,
This shit is going to take all day! Ain't no way I'm going to
wait until these niggers are through! Waverly should have
been here her damn self!*

Then one of Keith's employee's turned off the shampoo
machine and signaled Keith who was, at that moment,
bugging the office telephone. Keith finished quickly and left
the office to investigate how he could be of assistance to the
"good" Doctor.

"This is a big house you and your wife have!" Keith said
as he slowed down to catch his breath.

"Yeah, and it looks as if you guys are going to be here
most of the afternoon. I can't wait that long. Besides, Marie
will be in around two. Here's the check for the work my-
man. Just leave the invoice on the kitchen counter. Now, if
by chance you finish before Marie gets here, use the lower
level to exit. If you hit the garage opener twice, it will go
down on it's own – giving you sixty seconds before the alarm
is activated. So, you might want to have your crew leave
through the front along with all the equipment. I guess
Waverly will call you later today," Vincent said as he looked
around at the other workers.

But, then there was a loud sound that appeared to have come from the kitchen. Vincent gave Keith a look to imply...well I'm sure you could imagine. Then he quickly peeped down the hall leading towards the kitchen and back to Keith. Keith, being curious himself, yelled back to see if everything was all right. Meaning things were very much still in one piece. His worker responded,

"Yeah, everything's cool!"

Vincent shook his head then replied on his way out the door, "Try and keep an eye on your boys so they don't tear up my house!"

Keith just looked at Vincent and replied, "No problem!"

Being slightly uncomfortable, Keith waited until Vincent was not only in his car, he watched him drive half way down the driveway before he called Heather on the "two-way" to come down to get him. The boys as Vincent referred to them, were truly professionals. They were already on top of things. Keith simply nodded his head then left the Simmons home.

●●●●

*M*eanwhile, at the Prince Georges County Hospital, Drake Tyler was out on the parking lot just a tad frustrated because for the last hour, he had been adjusting and readjusting the twins' car seats. But for a man who wanted nothing more than to have several children of his own, you'd think a task such as this wouldn't bother him. I believe Mr. Tyler was still very much confused behind that whole Sickle Cell thing which, in my opinion, is causing his frustration. Meagan along with Waverly was preparing to leave the hospital. This had been a very long three days. In fact, to be exact, two days and eight hours was all Meagan could stand.*

As she gathered all of her things, including gifts received for the twins, Meagan had mixed feelings. But, when you think about it sensibly, it does make sense. She's wanted children her entire adult life, so of course Meagan Tyler was thrilled to finally have two beautiful girls of her own – even if one of them has a treatable disease. But, you must admit, if you as the parent knew, you were the one responsible... see my point!

Well Waverly, having her own dog instincts, which by the way had been turned up quite a few notches from her beloved hubby's love triangle was on to her good-good girlfriend as well. First, she sat there

*fumbling through one of those parent magazines. Then she finally
decided to say something to her friend.*

"Meagan Simone, now if I didn't know you any
better, I might assume you were still a bit dazed about your
new inheritance."

*Meagan immediately stopped what she was doing and looked
over at Waverly. Of course, feeling guilty for not sharing with her
closest friends, her eyes slightly swelled up with tears, as she stood
there vulnerable. Knowing she had to say something, Meagan just
couldn't decide what to share. So, she thought to herself, Do I tell
her what she already knows? No! But, why would she refer to
it as an inheritance? Who could have told her? Oh my God
Dra! Then Meagan took a deep breath and said,* "Waverly Corrine
– inheritance! What on earth are you talking about?"

"Your new life of course. Not less than three days ago,
you were carrying two babies. Today, Nia and Nyle are here.
You're responsibilities are endless now my friend. The whole
world is going to look and feel quite different now. This is
one of those things you can't change or take back. It's not
like the characters in your novels. You can't re-write their
lives. You will always – always be their Mother. And, neither
time nor distance will keep those little girls from being
yours," Waverly said as she sat the magazine down then
walked over to Meagan's side.

Meagan looked Waverly right in the eyes and said softly,

"But do you think it's the same if you never really knew
your Mother? I mean, what if I had adopted the girls? Would
that make their biological Mother their true Mother? And
let's just say that I've raised them both and now they have
children of their own. Who would be considered the Mother
then?"

"Okay enough of the run around conversation! This isn't
about the babies, is it?"

*Meagan feeling transparent now and not wanting to lie to her
dear friend or reveal too much, simply closed her eyes then remembered
when the two of them first met. It was an unusually warm fall
afternoon. They were both in between classes when they crossed paths.
Well, to be more precise, Meagan was rushing to get to an advance*

writing class, at which the doors would close not more than five minutes after the class begun.

But, on this particular day, Meagan was really running behind. And, if that wasn't enough, half way across the campus, Girlfriend dropped most of her books and notes on the grass. Now Megan's parents were well off, but Missy refused to buy a quality book bag – thus dropping her books. To this day she is still quite thrifty. I'm sure you can visualize one of the straps breaking causing her bag to tilt and most of its contents to fall to the ground. And at the same time, Miss straight and narrow, Waverly Corrine witnessed this scene as she was exiting the main auditorium. Smiling just a bit, Waverly knew this skinny little stay to herself white girl wasn't about to ask for help. So, she helped her anyway. Meagan gave her a big smile while adjusting her glasses and stuffing her papers back into her last year's high school book bag, then ran as fast as she could to the her class, never pausing for introductions. At a later time, the two bumped into each other again at the library and have been friends ever since. You could say that Waverly Corrine saw something then that wasn't being said and surely she sees something now. So, Meagan opened her eyes, paused then replied,

"You have been my friend for a long time and I can't recall one time when you didn't sense my anguish. My Mother wanted mc to say nothing until she found some answers, but I know she knows more than she's telling."

"Answers to what Meagan! What's going on?" Waverly asked.

At that moment, Meagan's eyes were filled with tears that began to flow softly down her cheeks. There was no doubt in Waverly's mind that something was terribly wrong with her friend and chances of it being the twins were slim to none. So Waverly wiped away Meagan's tears with her hand and said,

"You might as well tell me. We're friends, there shouldn't be secrets between us. Plus, secrets can eventually kill you, or worst hold you hostage in fear of it ever surfacing. Besides, you little Bunny, you're not the only one going through something right now. Just be thankful Drake's not licking someone else's ass. Well, pick your bottom lip up! That's exactly what I said! My wonderful husband of 15 years is fucking around on me. Not once, not twice, but who knows how many affairs that bastard has had. I don't even know if he's practiced safe sex all of this time!"

Meagan shook her head and mumbled under her breath, "I don't know, it sounds better than finding out you've been adopted 37 years later. And to put icing on the cake, this white skin is just a façade. Either my Mother or Father has black skin."

Waverly's eyes opened wide along with her mouth. At the same moment, Drake and Katherine entered the room, both a bit exhausted. Meagan looked over at them with a surprised expression on her face, while Waverly stood there tongue tied. Drake walked over to the babies, adjusted Nia's cap not knowing which baby she was and said,

"Why is Mommy and Auntie Waverly looking so silly Baby Tyler? You'd think they just saw a ghost!"

Waverly not thinking too clearly now blurted out,

"What in the devil do you mean you're adopted? And I know you didn't just say your real parent or parents are black!"

Meagan just closed her eyes and shook her head. Then Waverly's cell phone started ringing and without checking her caller I.D., she simply never bothered to answer, just waited for the ringing to stop. But of course it rang again. This time she peeped to see who was calling, believing it must not have been that two-timing Vincent. And it wasn't. The caller I.D. displayed Dominique's cell phone number.

Now you may recall, last we visited with Dominique, she was contemplating whether or not to help Sherian get up from the hospital floor or go to find out what was causing her best friend Sidney's histrionics. Well, now it was known that Miss Phyllis Maple had died during surgery due to complications with internal bleeding. Unfortunately, the doctors were unable to control the situation. So after about twenty minutes of peeling Sidney off of her Mom and out of the O.R., Dominique was able to calm her down just enough for Sidney to notice that she had become ill from the whole ordeal. And where would one go? Yes, to the nearest restroom! Poor Girl was on her knees, hands thrown over the commode, bringing up Mocha from earlier and everything else she had consumed the night before.

So, Waverly Corrine placed her finger in the air and said quickly,

"Hold that thought! Hey Diamond, what's going on? What's that noise?"

"Waverly, Miss Phyllis *died* during the procedure! Sidney starting zapping out! Then when I finally calmed her down, she got sick on me! Now she's locked herself in one of these damn bathrooms! I know she's throwing up Lord knows what! And she refuses to open the door!" Dominique shouted as she continued banging on the bathroom door.

Then Sidney yelled, "Just leave me alone, I'll come out when I'm good and fucking ready!"

Waverly exhaled and replied, "Diamond slow down. Did you just say Sidney's Mother died? And is that Sid screaming?"

Frustrated, Dominique whispered, "Yes and yes!!"

Then Meagan interrupted, "Sidney's Mother died? Oh God! What could have happened! When I spoke to Sidney last night, she told me the surgery was minor! Those damn doctors! Where is Sid now?"

"Wait a minute Meagan, I can't hear you both! Diamond, is Sid all right?" Waverly asked as she grabbed her purse then reached for her keys.

Dominique replied, "Outside of throwing, among other things, two technicians around in the operating room, then falling out on her Mom, followed by almost being dragged out of the O.R. and then getting sick, finally locking herself in the bathroom, screaming and shouting to the top of her lungs, refusing to come out of a restroom stall – yeah she's still Sidney Sharpe, but she's in really bad shape!"

"Well where is her sister?" Waverly asked.

Dominique scratched her head and answered, "Now that's a whole other story. Miss Sherian thought it would be best if she took matters into her own hands. Girl is down the hall being held by the hospital security for punching out the Doctor who operated on Miss Phyllis. He refuses to talk to either one of them. And can you blame him? They are two of a kind."

"She hit the Doctor!" Waverly shouted as she placed her hand over her mouth. Then Meagan interrupted again, "Sidney hit the Doctor!"

Waverly shook her head "no" and replied, "Sherian hit Miss Phyllis' Doctor... Look, we're on our way. Stay with Sid until we get there!"

Next thing you know, Meagan started stuffing the rest of her belongings into the overnight bag along with the few items of the babies that were still lying on the bed. Then she basically told Drake and her Mother to take the girls home and that she would be there as soon as she possibly could.

As she kissed her husband and was about to leave, Drake stood there with his mouth slightly opened in total agreement, but Katherine said,

"Now Me-Me, you're just going to go over there right now? I mean shouldn't you be resting? I can see that you want to help, but you've just had two babies! I think you should come home with us and call Sidney later. There's nothing you can do right now."

Waverly turned her nose upside down and looked at Katherine, shocked by her comments. Then she looked back at Meagan waiting anxiously for her to put her Mother in check.

Meagan simply replied, "Mother, Sidney is one of my closet friends. I would even consider us sisters. And if she needed me and it was in the middle of a storm, I wouldn't question the distance or my physical safety. That's how much love we have for each other. So yes, I'm going and I would like you to help Dra with the Girls!"

Still confused, Katherine reiterated, "I can understand that, but!"

"But what Mother! No disrespect to you but, do you even know the real meaning of the word friendship? It's truth! Being totally honest no matter what! Just being there even if there is absolutely nothing you can do!" Meagan said just before she kissed Drake good-bye then grabbing her jacket on the way out of the room.

Waverly kissed Drake as well, on this his cheek, then whispered into his ear, "I'll get her home soon"

Next, she turned toward Katherine and gave her a half smile letting her know that it was okay – then left the room. On the way to the hospital, Meagan and Waverly were both consumed with the same energy the entire drive over – fear! But isn't it mind boggling how having no known knowledge of what's to come can get your heart racing? Literally causing one to question whether or not you even wish to continue. It's like you know something's there and no – you can't see it. It only exists within you. Kind of like Love and you can't bottle it.

It doesn't have a face. And it can't be taken. It sought of comes and goes freely without notice. Although unfortunately with true love, that too only exists within you and the stakes are much higher. Almost every other moment you fear losing it. I guess that would explain all the different masks people wear. Come on! I'm sure you have at least a half dozen. First, there's the one you'd like to believe you are. Then there's the reserved one you pretend to be. And what about the one you press hardest to be like. You know... that perfect one with maybe one flaw. The list is endless. And the one thing that's totally unavoidable always – always happens when the issue's never addressed, you pass it on to your children. They then begin to pretend to be what they are not as well just so you'll continue to love them. I would even venture to bet my last crumb that's exactly what happened with Victor Simmons, Waverly and Vincent's only son.

●●●●

*V**ictor was in his second year of college. Being born with the curse of having a Judge for a Mother and a well-known physician for a Father, Victor's 4.0 G.P.A. was unquestionably expected. So too was his behavior. All of his friends from his former high school and of course the ones from college knew exactly who his family was and what that meant. As for Victor Simmons, trying not to follow in his parents' footsteps, but then at the same time not causing shame to their good name, left very little room for him to be the person he wanted to be publicly. So with his twenty-first birthday only days away, which in fact fall on the very same day as his Mother's – yes Waverly's! Well, Victor's contemplating very strongly about telling both his parents who he really is! And isn't it amazing how much more at peace we feel when we finally stop pretending?*

"Victor, one of these days I'm going to stop letting you beat me at this game. You know the only reason you're so good is because you've been around these white boys all of your life!" Jackson said as he placed his racquet over his shoulders then wiped his forehead.

"Jackson, you have been saying that for the last two years. Racquetball isn't just a sport for white people. It's more of a sport for the fit and the strong. Perhaps if you ate a little healthier and exercised," Victor said just before Jackson interrupted.

"I eat what I want because I can. And exercise is for old people! Besides, if I recall, the last time we were together, I believe you told me that my body was lovely. In fact, you were moaning something about, I can't get enough of you Jackson, Oh Jackson!" Jackson giggled.

Victor then replied, "Maybe I did! I'm not suggesting that you don't look edible, not at all! But, if you spend half the time on working out that you spend in the mirror admiring yourself, you may see some improvement in your game."

Jackson just smiled at Victor and said, "What time is your next class?"

Victor picked up his gym bag and answered, "One O'clock, why do you ask? What – are you going to treat me to breakfast?"

Jackson giggled again then replied, "Actually I've already had some Fruity Pebbles earlier. I was thinking maybe I could show you another way I've improved my game."

Victor looked at his watch first then chuckled, "Okay, but whoever screams first, buys the other breakfast or something."

Jackson and Victor both smiled at each other then one winked his eye at the other. On the way out of the racquetball room, Jackson stopped and stood directly in front of the door and said, "One more thing!"

"What now?" Victor shouted.

Jackson paused then answered, "Now the last time I was bottomed-up. This time it will be your turn…"

Victor just shook his head and said, "Makes no difference to me – anyway you want it!"

The two of them went off to shower… Well, well, well! Sounds to me as if Victor's been hiding the fact that he's a stud-muffin. Or would that just be a muffin. Whichever the case, Boyfriend's parents are in for a rude awakening. If you ask me, this page-turner should not have been called Common Lives! Sounds more like Common Lies!

Anyway speaking of common criminals, I mean common liars, what do you think of those Hernandez's?

●●●●

few days have passed since Tony Hernandez was arrested and with all the money dirt-bag has, I can't say I'm surprised about his lawyer getting him out so fast. Respected citizen or something, they said.

    On their way out of the police station and in the presence of his high paid attorney, Marshall Hunter, who by the way is referred to as the head-hunter; Gina Hernandez just told Tony that Charles Davis is awake and has amnesia. But, when she tried to continue with what happened during her visit with Scott, Tony stopped and gave her a very evil look, indicating to her to wait until the two of them were alone. Of course, Marshall Hunter felt the vibe and like a well-paid mouthpiece, he pretended not to hear it.

    Gina of course drove herself down to the police station in their Canary Yellow Hummer so that when Tony was released, they would at least have a few minutes alone on the way over to Hunter's office. Hunter already had a profile on the Hernandez's so he knew exactly who he was dealing with – therefore giving him the upper hand as to what he would charge them. In other words, Hunter could care less about the stories they told one another to later convey to him. He's strictly in it for the Benjamins!

    "Where are my smokes?" *Tony said as he looked in the armrest. Gina reached into her Burberry handbag, which matched her Burberry shoes, which matched her Burberry cape, which unfortunately matched her Burberry pants, to get him a fresh pack. She then freshened up her ruby red lips and said,*

    "I knew we should have stopped for a while after that episode that happened on the Coast. But no – no you said! Just one more baby! Stupid Man!"

    Tony, who was enraged at this point, not only for spending the last few days in an eight by ten jail cell or for being spit on by the local authorities, but I believe Gina spread the icing on the cake when she totally disrespected her husband by bringing up that incident that occurred on the Coast. What's more, teasing him about it after he had just spent his last 24-hours with one eye opened because his cellmate tried to have his way with him... So, with nothing else on his mind other than choking his beautiful wife... With a Newport in his left hand, Tony grabbed Gina's throat with his right hand, breathing very hard and yelling,

"Is there something wrong with your tongue? Maybe it's your brain!"

Then turning her head to face him while tightening his grip, he kissed her lips softly then whispered, "I do love your spunkiness. It sought of excites me. But right now isn't the time."

Finally, Tony removed his hand from her throat. While catching her breath, Gina tried to compose herself, quickly wiping the tears that ran down her face. Tony cracked the window just a bit so that the smoke didn't cloud up his truck. Then he looked back at Gina and yelled, "What!"

Gina inhaled deeply and replied, "You're right, I'm sorry. I shouldn't have said anything. It's just this time Tony, things got really out of hand. You wouldn't stop! Even when that boy Charlie fell out, you just kept on giving Scott those uppers so that you could finish the tape. Some tape! Well, I can't go to jail! Not for dis! Not for you, not for no'ting!"

Well, to put it mildly, Tony Hernandez was a smart, calculating, self-absorbing son-of-a well-trained female pit bull that's just given birth then ate half of the litter. He knew exactly what strings to pull to place him in a better position. So after plucking his cigarette out of the window, he reached over, rubbed the middle of Gina's thighs and said,

"No one's going to jail my little puppy. I'll have this mess cleaned up in just a few days. You'll go shopping and I will be back on the golf course doing business as usual."

Then Tony sat there smiling while thinking to himself, And after the smoke settles and the air is crisp, I'll make a fortune on those tapes...

Now what's that saying? "Birds of a feather flock together." Or was that, "It takes one to know one." Basically, Gina knew her husband very well and in some ways was just like him. She wasn't about to trust Tony without having an alternate scheme; I mean plan of her own just in case Tony's backfired. So she too sat there thinking to herself as well, Yeah, that's what I'll do... empty all the accounts, including the two million in the vault underneath the hot tub. That's should be just enough to start a new life in

Greece or perhaps the Philippines. As long as it's far, far away from here...

• • • •

1 guess Tony's not the only slickster primarily thinking of one's self. Actually, we have a hand full of self-indulged folks in this story. But why is it that when I mention words like self-absorbed, self-indulged or even slickster, I can't help but think of the good Doctor. Sure, we know he's fine. And being conceited is no crime. Unfortunately, though for Dr. Vincent Simmons, cheating on your spouse ranks second of the ten worse things you can do to ruin a relationship. Number one is murder!

However, even with a man like Vincent, I believe that he would have to be pushed pretty far over the edge for him to merely consider placing his hand on his lovely wife. Maybe being that charming lady's man forbids his conscious from swaying him in such a direction. I guess that would too include his chick on the side and speaking of chicks on the side; do you recall that old song by the Pointer Sisters. Sure you do! I believe their exact words were, "I betcha gotta chick on the side — sure you gotta chick on the side," In fact that would describe Waverly and Vincent's entire marriage.

Okay, besides the first eighteen months. After that, let's just say that the good Doctor always played on both sides of the fiddle. But, I wonder does he take it like a man when he's the one being played. You may recall earlier today that one of the reasons Vincent agreed to vacate his home was because of his previously planned lunch date with Payton. Now although their love affair was fairly new, Payton saw no reason to pretend that Vincent was the only thing of importance to her. In fact, if something else she wanted to do came up, even if they had plans to spend whatever little time they had together, she'd cancel at a moment's notice. And, this was one of those moments. Not twenty minutes ago Payton called her lover while she was still at home getting herself together for a different appointment, to cancel their lunch date. Vincent thinking that her call was to confirm their plans answered eagerly.

"Well hello there!" He said in a sexy manner.

"Hey baby! The way you greet a woman makes it hard for me to say why I'm calling. But, as you always say, business before pleasure," Payton said as she brushed her hair while taking one last look at herself in the tall oval shaped mirror that stood in front of the bay window in her bedroom.

"Business, you can't...Wait a minute! I thought you said today was your day off and besides, we had plans!" Vincent reminded her as his voice became deeper.

Payton, not paying Vincent any attention politely explained, "Vincent I know we had plans and I had special plans for you. But, something really-really important came up. Remember that photo shoot I was trying to sit in on with "Buttons and Bows," the hottest new fashion magazine since "Ebony," Well, the photographer's tech got sick at the last minute...I'll give you one guess who he called?"

"You..." Vincent murmured. Then he said, "And you couldn't tell him you were busy?"

Payton smiled and replied, "You're joking right? I promise I'll make it up to you. You know this could place me precisely where I need to be. And while we're speaking of needs... I need about fifteen hundred dollars and it would be perfect if you could leave it at the desk for me so I don't have to chase you around the Baltimore/Washington area."

Vincent shook his head and said, "What makes you think I'm even anywhere close to Baltimore. And why do you need fifteen... Never mind! This is the second time today... Can I ask a question?"

"Anything Baby," answered Payton.

"May I assume you do whatever it is you do when assisting the photographer by passing him or her what they need during a shoot? If so, how is doing that going to help you become discovered as this rare photographer yourself?" Vincent asked with a puzzled look on his face.

Payton chuckled then answered, "You're too funny! Things do happen! Were you always the famous doctor?"

"Yes, believe that," Vincent said laughing.

"Look, I've gotta go lover. Maybe we'll chat later," Payton said just before she ended their call.

Vincent, still laughing at his own joke suddenly realized Payton had hung up on him. A little disappointed, he wished her good luck anyway then headed for Baltimore knowing he'd score bigger if he left the money at Payton's job as she requested.

I don't care what you're thinking. Vincent only thinks of Vincent. What's that saying, "you can catch more flies with honey…" And believing such a thing's true, who would be foolish enough to steal honey from a bee whose known for its stinger. But, I do know of one bee for sure that's going to place her stinger in someone's rear end as soon as he's caught with his hand in the cookie jar. Unfortunately, Vincent's so detached from his true identity that this, I'm afraid has already gone way over his head. In fact, after being stood up by number two in his life, Boyfriend's still thinking with his other head, which caused him to call number one in his life.

Waverly, by the way, has just arrived at Howard University Hospital and is stuck in the parking garage with one of her best friends – waiting impatiently for a slow-poke to pull out of a space so they could pull in to it. So far, this morning wasn't going too well…

●●●●

W hat does he want now?" Waverly whispered just before answering, "Hello!"

Meagan just looked over at Waverly still astonished about the state of her marriage.

"Hey beautiful, how is your morning going?"

Waverly frowned and answered, "Not very well…"

"How about meeting me at the condo for a quiet lunch? I can bring your favorite – then afterwards rub those soft sensuous shoulders of yours. I was thinking, maybe we could finish what we started the other night."

At that moment, the parking space became available and considering that she had absolutely no desire to eat or sleep with her husband, Waverly quickly blew him off by saying,

"Right now is really not a good time. Sidney's Mother just died and we've just arrived at the hospital. So, if there's nothing else you want…."

Vincent being somewhat taken by surprise, for a moment, forgot about how horny he was and felt a sense of sorrow for his wife and her best friend Sidney. Numb by Waverly's comment, he slowly replied,

"No… I'm sorry to hear that baby. I guess I'll just see you later." *Damn!* He thought as he let the cell phone fall into his lap.

But just as I said, Vincent once again only thinking of himself, continued to drive all the way to Baltimore with Keith and Heather on his coattail imagining how nice it would be if he was the lucky one in the position to comfort Sidney Sharpe at such a time.

Vincent's always, always found Sidney irresistible. I'm sure the only thing that stopped him was his fear of Waverly's reaction if ever she found out. That was too close for comfort! So he handled his lustful desires by simply drooling from a distance. But, I once heard somewhere that just like animals, people can sense these things. And I bet you Sidney knew of or felt Vincent's lust. Maybe this was her reason for not trusting him. I mean really, feeling vibes from your best friend's husband. If by chance you are or are not attracted to him, or wanting or not wanting the same thing, you know that your actions would cause an irreconcilable situation. It would ultimately end up with disastrous results. Besides, with all the stones yet to be turned, this need not be one of them.

● ● ● ●

Speaking of stoned! I wonder if our recovering alcoholic is considering a drink. It's hard to tell by watching her sit so still. Poor Sidney, she almost looked a little ghostly with her dried face yet dampened tussled hair. And I guess she's ignoring the "no smoking" signs since her cigarette is nearly burned out. I always saw that as an art to be able to keep ashes from falling while you're having a smoke.

As Dominique stood at the window with one eye on Sidney and the other on the parking lot wishing Meagan and Waverly would hurry, she couldn't help but think to herself, "God only knows how this is going to impact our friendship!" Death does have a way of either bringing people together or tearing them apart. One can never tell! Although I believe there's more than meets the eye. If you recall, just before Miss Phyllis went off to surgery, she practically insisted that Sherian do right by Sidney. Almost transparent, her demeanor revealed to me that Sherian knew exactly what her Mother meant as she sat directly across from Sidney scanning her up and down.

At first it was hard to tell what Sherian was looking for exactly. But, then it became crystal clear. Sherian was looking for the little girl she believed still existed somewhere deep inside of the "sister" she knew long – long ago. Back then, Sherian and Sidney were very close. Sidney looked up to her older sister, respected her opinion and *practically wanted to do everything she did. Well, that was until Sherian started working and wanting to spend more time with friends her own age. I would imagine it's that way with most siblings. Unfortunately though, for Sherian and Sidney Sharpe, it built a bridge between them that neither was willing to cross. And occasionally when they were together, as Sidney grew older, Sherian treated her like a child instead of respecting her as an equal, causing Sidney to pull away. Sounds like someone you know? Anyway, Big-Sis is now desperately looking for an open window to connect with Lil-Sis. And from the looks of things, she's going to have to keep looking because Waverly and Meagan are now stepping off the elevator to be with their good girlfriend.*

Out of breath, Meagan ran over to Sidney giving her a big hug almost bringing Sidney to her feet. Waverly being the mother of the four, not only noticed Sidney smoking in a non-smoking building, she also saw the stack of ashes finally falling on the hospital floor as Sidney held on to the butt. Shaking her head, knowing this was just one of those things, Waverly politely removed the cigarette butt from Sidney's fingers and scooped up the ashes, discarding them both.

Dominique, relieved to see Waverly and Meagan, finally exhaled as she smiled then moved closer to be with her friends. Sherian, with mixed emotions, was again disappointed. Not at all by her sisters' friends being there to comfort her, but solely because she herself was unable to find an opening for such a connection...

● ● ● ●

Maybe later, Sherian thought as she got up heading towards the elevator. *Sidney, having more love for her sister than Sherian believed noticed her leaving and said as she pulled away from Meagan,*
"Cher, you want to meet at Momma's later!" *Hearing Sidney's voice and realizing she was speaking to her and not to someone else, sounded like the voice of an angel. It was almost as if Sidney was that little girl again Sherian once knew. Overwhelmed, Sherian quickly turned around and made her way back to her sister. The two simply embraced each other as the reassurance of their commonality was revealed....*

"How about five o'clock," Sherian said.

"Five o'clock is cool," Sidney replied just before kissing her sister good-bye.

Sherian then turned to the others, hugging and kissing them good-bye as well. As a single tear rolled down Sherian's cheek, Waverly wiped it away then whispered,

"I can't begin to imagine what this means for you to have to assume the role of Sid's Mom. But, if you need anything – anything what so ever, please call me. We're here for you as well Sherian."

Sherian closed her eyes, opened them again, took a deep breath then walked away. Suddenly at that moment, the little chilled hospital waiting area became slightly brighter. It was as if a soft, comforting energy was moving through the room. And I saw for the first time, in a very long time, just what true friendship really means. Just in that small window of time, the focus wasn't on Sidney's loss. No, it was channeled to what she shared with her three best friends. Unconditional love!

This was not a give and take arrangement. These four women gave of themselves always – always in exchange for nothing – almost as if they were a part of one another. They were somehow able to feel just what the other was feeling even if several miles away. One could say that this friendship was priceless. You couldn't buy your way out of it.

Before long, these bunnies were giggling again and making fun of each other. Somehow they had gotten on the subject of Meagan's delivery of the twins. And with Dominique playing charades of the whole scenario... Well I'm sure you get the picture. Sore and all, Meagan still had that unchangeable grin covering her face. While Waverly sat there with one arm around Sidney and the other on her head laughing at her silly friend, not thinking once of her unfaithful husband. And let's just say that Sidney Sharpe looked as beautiful and innocent as she always did while thinking of and feeling every moment of her best friend Meagan's miracle. Before long, two hours had passed and these four stooges were still enjoying each other's company. And you know what, I believe this is just what the doctor ordered. To get Sidney's mind off of the tragedy she just experienced, they switched their focus to Dominique.

●●●●

"So Diamond, with all of this pretending you're doing, I must admit that maybe you are ready to have a baby of your own," Waverly chuckled.

Sidney frowned then added, "Not unless she's getting a sperm injection. Remember, it takes two to tangle. But wait a second! Just last night, Dominique told me something about having a new piece. In fact, he's supposed to be coming to visit soon. Diamond, no more holding out on your sisters. Is this new lover a candidate to be your baby's Daddy? Truth!!"

Dominique glanced at her watch remembering her appointment with the social worker and yelled, "Damn...Damn...Damn... Oh no! I can't believe I did this!"

Meagan being curious about Sidney's comment to Dominique looked at her in utter surprise. In her mind, she was truly happy that Dominique had finally found someone special. Just maybe Dominique would also have a chance at true love. It's kind of hard to explain. I mean Waverly and Meagan, before Waverly hit her with all of the drama about Vincent, were already happily married, and had been for a very long time. Now Sidney Sharpe on the other hand, had been in and out of more sex-ships – I mean relationships than one dared to count. Something to do with one man never having all she needed or something – if you can comprehend that. Well, that leaves Dominique Alisa Blake, who in the opinion of her good-good girlfriends hasn't had much luck with men in years.

Now it's true that Miss Blake's a bit private with the sexual aspects of her life. Not everyone kisses and tells. Maybe on occasion, Dominique has mentioned a friend, but never ever in detail. Funny though, with her clock slowing ticking, Waverly already having a son, and now with Meagan finally having children of her own... What's that saying, "Monkey see-monkey do" My guess is, Dominique was also ready to play Mommy knows best!

"Is it true Diamond?" Meagan asked.

"What? Well, maybe half true! I was going to tell all of you as soon as our first visit with this social worker pans out," Dominique explained with a curious look on her face.

"Sure you were!" Waverly added.

At that moment, Sidney remembered Dominique's appointment as well and said, "Awe damn! With everything happening at once, I completely forgot about your appointment. I'm really sorry Diamond. Is it too late for us to still make it?

"Make what?" Waverly asked.

Dominique shook her head and answered, "No not yet!"

"Make what!" Waverly repeated.

"Well Mommy Dearest, my friend and I were supposed to be meeting with a social worker regarding my desire to have a child. And before you go into asking me why, the answers are complicated. Unfortunately my friend's unable to get to town soon enough. So, I asked Sidney if she would accompany me to my appointment. But when the morning exploded, I don't know, it kind of slipped my mind and now..." Dominique whispered.

"And now what?" Sidney added.

"No – Diamond might be right! Maybe Sidney should be home resting," Meagan said.

"I don't think so! I'm not ready to go home and do anything right now. I promised I'd go with Diamond and I'm going. Maybe helping her will help me!" Sidney explained.

"Okay – okay – okay, now your time's up Meagan! You have our undivided attention! It's time for you to tell us what on earth you were talking about earlier. And don't leave out one detail," Waverly said as she looked Meagan right in the eyes.

Finally! I thought all of the excitement gave Waverly Corrine amnesia. Meagan blinked her eyes at Waverly, not at all comfortable with her questions and replied, "I'm not even sure if my Mother's telling me the whole story now..."

Dominique and Sidney both shouted, "What story?"

Waverly nudged Meagan and said, " You may as well tell them!"

Meagan closed her eyes then dropped her head knowing there was no way she would be able to keep this secret from her best friends any longer. She not only told them about Katherine sharing such fragile news with her on the same evening that she gave birth to the twins, Meagan also told them about Nia's illness and that she was the one responsible for passing on the trait. Sidney already overwhelmed with her loss, felt Meagan's pain and began to cry. Dominique feeling bitter about her parents felt no compassion for Katherine what so ever. In fact, her comments were,

"You know, sometimes parents can do some of the dumbest things. I know one thing for certain, I'm never going to lie to my child."

"Never say never Miss Blake. One should not judge unless you've been down that same road. Sometimes as parents we think it's better to live with little white lies than unthinkable truths. I've done it! And have thrown people into jail for it. The line is a thin one to cross, and once you've crossed it...basically convincing yourself that your pretend world is real, it literally takes a mass miracle to return you to sanity," Waverly explained as she reflected... having lived on both sides of the issue.

"But telling your daughter that she's not your daughter on the exact same night she's just given birth to her two daughters, knowing the hell she's been through with the other miscarriages... That's just too off!" added Dominique.

Sidney wiped her face dry with the end of her sweaty sweatshirt and said, " But when is it a good time! I mean when do you ever think it's a good time to share devastating news? You can't say what you would do. You're not her Mother. It's true what Waverly said. Only if you've been there! Only if!"

"I know, but it's still messed up," Dominique whispered.

Waverly put her arm around Dominique and said, "Yeah, but it could have been worse."

Meagan on the other hand just stood there thinking, *It better not get any worse than this!* then she said, "Come on little girls, lets get out of here!"

Waverly took Meagan home just as she promised, while Sidney accompanied Dominique to her appointment with the social worker. Sidney had no idea what she was walking into. The entire drive over, Dominique hoped everything would go smoothly. She had it all planned. Sidney basically would wait in the lobby while Dominique would prove herself worthy of adopting a child, even if she was secretly in love with another woman.

I mean, how much does it really matter if Dominique and her new lover Hannah only has a one sided view of raising children. Who knows, maybe they will confer with a real man when the time comes. And it looks as though Dominique's time has come! What girl fears most is about to become face to face with her. As she and Sidney stood at the front desk of the office confirming her appointment — just beating the clock, Dominique heard a rather deep voice asking the secretary if she had arrived.

● ● ● ●

" **O** h no – not a prick!" she thought as she gave the social worker a phony smile, waving letting him know that was his next appointment.

"Good! Are you with her?" he asked looking directly at Sidney.

Sidney nodded yes, but before Dominique could tell her to wait in the lobby, the social worker invited both of them into his office. Ironically, the first ten minutes went quite smoothly. But, then it came! The one question Dominique did not want asked in Sidney's presence. In fact as she watched the words slowly come out of the social worker's mouth, Dominique's palms became sweaty and Sidney Sharpe's bottom lip dropped... My bad, let's rewind that for you!

"Just a few more questions and we'll be all done. Well Miss Blake, I've heard enough from you. Why don't we let your partner answer the next few questions," *The social worker said just before the ringing of his phone interrupted them. Well, like I mentioned before, Sidney's bottom lip dropped as her head turned counter-clockwise while thinking to herself, I know this Ding-a-ling doesn't think Diamond and I are fucking. That's my Girl... I mean... Shit!*

Dominique feeling Sidney's reaction but trying very hard to calm her good-good girlfriend down, discreetly politely reached over and closed Sidney's mouth then softly said,

"Close your mouth before a fly gets caught in it. It's going to be okay. I'm just sorry you had to find out this way!" After he was done with his call while fumbling through his paperwork, he looked back to Sidney and said,

"So what is your view on *lesbian* women raising a child? Where does the *balance* come in?"

Sidney simply sat there, this time with her mouth sealed shut just shaking her head, eyes wide opened and lost for words. At that moment, Dominique interrupted, rescuing her friend by saying,

"Excuse me, this is my girlfriend Sidney. We're just friends! In fact, best friends! My partner, Hannah Wong, is going to be tied up for another week. We were hoping we could meet again when she arrives."

"Oh!" He said as he got up from his desk.

Sidney's bottom lip fell open again. Dominique gave her a silly look and whispered, "I see your tonsils again!"

Sidney shrugged her shoulders then whispered to Dominique, "I'm going to get you when we get out of here!"

Dominique merely smiled as if to say "Things couldn't possibly get worse than this!"

Now that may well be the case for Dominique, but I'm not so sure about Katherine and Meagan. By the time Meagan arrived home, greeting her at the front door were their two German Sheppards.

●●●●

*M*eagan and Drake's newly renovated Brownstone, once so quiet it almost seemed like a library, now sounded more like a circus. Of course she was delighted to have Albert and Costello greet her at the door with much love, but had even more appreciation for just being home again.*

As Drake came down the stairs with one newborn in his arms rocking her as she cried softly, Meagan looked up at him smiling while wondering where her other baby was because she could hear her crying rather loudly. Remembering that she dressed Nia in powder blue and Nyle in pastel pink, it was clear to her that Drake was holding Nyle.

"What is Mother doing to Nia?" she asked looking somewhat puzzled.

"Not too much of anything considering she left me here with the girls alone over an hour ago. I thought she was going to stick around at least until you returned. But, it was obvious that she had something on her mind," Drake said as he attempted to give Nyle her bottle to calm her.

"I can't believe my Mother! I asked her to stay with you until I arrived. What do you mean she had something on her mind?" Meagan asked as she started up the staircase.

Drake politely got out of the way then answered, "You know what I'm talking about! You and your Mother have a lot of crap with you! So what now! Are you going to give *me* information in pieces at a time? I've had it up to here with being the last to know what's going on! This whole Sickle Cell thing is too strange! And Meagan, Dr. Stone tested us both! You're the one with the trait! How did that happen? Is your Mother half Black?"

By this time, Meagan was standing at the top of the staircase holding Nia close, rubbing the infant's tiny little back, soothing her. At that moment, their Brownstone was unbelievably quiet. Meagan then walked slowly down the stairs and over to the tall bay window which was at the front end of the house. She turned around slowly still rocking Nia and softly said,

"Why are you doing this Dra? Is my Mother half Black? I really don't know… These last two days have been really hard for me. And to think that after all of these years, we've been together, I never imagined trust would be an issue with us."

"Oh no you're not going to turn this situation around on me! Something's been different about you ever since we had the girls. At first I figured it was that…that baby blues thing. But, after Dr. Stone told us that Nia…" Drake said shaking his head.

"What! You can't say it! Is it that hard? What exactly did my Mother say to you before she left?"

Drake hesitated first, gave Meagan a half smile and answered, "Okay – Katherine basically talked on the telephone the whole "freaking" time she was here. And, you won't believe who she was talking to"

Meagan's closed her eyes and whispered in defeat, "Father Murphy…"

Oops… Drake knew then that Meagan had not been totally honest with him.

"You just stood there and practically swore to me that you really didn't know what the hell's going on! And we should trust each other? Bull$%#@!! I'm not sure if I even know you anymore Meagan Simone! Is that even your real name?" Drake said in total disgust.

Meagan started to cry.

Drake just turned his back to her and said,

"I have no idea what Kat and Father Murphy were talking about, but she abruptly ran out of here to meet with him."

Meagan being equally *hurt* and *confused* said, "I can understand your distrust right now. And I know that you love me. Believe me Dra... As soon as I sort this whole thing out, I will come to you with the absolute truth. Dra... Drake Tyler.... please promise me you'll be there when I do. Promise me!"

Drake said nothing. Meagan walked away. Albert followed her while Costello stayed with Drake. Can you believe this family? The Tyler's were damaged. Was it really worth it? Was Katherine the only one to blame? Was it a simple case of a "failure to communicate" by all parties involved?

●●●●

Speaking of cases! *Judge Judy – I mean the honorable Judge W.C. Simmons is hearing a rather interesting case in her courtroom this afternoon. A young girl is accusing her employer of Sexual Harassment. But, because of the girl's previous record – being convicted of prostitution, the man's attorney is going to down play the incident shifting the blame to the young girl. So after reviewing the case, Waverly mumbled to herself,* "Not another one!"

Then for a brief second, it happened again. Waverly drifted into one of her daymares. And this time it was crystal clear! Waverly was rinsing out color from the hair of her last client at a salon owned by Gina Gonasales called "Styles... which later closed down because of similar allegations then reopened three years later under a new name, "Colors and Cuts?" Sounds familiar! Anyway, as soon as Waverly was done with her client, the lady gave her a five-dollar tip,

"Thanks Corrine!" she said.

Gina, who was referred to as Miss "G" at the time, noticed the amount of the tip and said to Waverly with a very seductive look on her face, "A girl as pretty as you shouldn't have da work dis hard for such little money. You could earn more in one night with me din you can make in a week, sucking up to dese hussies."

Waverly hesitated first then replied, "Exactly how much money are you talking about and what will I have to do to earn it?"

Surprised by Waverly's response, Gina quickly replied, "Oh Corrine my dear, you're not telling me you are a virgin" . . . Then Gina thought to herself – *however, dat would be nice!*

Slightly embarrassed, Waverly shouted, "I'm not really a virgin. It's just; I've only been with one boy once. I could do it! But I'll want the money in advance."

"You can *trust* me Corrine... You can trust me Corrine...trust me Corrine...Corrine...Corrine.

Awe Man!! Just when it was starting to get interesting! I knew I smelled fish. Waverly Corrine has had her own trick or treats or would that be tricks for treats? Whichever the case, Judge Simmons has danced with the devil herself as well. But you know what? In my opinion, with everything else that's going on in Girl's life along with this sudden mis-hap – falling back to one's past mentally. I'm just not in favor of there being able to stomach much more. So now with her courtroom full and opposing counsel waiting, standing by the way, Judge Simmons is not only looking as if she has something to say, she's actually biting her bottom lip, of course the brows are raised and she's looking kind of straight through the people in the courtroom.

Now, no judging the Judge for she's known as the Black "B" in a Robe. Even if now she's caught up in a daze. And please spare me. I know you too have been caught up in something... Besides, Waverly's smart. Rather than torturing herself, she finds a strategic way of postponing the trial to another day, giving herself time to shake off those bugs. I mean visions!

Afterwards she tells her secretary, Grace, that with all the things going on right now with her best friend and their family, meaning Miss Phyllis' death, she'll be taking a few days off. She asked Grace to push her remaining cases to Judge Michaels. Waverly then went to her freshly painted chamber, pulled off the white sheets from the mini-bar and made herself a Long Island Ice Tea – a drink she preferred when all hell was breaking loose in Girl's world.

I have got pull myself together, she thought as she stood there sipping her drink and gazing out of her office window admiring the beautiful view of Washington, D.C.

Chapter Seven

Fairy Tales

ome may say that dreams come true. I myself might differ on that notion. Although there are some that do in fact come true, there are some who say that the tooth fairy's a myth. So, if that were indeed a fact, then would it be fair to say that it's originator's a fake! Oops!

Remembering back, I recall hearing someone say, "It's best to tell the truth because it needs no support. However fibs needs other fibs on top of fibs just to stand up. And where does it all begin? I would imagine with humans, such a thing would begin with one's primary caretaker. You know, your mother or perhaps even one's father would suggest something, literally attempting to convince you of its validity. But oh what a shame! Be truthful, you too once looked up to your parents to help you with what was right and what was most definitely wrong. At least that was until you entered grade school! And how would that factor in with those little white lies. Or even never saying anything at all. Would that be considered worse? What's that old saying, "What's the worse thing that could happen?" Or, was that an old movie?

Nevertheless, my guess is Katherine's surely chewing on all those unspoken words that were never said almost thirty-some years ago. In fact, from up here, Girl looks speechless. She's practically frozen her entire existence to finally search out her adult daughter's true identity. But then at the same time, she acts as though she's surprised at Father Murphy's answers. Katherine always – always knew that if she were ever found out, the price to pay would be high. And now since that cat is out of the bag, it's time to pay the piper. So as she sat there in the third pew from the front, center row, waiting nervously for Father Murphy to come down from his office, Katherine couldn't help but to think back to when she told Meagan that she was not her biological Mother. And unfortunately the only words that continued to race through Katherine's mind were "Yes – you're crazy! Say I'm wrong Mother! Say it! Say something!"

Poor lady, just as before, Girl really didn't have much to say and now she's still lost for words. Suddenly, the church bells started to make that really loud bonging sound. You know, like in the movies when it's letting you know what hour it is. Or that something's getting ready to happen. Katherine was naturally startled by the loud noise, so first she jumped! But, after she realized the sounds were coming from the church bell, Katherine relaxed her shoulders, took a deep breath, exhaled then, closed her eyes attempting to calm herself.

The church bell continued thundering as she sat there crying at it's every bong. Finally the sounds were silent! So she slowly opened her eyes and to her surprise, Father Murphy was standing just to the left of her. Startled once again, she said,

"Please tell me you've found out something about my Me-Me. I'm so afraid that this one secret has already caused a grave distance between my son-in-law and Meagan. How could I have known that keeping this from her all of these years would be so disastrous?"

Father Murphy sat down beside Katherine; place his right hand on his cross, which hung from his neck, said in a very softly,

"Now Sister Katherine, you have been a very good Mother to Meagan her entire life. Surely you couldn't have known what was to come of this. I've already prayed and asked God for his grace in your time of trouble."

Katherine wiped her nose with her sleeve, opened her eyes wider and asked,

"And what did he say? He did answer you Father, didn't he?"

"Patience my child, of course he answered. And he sent a word of good news and of the opposite," answered Father Murphy.

Shaking her head in disbelief, Katherine asked to hear the negative findings first. Father Murphy went on explaining to Katherine how there was going to be no chance at all of ever finding Meagan's biological father because her biological mother heard that he had died in a fire over thirty years ago. He went on to say, Meagan's real Dad moved to Philadelphia and became a local fire fighter right after he heard that his newborn was placed in adoption. Still having strong feelings for Sophia, Meagan's biological mother, he stayed in touch over the few years he lived up until his death.

Sophia was not only bittered by Richard's death, she also felt some what responsible for losing her very first true love because she was unable to face her parents with her involvement in an interracial relationship – the same reason Sophia abandoned Meagan just two days after giving birth. Somehow, ironically though, these nightmares continued to haunt young Sophia as she approached her twenty-first birthday. So, rather than telling her parents the truth about what happened between she and Richard, Sophia sought comfort with a young priest at a local church. As Katherine sat there with her mouth opened and tears rolling down her face, she couldn't help but think to herself, This is so sad, and where have I heard that name before . . . Sophia. It couldn't be . . . Mother Sophia, yeah right.

Then she whispered, "I had no idea. Sophia must have felt so alone. But, how on earth did you discover that this Sophia was in fact the same young woman that gave birth to my Me-Me. Now I do recall your involvement in the adoption. But, you said then that there really was no need to worry about the baby's birth parents because they would never come for her. If that's true, then you must have known them. Did you Father?"

Father Murphy looked Katherine right in the eyes and answered, "Yes my child, I knew them both. Richard was a bright young black fellow who had just turned nineteen that same summer he started working at the church. Sophia was a beautiful young girl, but only sixteen at the time. She and her parents attended Mass almost every Sunday. Sophia later disappeared for several months without any explanation. I had no idea she was secretly dating Richard. It wasn't until three years after you found Meagan that she came to me with the truth. She repented for her sins and we vowed to never speak a word of it again."

"Oh my God, Father! You know where Meagan's birth Mom is?" Katherine whispered as she cried even harder.

Father Murphy smiled and replied; "I did say that God had given me a good word for you sister Katherine."

"Please tell me Father! I really need to know!"

"Calm yourself child! This is still the house of the Lord. I cannot tell you everything at this time. But I can tell you that Sophia has always – always been close," Father Murphy said as he stood to his feet.

"Close! What are you saying Father?" whispered Katherine

"That's enough for now my child. Go. Go home and be with your daughter," Father Murphy said as he walked away.

Katherine just sat there for a few minutes, rocking back and forth thinking, "This can't be so! What am I supposed to say to

Meagan? This isn't enough!" Well maybe it's not for Sister Katherine, but what about Ethan and Daisy Davis? Do you remember them?

●●●●

*Y*ou'd think those two have had enough? I'm sure by now the only thing Charlie wants is his fair share of the money – with interest of course! Now Scott on the other hand along with his dear Grandmother, Miss Nelson, seems to be the ones more likely to play hardball. And who better to play it with? Tony and Gina Hernandez, one of the riches couples in Prince Georges County.

In fact the Hernandez's hard nosed attorney, Marshall Hunter has already contacted the Davis family regarding an out of court settlement. I'm sure I don't have to remind you that Charles' Dad Ethan is more concerned with this mess never surfacing, than he is with justice being served on his son's behalf. So considering the fact that the Hernandez' are offering the Davis family a whole lot of money to drop all charges, one might think it's not such as bad idea after all. I mean think about it? You know, without a shadow of a doubt you're lying? And let's just say that the public humiliation could be far too great to live down. Plus, giving in is usually easier than fighting, Amen? Ooops – sorry I thought I was still in that church! The question now would be as Waverly Corrine stated earlier... Exactly how much? How much would you take to keep quiet? And let us not forget that your only child has just spent the last weekend in the intensive care unit after being found in a near by park not two feet from a wishing pond – left for dead. Talk about drama! Oh and how convenient is it for one who's guilty as hell to wake up from a coma with a slight case of selective amnesia. I couldn't have planned it better. Charlie's crazy! Besides, the way he's lying there, and I do mean, "lying" there! He looks as if he's trying a tad too much to be believable. And I'm sure Charlie's Mom believes in him even if she too finds this somewhat strange. But, how about his Father? From up here, he doesn't seem to be too comfortable. Let's see what Mr. Ethan Davis is crying about, I mean talking about...

"We need to just take it!" he shouted.

"Ethan, I hope you're not basing this all on your career! We've had that discussion! Charlie's the one we should be thinking of," Daisy yelled as she moved away from Charles' bedside.

At that moment, Charles set up in that terribly uncomfortable hospital bed and yelled at the top of his lungs,

"Will you two just quit it! Mother, Dad's right! I think we should just take the money! What harm can it do? I don't' want to go to court! They'll just try and say it was me and Scott's fault this happened to us. I'm tired! And, I'm tired as hell of being in this shity little hospital room! I just want to go home and get on with my life."

Ethan looked at his son in amazement then whispered, "You mean, your "Gay" life with that good for nothing Scott Griffin!"

Dag! Someone's a bit bothered by his son's lifestyle. I thought parents were supposed to encourage their children to be themselves. My Bad!

"Charles Ethan Davis, you should be ashamed of yourself! You've known for years that Charlie's – you know –" Daisy said shaking her head.

Charles chuckled and added, "The term is Gay Mother. And I don't believe Dad's ashamed at all. Say nothing if I'm right Father! I thought so. Dad's always – always wanted his only son to be one of those ball players or something. But Dad, a lot of them are Gay or Bi-sexual too."

"Charlie, stop making fun of your Father. He does that all too well all by himself," added Daisy.

Ethan looked at his family, not at all surprised and replied,

"You know sometimes I ask God – How did I get stuck with you? I mean, I am a fairly good man – good provider – perfect role model! Good looking! I even dress pretty well, so why?"

Daisy smiled knowing their quarrel was over and said,

"Well you chose me! So blame yourself! We'll take the money. But every single penny will go directly to Charlie's college savings, where none of us can access it. Agreed? Do we agree gentlemen?"

Charles nodded his head in agreement while thinking to himself, This is fucked! I still want my five hundred that was promised!

Ethan on the other hand simply whispered under his breath, "Yeah"

"Well it's settled! I'll just have to call Miss Blake in the morning," *Daisy said as she kissed her son good-bye then gathered her things which signaled to Ethan that it was time to go. Ethan gave Charles a half smile and left the room. Daisy shrugged her shoulders then whispered,*

"He'll be okay son. You know how your Father is, give him a little more time."

After watching them both leave, Charles jumped out of that tiny little hospital bed as fast as he could, almost tripping as he reached the bathroom because he had held his himself entirely too long. While making a slight mess of the commode, he thought, Oh well, I'm sure straight dicks miss the mark too sometimes.

Charles then took a really long look himself in the glass mirror which hung over the sink in the bathroom. As he began to wash his hands, Charles noticed that he was still very much sore from the operation along with all the other tubes running to and from his young body.

Damn, he thought as he shook his head with remorse from his need to do just what he wanted when he wanted – once again totally disregarding any repercussions – what so ever!

"Maybe this time the joke is on me," he said smiling, but then too, thinking at the same time. *Yeah, it's really time for me and Scott to exchange a few words...*

••••

*O*nce again, he attempted to call his partner in crime, Scott Griffin. And let me just say for the record. There is no need in believing in coincidence – period! There's no such thing! So, I don't have to tell you who's just snuck out of his Grandmother's two bedroom apartment, to try and secretly call his former partner in crime... trying to inform him of who's now engrossed in a deep conversation about, what else? Settling out of court! Talk about **waiting to exhale**, I don't think so! Okay, breath... So now with Charles on one line trying persistently to get through, yet getting another busy signal... Scott is on the other line holding while the hospital operator is trying to connect him to yet another preoccupied line. Okay, maybe I am just a Fly, but doesn't everybody have that thing called, "Call waiting?" Well, Scott being a *bit overzealous practically begged the poor operator to just try one more time, claiming he was simply unable to go see his stepbrother while he had been there. Ironically, Charles had just slammed the phone down, frustrated again by his attempt... And what do you know...*

Ring...! Ring...! Ring...!
Startled by the sounds, he first hesitated before answering...

"Hello..."

"Dude!" Scott replied with a big grin on his face from ear to ear.

"Scottie, Boy we need to talk like yesterday!! This is not what I bargained for. This shit has gone way over the edge! Man! You said we would be in and out! A few dollars! A little excitement! A free blast! And maybe even get our Birds wet! I barely remember anything! All I know is – I woke up in a whole lot of pain, Man! Confused and with unknown objects running in and out of body parts which I care not to mention! This is fucked, Man!" *Charles explained, really not understanding it clearly himself.*

Scott chuckled then replied, "Calm down Dude! Take another one of those valiums that they gave you or something. I hear they're like that. And put aside a few for me. I'm looking at my last two now. Not good!"

"Stop joking me Man! I'm cold serious! Besides, what makes this even more far out is, my parents were really hell bent on taking that Gina woman and who ever that is – Man, to court. We can't let them push it that far, Man! I'm supposed to be visiting colleges soon, not stuck up in some doctor's office trying to figure out how I ended up this way! I was enjoying my teen years, at least up until now."

Charles said as he began looking around the room. Then Scott thought he heard his Grandmother calling him so he placed his hand over his cell phone, then pressed his ear up against their apartment door. Charles hearing nothing on the line, thought they had gotten disconnected, became even more anxious and shouted, "Scott.. Scottie!"

"Shhh..." he whispered. "I thought I heard my Grandmother calling me. You know how she is... Nah! It's cool! I must be slipping! Now did I hear you say that Daisy

Davis and Easy "E" were going to drag us all into the big house? But now they're suddenly having a, let's push this under one of those Persian rugs they claim to love so much ideas," Scott said smiling in total agreement.

Agitated, Charles replied, "You know Man, I really wish you would stop referring to my parents as Daisy Davis and Easy "E". You make them sound like rappers. Plus, it's down right disrespectful!"

Scott began laughing...

"For real Man! You wouldn't find it as amusing if I started referring to your Grandmother as "Old Man Hatched! Since everyone suspects her of being a cross dresser who needs to take it one step further and shave that Rumplestellskin beard of hers. And how about the fact that your apartment smells like one of those corner bars because when she's not running numbers or hustling people, she's smoking cheap cigars! And what about her over-sized..." Charles added just before Scott interrupted

"Okay, okay, you've made your point, Dude! No harm intended. So are they really going to accept Gina and Tony's offer?"

Charles raised his brows and replied, "Pretty much. But how did you know about the money so fast?"

Scott smiled and said, "You're not the only one that was so-called sodomized and drugged, then left for dead. Although you and I both know that your under-experienced self passed out just before round two began. I, on the other hand, finished the tape. Therefore, technically we're due the remaining balance of all funds that were promised. And, from the looks of things which is why I called you in the first place, my Grandmother, "Old Man Hatched," as you said it best, is about to get us more than we both bargained for. Talk about wheeling and dealing! I may even consider taking the old lady with me on my next quest. Sike!"

Still puzzled, Charles shouted, "Next quest? And what do you mean your Grandmother is getting more! More what?"

"It's a good thing that you're finishing school and going to college. There's still so much more for you to learn my naïve friend. Try and keep up now. If your parents agree not to go to court and my Grandmother's talking on the phone to a "Mr. Hunter" (Tony's mouthpiece) right now about settling out of court... Now, what would we be referring to stupid? And let's just say – it's the next best thing to food stamps... Time's up, Dumb-Dumb! I can't believe you're so slow... Money, Charles! More money," Scott shouted.

Charles, not knowing exactly how much was offered initially asked, "So what are they offering you?"

Scott chuckled then replied, "I have no idea, but what ever it is, I heard my Grandmother saying something about it's supposed to be divided up between the two families, meaning us. Although..."

"What? What could they possibly want from us? The truth, which I'll never tell," Charles said firmly.

"That's not it Boy wonder. They basically want you and me both to sign papers saying something to the effect that we would never discuss this indecent proposal publicly. Or, when we're of age, never trying to resurrect the dead for any wrong doing. This whole thing is a trip. But, it makes sense – I wouldn't trust me either," Scott added.

"Damn, I guess your days as the head shampoo girl at the famous Colours and Cutz are no more. And you know that also includes your fantasy of that gorgeous Antoine ever bending you over one of those backwashing bowls, having his way with you... That's now basically obsolete. But as you always, always say, "When in Rome – Do as the Romans do!" Charles said as he began to laugh.

Scott knowing just how creative his friend is, asked as he giggled to himself, "And, what exactly is it that they do?"

"Get over it my dear friend! Move to Hollywood, change their name to hide from his predators and become one of those most talked about over-paid superstars!" Charles answered.

Scott laughed even more and said, "That is what they do... But once again the phony, oh I'm sorry. The Tony award goes to none other than yours truly, for waking up from a coma and conveniently forgetting what ultimately could destroy our scam against those Spanish Flies. Drum roll please...Charles Ethan Davis, the 2nd! I knew you wouldn't punk-down on us. There might be hope for you after all."

Charles just smiled then replied, "I was good! But all this talking has me famished. Why don't you find out how much money we'll be receiving? But, keep in mind that you will owe me something from your portion because my parents are making me put all of my coins into a college fund which they started years ago for me. Of course, they'll swear it's for my own good. But, for true – they will be the sole beneficiaries in this case. It's true! If by chance, we make out the way I'm thinking, I see six digits easy for the both of us which means less money for Mr. and Mrs. Davis to contribute to the college fund, meaning more money for them to grow old and stupid with. So, in all actuality, it's for *their* own good."

Scott just shook his head and replied, "You're so bad... How about we stay off the air for just a few days – you know, wait and see how this story plays out. Let's just say, I have an itchy suspicion that we'll be giggling over one of those cheap bottles of wine my Grandmother hides in the kitchen cabinets behind the cereal, in record time. So, do we have a deal?

Nodding yes, Charles said, "I would say, we do."

"Okay?"

"Well okay."

"Well I guess that's that..."

Chapter Eight

Twisted Fate

*O*h what a tangled web we weave. *Although with many – many lessons to choose from, somehow we choose only to deceive. And, knowing deception has no bedside manners what so ever... But, then at the end of your day, when it's all said and done, you say... "Now I lay me down to sleep, I pray my lies never catch up with me!"* Saying this, still not convinced you believe apologizing in advance will suffice. But, is it really enough? How many times since the last time, when you were in a similar situation, did you say you were sorry? Only apologizing simply because once again, your back was up against the wall and or basically you'd run out of fix it ideas, leaving one's vocabulary limited. So, I would imagine the phrase, "I'm sorry" would come to mind. In fact, it's the only thing that comes to mind.

Remember earlier when Sidney's eyes were first opened to the fact that her good-good girlfriend Dominique is most likely Gay? Floored by the implications, Sidney was tongue-tied. And at that same moment in time, Dominique knew she was busted. Reluctantly, with no other straws to grasp onto, she jacked. Politely apologized and tried to move forward. But, you know what... I believe even in the most unexcused situations, after the anger subsides, you will either laugh or cry wondering, how on earth could you have been so naïve? But, I guess that is better than openly admitting you've been made a fool of. Who do you know who likes to think of themselves as being anything less than smart? Now I'm sure Sidney Sharpe sees herself as being highly intelligent, even if her past shows she has been unable to stay clean and sober for more than ninety days at a time. As for Dominique Blake, the position she holds alone at the law firm proves her ability to think a cut above the rest. Well at least from an attorney's point of view. However, right about now, it looks as though Dominique's lost several points considering the way she's sitting there not at all noticing the light has been green for at least ten seconds. Sidney on the other hand, still blown away by what she learned earlier, waits as well. Not just for Dominique to cross the intersection – my guess is the subject placed on the table earlier was still up for grabs. Now impatient Sidney says,

"The light is green New York Undercover. You can go now."

Delayed by Sidney's comment, Dominique first giggled while shaking her head then looked at Sidney from the corner of her eye and

replied, "Okay, okay… I know this is a bit much for even *you* to swallow. Maybe it's more than a mouth full, but I don't know what to say! Believe it or not, I never knew what to say. Not to you! Meagan! And especially our straight and narrow ass Waverly Corrine. Our friendship has been the one thing *most* important to me always. The thought of compromising it because of who I choose to be sexually intimate with…Well, that wasn't going to happen!"

Sidney turned her lips upside down and said, "I think describing this as being more than a mouth full, even for me is truly an understatement. And if you expect me to believe that you – one of my oldest and dearest friends… Washington, D.C.'s best mouth piece, has somehow misplaced her train of thought… now who's asking too much??? Dominique Alisa Blake, I have never doubted my love for you. No, I don't see us in the sack together, but I can't honestly that say your fetish for women would split us up either. Now as for Meagan and Waverly… don't worry about them. They're happily married; well at least they *were* both happy. What I'm trying to say is, you cannot continue to live your life as a lie in fear of what the s whom you say love you *might* think. That's not the way it's supposed to be. That's not God's will."

"I can't say it's his will for me to be with other women either," Dominique added.

Sidney smiled and said, "You're tripping now girl… You know what I think…"

"What?" *Dominique asked as she pulled her truck on to the shoulder of the road.*

Sidney then took a deep breath and said, "I not only trust in Him, I truly believe that God's love for all of us is unchanging *and* unconditional. He loves us in spite of ourselves – which means – silly, before you were formed in your Mother's womb, he *knew* you Dominique. God knew who you were before you even noticed that first hussy in your space. So what! I can't totally understand your desire to be with … Umm…"

"Hannah!" Dominique said.

"Yeah, but I do know what it feels like to love someone. And if, Hannah makes you happy, then who am I to stand in your way? Let alone judge your commitment to your feelings," Sidney added.

Dominique just shook her head in awe of Sidney then replied, "You know you're really tripping me out. I guess I'm feeling really naïve right about now. I had no clue that you would respond this way. All of this time, I've been creeping and faking – afraid to tell my friends who I really am. I feel very much like one of those crazy adolescents right now. I am truly sorry for deceiving you all of these years. Thank you for always, always being you Sidney Sharpe."

Sidney chuckled and said, "And who else would I be. Can you really imagine me being anyone other than myself?"

Both girls looked at each other, smiled then shouted at the same time, "I don't think so!" *Well the next sounds that were heard were laughter. It was obvious they were equally amused by each other's response. By this time, Dominique felt a sense of relief so she pulled off. And yes, Sidney Sharpe and Dominique Blake were still giggling.*

"Okay, enough about me. Tell me Diamond – is this Hannah Girl all that and a bag of chips?"

Dominique looked over at her friend and answered, "Well of course she is *Nigger*. I don't do trolls!"

Sidney smiled then added, "But is she prettier than me? Sounds as if Girl's not from these parts... You know those Asian chicks have speed bumps as asses and very few curves to work with as well."

Thrown by Sidney's slur, Dominique answered while shaking her head, "Just for the record, I don't believe there's anyone on this earth as pretty as you – Miss Sidney Sharpe. Now as for Hannah, why don't you wait and see for yourself. But, in the meantime, no girl jokes! I'm going to have to find an easy way to tell Meagan and Waverly as it is... So be a good little bunny and hold on to this as if your own life depended on it."

Sidney shook her head indicating that she understood completely. Yet, Miss Sharpe had her own curiosities so she asked, "Okay... But can I ask you something?"

"Sure, as long as you're for real Sid..."

Sidney paused then said in a very soft tone, "There is one thing that I've always, always wondered about those kind of sex-ships..."

"What?" Dominique asked wondering what in the devil Sidney was talking about.

Sidney paused again and said, "When you're right in the middle of hitting it... I mean close as hell to reaching your climax; can you *really* tell you're with a woman instead of a man? I mean, is it really... I mean, I know it's some kind of difference. It's just that a real man has a way of making a woman feel ah... helpless and crazy out of her mind and shit. You know, your body starts going into uncontrollable convulsions and stuff. I just think if it was me, I would know . . . .

Dominique looked over at Sidney in disbelief and said as she tried hard not to laugh,

"You would know what crazy?"

"I would know if I was with Denzel or Halle, silly," Sidney replied.

Now – by this time, the girls were pulling up right in front of Miss Phyllis' brownstone where Sherian had been waiting for her younger sibling to arrive. Sidney knew this was her cue to stop, but curious minds still wanted to know. So she blinked those bedroom eyes as she always, always referred to them, placed her hand under her chin and waited for Dominique to answer.

Dominique started laughing. Next she put the gear in the park position. Still amused by Sidney's comment, she pulled her hair back off her face then turned a little to the side so that Sidney could see her more clearly when she answered her. After taking a deep breath, she said,

"You *really* want to know?"

"Yeah, I really want to know!"

With her lips turned upside down, very slowly she said,

"Okay... Let's just say... imagine those nicely curved hips of yours, slightly turned upside down. Imagine your head tilted slightly back allowing just a bit of air to push through in spouts. Imagine your moist body running a fast temperature of 360 degrees still climbing causing your heart to race and your limbs to tremble. Now of course when you begin rubbing your breast that's just a bit more than a mouth full in size, your sweaty palms signals your mesmerized mind that they are now saluting to the flag. Still with me?"

Sidney just blinked...

"Okay now imagine those well-toned thighs of yours raised at a 45degree angle moving back and forth. And last, imagine that soaking wet, well-experienced, all American pussy of yours, regularly giving it to the needy and offering seconds to the greedy; throbbing almost ready to explode as if you're a fat woman stuck in an elevator hours after over-dosing on Exlax. At this point my curious little friend, you could care less about who's having you for dinner – let alone be able to distinguish if the culprit's a dick or a split," Dominique said as she politely closed Sidney's mouth with her hand.

Sidney still tripping off of the track door, turned her head back to Dominique and said, "I still adore you but you know that you are really full of shit! I cannot believe you set me up like that... I hope it haunts you for your entire drive home. Now I have to go in here and attempt to console my second Mother, Sherian. I guess I'll see your bad-tail-self in the morning Nasty Girl. Bye Girl!"

Dominique simply smiled and said, "I love you!"

Sidney returned the gesture and replied, "And I you!" And the moment was over.

●●●●

ou know what? Life is puzzling most of the time. Take a word as simplistic as "moment." What does it mean? To be brief? That's just it! Let's say while Sidney was enjoying Dominique's company, in that moment, Girl felt good. She was as close as she's ever been to her friend, yet totally safe and secure within herself to say exactly what she felt. Well, that was that particular moment in time. Brief! But when Dominique pulled off, just that fast, that moment in time was no more. Brief! Over! Chances of it ever resurfacing were none! And Sidney, now moving slowly up her dead Mother's walkway is in yet a different difficult moment of disbelief and fear. Fear of never being able to call upon her Mother for guidance. Never mind her role as the younger sibling with respect to honoring her only sister, Sherian as the elder while in return insisting she respect her as well.

As unexplainable as it is, feelings can and do change usually without warning. Now you feel it, now you don't. And speaking of feeling things... You wouldn't believe how fast the feeling of relief came over Sidney Sharpe as she stood on her Mother's front steps noticing a little girl getting her hair combed by her Mom as she looked through their living room window. It looked as if the girl was in some sort of pain. Nevertheless, as Sidney watched, she couldn't help but reflect back to when she was a little girl getting her hair combed. Tender-headed herself, Sidney would never sit still long enough for her Mother to successfully braid her hair because Miss Phyllis was unmercifully heavy-handed. Sherian remembering how it felt being torched under her Mother's grip, always-always volunteered to comb Sidney's hair. It's funny though, recalling that small little piece in time – yet another moment, gave Sidney Sharpe her much needed comfort.

As for Sherian, neither Rolaids nor Exlax could restore the old tapes that are playing in her head right now... Who knows, maybe Sherian's now overwhelmed with guilt from never acting on that "ill conceived tale" her Mother encouraged her to tell all of Sidney's life. But I can't help but wonder... Can one's support system really have that kind of impact on their decisions? How would that work? One person, who feels as though they are either older or wiser, suggests to you that what they believe is best for your situation is better than what you feel is best? But in actuality, because they are not you, their opinion of what you should or should not do, leaves them blameless when consequences happen. I know it doesn't make much sense. You can even say that it's somehow trying too hard to be accepted. A "People Pleaser!" So, I guess it does play a significant part. One's environment can alter one's mind, especially if the support system being drawn from is dysfunctional to begin with.

Now 35 years into her spiral-cased, domino affected game of charades, Sherian's haunted by the mere thought of spilling her guts. Just by the way she sits there in her dead Mother's kitchen now somehow blaming Miss Phyllis for what ultimately was her own selfish final decision. It certainly appears all too convenient now. It sure is less convincing to shift the responsibility to the one who's no longer here. Who can contradict her version now?

One thing for sure, if she doesn't pull herself together sooner than later, her guilt alone will reveal the real means behind that unspoken tale. And if you ask me, Sherian should start by having less conversation with herself. This way, she can stay in the present while waiting for something as simple as tea to boil so that she'd be able to hear it when it's ready. This time, however, she's taken a death ear to it. Talk about blocking things out! I believe shrinks refer to them as being emotionally unavailable or mentally detached from your own reality. Poor lady! You think maybe if I get a little closer to her she'll snap out of it...

●●●●

"**O**h my Lord – what in the devil was that? Now I'm hearing things! Mother, it's really too early to assume I need help with this! I promised you I'd tell her and I will! I wanted to be honest with Sidney on many, many occasions, way before now! But no – you somehow always changed those thoughts! Even this is so much like you... Dead, yet still having the last word."

Tears rolled down Sherian's face. While trying to blink them away, she noticed her tea was ready. Viewing her watch first, Sherian finally got up from the chair and proceeded to prepare herself an unusual cup of tea. First she placed two different kinds of flavored tea bags into her mug, followed by a half spoon of honey. Then Miss Lady went down the stairs to the basement where Miss Phyllis had a wine-cellar installed almost 20 years ago. She claimed it would not only add appeal to her brownstone, but it would increase the value as well. Although at the time Sherian thought of it as an excuse for her Mother to waste some of their new found fortune, she somehow managed to find use for it anyway. So from time to time, when Miss Sharpe wanted to relax her mind, she'd sneak a bottle of brandy or cognac from the cellar and add a little to her over flavored tea. Now with Miss Phyllis being unable to monitor her vintage collection of priceless potent portables, the satisfaction that was gained through Sherian's deceit was no more. So instead of carefully placing the borrowed item back in its place, Sherian took it up to the kitchen where she finished preparing her tea and continued her chat with her dead Mother...

"What am I going to do? Yeah, now you say tell her! You're not even here to confirm this charade. So now I guess I'm supposed to call on her Father. The same father who we told Sidney she never had. Let alone the fact that he's old enough to be her grandfather. And let's not forget he has a family of his own, who's not only pure as snow, they're white as snow! And what about all the years of accepting money in exchange for secrecy... The more I even talk about being honest with Sidney, this late in her life, considering all the factors that will come into play... This is not only an act of insanity, this shit is cruel Mother!!! I guess payback is a bitch! But then you would say that it's time for your spoiled, self-indulged, self centered, bewitched daughter to step up to the plate and be a Mother to her own daughter. After all, its Sidney's birthright, especially since the Mother she's always – always known has past on."

Still hurting, Sherian cried even harder... So much so that her stomach began to ache. She tried calming herself by wiping the tears. But, the more she wiped them off, the faster they covered her face. Next, she tried covering her mouth with her Mother's favorite hand towel that usually hung over the door handle of the oven, thinking if she could just silence her cries the tears would stop. Well that didn't work either. Finally, she closed her eyes really tightly biting her bottom lip at the same time as she clinched on to the hand towel in a prayer position. Then it happened... Sherian's eyes began to dry. And as she continued standing there in hopes of regaining her composure, she couldn't help but think back to when it all began...

It was early one Saturday morning when Sherian was supposed to accompany her Mother to the city to do some shopping for her employer's planned birthday celebration. Miss Phyllis, being his most valued worker, was assigned the position of making certain that everything would go as planned. And as usual she was not taking this assignment lightly. As for Sherian, she was moving extremely slow that morning. It was obvious something wasn't quite right. Well after calling her several times, Miss Phyllis, being impatient now, decided to go and see exactly what was keeping her.

Surprisingly Miss Phyllis found her daughter in the bedroom which they shared located on the third floor of her employer's home, at the foot of her bed curled up in a fetal like position. Convinced once again

*that Sherian was indeed up to her usual trick of simply not wanting
to go, Miss Phyllis stormed over to her pulling at one of her legs
forcing her out of the bed. Now on this particular morning, young
Sherian was really ill. So when she turned around and attempted to
get up from the floor, her jaws filled rapidly with vomit and although
Sherian covered her mouth quickly, a little managed to spit out.*

*The two looked at each other in disbelief, and then Sherian ran as
fast as she could to the nearest bathroom. Miss Phyllis using her
animal instincts... I mean Motherly instincts, knew right then that
her fifteen year old grown acting daughter was without a doubt
baring a child of her own. So as she watched Sherian on her knees
with her hands thrown over the commode, and her face practically in
it, the feeling of anger and contempt quickly overwhelmed her.
Ironically, with all the seasons that have come and gone since then
including the ups and downs, good and not so good times, the one
thing that's always-always stood out in Sherian's mind about her
Mother was... on that particular day when she thought she needed
her most... In spite of all the times that she cried wolf before, Miss
Phyllis chose not to embrace Sherian as her daughter. In fact, her
exact words were,*

"You're pregnant aren't you? Don't you dare deny it!
How could you shame me this way? After all the sacrifices
I've made to keep you here with me. I should have never
listened to my family. I wanted to leave you with my aunt
and then send for you when you matured. At least then, I
wouldn't have been made a fool of! You disgust me! Well
this time little girl, you will know exactly how it feels to
carry someone inside of you, feeling it grow as the latter days
get harder... Yet, never really knowing if you'll be able to
care for it properly! Maybe not even wanting the child! Yes
you'll know this time! And after you've endure the pain of
birthing your child, only to have it taken from you as if it
never ever-ever happened... only to have it taken... have it
taken... as if it never ever... ever happened..."

● ● ● ●

ag, I imagine those thoughts would stay in my head as well...

"This shit still feels like yesterday," she said aloud as she poured another shot of cognac into her tea.

Just then, Sidney walked into the kitchen, catching the tail-end of Sherian's statement and replied, "What feels like yesterday Cher?"

Startled, Sherian hesitated answered, "Nothing, I mean everything! All of this! This house... this kitchen... these damn mugs... the same flavored tea and her oh so lovely voice in my head!"

Sidney smiled slightly and said, "I see you're still sipping brandy and tea..."

"It's cognac and how do you know?"

Taking the cup out of Sherian's hands, smelling it first, she added, "For one, it's late. Second, through the years, Mother's priceless collections have always-always had a way of lingering in the air. And you usually drink when you're defenseless. Unfortunately for me, I've abused that luxury all too many times."

Both girls simply smiled at each other in total agreement... Then Sidney shouted, as she sat the cup down on the kitchen counter pushing it out of Sherian's reach, "I have an idea!"

"What?" Sherian asked looking strangely puzzled.

"Why don't we go upstairs to Mama's room?" she replied

"Light the fireplace, kick off our shoes and climb into her bed...," Sherian added.

"Just as we did when we were little girls once you finally gave in after running out of your famous fix it ideas, leaving us helpless till Mama returned," giggled Sidney.

Nodding yes, Sherian said, "Okay that will probably make us both feel better because right now it does seem a bit unbearable. But, just for the record, you were the only little girl in this house. I was born grown up!"

Sidney laughed then replied; "Now that explains why you cried more than me Cher! That's right – I was the one consoling you!"

"Who asked you little girl? Big girls cry too!" Sherian added as they headed up the staircase.

"Only until we get our way Big Sis... But let me say right now! If you even look at me like you want to start playing in my hair, thinking I'm one of your lost and found baby dolls! I will cut you!" Sidney said as she placed her hands in the air mimicking a true Ninja.

Sherian chucked first then added, "This is not General Hospital and you switched practices almost two years ago."

"Maybe so, but it's just like riding a bike! One never forgets! And it's been over two years since I've held a scalpel," Sidney said as she turned her lips upside down.

Sherian with her need to have the last word, added, "Okay... Okay you little elephant, since you don't want me playing in your hair, and by the way, it looks as if you need a relaxer and a cut... But then I'm not your stylist!"

"No, you're not!"

"Anyway, I hope you didn't forget to wash those stinky toes of yours. Because if my memory serves me correctly, I believe the term was Cheetos! Or was that Corn Chips!"

"Oooh... see... that was not right!"

"Well, you started it Sidney Sharpe!"

"That's okay, I owe you one..."

"Sure you're right! And as long as you owe me, I'll never be broke!"

Now where did I hear that before? Nevertheless, these two Bunnies look as though this particular episode will be worked out. And that's kinda all right. Just by the way Sherian and Sidney are able to talk; pulling on one another's strengths in a time of need has to be a learned behavior. Maybe there's more to this than meets the eye. Maybe Miss Phyllis Maple did her part to the best of her ability considering the tools given to her by her caregivers on child rearing. Now with her out of the picture, I'm certain there are many-many items to sort through. From her liabilities to every deed... Who knows how many treasures that old lady managed to put away. Surely you yourself have questioned that! Remember the watch! And how about that old antique jewel box! Lord only knows what lies in that. I suppose we'll have to wait and hope we'll see!

But as I stated before, time waits for no one. That includes Sidney and Sherian... In fact, they used the next few hours to reminisce about every single moment shared together and with the late Phyllis Maple. I suppose doing that helped to smooth over the rough edges for the conversation that was about to follow. Before long, it was late. Ironically, both Sidney and Sherian had exhausted themselves with topics ranging from Sunday school lessons to what was to be worn at their Mother's funeral. And just in case you're wondering – Miss Phyllis Maple requested that everyone, meaning all of the guest attending, dress in ivory. That's cream or off white for the slow pokes! Oh, and she also wanted her going home services to resemble a party – rather than a morbid farewell. I believe Miss Maple's exact words were, "Give me my flowers while I'm still alive. Bring nothing to my grave other than rose petals. Sprinkle them about so that when you see them scattered, you'll know I'm with you..." Crazy huh! Well, that's what she said. So now as the fireplace crackled, the only other sounds heard were the soft whistles that came out of Sherian and Sidney's nostrils as they slept. I did mention before, like mother – like daughter! That's simplistic!

● ● ● ●

oo bad life's not so simple for Mr. and Mrs. Simmons. It's true! Take Vincent... Here we have a successful young doctor who on one hand has the best of both worlds. But then at the same time, "Boyfriend's" double standard lifestyle is about to do a "nine-eleven any day now" So as he stands there, chocolate body, slightly damp from the shower he just finished, Boyfriend's clueless to what really lies ahead of him. Even now, as he dries off his oh so buffed muscular body, Vincent ponders the idea of his lovely wife giving him "head" while his mistress Payton fondles her. Which leaves me to wonder, do all men secretly daydream about having sex with two women? Anyway, Vincent's weakness to continue to commit adultery along with his blatant fictitious attempts to cover his tracks, have now pushed Waverly over the edge. Not to mention her insecurities about turning the big 40, this in fact is running neck and neck with those daymares of hers. But, isn't it amazing though – how one's past has a way of inviting itself to the present. So, it would be safe to say that while Vincent is thinking of Waverly, Waverly's thinking of Vincent. And with him being all too conveniently butterball naked, it gives her plenty of room to go up in her head as well…

Look at you… You really think you've got it going on… If your brain was half the size of that dick of yours, maybe you could see the senselessness of fucking everything in sight. You're the joke – always trying to mind-fuck a sister with those worthless gestures in hopes of bringing back the way we were. But that's okay… the next game will be played on you my dear. So from this day forward, consider yourself cut from the waist down! And as soon as I confirm you're fucking around on me again for the last time, I will not only throw you out of my home… But, by the time my attorneys are done with your black ass, you'll be working ten jobs to live one life – you sorry ass motherfucker!

Well, I wonder how this night will play out…

"So Baby, would you like me to get you something before I come to bed? You look a little worn-out from all of the excitement surrounding Sidney's Mother's death. What happened to her anyway? I know she was old but…" Vincent said just before Waverly interrupted.

"Miss Phyllis was not that old and I don't believe there was anything exciting about her death!"

"I guess that came out wrong. My day didn't go so well either. First I had to kick out a thousand bucks to some cleaning service because you my dear failed to mention they were coming or leave a check. Then…"

"Cleaning service!"

"Picky People or something. Don't tell me you don't remember them… Bald-headed tall dude. I think he said his name was Keith. You know you really need to ease up on doing so much… Maybe after the funeral, we can steal away for a few days?"

Smiling, Waverly's first thoughts were, Not even if my life depended on it! However reminding herself, that she needed to keep her cheating husband off balanced, she said in a very soft tone, "I would like that…"

Now after hearing the answer expected from his mourning spouse, Vincent's ego was immediately inflated. He was not only certain that his pretending to be the receptive loving husband was without a doubt working. But once again Dr. Simmons was confident his dog tracks were covered. So with the night being young and the good Doctor still unable to satisfy his thirst, he preceded to climb into their bed naked and push up on his wife to encourage her to make love. Waverly had not so long ago got into bed herself in hopes of relaxing her mind by reading one of her favorite novels, "Love or Lust" by Toni Chance. Vincent, always-always seeing things through his eyes only – believed this was yet the perfect moment. So first he began by rubbing Waverly's shoulders with some aromatherapy body oil he kept close by in the nightstand beside their bed. Waverly, not wanting to reveal her true feelings by acting indifferent, decided to play along. She thought, What the hell, at least this will save my seventy bucks at the Spa!

Well with only ten minutes of feeling her cheating husband's firm but gentle hands, mesmerized her tense body, Waverly had the hardest time pretending not to be aware of Vincent's present misbehavior. Thinking relentlessly that the way he touched her, with the ability to make her forget about her troubles and desire only him, was precisely the way he touched his mistress.

Well this made Girl even more pissed by the second and at that moment, Vincent's warm hands began to burn Waverly's back like hot coals. So by the time the good Doctor reached his wife's favorite spot, just a half inch below her posterior on the inner pat of her thigh, Waverly jumped up screaming "Don't," at the top of her lungs.

"Don't! Baby you can't be serious…"

Nodding her head yes (I am serious) while forming wrinkles between her hazel eyes, she went on to explain why she felt unable to perform tricks or have them performed for her on what appeared to be a perfect night. Vincent, with his dumb self, looked at Waverly not hearing her at all. He seemed to be looking right through her! He acted as if through his lion eyes, he visualized a raw tender piece of fillet migeon which he planned to devour as soon as she put a sock in it. In fact, Waverly soon noticed that her husband was not at all buying her excuses on this particular night. So when she moved a little closer to him with hopes of making her points more clear, Boyfriend pulled her down on their bed, wrapped his tree limbs firmly around her and forced his lizard tongue right in Girl's mouth. Knowing at this point it was simply hopeless, she thought to herself, I know this little mother-fucker is not going to just take the pussy!

Now I know what you're thinking, "poor-poor Waverly." But why not? I thought that a wife's duty was to give up the bootie! And besides, how does one take what is **supposed** *to be his in the first place? You try and figure it out... They say that it's always-always two sides to a story. You have the advantage of knowing both sides. Now as for myself, if I was Judge W.C. Simmons and a tall dark simply gorgeous hunk of a man who just happens to be my husband was rubbing all up against me, for that moment, I would say to hell with what's going on in and around me. You know what the "Nike" commercials says – "Just Do It!" I mean really... Who cares and who would know? If it helped, you could even force yourself to find the good in it. You know, pretend that it's all about you. Get your needs met or just get yours! However you want to look at it...*

And speaking of looking at it, from up here it looks as though Dr. Simmons has already established his point of view for his lovely wife which is to make love to her – period! Even with her now being breathless from his warm sensuous kisses still squirming trying desperately to get away, Vincent with what appears to be sweat beads rolling down the center of his back, is determined to get his way. He doesn't have a clue that this is not at all what Waverly wants right now. The only thoughts that are skipping through his mind are, "Man–oh–man I need this" and "I swear that out of all the lovers I've had, this pussy fits my dick like a glove. No wonder I'm still hooked!"

Now that's just like a man. Dude's ego is still most likely inflated more so than his "you know what." Anyway as the long strokes multiply, I mean minutes past by, Waverly's resolve is beginning to subside as well. It's true! If you dare to turn back a page or two, you will find Girl screaming "Don't" as if she had no desires what so ever of being sedated in this way by the good Doctor. However, now with him stirring up things literally, poor Girl's body is responding quite well – contrary to what her mind tells her. I believe a young artist wrote a song about it... It went something like, "Say my name – Say my name."

Anyway, whether she wants it or not, Girl's getting it and loving it! Alright now I'm convinced maybe the saying's true, "A good piece is hard,... or was that hard to find. No – a good man with a good piece is hard to find." Yeah! Oh well, you get the picture. And – too, there's no need to wonder how this night will play out. Vincent's giving it all he's got while Waverly's taking it like a man, I mean woman. I guess this goose has been cooked. Maybe we can check in on another Bunny... Oh maybe not... Would that be a phone I hear ringing? Sounds more like a cell phone and I'll give you one guess as to who's... "Wrong!"

Well pretending not to be bothered, Vincent went on doing what Vincent was doing. In fact, Boyfriend began to speed up the process. I believe the term "Ejaculate" would describe the moment to come...

"Don't get that Baby! Wait a minute! Not now – just..." whispered Vincent seconds before he was to burst.

But life is funny... How about the phrase, "Flip-Flop"! That annoying sound which is supposed to be a tune caused Waverly Corrine to snap out of it. So when one cell phone rings, one answers. And with it conveniently charging on the nightstand beside her bed, she answered just a little out of breath,

"Hello..." *The voice on the other end said,* "Corrine" *Now knowing she had given her middle name only to Keith Sheppard of Sheppard Investigations, "Mary", I mean Waverly jumped out of position faster than a blink of an eye. Well that sudden movement caused the ever – so – horny Dr. Simmons to ejaculate on their white satin sheets as opposed to in his wife's "you know what."*

"Damn Waverly!" *Vincent shouted. Undecided, Waverly just looked.. Unsure as to if he had dialed the correct number,* Keith said, "I'm sorry, I was trying to reach a Corrine. I must have mistakenly dialed the wrong number..." *Still in shock, Waverly uttered,* "No this is Waverly – I mean this is Corrine" *Now Vincent's brows rose slightly as he slid his messy-self out of their bed while Waverly sat up straight, more so at attention, but puzzled at the same time.*

"Did I catch you at a bad time?" Keith asked.

"Mmm... no, why? What's up?" *she replied trying to pretend to be talking with one of her girls and not to this new found – too bad he's not my secret lover on her cell at the most inopportune moment...*

Well sensing that Waverly was not alone given her reaction to his call and keeping past experience in mind, Mr. Sheppard ended their call telling Waverly that he'd check back in on her by early afternoon on the following day. Of course Waverly concurred and with hanging up just as fast as she answered, she allowed Vincent to believe that as untimely screwed up as their interruption was, maybe it really was one of her emotional friends on the other end after all. I mean it seemed almost believable. And too, there were a lot of things going on that day. Besides... even the irresistible, emotionally unavailable Dr. Vincent Simmons knows that it is sometimes better to pretend to believe what your mind tries to persuasively have you believe, rather than what your profound first instinct tells you is unfortunately true.

Most people do just that on a daily basis. You know, instead of stating what's really on their mind they force themselves to believe in what one desires, which is usually what feels tolerable or better. That way, one can avoid challenging decisions that alter one's reality. Make sense to me!! Anyway, once Vincent closed the bathroom door behind himself, it gave both of them just what they needed... an opportunity to return to their fake selves... time out...

Chapter Nine
Deja vu...

ell day four of this unpredictable mood twisting saga has finally come.. And yes, with just minutes past the hour, the drama continues... And what better place to start... How about Dominique Blake's house? Where is she? "Come out-come out where ever you are..." Okay, she's probably in the bathroom since I hear water running. Although it sounds like Girl has company... But the fog, I mean the steam is a bit thick in here and I can't quite see yet... Good, well at least she's courteous enough to wipe the mist from the mirror. Okay, now I see that she's on the phone.

"So Baby, you never said how your first visit went with that Social Worker? Did she go easy on you?" asked the voice on the speaker phone.

Now we know Dominique's a mess... While flossing she mumbled, "at wu okay – okay ut at- was- a dick."

Of course understanding nothing she said and knowing just what her predictable lover was doing, Hannah demanded first that she turn off the water knowing that her bath was full and second she reminded Dominique that she had been flossing since the beginning of their conversation and now would be a good time to stop. Then she asked Dominique to repeat herself. Smiling, not wanting to believe she had been peeped, Dominique replied...

"You do not know me that well Little Girl!"

"Oh but I do, all too well... In fact I know that you are probably topless with your white "Vicky" briefs on. And I also know that you're minutes from covering that flawless carmel skin of yours with all those gels and creams you swear by – which would also mean that the beautiful silky black hair I first noticed and fell in love with is pulled back off your face and tucked ever so smoothly behind your little "elf ears." Need I say more?"

Speechless Dominique merely shook her head and continued to floss.

"So stop holding me in suspense by stringing me along. Did she give you a hard time or not Dominique Blake?"

"First off she was a "he". After he realized that Sidney was not you, he thought we should continue our session once you got into town – so there."

"My-my... I bet that was a bit uncomfortable. Don't tell me you weren't able to warn Sidney. Tell me you told her before you met with the good doctor – please..."

Dominique hesitated...

"Dominique – she's your best friend! How could you allow her to walk into something like that?"

"I talked to Sidney about it okay Hannah!"

"Good, thank God!"

"Well kinda after we left the prick's office..."

"Dominique you know that was totally unfair. So how did she take it? And did you tell her about me, I mean really about me?"

"Well she in fact took it quite well...Actually, more so than I expected. And yes, how could I *not* tell her all about you? We will be spending the rest of our lives together. I just..."

"You just what Baby?"

Hesitantly, Dominique added, "It's just – I pray that Waverly and Meagan are equally accepting."

"And would that really matter one way or another? You do know that the only way for us to go forward is for you to be honest with yourself and your friends. And if..." *Hannah said as Dominique interrupted her.*

"Don't say it! I've already been told! If in fact we're truly friends, they will understand."

"That's right! So my dear..."

"So nothing... Besides, the last thing I'd prefer to engage in at this time is this conversation. It has unfortunately been at the forefront of my brain longer than I care to remember. What will they say? Will they say what they truly mean? Can this small omission change our friendship and if so in what way? So you see "Darling" I've played this tape over and over again. So much that now it's playing me..."

"But Dominique, what you're thinking is not real and none of us are back in college. What about this new era?"

"What about it? Some people still go on old information."

"Not Sidney Sharpe!"

Laughing, Dominique added, "No – Sidney's in a class all by herself."

"And so are the others! You've said yourself how unique and special they *all* are. I think its way past time you trust them and be okay with it. And just so you know, when I get up there on the weekend, I will not pretend to be a casual friend! We are soul mates and great lovers and like it or not... Or should I say – accept it or not, we will act accordingly."

"You're a trip!"

"I've been called worst... So until then, my love..."

"Until then my love..."

Well this should be interesting. The two ended their call on that note. Hannah went back to sleep, while Dominique finished her facial then climbed into the bubble bath awaiting. And as her little petite body disappeared in the soapy water underneath the bubbles, Dominique kept repeating the phase... "This is the day the Lord has made, I will be glad and rejoice in it" Well this is yet another day and if what she says is true, then so be it!

I once heard someone say, "Nothing just happens – Everything is as it should be." Meaning, you are right where you're supposed to be based upon the work you've done. Basically, lots of work – much progress! Little work... well you get the picture. But how would that equate with pretending, especially for long periods of time? And what if you never had a clue you were pretending to begin with? You know something like living all of your childhood and a portion of your adulthood believing you're this person, attached to a particular inheritance, but all along it's simply not true. Now I've heard of many instances where people find out their birthday is not really their birthday. Meaning, the month, day or in some cases, the year have been mistaken. But, what if the parents you thought were your parents were not? Could that be so easily forgiven or overlooked? But in all fairness, this question could only be answered by one who's experienced such a thing. Isn't that what kind of happened to Meagan? Last we checked in on her, she was at the end of a small beef with her supposedly loving spouse... Well, hours later and yes with things still weighing heavily on her mind – not to mention this new found life of hers, Meagan's up bright and early walking both of her Sheppards. Now she just finished giving Nia and Nyle their two-hour feeding but with all of her unresolved issues floating about, she thought maybe she could save Drake some time by taking the dogs out earlier than usual..

I believe Girl just had a hard time falling back to sleep. I suppose that would be normal. I have never had the graceful pleasure to experience such a thing. But if I did give birth to two beautiful daughters, and one of them carried an illness known only to be transferred via the gene pool... The same gene I believed my entire life I didn't carry... well, that alone is enough my friend and would be more than enough reason to crumble my foundation thus keeping me up all hours of the day and night. But you know what? Meagan's not only wise; she possesses an unbelievable hidden strength that somehow only manages to surface itself when her back is dead up against the wall. So, even though her mind is playing tug of war, Meagan clearly hears her Father's words of many-many years ago saying,

"Meagan, you know Daddy loves you more than anything on this earth. And, my darling "Princess" you will always-always be. But one day when you're all grown up, another good man will touch your heart in such a way that you will want to become his "Queen." But the one thing more than anything else I want you to remember, even if I'm dead and gone... No matter what this life throws your way, always-always put "you" first. Go to God for His divine guidance for those things that may confuse your thoughts. Feed your spirit with his words and keep your temple clean of any hatred. And no matter what the adversary tries to have you believe, always-always have compassion for your fellow man!"

Well, if I had an old tape like that I guess I would be eager to stay busy right along with "Little Missy". So with the morning being at its peak, just about an hour before daylight, what thoughts do you suppose ran through Meagan's mind? Run – and Fast!! I mean why not? That is what she's always done in the past... Well at least until her pregnancy made it simply impossible. So immediately she took the dogs back into the house while thinking,

"I'm not waiting for Dr. Stone or anyone else to say different!, I'm going running!"

And before she could give it a second thought, Meagan grabbed her cell phone, wrote Drake a note and headed for the Rock Creek Park where she knew her good-good Girlfriends would be. And just like clock-work, there they were...giggling, half sleepy and a little unavailable. And starting from the youngest to the oldest, Sidney was saying something about being tired this early in the morning so she said and I quote,

• • • •

"**N**o, why would I brush my teeth just to go running with women! This isn't a date! The only thing I do this early is gargle and pop in a mint. Then of course when I return home, I shower and brush…"

Dominique saw that as being nasty, but funny at the same time. So of course she teased Sidney about it. Her opinion was one should brush and floss after meals. Naturally her response to Sidney's comment was,

"You're nasty! I still love you but you're nasty. You see my teeth? I'm at the dentist four times a year. I've never once had a cavity or one of those gum diseases. I probably could even do a commercial or something. What do you think Waverly?"

Now Waverly was indeed thinking, but not about her Girlfriends. And not at all about how often one should brush. Her thoughts were "About Last Night."

"Waverly Corrine! Are you still with us?" Dominique asked as she waved her hands in front of Waverly's face.

Noticing her, Waverly answered,

"Yes, what were you saying?"

"Do you know Sid does not brush her teeth before she runs with us in the morning?"

Confused, Waverly answered, "No, how could I know that…"

Sidney and Dominique just looked at Waverly then back at each other and continued to laugh even more. Waverly not understanding the point of the question or why it was asked to begin with simply shook her head smiling and said,

"You two have a real problem."

"So how often do you brush your teeth?" Sidney asked looking directly at Waverly.

"Enough!"

"No, I said Sid was nasty because she didn't think that she should brush before we run in the morning. In fact, "Little Miss Nasty" thinks once is enough... Then your response was "enough"! Now according to the nasty girl, enough means once. What is it to you?"

"Oh I see – you're also fixated on your pearly whites..."

"No-no, that's not it! You both are a little nasty! That's it I have two nasty girlfriends!"

Now I thought these women were supposed to be exercising. Instead they had jokes for one another. Anyway, while the three of them were joking each other about their personal habits guess who walked up looking a little whipped from her evening as well. Noticing her – first Sidney whispered,

"Meagan..." Dominique knowing Meagan for her big beautiful smile, added,

"Yeah, she's not nasty like you two!"

But then Waverly noticed that it really was Meagan and shouted, "No Diamond, Meagan's here!"

Finally, Dominique turned around and surprised herself, she shouted, "Meagan Simone Tyler, what on earth are out doing here?"

"And looking like you've walked straight out of *Hell*, I might add," Sidney said looking equally surprised.

"You try having twins at my age," answered Meagan with a half of smile on her face.

"Oh you poor-poor baby..." Waverly said a as she pushed Meagan's hair off of her face, kissing her on her cheek while giving her a big hug.

Next thing you know, all three girls were embracing their friend. They were all surprised, but at the same time, elated to see that Meagan was ready to get her life back on track.

"Well Waverly Corrine, you're in luck today!" Sidney said smiling as she began to walk swiftly up the path.

"And why on earth would you say that little girl?"

"Easy, since Meagan's joining us, you won't have to pretend you can run today!" chuckled Sidney.

Now knowing every day that Dominique and Sidney makes it their business to joke her about her inability to keep up when they're all exercising, Waverly chose to ignore Sidney's slur and followed her up

the path anyway. Dominique on the other hand, saw this as being too good of an opportunity to let go, so she quickly grabbed Meagan by the arm and headed up the path as well giggling and making funny sounds with her mouth as if she herself was running out of breath as well.

Noticing her, Waverly replied "I see, you find Sidney's comment to be amusing too!"

Trying hard not to laugh, she answered, "But you have to admit, "The Nasty Girl" has a point. You will be turning the big "4-0" soon. Isn't that considered up there or do they call that over the hill?"

"I'm not receiving that," *Waverly shouted as she walked even faster. Then when she finally reached the top of the hill, making it her business to pass Sidney first, she turned around to catch her breath and added,*

"And just for the record…, Meagan close our ears!"

"Not this time, I think I want to hear this!"

Well suit yourself! Anyway… as for you and "Miss Nasty," both of you can go straight to Hell!"

Laughing, Dominique replied, "I knew Judge Judy was coming out of her mouth with that!"

Nodding in total agreement, Meagan added, "Well that is Girlfriend's response to just about everything that manages to crawl up under her skin. But past all that, we know that's just Waverly! What I'm confused about is… Why on earth are you guys referring to Sid as "The Nasty-Girl?" I mean everybody knows she's a little loose."

"Oh, now I'm loose!"

"Well if the Gucci fits!" chuckled Waverly.

"That's not what I meant! I was just saying that you normally have many choices…"

"Save it my Sister in Christ! I'm certain all of us know your intent. Anyway, I first noticed Sid's breath was a little tart so… Okay, my bad… let's just say it didn't have that Colgate aroma!"

Next thing you know everyone including Sidney Sharpe was laughing like hyenas… Finally, with her belly hurting just as mush as her over-worked legs, Waverly shouted,

"Stop…Stop it Dominique?"

"You're crazy as shit! I'm not sure who is worse – you with your sidebar humor or Meagan with her need to be nice while cutting you! I believe this whole thing stared when the health addict and the "Nasty Girl" I mean Sid were debating about how many times a day healthy individuals brush their teeth. My guess is – Sid... maybe she brushes once or twice..."

"Once!" shouted Dominique.

"Okay counselor.... Anyway, it's safe to assume that Dominique disagrees. Then Sid asked me how often I brush my teeth within a day – I mean really!!"

"And just like most of our judicial rulers and their evasive opinionated comments, she said "enough", Dominique added with her lips turned upside down.

Shaking her head, Sidney replied, "That's not an answer!"

"Sure it is!"

"Maybe a less convincing one..."

"So what are your thoughts Counselor? How often should one brush and floss daily?" Meagan asked as she glided her tongue across her pearly whites. Shaking her head, Dominique answered, "Come on now any hygienist will tell you to brush at least three times daily and floss after each meal unless you're nasty like some of us!"

"I see that's why you guys keep calling Sidney out of her name."

"So what do you think Meagan?" Dominique asked.

First Meagan smiled, revealing her pearly whiles as well. Then she said without hesitation,

"I'm sorry Nasty-Girl, I mean Sid I totally agree with Diamond. How could you stand all that buildup and junk on your teeth? That is a lil' nasty..."

"Forget it! Forget the whole thing! I am okay with me and that's enough. You all are too serious," Sidney shouted as she continued down the path. "But just so you know, there are times when I brush more than once or twice as you call it!"

With her brows raised, Waverly whispered, "Oh lord, I'm afraid to ask..."

But eager to know, Dominique shouted, "When – When, tell us all!"

And with a smirk on her face Sidney softly said, "When else... before and after I give "Head".

"Oh that was gross!"

"Well you wanted to know kid-O!"

"I just cannot believe she just said that! Beyond nasty! Crazy prefers a clean mouth before and after sucking a "Dick" as opposed to just because..." whispered Waverly as she shook her head.

Now that was not right. But who's to say it was wrong either? Sounds healthy to me. I guess only a true friend can dare to step to one in such a manner. Anyway, after the giggles subsided and the minutes continued to pass them by, the girls managed to finish their daily work-out. Afterwards, they all sat under their favorite Maple tree, swapping horror stories and of course, many-many suggestions as to which none of them were truly willing to follow. And, along with the many suggestions everyone agreed, including Miss Sharpe, that it was indeed time to change her look and yes, get a relaxer. Sidney had been wearing her hair natural for well over three and a half years. So when the subject came up for her to go back to straightening her hair permanently, Girl unwillingly agreed. In fact, she thought "Maybe Cher was right..." But of course with Sidney being Sidney, she had to have her friends believe she had already come to the very same conclusion several weeks ago – all on her own. In fact, Girl even exaggerated the story by claiming to have an appointment later that same day. I believe her exact words were,

"It's beyond me how I never knew I would need my hair done or even want to change my look for my Mom's farewell..."

"So did you and your sister decide on a date?" Dominique asked as she thought to herself, *I just hope it doesn't fall on the same day Hannah arrives...*

"Kinda sought of ... We were hoping for Friday. You know, have everything on one day. I don't want to draw things out..."

"Too bad you're not Jewish like Meagan. If you were, you could avoid all of the hoopla."

"Yeah, but "us" black folks... we have to write an entire screen play and then act it out line by line," Waverly chuckled as she shook her head.

"But you know what gets me? People you haven't seen in eons all come together... I think to be nosy, smothering you with false pretenses of how they're (now) here for you, only to once again vanish within days of the burial."

"Damn Counselor! You certainly have a point..."

"Well, all that may be true, but still at times like these; we need our families even if we're not familiar with them all. Besides, without weddings and funerals when do you get a chance to meet them?" Sidney whispered as her eyes watered.

At that moment, everyone could see that Sidney was beginning to re-live the pain she felt when her Mother died. It has only been twenty-four hours since they last spoke. And although she tried to stay busy, everything reminded her of Phyllis Maple.

"No more wake-up calls" she whispered as the tears rolled down her cheeks.

"I'll call first thing everyday. It's not like I get much sleep with the girls anyway..."

"Yeah, I can call as well. You know I'm an early riser!"

Then they all looked at Waverly.

"Well, when you call Sidney - call me too! I have a hard time in the mornings..."

The tense moment was broken by their laughter...

"Okay Sid, why don't you let one of us accompany you to the Salon? You know... cheer you on while you're becoming a new woman," suggested Dominique.

Knowing that there was never really an appointment to begin with, Sidney uttered,

"No-no-no-no- that's not necessary!"

"Sure it is! You just said in times like these we need one another. Although Meagan could truly use a trim or something, I'm sure she can't possibly stay out all day. And I really have to go in and work on a case, so that leaves you Judge Judy. I'm sure you of all people can make-up something to get out of court today..."

"I believe you have me mixed up with yourself Counselor."

"Anyway, I'll go fight with the sleaze-balls. Meagan can go do whatever one does with two babies, two dogs, a horney white man and an over protective mother. And speaking of mothers, did Katehrine ever find out anything else about your biological parents? I mean that could really be the mystery behind Nia's illness... And to be frank, I'm not at all surprised. I've seen some strange things!"

"Okay Counselor, you've made your point! You go from one thing to another! I'm sure if Meagan's found out anything else about whatever's going on with her private life, she would have shared it! So, enough said! Sid why don't you swing pass and pick me up on your way to the salon? In the mean time, I'm going home. I am expecting an important call," Waverly said as she signaled her friends' good-bye.

And with that said, the other three quickly followed and went their merry little ways also. Well at least two out of three... Unknowingly and to Mrs. Tyler's surprise, Mr. Tyler would not be waiting with open arms alone. Katherine with her need to overreact and obsess over just about any and everything pertaining to Meagan Simone (A.K.A) MeMe, was there waiting as well. You'd think by now even she, given the facts, would be the first to provide Meagan with all the space she need to work things through. But, then what am I saying... Don't most mothers usually try to run their children's lives, grown up or otherwise? Well anyhow, seconds before Meagan's foot hit the front steps, both Albert and Costello were at the window panting hard and wagging their tails excited to see her. Then when her key made that distinctive sound in the lock as the doorknob turned, Drake also noticed his lovely wife was home and shouted,

●●●●

here she is! It's about time!"

66T *Now where have I heard that before? And why is it usually the first thing that rolls off of the tongue of most humans? It's almost as if you are expected to do what someone else wants at any given moment. I mean, did she not leave a note? And last I checked, Meagan's well over thirty years of age... Anyway, since Drake felt the need to open the door seconds before*

Meagan had opened it for herself, Girl naturally stumbled in over the stoup.

"Where have you been all morning and why on earth didn't you wake me?"

"Excuse me? Well good morning to you too dear..."

Then Katherine walked in...

"Hello Mother, long-time no see..."

"Meagan, don't change the subject... Why would you just up and leave me and the twins? I mean this is totally inexcusable... especially given Nia's condition! And how about the fact that you worried the hell out of your Mother and me!"

"MeMe Drake is right. You should have at least told him before you left."

"Okay hold on! I left you a note, sweetheart, right here ... Well, it *was* here earlier..."

Then she looked over at her dog, Costello, knowing that his favorite snack is paper...

"Did you eat Mommy's note?"

"Come on Baby, stop blaming our dog for your inability to be considerate of anyone other than yourself"

"Inability... who's being inconsiderate now? I did leave you a note! Besides, I only went to the park with the Girls for our morning run."

"Oh my Lord MeMe – did you really think you were ready for that?"

"Well Mother, I wouldn't have gone if I didn't think so," Meagan said as he kissed Drake on the lips then proceeded up the staircase looking for her twin daughters.

Shaking his head in disbelief, Drake asked his Mother-in-Law if she could possibly talk some sense into his wife. So honoring his wishes, Katherine followed Meagan up the staircase, down the end of the hall to the twins' room. There she found Meagan not checking on the twins as she thought, but looking herself up and down in the mirror as if there might have been a little truth to her statement after all.

"Are you looking for something?" Katherine said as she made her presence known.

Startled by her Mother's voice, Meagan quickly answered, "No, of course not! What is there to look for? Some ugly stretch marks?"

"Now there's a question I have no answer to. You see, I have never had a child the old fashion way. In fact, I've never gotten past the first trimester. So after the forth miscarriage, your Father and I thought it best to stop trying to conceive all together. After praying to God so many times for a healthy child of our own, I started becoming bitter and resentful, thinking he didn't find me worthy."

"You never told me that Mother"

"What was there to tell? All I know is that when we found you, we fell in love. You were simply breathtaking."

"What do you mean found me? Great choice of words Mother! Just say the first thing that pops into your head! Why not! You conveniently wait until I'm all grown-up, damn near forty with children of my own to even mention this tiny little fact – I'm not yours! And now you're not even selective with what you say! You say you found me! Way to go Mother! This is too much…"

"Me-Me! First off, I've always viewed you as my gift from God. Never once have I regretted the way you came into our lives. Back then, it was so hard to adopt a healthy white baby, let alone request a gender preference. Understand I had my concerns in the beginning… So, I went to the church for guidance! But, Father Murphy assured us that there would be no one to come for you. So we asked God to forgive us for never taking you to the authorities and basically moved on with our lives. After the first year, we told our families that we adopted a beautiful baby girl and gave you our name. I found out about the bloodline disorder within weeks of having you and convinced myself that it would be best to keep it from your Father. He had enough to deal with back then. You never got sickly so, I never recorded it. I changed doctors and that was that."

"This is all so much to take in… I guess it has to be true. I'm not yours and Daddy's… So then – who's child am I Mother? This is just so crazy! So now what? I can't just pretend none of this has happened. You couldn't have thought that! What about my real parents?"

"Theodore and I – *are* your real parents' young lady!"

"Not according to my blood work!"

Then Katherine started to cry. It was obvious that Meagan's choice of words was hurtful and inconsiderate and she saw no need to apologize. Her thoughts were, My entire life has been a lie!

Now before you take sides, know that all of Meagan's life – she has been taught to tell the truth no matter what the consequences. Now thirty-six years later, who will pay the price for this unspoken tale? Indeed something will be sacrificed, but what or who?

"Okay, maybe that did come out wrong. I really didn't mean to be hurtful, to you or anyone else for that matter. It's just… it's just that I'm so angry Mother. How could you wait so long to trust me with the truth? I don't understand…"

"Me-Me I can't make you understand what was going on back then or how we felt. What I do know is… I was very much afraid. I practically swore to Theodore that they would take you away from us if we reported finding you. We didn't have much money then and I believed strongly, that if you were taken into foster care, a wealthy couple would have been considered more suitable."

"All right, all right… But did you really find me? I mean like on a stoop or something?"

"That's not important. I've always believed you found us."

"You're something old lady… I suppose that's why I love you as much as I do… But, can I ask you something and will you be totally honest with me?"

"Of course MeMe."

"Do you know who my birth parents are? I mean it's not like I want to go to them and tell them who I am or anything like that. I just want to know…"

Thinking first about all the things that could possibly go wrong, Katherine tried to avoid answering her daughter's question. She said,

"You already know enough about your past. Why dig up old bones? You may want to think long and hard about what you're asking… All right, we know you and Nia have the trait. But look at you – you've gone your entire life healthier than anyone I know. Trust me, Nia will be just fine. I even believe I know where it came from and that loose end is...."

"Is what Mother? Tell me! Was it him or her?"

Hesitating, Katherine whispered, "It was your biological Father. And there's no need looking for him now... He died a few years after you were born. I'm so sorry Me-Me..."

"He died too Mother? Oh my God!" Meagan whispered as tears rolled down her face.

Quickly trying to comfort her, Katherine reached out her arms for Meagan to embrace her. The two just stood there holding each other for several seconds both crying softly. Nyle slept endlessly on her tiny little back while Nia had somehow managed to turn herself over onto her stomach lifting her head slightly just enough to capture the view.

"Incredible!" Meagan thought to herself when she noticed her daughter looking at them as if she knew just what they were discussing.

"Oh... You're right Mother. Nia will be just fine," she said as she went over to her daughter, picking her up with gratitude, knowing she too was her blessing from God.

What's that saying? "Some blessings come in small packages..."

Well what about the ones that arrive in rather large packages. Then there are those that show up at your feet unpackaged, bare, and literally stripped of forewarning. Now I'm certain by now you may be a tad confused, but to explain... I'm referring to "death." Sudden death. Now some might say, there's no blessing in that. I totally disagree. If you look past its face, you'll see that the blessing came long before the passing. Look at the life lead instead of the tears shed. Most who've died came first to leave something. And when that deed is done, then so is the life. I know it sounds selfish, but it's really a blessing. Surely it's customary to morn the dead, but I challenge you to rejoice the season spent.

●●●●

hat's what the late Miss Phyllis Maple wanted. In fact, she asked her daughters to make her going home service resemble a party rather than a morbid farewell. No traditional black and no flowers. I believe this woman wanted her girls to embrace what they shared as a family and not what was to believed missed from her passing. I know, easier said than done was the exact thing that came out of Sherian's mouth not seconds ago as she sat in their attorney's office trying to discuss her dead Mother's estate.

"So what's with the box?" *Sherian asked rudely, knowing Mr. Hoffman knew much more than he was saying.*

Shaking his head, he replied, "Sherian, I told you earlier to bring Sidney along. Then, I could explain the contents of your Mother's box. Now what I can tell you is, your Mother's entire life – who she was and why she did all of the things she did, rest in your hands. And, I'm afraid to say that your younger sister Sidney holds the key..."

Key... It's that damn watch, Sherian thought as she sat there looking completely blown away."

Several seconds passed so concerned, Mr. Hoffman asked Sherian if she was all right and if there was anything he could do. Sherian, angry to say the least, merely shook her head with contempt, got up very slowly from the chair and with her timely tunnel vision, seeing Mr. Hoffman's office door as the only thing that stood between her and her dead Mother's watch which Sidney kept within arm's reach.

"Not so fast Sherian, you can't just run off half cock and blinded on your own self-will! I believe we should first discuss your plans," he shouted just as her hand reached the door knob.

Turning her head back towards him with what looks like actual steam rising off her neck, she murmured, "Pardon me..."

Now tongue-tied, he tried to explain how it might be best to approach the situation, delicately with more thought in mind. Sherian went on to say how the contents in her Mother's mystery box as never left her mind. In fact, she now believed good old Mr. Hoffman has reluctantly revealed the whereabouts of the never seen key. I believe Miss Sherian knowing their issue, has her own plans to first examine the contents thoroughly before sharing them with Sidney.

"So that's – that! You're just going to take the watch from your sister without her knowledge?"

"Basically! And what do you know about the watch? My Mother has had that damn thing, I know since I had Sidney! You heard me correctly! Don't look so surprised... You too have been around that long. All of this has to do with Houston doesn't it? It's that money. I don't believe this..."

"Sherian, your Mother has already spelled out her entire estate to the letter. And I was placed in this position to ensure just that."

Looking straight through him, taking a death ear to every word, Sherian whispered, "You know all about the charade. Houston, the money, the store, the house, the fact that I was in love with him and all the years of unbearable silence! No need to lie now! You messed up when you mentioned the watch. No one else knew anything about it. And just like this damn box, Mother held on to her priceless watch as if her whole world depended on it."

"Why don't you come and sit down Sherian..."

"Not this time! I've been sitting much too long. And I'll take your silence as a "yes" to my gut feeling. Hah – it's funny... All of my adult life, Mother always insisted that I trust my inner most self. "Trust your guts, Cher" were here exact words. She would say there lays the uncontaminated truth. Some truth! I just wish she would have shared that with me when I first fell in love with Houston and had our baby girl Sidney. You know back then, I had this antique porcelin doll. It was a shade darker than me and I had never seen anything more beautiful. Houston gave her to me when I turned twelve. Even then, I knew I loved him. So I named her Sidney."

Then Sherian started to cry...

"When Mother found out I was pregnant and that I had been secretly sleeping with Houston, she went on a rampage. I'd never seen her like that up to that point. And that was when she swore to me I would never raise my child as my own. Hours after I had given birth, she took my baby and sent me away to boarding school – claiming it was for the best. Best.... Bull! Trusting her, I went without question. It wasn't until I returned a year later for the Holidays that I learned she named the baby "Sidney" and claimed her as her own. Houston's Dad, my Mother's employer who was white by the way, sent him practically across the country to attend college. The money which I never wanted was just a buffer for all the lies told. As for the wealthy Houston's, they have been living happily ever after. Mother's gone, leaving her blameless. Houston, last I heard was married with children. Our only daughter together knows nothing of this tale. And I'm left here alone with zero support to attempt to explain this shit! So you tell me, with your loss for words useless self, what to do?!"

Sitting back on his cherry wood desk, Mr. Hoffman again had nothing to say. Wiping her eyes, Sherian grabbed her coat hanging from the horseback and proceeded to walk out the door. In her mind, there was no need to look back. All of her answers which had been there all along were staring her right in the face. There would be no other way, no short cut, nothing left to do but tell Sidney that SHE – not Phyllis Maple – is her biological Mother.

Unfortunately for Sherian though, she's going to have to push past those refreshed, unresolved feelings that are now beginning to revisit her.

"Oh no you don't! Not this time! I'm going to find Sidney and nothing will stop me from telling her who I really am this time! Not Mother nor that false disbelief! To hell with the money and the Houston's! I will not live another day with this lie standing between me and my only daughter. It's time to stop myself from continuing this lie. May God forgive me…"

Well I guess that's that! You know… it's funny how things can get so backed-up. It's like only so much can be put into any one thing. And when the rest is forced in, it overflows.

● ● ● ●

*A*nyway, *Waverly Corine is now sitting in the bay window of her beautiful kitchen over looking the hot tub connected to the heated pool she and Vincent had built less than five years ago to make their mini-mansion paradise at home. Some paradise! I guess not all story book romances last forever. Unfortunately though, that feeling known as pain has a way of never really vanishing completely. It's true, unseen feelings begin with a thought. No matter how old the mind reminds the body just how bad it felt, way back then… Literally erasing all the time lapsed in between… Making it as fresh as baked bread straight out of the oven. So I guess in Vincent's case, reluctant* *to do just what he has always done which is convert back to familiar behavior after being forgiven time after time. Waverly's continued feelings of hurt and disbelief in their marriage won't allow her to rest. So now as she sips her morning coffee, Girl watches her cell phone with anticipation waiting for Keith's call.*

"That's quite all right. I'll show you," she said just as her cell phone vibrated signaling her that it was about to ring.

Glancing at the caller ID first noticing it was indeed the same number as the night before, Missy tried to answer rather calmly. Not!

"Good Morning Mr. Sheppard – How are things going? Or is it too premature to ask? I hope you didn't run into a problem! That was you yesterday... here at my home...wasn't it?"

Grinning from ear to ear, Keith answered, "Well Good Morning to you... And yes, we are making progress... and no – it's not too soon to ask. There are no problems and yes that was me at your home yesterday. Now, can we slow down and "Keith" sounds better than "Mr. Sheppard." I'm really not that old..."

"Okay, but on one condition."

"Name it..." he said chuckling.

"First, take that smile off of your face. I find it very hard to see humor in infidelity. You couldn't possibly imagine how hard these last few days have been for me."

Hesitantly he replied, "How did... my apologies. It's just that in my line of work, I'm always the bearer of bad news. So when I have none, I try not to take myself so seriously."

"Well then, maybe I should be the one to apologize. You know when I was a little girl, my Grandmother would always say, "Be careful what you pray for because you just might get it."

"Are you having doubts about the investigation?"

"No, not at all! It's just... how can I say this...wondering and doing nothing can keep a person like me hopeful. In a sense, a small part of me thinks that maybe things will get better. Maybe he'll see what a prize I really am. Maybe he'll stop before it's too late."

"But then once you know, then what? You two have been married for quite some time. I'm sensing that this is familiar territory for you. Am I right?"

"More than you know... more than you know... So in a way, this could be my passport out of Hell!"

"Okay then... on that note, let's get down to the business at hand.

Your Dr. Vincent Zachary Simmons is most definitely up to something – in most cases...someone. Just to bring you up to date, let's see... Where is it? Okay, here we are! As you are already aware, we tagged the "Good Doctor" at your home yesterday morning, placed all the necessary bugs into position and then proceeded to follow him most of the day."

"Bugs! Huh, I would surely like to be the fly on the wall! I can't wait until we catch his black-ass right in the midst of his mess. And, I want it all on film..."

"Oh, no doubt! By the time I'm done with him, I'll not only have him on film, there will also be audio tapes for a voice match, fingerprints to place the "Good Doctor" at the scene, his DNA and the accomplice's DNA to show that you were not a participating party, and a reputable eye witness just for the fun of it..."

"Good! Serves him right!"

"I believe 'Tony the Tiger' said it better... GREAT!"

Well, the next thing heard was laughter on both ends. Waverly somehow, contrary to her belief, finally saw the humor in infidelity. While Keith managed to move a little closer to her, emotionally as evidenced by the smile he brought to her face. Continuing, he went on explaining Vincent's weak reasoning for being in Downtown Baltimore. But at the same time he tried not to disclose any misinformation about the alleged money left for the presumed Mistress, "Payton Von-Lee." Cunningly, Keith toyed with his wording until finally Waverly demanded the uncut version. And with his arms twisted behind his back, Keith told what he believed to be the truth...

●●●●

"T he Good Doctor was photographed leaving an envelope filled with cash at the front desk of the Harbor Courts Hotel for a Miss Von-Lee."

Surprised, Waverly replied... "Von-Lee! That's Payton... I don't believe this... Now he's banging the help!"

"So, you're familiar with Payton?"

"Of course I'm familiar with Payton. She's the in-house Manager at my condo development. But she's always been so respectful... It's seems unlikely picturing her with Vincent... But then I guess you never really know people – huh?"

"Well, let's slow down for a moment. We don't want to draw any wrong conclusions. Besides, the money could have been left for any number of reasons."

"I doubt that very seriously. My husband has been known to buy his "women on the side" anything from fine jewelry to fine art. He has even taken them to some of the very same places we've gone. Payton also resides at the same condo which Vincent insisted we keep for get away purposes only. But you know what? I always felt it was something more..."

Believing Waverly's instincts to be true, Keith remained silent as he took a deep breath then blew it out very hard. Hearing this, Waverly knew just what Keith was thinking and trying not to be emotional, she quickly replied,

"I'll tell you what... make it your top priority to nail his ass as soon as possible! The sooner, the better!"

"You have my word on that."

Waverly, unable to hold it together any longer and without saying good-bye just hung up the phone as her eyes watered rapidly. Remembering their vows and all of the many times Vincent swore to be faithful, Girl could only shake her head in utter contempt. Between recalling his past indiscretions, terminating her marriage, her best friend's mother dying and turning forty, she thought... This will not be easy!

But then something remarkable happened. Waverly, for a brief moment remembered the unconditional love shared between her and her best friends. She reflected way back to the night when they all swore to be friends until the end. She remembered the laughter, the hugs and all of the many times they have held on to each other in seasons such as these. And knowing the fat lady had not begun to sing, a smile came across her face as those salty tears rolled down her cheeks...this time switching to tears of joy and great appreciation.

And right on cue, as always, Sidney pulled up the driveway honking her horn like a bat straight out of hell. Knowing it was her, Waverly quickly rinsed her coffee mug, grabbed her sunglasses and purse then headed for the door. Sidney, unsure if Waverly had even heard her, continued sounding off as if her life depended on it. I believe girl was just excited about the idea of having another brand new sports car. Talk about "vanity..." Anyway, when she finally got to Waverly's front door, she noticed a bug resting on her windshield. Luckily, it was not I! Well before crazy even put the car in the parked position, she flipped on the automatic wipers to assist the poor creature in getting off her new windshield. Now, by this time, Waverly was standing on her front step grinning and shaking her head at her hopeless young friend.

●●●●

"Little lady," she yelled. "You surely got it bad! I thought you were kidding about buying a second sports car!"
Ignoring Waverly's comment, Sidney turned off the wipers, put the car in park and then got out with a tissue to check the windshield for any smudges. Still searching for a reasonable answer, Waverly added,

"Come on now Sid, I'm serious? Why have two vehicles that are so much alike?"

Shaking her head, Sidney answered, "You really don't know, do you?"

"No – enlighten me!?"

Eagerly, she replied, "Every woman over the age of thirty-five should have either two really great lovers or two extremely fast cars!"

"What?"

"Think about it. Two is always better than one. It's the law of the land as far as I'm concerned."

"Oh, I see. So, if you were a man it would be a bike and a bitch."

Tongue-tied for the first time in a long time, Sidney had no come-back. She thought, "Waverly Corrine must be really fed up with Vincent stepping outside of their marriage this time. Maybe an afternoon of beautifying ourselves at Colours & Cutz is way over due for more reasons than one…" So she quickly changed the subject and insisted that they hurry to the salon to get pampered. Waverly, trying to lighten up, said something about she would much prefer a total stranger having his way with her over an afternoon at a salon watching her girlfriend relax her nappy hair any day of the week. Sidney, snapping back to her witty self replied and I quote…

"No, I think maybe you've just had the same old "Dick" for twenty years too long "Boo!"

Knowing she'd been fingered once again, Waverly gladly agreed by giving her girlfriend a high five shouting, "Well, maybe you're right "Boo-Boo!"

Maybe you're right Boo-Boo???… Is this the same woman who has for the past twenty years, lived by the parable, "Image makes the "man" slash "woman" in this case?" Now she's come to the realization that "two heads are better than one." What about the phrase, "Two wrongs don't make a right" or does that only apply when Judge Simmons is addressing known offenders. Talk about contradictions…

Well since the cat was already creeping out of the bag, Waverly immediately pulled the clip from her hair running her fingers through to her scalp as if suddenly she had an irresistible itch. Then with her favorite hairbrush being conveniently in her purse, she reached in, removed it and began to brush her hair back into a ponytail. Next, Girl adjusted the seat back slightly and tossed her purse on the seat in the back. Waverly then, reminding herself to think happy thoughts sat there and seriously contemplated the idea of being with another man the entire drive over to the salon. Sidney, for what it was worth, just played it sort of cool from the outside. She knew what it was like…sleeping with the enemy. And although the feelings weren't always pleasurable, in her mind, rule of thumb – 101 insist that living with one's closest friend while she's going through an emotional roller coaster measured far worse on its best days. Besides, she knew Waverly was serious this time and there's nothing worse than laughing at a scorned woman …especially if the laughter doesn't come from her first. So, Girl just giggled to herself about her girlfriend's theoretical conclusion for the duration of their drive. That's funny…

I once heard someone say, "Although it may be a mistake to live with one's closest friend, the true mistake comes from never finding one."

• • • •

*W*ell *as the minutes passed by and upon reaching their destination, they both sort of gave one another a look, suggesting, "Okay, let's just get this over with." So after simultaneously inhaling and exhaling from the moment of excitement, Waverly Corrine and Sidney Sharpe proceeded kind of quickly up the long redbrick walkways which lead to the 8ft double stained-glass doors that carved out the entrance of the upscale beauty salon.*

"Well, this is special. Maybe I should have worn something more flattering for the occasion."

Waverly uttered as the stained glass doors opened automatically. Taking her by the hand and pulling her through them, Sidney replied,

"Now that's a new one. I didn't know flattering was even on your list of things to do!"

"Oh don't let the robe and twenty years of marriage fool you! It's on the list! Indeed, it's most definitely on the list. In fact, it's right next to you relaxing your nappy bush."

"See… this is why I choose very carefully in keeping your company before the sun rises and long after she sets. You my friend, lack tongue control."

"Why… Because I'm honest with you?"

"No, it's not that. It's your infamous timing. You know, like taking charge of things without being appointed…trying so hard to run our lives simply because you're older. And since we're being honest, personally, I think you waited way too long for Vincent's sorry ass to change."

"Oh, now that was blunt!"

Luckily, before Waverly could chew into Sidney's you know what, Rebecca the Salon receptionist with great enthusiasm said, "Hey there! How you-all doin today? My name is Rebecca. Welcome to "Colours & Cutz! Now how may I help you ladies today?

Surprised herself, Sidney simply smiled at the woman disregarding the name tag on Rebecca's jacket, labeling her as the receptionist slash assistant manager thinking, "This can't be so!"

• • • •

averly, proving Sidney's previous statement to be true quickly leaned over towards the counter and whispered,

"You are joking right?"

"Why gracious no, this is a beauty salon where we's here specialize in total makeovers for the woman of today. And you all are most definitely looking as though…"

"Looking – the only thing I'm noticing is a tired…"

Waverly went on to explain just as Sidney nudged her signaling her good friend to take a time-out. Then Sidney cattily apologized for any misconceptions and told Rebecca of her appointment with the one and only "Clay" their most favored Senior Stylist. But still quite confused, only understanding the tail end of Waverly's comments, Rebecca smiled politely and replied, "He'll be right with you-all…"

Annoyed slightly, but then amused at the same time, Waverly with her nose turned up tipped over to the waiting area which set in the middle of the salon, giving her the perfect view of everything and almost everyone. Needless to say, if Girl had a clear view so did most of the staff. And with her brushed down picture perfect pony-tail, posing as a hair style, Waverly was mistaken rather quickly as a potential client in need of a make-over. In fact when "La-La," Clay's assistant, first took notice of her. He told Clay to and I quote, "Stop the presses! Sade is in the house in need of a color and cut." Clay merely responded with a giggle. Then he and La-La both went over to greet her with the assumption that she was Sidney…their next appointment. Sidney, at that time, was still at the front desk sampling their retail lotions when Rebecca pointed out Clay and La-La. Eager to get started, she too went over to greet them.

"I knew I should have brought my camera to work today. Well I guess the camera phone will have to suffice," La-La said as his way of saying hello.

Not being certain if his comment was intended to be negative, or otherwise, Waverly just looked at them and said,

"I believe you have me confused with my Girlfriend…"

Well before things could get even more twisted, Sidney came over with her over curly locks and a big smile introducing herself as their next appointment, who was a little hesitant of a change. She introduced Waverly as her partner in crime and Waverly then smiled. La-La immediately, with his short gloves on, started going through Sidney's hair mumbling something about this taking all day since Sidney was in need of the works. He wondered out loud why it has taken her so long to come back to reality. Sidney, knowing that this was just salon talk coming from the mouth of a young babe who was also gay, smiled in amusement. So reassuring her, Clay placed his muscular arm around Sidney's shoulder escorting her to the prep-station in the rear of the salon. La-La attempting to patch things up with Waverly politely apologized for joking about her homemade hair style. In fact before switching away, he said something about her greenish-gray eyes bringing back that ponytail hairstyle, he some how figured was still "frozen in time." Bothered just a bit, Waverly sat there mumbling,

"Frozen in time... The only thing I see stuck in time is that paste-down hair style you're wearing confused whether or not it wants to be finger waved or straight..."

But then something totally unbelievable happened... How can I say this? Well, after rolling those greenish-gray eyes around her already agitated head and finally reopening them, Waverly saw the vision of a female fire-ball straight up from hell. Focusing, she thought to herself... "It can't be... It just can't be..." But, it was...Out of the hundreds of salons available for Sidney to get her makeover done, she unknowingly chose the one "Colours and Cutz" who unbeknown to her was really the one and only "Strands" owned by none other than Tony and Gina Hernandez, the two individuals Waverly vowed to get back at one day when she was older and wiser... They stole her innocence and she has never forgiven or forgotten them.

●●●●

"**B**itch...it's you!" *Waverly uttered under her breath just as her stomach began to turn. One would think now is not the time to get ill, but she did. Who knows, maybe seeing one's past in the present is all too much for any human being to handle... and first things first... When your stomach turns, it's either time to sit on the commode or throw one's head over it. Poor Girl, the way she slid off that sofa and switched harder than La-La to the ladies room... Let's just say she definitely brought attention to* *herself. I once heard someone say, "Regardless of where you are in life, you never forget who you owe or who you slept with." So just as her hand reached the doorknob of the ladies room, Waverly's head turned slightly counter-clockwise at the exact moment Gina was finishing up with Rebecca. Therefore giving Mrs. Hernandez precisely enough time needed to recognize Waverly as well. Talk about thunder and bolts... or was it just nasty gestures going through the veins of a perpetrator/child molester. Well upon entering the single bathroom and managing to lock the door behind herself, so she thought, a horrible rain of sweat came over her. Exhausted and caring less if she was unable to get to the toilet; Waverly expelled what seemed like everything she had eaten that day and the day before in the sink. What a mess! And with the water running in an effort to force it down, that almost seemed to make matters even worse.*

"Oh shit!" *she said when she noticed the sink filling up. Fortunately after a few seconds, the smelly vomit began to dissipate.*

"I can't believe this shit is happening again. I've got to pull myself together. That was then and this is now..." *she whispered as she washed and rinsed her face thinking back to the last encounter she had with the Hernandez's.*

It was the night of their first so-called year anniversary of sleeping together. Gina was excited more than ever this particular time because she would finally get her wish of having a threesome with Waverly and her soon to be husband – slash partner in crime, Tony Hernandez. Now I'm not sure if Waverly had saved up enough money or simply got tired of being their trick after hours... Whichever the case, Girl was having second and third thoughts about this... But there she was again, all dressed-up in one of Gina's home made nasty costumes, looking in the mirror seeing herself this time as the prostitute she had become. From the bleach–blonde hair to the overly done make-up, resembling a drag queen, even she found it some what difficult remembering who she was underneath of it all...

"I can't do this... not any more," *she whispered as she felt her stomach began to turn again just as it had done before when she saw herself as being vulnerable and out of control. Seeing this but caring not the least, Gina walked up behind her stroking her hair slightly annoyed by Waverly's hesitance and said,*

"Dere ya go again acting like a little girl. Ya tink by now ya would enjoy our times together and stop letting your immaturity upset your stomach. You are in college now after all...soon to be dis great attorney; you should be able to handle... You will do dis and love it, especially cause I pay for your time missy! Comprenda!"

Gina then placed both of her hands on Waverly's shoulders, squeezed her tightly while pulling close enough to kiss her and said very nastily... "Ya see Corrine my dear, I know you like and wish to please me. So dis is why I will forgive you, but next time... you will regret such language."

"No Miss G, this time I say no. This is not who I am and I will never grow to love this sorted situation with you and that perverted boyfriend of yours. I don't need your money anymore. I don't even want it anymore. Besides, this whole fucking shop is probably a front for one of those child pornography things cause it's sure is hell not enough clientele to keep the doors open!"

Well insulted by Girl's comment, Gina raised her hand up high back-handing Waverly across the face so hard, it knocked poor thing into the mirror causing it to break. Hurt and feeling the warmth of blood sliding down the back of her head, Waverly with her little self, leaped up on Gina with her knees in her chest forcing Missy to the floor, choking her until her flesh tone was pink. And although seeing Girl's face turn right before her eyes, yet still so far removed from the consequences of what could be, it took Girl's own tears to shower her face before she could snap back and realize just what she was doing. Gasping herself and too shocked by her own reactions, Waverly then began to cry out angrily as she slowly removed her hands from Gina's throat.

One would think now's the time to back off...Not Gina... she thought it was best to threaten young Waverly. What she didn't realize is that although Waverly was strong and very bright, once her mind was made up, there was no turning back. Granted she was a bit green a year ago when she agreed to being tricked after hours...thinking easy money. But still, in doing that, she managed to build up a resistance to pain and pleasure at the same time while hardening her heart which allowed her to fear no one. In other words Gina's threats had no hold over her this time. Waverly was leaving and cared even less about the consequences. In fact she told Gina, if their paths were to ever cross again, she'd kill her for sure... Well okay if that's true – why in the devil is Waverly now in the commode tripping? Could it possibly be the fear of the inevitable? Whichever the case, one thing is for sure, Girl needs to come back to reality right about now because her "Daymare" is standing directly behind her. Tis true! Gina, with her pretend to be concerned nasty self, has once again violated Waverly's space by letting herself into the ladies room with her master key. Now I'm not sure about you but the phrase "Death Wish" comes to mind...

"I see some-tings never change... you still lettin da intensity of da moment upset your poor little stomach," Gina *said as she stroked Waverly's ponytail. Now contrary to what should be Waverly's natural reaction, knowing from the bottom of her guts that the woman that stood there was somehow just the opposite. Girl simply shook her head while opening her eyes and said with much certainty,*

"You know long ago when I was a little girl; my Grandmother would constantly say to me that the scent from bad works will always linger even in fresh air. And the only way to get rid of its stench is to be at peace with yourself."

Laughing, Gina replied, "Seems to me your Grandma-ma was a stupid old woman who had little or no meaning to the tings she said...unless of course she was referring to your lack of ability to control your insides Corrine."

Now even more pissed, trying desperately not to retaliate physically, (meaning, bang her in the mouth), Waverly turned around, looked Gina dead in the eyes and said,

"No, actually she was a very wise old lady because you see... even your shit for brains, ass-wipe self understood that!"

But actually, Gina was quite tickled by Waverly's slurr. In fact she just stood there in total silence lusting over the idea of having her once again, now that they were both more mature. So without hesitating, blocking any means of escape, Gina slid one hand slowly down her own skirt seductively fondling her "you know what." Then if that wasn't rude enough, she pulled out her nasty fingers and wiped them across her lips just before rubbing them all over her previously altered breast. And too, knowing she was being totally inappropriate but loving it, she merely smiled and said,

"So, how bout it Corrine? Once again for old times sake?"

Well Waverly, who was already pushed to the edge, was now reluctant to even recall the oath she had taken. Girl ...without thinking pushed her so hard that in order for Gina to keep her balance, she had to use her elbows to brace herself against the hollow walls of the lady's room. Naturally, this was heard in the work area. But wanting to rid herself from all of the shame, she believed Gina and Tony had left her with all of these years through massive manipulation causing her panic attacks, the only words she could put together were,

"Well if you're referring to me whipping your Spanish ass, why not!"

Still amused with a sneaky kind of look on her face, Gina straightened herself up as if nothing had happened... then moved close enough to whisper,

"No actually I meant licking it..."

Unknowingly to Waverly's surprise before she was even able to blink, Gina grabbed Waverly's arms pushing her back against the sink, kissing her right on the mouth forcing her tongue almost down her throat. Wrong move! Well how about the phase, "Carry-out"... Confused? Then pretend for a moment that you are Waverly. Your arms are pinned down and outside of kneeing her in between the legs taking a chance of missing, knowing you want her off of you. Not to mention her scent is going right up your nose while the taste of her body fluids are now in your mouth thanks to her "vulnerable" tongue resting on yours. What do you do? Well Waverly decided to bite her until Gina released her or until the taste of her blood was in her mouth. Therefore knowing she had hurt Gina just enough to give her the upper hand and to finally finish what was started nearly twenty years ago. Poor Gina, you could almost here her cursing Waverly through the intense screams. And foreseeing one's natural response, Gina immediately released Waverly's arms and began scratching her right in the face. Waverly still determined to hold on... used even more force, kneeing her and stomping on her opened-toe shoes while desperately reaching for anything to hit Gina with. Well, the knocks got harder and the screams were even louder. The staff was without a doubt convinced that there was a fight going on in the ladies room. But with the door locked and the only key on the inside, confusion spread across the salon faster than burnt hair or a bounced check. In fact, Rebecca told a member of the staff that Miss "G" was indeed in there but the identity of the second or third person was unknown. Another suggestion was that it was most likely one of her mistreated tricks coming back for revenge. Hearing this, most of the clients began to leave unfinished. Sidney unable to do anything... expressed her concerns about locating Waverly, to her stylist Clay who was in the middle of applying her relaxer.

Not missing a beat, La-La immediately interrupted,

"You talking bout Sade?"

"Yes stupid, but don't call her that. Her name is..." Then Clay looked in the mirror at Sidney and she replied, "Judge Simmons."

Both surprised, Clay and La-La just looked at each other as if to say "oops"

Then La-La added, "Well, if I'd known she was a Judge and all like that, I would have at least said your honor or something to that effect!"

He was trying to patch things up in hopes of Sidney staying until her hair was finished after seeing all of the other stylist's clients leaving because of the commotion. Clay merely shook his head in an attempt to look concerned and said,

"Good help is so hard to find."

Meaning, La-La wasn't necessarily good help. Sidney just stared at him ready to get up and find Waverly. Seconds past and just as La-La had cleared the corner, out of sight, the sound from a shattered mirror went through the already disturbed "Little Shop of Horrors."

Well, like a "punk in boys town," La-La ran back around the corner very much excited and shouted "Damn this! It's time to bring in the troops! Somebody's whipping Miss "G's" ass and it's our duty to protect this establishment!"

"You need to calm down and stop scaring my client."

But before he could, the banging had stopped. The salon was silent for about a hair of a second just long enough to hear the door to the ladies room unlock. The staff and the few clients who were still there had their ears almost pressed against the door began to back away slowly, not knowing what to expect. La-La, with his need to know-self, switched back around the corner with a pair of Clay's sheers in one hand and Clay's cell phone in the other just in time to witness Waverly exit the ladies room first.

"Sade!" he shouted as Waverly spit out the remaining blood left in her mouth from Gina's tongue as she quickly exited the Salon...

Uncertain of Miss "G's" well being, La-La was the first in the ladies room to help Gina up from the floor. Noticing she was bleeding from the mouth, he quickly dialed "911." Gina knowing there would be more to lose than gain, meaning Tony's future was already at stake, grabbed the phone and threw it up against the wall shouting, "NO!"

Chapter Ten

Keeping

Secrets...

*N*ow... *the odds of keeping a secret, for what it's worth, I heard were slim to none. And the few that weren't discovered, never really existed at all. Think about it... A secret is only a secret until it's revealed to someone else. Once it's exposed, its value diminishes. So tell me, is the one you're holding on to worth more than what you stand to lose if it's ever revealed??? You know like the many lies told in this tangled tale. The list although unfortunate is so long, one couldn't help but wonder. Is there any truth to any of it?*

Take for example, the first lie told in "Common Lives." Katherine and Meagan... Now Katherine's version, however complex, claims there was no other way but to keep her daughter's true identity from everyone, including Meagan herself. And considering, just how hard it's been holding on to a lie of that nature, believing in your heart of hearts you'd lose your daughter. Who are we to say that her judgment and the time she chose to confess the truth was without empathy? For all we know, there could have been someone else as well turning the cards.

Think about it! In the very beginning when Meagan asked who she really was, Katherine called Father Murphy. Then, insisted to see him as if he knew more about Meagan's true identity than she did. Meagan on the other hand, just as many adopted people have, maintained a yearning desire to at least know the truth about her biological parents. Sounds believable to me... But then again, "I'm just a Fly on the wall..."

• • • •

*S*o, *back to the story at hand... And, what better place to continue... How about Katherine and all of the unanswered questions she posed to Father Murphy...*

"But with all due respect Father... What would you suggest I tell her? You of all people know how persistent she can be. And please forgive my saying this, but I cannot accept not one more of these church-tale lies of how my daughter ended up in your pew, less than three days old, thirty-seven years ago! We both know that *you know* exactly who left my Me-Me there! So maybe it's time for you to confess the truth. Tell me who she is!" Katherine said as she hung her head in disbelief.

But again, Father Murphy said nothing as he held the phone to his ear looking directly in the face of Meagan's biological mother. So Katherine with much certainty, repeated,

"Father, the choices have been made. You must now take your place as the leader of our Parish and force this cowardly woman to come forward. This can not be God's will for us!"

Now at that moment, Father Murphy stood there literally frozen. It was clear that this man of faith was torn between the two women; both of whom he swore to keep their secrets. Now one might say... how could that be?. Well allow me to explain...

Forty years ago, young Father Murphy, against the few blessings of his community, was selected to lead a small parish. And although the stakes were high, many sat patiently awaiting his failure. The young priest secretly made a vow to himself to uphold the rules of the parish and no matter what... never betray the trust of another. And be it may, the first couple of years were far too easy. You know, people coming into confession, laying down their souls, the young priest telling them to go in peace and basically never having to speak of it again. But, one evening just as Father Murphy had finished his prayers, he heard what sounded like a young girl in tears already behind the long dark curtains, in need of forgiveness. Not knowing to what extent, the self assured priest entered into a lifetime journey that would not only effect the sobbing girl, but another family and the church as well.

To be brief, the young girl confessed that she was the one who had left the newborn in a pew of the church in hopes that someone with less confusion in their hearts could care for her child. She went on to tell about the interracial relationship she had engaged with a young black man which in those times would forbid them from raising the child themselves. Therefore, believing their hands were tied, and trusting the church, young Sophia asked for forgiveness and swore to never return. Witnessing this, Father Murphy knew then that his not so complicated position was now compromised.

You see, a week ago to that very day, a young couple whom he had been praying with, came to him in secrecy sharing how God had answered their prayers by giving them a baby girl. Amazed, Father Murphy asked,

"How is this so?" *He knew of the four miscarriages and how rare the possibility was to adopt a healthy white baby.*

"It was God himself!" *Katherine stated as she explained how they had arrived early for Mass and found the newborn in a pew cooing in fresh linens with a sparkle in her eyes... waiting for them as well. Searching for reasoning, but clearly unsure of what to do, nothing was done. Well, almost nothing... Believing in their faith, Katherine literally begged the young Priest to never tell another soul. So when he found the young girl in confession and all of the puzzle pieces seemingly connected, he immediately went back to Theodore and Katherine and convinced them that no one would ever come for the child. Seems easy...*

But, then a few years passed and conveniently enough, Theodore and Katherine who were well liked members of their parish had no problem easily convincing the others of the adoption which had no legal binding to begin with. They figured they were out of the woods. But I once heard someone say, "What's the worst thing that could happen?" or was that a movie... Anyway, it happened... Young Sophia who was now of age, returned and with no desires to claim Meagan, asked for a refuge from the church... She spoke of her journey, told how Meagan's father had died and expressed her deep sorrow. She went on to explain how she wanted nothing more than to give back to the church for keeping her secret and finding a loving home for her baby girl. Simply taken back by Sophia's courage, the young priest took her in and like him; she became a part of the church. From cleaning it to eventually becoming a Nun, Sister Sophia after many years of commitment to the church giving back all she could while watching Meagan mature, ultimately earned the position of Mother Superior. And how awesome it was for her to stand back and secretly admire Meagan and Katherine's relationship as Mother and Daughter, knowing she too was part of that history. Talk about "Daymares!" Is she for real? I guess she is standing there, no doubt paralyzed. And what would one say... almost forty years later? Oh, I'm sorry Katherine. The cowardly woman you speak of is your own Mother Superior... Will someone simply end this and just "swat" me. Now she speaks....

●●●●

T ell her I'll meet with Meagan. Tell her we'll need a little time but I've agreed to meet with her."

Overhearing her soft spoken voice and agitated even more, Katherine said,

"Is she there now Father? I can't believe this... And to think I've trusted you all this time!"

"Your trust has always been in the Lord my child. When the time comes, Meagan shall have her meeting if she so desires. And to keep as such with our beliefs, neither you nor the birth Mother shall ever meet. So until we speak again..."

"Until we speak again...Father...."

The two then ended their call. True... there was a sense of relief in Katherine's heart, but still an equal amount of fear rested there as well. Her thoughts were, When will I tell my Me-Me, I've found her Mother.

Beats me! Babe! What's that saying ... To be or not to be a Mother.

And to think most women live for that...Yeah right! You know, right next to Romeo. But then again... for some women in or out of the closet... They long for Juliet!!! And speaking of closets, when on earth is Dominique Blake "coming out." You know, it's kind of hard to tell by the way she's sitting there biting her nails, clearly disassociated from her work. In fact, her mind was on a baby as well. Beyond that, how in the world was she going to explain her involvement with another woman to Meagan and Waverly, the two whom she believes expect more from her. So while Franklin tries to review their case load, Dominique's, as the songwriter sang, "Mind is on the other side of town" or better yet- in Japan...

"So how are you going to do this?" Franklin said.

Unavailable, Dominique answered, "I've decided that the best time to tell Meagan and Waverly I'm a Lesbian will be when we take Waverly out for her fortieth birthday celebration."

"Damn, I was referring to the Hernandez's. But if you've finally got up enough balls to say who Dominique Blake really is... Well then, good for you."

"I'm sorry Frankie, I should be thinking about work, which is how we eat..."

"Praise the Lord..."

"You are so crazy, but really... between trying to adopt a child and Hannah arriving on Friday which happens to be the same day we bury Momma Phyllis...It's been extremely difficult to keep my mind on any one thing, including this crazy case."

"But still, I remember when I told *my* girlfriends."

"What girlfriends, Franklin? I'm your only girlfriend."

"You see what I mean, they all left..."

"You are a fool and I'm trying to be serious."

"True – true that. And be it may, one stuffed shirt around here is more than enough. Besides, your parents are both dead. What in God's name will they do to you? Disown you! Or better, send you back to Jamaica! Gracious, all of that crap went out with the "Golf War.""

"I know – I know. But..."

"But nothing! Have you looked at yourself lately? You're over thirty-five, beautiful, smart and very successful. In my opinion, your so-called friends would be foolish to love you any less."

Almost convinced, Dominique added, "Yeah, you're probably right because Sidney didn't seem to care very much when she found out."

"So you see, there you have it! I like her anyway..."

"Don't you start Franklin Lewis, take your files and get out of my office!"

"My files!"

"You pretend to be the boss anyway..."

"But what about Mr. and Mrs. Freaky Deaky?"

"The Hernandez' will probably agree to a very large settlement. Something tells me that there is more to this but our clients would much rather settle so, be gone with your cattiness."

And with his brows raised, Franklin politely gathered his files, pushed the chair in gently with his hip and respectfully strolled out of Dominique's office. Watching him role play, she couldn't help but giggle. But after the door closed behind him, reality seeped right back in and poor Dominique began to imagine all of the things that could go wrong once her secret was revealed. And with only one friend in her corner, she immediately called Sidney. Sidney had not so long ago left the salon highly agitated and a bit confused about how their girlfriend ended up in the bathroom of this upscale well known salon, in a cat fight with the owner of all people. So without checking the caller I.D., she quickly answered in the ugliest voice believing it was Waverly.

"Waverly Corrine, out of all the people I love and choose to hate, how in the hell did you end up in a fist fight with some crazy-ass woman, in the toilet while I was trying to get my hair done? You were supposed to be waiting in the waiting area! Tell me they were all wrong! Please tell me it was a case of mistaken identity! Please!"

"Excuse me... this is Dominique and what the fuck are you talking about! I know you didn't just say that Waverly was fighting in nobody's beauty salon!"

"Oh Diamond thank God it's you because I'm not sure if I'm ready to hear her reasoning right about now!"

"So, she really did get into a fight at the Salon?"

"Yes damn-it! What part of this aren't you getting? And yes before you ask again, it was with the owner, Gina Hernes or something... Her staff refers to her as Mrs. G. I cannot wait to find that damn girl! She not only embarrassed me! She could have lost her seat on the bench over this shit!"

Quickly placing pieces together, Dominique knew exactly who Sidney was referring to... and knowing the capabilities of the Hernandez', Dominique immediately sided with Waverly.

"Now hold on Sid, you and I both know Waverly. And as tight as she can be at times, there must have been some horrendous force pushing her in that direction. Why don't we find her first, get to the bottom of how all this came about and go from there..."

"Oh it's so like you to try and mediate shit. I tell you what though, it's going to take more than your court room bull-shit to get pass this one!"

"Just find out girl – capiesh!"

"Capiesh my ass!!!" The line went dead...

● ● ● ●

*M*eanwhile, on the out-skirts of town, Keith Sheppard had just stepped out of the shower and into his favorite workout clothes when Waverly called him on his cell phone. Recognizing the number to be Waverly's, Keith quickly answered.

"I was just thinking about you."

"And right now, you're probably not the only one…"

Sensing something was wrong, he asked, "Are you alright?"

"Well if you exclude my snooping around after my husband, turning forty in a couple of days… and oh getting into a nasty fist fight with a bitch from my past, then I guess I'm okay…"

"Wait a minute, back up!! Did you just say you were fighting someone? Where are you?"

"Right outside… by the way, you have a lovely home Mr. Sheppard."

"It's Keith and how did… never mind…I'll be right out…"

Baffled, Keith hurried outside as if Waverly was married to him rather than Vincent, the man whom he'd been investigating for the last two days. And it was easy to see that Keith was very concerned about his client's well being, but perhaps Mr. Man's allowing his emotions to rule. If so, do you suppose he'd make a better impression if he'd remembered to put on his socks and shoes…

"You didn't have to rush on my account…" she said, noticing he was barefoot.

"This is not the time to be concerned about my shoes… Are you all right? What's this about you getting involved in a fight? Damn, is that a cut on your forehead?" Keith said as he opened the car door to help Waverly out.

"I'm all right Keith… I just couldn't think of anyplace else to go. Home is not an option. To be perfectly honest, the shame and disappointment I feel at this moment, which I've mastered techniques to cover all of these years, is exactly why I have been unable to be straight with my best friends. How could I have allowed that bitch to play me like this? I should have taken care of her years ago…"

"Ho-Ho hold-up right there! When you say words like take care of …to me it suggests straight up murder!"

"Oh I know exactly what it means. And if I'd had sense twenty years ago, I could have probably gotten away with it…"

"Come on now Corrine… This is just another one of those fucked up moments in time. It's not necessarily who you are… Shit if that was the case all of us would be locked-up in an institution."

"Maybe so, but you and I would have to totally exchange places for you to even begin to understand. Right now, from where I'm standing, my life's a total mess," she said as she looked down noticing her silk blouse was covered in what appeared to be blood and saliva.

And now, realizing her options were almost null and void, tears began to trickle down her face.

"Hey, the worst is over. You have nothing to be ashamed of… Let's go inside, clean up and take it from there. I bet you're hungry…"

"How can you tell?"

"Well, altercations and sex usually keep me famished," he answered with a big grin and a shrug of his shoulders.

Returning the gesture, knowing his intent was to make her smile, Waverly did just that and said, "Oh really!" as they both walked through the side entrance of his newly renovated rancher and newly renovated… was an understatement.

From a glimpse of the massive room, it was clear to see a stone fireplace at the end of a long sleek hall which opened up about midstream of this indoor/outdoor bungalow. Keith had always referred to his rancher as an indoor/outdoor live-in space because of the oversized sunroom off of the gourmet kitchen. From almost any corner of the house, the tall eight-foot automatic double glass doors were only part of its revealing appeal. In fact, when Keith purchased his home almost three years ago, the first thing he changed was the floors in that room. Avocado sixteen by sixteen marble is what he had in mind. So after falling in love with them, he decided (excluding the master suite) to change all of the flooring to marble Avocado. Waverly, to say the least, was amazed at his rugged but elegant style.

"This home is beautiful," *she whispered while walking through the kitchen headed straight toward the sunroom, as she noticed the fifteen foot ceilings looming above her head. Keith just stood still, watching from a distance with his hands in his pockets.*

"Did you do all of this yourself?"

But before he could answer, his office line started ringing.

"I'd better take that. I was kind of waiting for Heather to get back to me just before you called. It is about that time."

"I'm sorry, maybe I should go..."

Shaking his head to indicate "no"... Keith replied, "The only place you're going is through those double doors to take a nice hot bath and relax your mind. I won't be long. When I am finished, maybe we can order take-out and exchange stories... okay?"

Flattered and tongue tied, Waverly clutched on to her purse and did as he suggested. At first she was all for the idea of stealing away some time-out for herself, being rescued by this simply gorgeous stranger... But then as she sat on the side of the tub completely naked, watching the hot water hit the bubbles, she couldn't help but think, What the hell am I doing?

Tears rolled down her cheeks again as she slid into the tub. She closed her eyes, laid her head on the bath pillow and before she could think back to where it all began, Waverly Corrine fell fast asleep. About an hour passed and Keith being the gentleman he was, not only found Waverly something more comfortable to wear, but he also ordered pizza and Chinese, not knowing what her preference would be. Entering his bedroom, the scent from her wet body lightly filled the air. Noticing her clothing at the foot of his bed, he gathered then up, piece by piece and placed then in the washer on the gentle cycle.

What a woman, he thought while resisting the urge to smell her garments. But, who could blame him; there was indeed a spell of chemistry between the two of them and no matter how hard they tried to ignore it, only time itself stood in their way... Well Waverly's time was up! While she had entered la-la land, Keith unknowing she had fallen asleep, was standing at the bathroom doorway completely taken by the natural beauty of her naked body seemingly floating in the bubbled water. Resisting the urge to join her in the tub, he politely placed a towel on the side of the tub and turned the power jets off. Sensing his presence, Waverly opened he eyes...

"I'm sorry, I didn't mean to be rude," *Keith uttered, totally embarrassed for being caught red handed. But placing his mind at ease, Waverly displayed no fear or discomfort whatsoever. One would think Girl was used to Mr. Sheppard's piercing eyes admiring her naked body. To my surprise, she just smiled rather invitingly and said,*

"It's okay, I can't recall the last time I had a more pleasant bath. This almost makes me forget about all of the turmoil I've been going through…"

Unbelievable…These two might as well just get it on and get it over with. Tis true… Keith's biting his bottom lip, looking at her, while she's already "doing" him in the recesses of her mind. All the while, nothing's being said, leaving the window of opportunity wide open. Well after several seconds passed, with Keith now close enough to taste Waverly's lips, a sudden sense of reality came over him as he realized maybe what he was contemplating was in fact, wrong. He stood to his feet, turned his back towards Waverly and politely excused himself…

"I'll wait for you in the other room," he said as he walked away.

After hearing the bedroom doors close Waverly exhaled and slid completely under the water.

I think I've died and gone to heaven, she thought as she blew bubbles to the surface. Anyway, after another twenty minutes passed and Girl was able to pull herself out of what was now a cold bath (how convenient), she managed to slip on the tee and short pajama set Keith laid out for her. As she examined the pajamas, she wondered with her nose slightly turned up, "ummm… who's pjs are these, since they're just my size and really cute."

"He's too charming and probably gets more ass than he knows what to do with…"

Now you see… that was not right… why couldn't he have just been being nice to her? Remember, on their first encounter, he suggested… and I quote "all men are not dogs!" Besides, how could she even think that considering the way he had everything laid out for her, take-out and all… Keith Sheppard had a mysterious way about him and Waverly Corrine, with her need to analyze any and everything, was already two-thirds of the way exposed for who she really was…

"I suppose I owe you an explanation..." *Slightly smiling, he answered,*

"I have to admit...as much as I would like to know what's really going on, I am not sure if we should discuss it on empty stomachs. So, what do you say we sit down by the fire, have some wine and only contemplate over Pizza or Chinese. Then you can decide what part of the truth you wish to share and what part you want to withhold."

Feeling transparent, she quickly answered, "What makes you think I'd lie now?"

"Who said anything about lying? We've only known each other for what... less than seventy two hours... and for real – for real, if I was a person of your stature, not knowing me from "Adam", I sure as hell wouldn't trust all of my whatever with a total stranger unless..."

"Unless what?" Waverly asked even more concerned

"Unless I had somehow fallen profoundly in love with you and thought for a brief moment you could change my world or if nothing else... understood it. Then I would...uh what would I have to lose?"

Hesitating for several minutes... Waverly replied, "How about everything..."

Now that I'm afraid was definitely not an ice breaker...Again, silence filtered the air excluding the soft music playing in the background. Keith grabbed a slice of pizza while Waverly picked the onions out of her shrimp-fried-rice. All the while, be very mindful that Girl's stomach was still in knots from all of the anxiety she was experiencing... She needed desperately to unload her mess onto anyone with some capability to understand. So with her lips turned up, she repeated herself...

"I suppose I owe you an explanation..."

Keith looked into her eyes attentively as he poured two glasses of white wine. He knew she was ready. And what better way to ease one's tension than with a glass of wine. Waverly's lips began to quiver and for the first time ever, she actually told her entire life story of how she came to this fragile place in her life... I mean Girl held back nothing! She told of what it was like being raised by a single mom, moving from house to house because of her mother's inability to maintain the few dollars given to her from child welfare. She told of

*her mother's promiscuous lifestyle and how that has always distorted
her views of men, including her husband of seventeen years. Waverly
also expressed her childhood dreams of becoming a woman of influence
and power some day until her dream was shattered when her mother
was diagnosed with an aids related disease passed on to her from one
of her "johns".*

"That would explain how you ended up with the
Hernandez family"

Shaking her head no... Waverly chuckled, "I'm afraid that
was just a bad decision on my part. I could only work part
time and Gina promised me a little more than minimum wage
plus tips at the time. I was just pressed financially... My
mother had been recently hospitalized and we needed the
money badly... I guess after she died, I stopped caring!
That's when I agreed to the sex after hours..."

*Keith just looked at Waverly with admiration and empathy... It
was clear that he understood her plight.*

"Like I said before, we would have to totally exchange
places for you to understand. I am not proud of my choices
but I always believed in myself to correct them when I could.
Shit... life's no picnic and the few who've managed to miss
its wrath... well more power to them. I knew even back then
that my behavior would eventually come back to taunt me.
My only question to God is...why now? "

*Wow! I suppose I too would have questions if I were Waverly...
Anyway, Keith and Waverly continued their conversation over
another bottle of wine. They even managed to move on to a more
uplifting topic... Vincent! Yes, the cheating husband... Keith
updated Waverly on his findings then reassured her that it was a
strong possibility of catching Vincent red handed. This, no doubt,
made Girlfriend feel a little better. Well, the evening's end grew near
and the two eventually fell asleep literally moments before the fire
fizzed out.*

● ● ● ●

*T*hursday morning... *Meagan, Sidney and Dominique were
all on a three-way call not only discussing Waverly's
alleged fight with Gina Hernandez, but also the whereabouts of their missing friend.*

"So Sid... do they know for sure that it was

Waverly?" Meagan asked.

"Yeah I'm afraid so. The receptionist identified her when she came out of the ladies room covered in blood with her picture perfect ponytail looking a damn mess."

"Old habits rarely surprise me. I bet that freaky lil bitch never even bothered calling the police!"

"How can you be so sure of that? Sidney was the only one there, not you…"

"Indeed I was the only one there, so what aren't *you* telling us Diamond?"

Dominique hesitated for a second then spilled her guts… She knew what she was disclosing, if ever found out, could have a negative impact on her career. But, trusting in their friendship, she wanted Sidney and Meagan to at least know a little about Gina Hernandez so that they too could consider Waverly's innocence. Maybe her judgment was premature but Dominique Blake, in her own words, said "To hell with hem all!" She believed in her girlfriend's innocence and was not about to let anything said cloud that…

Meagan on the other hand was having a difficult time understanding how in God's name her lifetime friend could be in any way tangled with a person like Gina to begin with… But as always, Sidney Sharpe sat in a class all by herself. Girlfriend was caught up into being totally embarrassed since she had disclosed her reasons for being there to Clay and any other nosy stylist with an open ear. And I do mean all of her business! From the struggles with her addiction… to the bickering for years with her older sister Sherian. She even thought it was appropriate to discuss how much money they all made including Waverly whom she described as being the most successful of the four. Some success story… But then how could she have known that the one person whom she most admired… secretly hid who she really was… and to top things off, allowed herself to be exposed in public. I suppose I too would be a little embarrassed… especially if I'd had a sudden case of diarrhea of the mouth…

Anyway, their conversation lasted for an hour and a half. Now my guess is, since Dominque ended their call, maybe she figured out a way to find Waverly herself… Perhaps if there were different circumstances, it would be easier calling the police. And, now since its been over twenty-four hours since Dr. Simmons, Waverly's soon to be ex-husband has seen or heard from her, he too is concerned…

"Where in the hell are you woman? I can't believe that Bitch didn't even come home last night! I just hope it's not another man because as sure as my name is Vincent... after I remove my hands from around her pretty little neck, I'll probably need some assistance in taking my foot out of her ass..." he said to himself just before his son Victor entered the kitchen.

Victor was also aware of his mother's absence from the home since the previous night, but thought to himself, Maybe she's just giving Dad a dose of his own medicine. He had no idea how bad things really were between his parents. Vincent spent most of his time away from home claiming to be working or at a work related meeting, while Waverly engrossed herself with her daily grind pretending to be content with a marriage she really wanted to end. Games would be a reasonable assumption for this family. And let's not forget Victor, he has been hiding his sexuality from his parents for quite some time. In fact, even as things stand now, the only thoughts that linger on his mind are... In less than a week, he will be twenty-one and when he and his parents are out celebrating, that's when he'll tell them he's Gay.

"Good morning Dad."

"Have you seen your Mother?" Vincent asked totally ignoring Victor's greeting.

Victor just looked at him, as he shook his head knowing his Father was not in the mood for any conversation unrelated to his Mother. So not wanting to make matters worse, he simply shook his head indicating he had not and proceeded to make himself a bowl of cereal.

"Do you think once you turn twenty-one you'll eat something other than fruity-pebbles for breakfast everyday?"

"You're not serious are you?"

"Yes I am... I just think it's time to do something different. Year in and year out, same old shit! I'm not sure where you are with this suffocating lifestyle, but I've had it!" *Vincent said with a peculiar look of distance in his eyes.*

Victor was no fool...he could see his Father's resentment. It was the same look that held Victor hostage... making it impossible for him to be who he really was for the sake of appearances. Having a doctor as a father and a judge as a mother, made it virtually impossible to admit that he possessed homosexual feelings since eight grade. It was

just unacceptable! Sure, he wanted something different... but
Victor's different would be to lower his parents' expectations just
enough so that they could accept him as being less than perfect. A
world within a world is what Victor called it. Being in it... but
unable to be of it... Another way he'd expressed it was, like a covered
sheep being born and raised by properly trained wolves. So as long as
everyone's pretending... personal responsibility would never become
an issue. What was once tolerable suppressed anguish, if left
undisclosed now, for Victor would be torture turned inward. In other
words, there was nothing on this earth that was going to keep him
from telling his parents the truth on his twenty-first birthday...

"Now there's a safe but true statement..."

"Are you even listening to me Victor? I'm not
suggesting life at twenty-one is going to be an easy
adjustment to change. What I am saying is... your time has
come."

"That's something Mother would say."

"What difference does it make who says it? As your
Father, my only responsibility to you is to..."

At that moment, Victor stood to his feet with body
movements suggesting to his Father that enough was enough. Seeing
that, Vincent knew there was no need to finish his statement.
Surprisingly enough, Victor respectfully placed the dishes in the sink,
put the box of fruity-pebbles back in the cabinet with all of the other
boxes of fruity-pebbles, turned to his Father and boldly said...

"I know because I've heard it a thousand times. The only
responsibility you have to me is to raise me to be a respected
member of society. But you know what Dad, if I may be
candid, the most twisted part of this lesson taught so
diligently by you and Mother which I was forced to
understand and believe is: What one does in this society
dictates who you are. Forget all about who you *really* are
once the curtains are drawn."

"Important people are only interested in what you can do!
Now how is that for one of your most meaningless quotes?"

Victor smiled... he knew his Father didn't believe it anymore than
he did.

"But that's not all true is it Dad?" he said as tears bubbled
up in the bottom lids of his eyes.

Vincent just shook his head "no" knowing the words he passed on to his son came from his wicked Nana. You see Vincent was taught at a very young age that the appearance of knowing holds just as much value as knowing itself. To question or to be unsure, in Vincent's grandmother's eyes, would be admitting defeat. So unlike genes, unaware of which one is passed down, Vincent knew as much as he hated what was forced on him, in turn forced the same misinformation on to his son.

"Look, all of what I've tried teaching you was not wrong. And maybe your Mom and I didn't do our best at showing all of the ugly sides of this fucked-up world. We did however give you what we had. Shit... half of the reason we've lasted this long is because of you."

"I've never once asked that of you guys."

"That's not the point," Vincent uttered as he placed his hand on Victor's shoulder.

They both just stood there silent for several seconds looking at each other understanding the feeling was love first, survival second. Knowing his son had so much more to learn and would have to learn it on his own, Vincent pulled him close and whispered the words, "I love you man," *in Victor's ear.*

"I love you too Dad. And yes I will be at dinner next week. And when Mom calls me, I'll three-way you."

Chapter Eleven

Coming Out...

*T*o be brief, this chapter's title is self explanatory... My only question is, with all of the lies already told and equal amounts of truth unexpressed, who will be the first to tell it all? They say credibility rests with the one boldest to come first... As for second and third... who knows...

It's Friday morning exactly one hour before Miss Phyllis Maple's wake was to begin. If you recall, Miss Phyllis, Sherian and Sidney's Mother, went to her doctor's office upon his request for test results. Once there, she was told surgery was necessary. Unfortunately due to complications beyond anyone's control, Miss Phyllis died on the operation table. Sad but true... And the most bizarre piece of this tale is, Sherian wished her secret of being Sidney's biological Mother would have died with her... Now she's left to choose an appropriate time for alienation. And if indeed Sidney chooses to do just that, what Sherian feared most would have become her reality.

Remember when Sherian set across from Sidney at the hospital right after Miss Phyllis died. Sidney was disregarding the "no smoking" signs while Sherian's frustrating thoughts overwhelmed any hopes of connecting with her then... Surprisingly though as preoccupied as Sidney may have been, she shared no distance feelings with her sister. Sherian on the other hand has always hesitated or second guessed herself with regards to Sidney merely out of guilt for allowing her own personal relationship with her Mother (Miss Phyllis) to dictate what was to be between her and Sidney. Now just like many times in the past, when she had the opportunity to tell Sidney the truth about her birth, Sherian's trying to approach it as her Mother would have instead of just explaining her own lack of courage. Personally, I believe with some support, a girl like Sidney Sharpe could have handled such a profound story.

Granted, a father has never been mentioned for neither Sherian nor Sidney. Their common bond was their dead Mother Miss Phyllis. And still even in her absence, the words of her last request are what is now forcing Sherian's hand. The same hand that is caressing Sidney's head and stroking her hair as she's curled up in a fetal position in the arms of her birth mother, mourning a woman who she believes is her natural mother, in the back of an ivory colored rolls Royce headed for the church to pay their last respects.

One would think they were having a celebratory affair instead of a homegoing service as indicated by the way, they were dressed and from *the selection of music they played. Sidney's dress was beautiful, simplistic spaghetti strapped, ankle length gown. As requested by Miss Phyllis' before her death, it was ivory colored with a satin finish. She accessorized it with a chenille beaded shawl and a jeweled purse. And... before I forget, that old antique watch Miss Phyllis asked her to hold before she went into surgery, Sidney held it in her right hand as if it would reveal something later...*

Sherian, to be brief, simply wore a two piece wide legged silk pant suit. And yes it was also off white. In fact by the time they had arrived, the entire church, upon Phyllis Maple's request, was dressed in ivory or off white. White catch lilies were strategically placed throughout the chapel so that where ever anyone's eyes wandered; you'd notice its beauty. The boys youth musical ministry sang while a renowned harpist played with the choir director on piano accompanying her. The melody was pure yet up lifting and most of the faces in the crowd were pleasantly smiling instead of sorrowful... just the way Miss Phyllis wanted it to be...

The overall vibe of the service took Sherian and Sidney by surprise. As much as they were different, like Mother – like daughter, their reactions to what they were feeling were very much the same. So, frightened to see just who had showed up for this life changing moment, knowing some were there to be nosey and some out of guilt; a few out of love and the rest just because someone died, Sherian knew she too fitted into one or two categories. She held her head up and began to pray while Sidney believed most of the people she'd meet on this day, she'd never see again. But, someone as always as most people do would say or do something to shame her feelings about her dead Mother. So she scanned the chapel for her lifetime girlfriends for the strength to get through the service. Meagan and Dominique however were the only ones she saw. Waverly was no where to be found.

"Come on Sid, it's time to say good-bye to Mother," Sherian whispered as she pulled Sidney by the hand and lead her to the opened rose colored casket.

Miss Phyllis was astonishingly dressed in powder blue just like a newborn baby. Her nails were frenched and her hair sparkled like white-gold. Loving fine jewelry, a beautiful three-carrot diamond cross laid on her breast and an eighteenth century ruby ring was on her index finger.

Noticing her trinkets, Sherian thought to herself, *I suppose you'll be laid to rest with your hush money gifts Mother.*

You see, Miss Phyllis would share stories with Sidney which were all lies of how all of her most expensive gifts were given to her by this secret male admirer. Sherian knew the gifts as well as the store they owned were in exchange for Miss Phyllis silence and protection of an important secret. But I guess now with Miss Phyllis being gone, the secret holds no value. Both her daughter and granddaughter were successful. What Miss Phyllis didn't spend, she invested. And with the four current insurance policies she had, the hush money taken for so many years was no longer needed. A sense of belonging is what was needed and unfortunately for Sherian, she would be it.

Sherian knew it as she stood beside her daughter looking down at her Mother. As angry as she wanted to be, she had to just believe with all she could and simply forgive her Mother. Maybe it was all wrong, so what! It was still their life and now minus one. Sherian hesitated for a second then looked over at Sidney who had tears streaming endlessly down her face. She gently rubbed her Mother's hand and whispered as she kissed her harden lips, "I forgive you Mother... I do... I really do..." This comment made Sidney's silent cries evolve into the screams of a wounded babe caught in a trap. Next thing you know, a woman started speaking in tongues so loud you could barely hear the choir singing anymore. And just like a domino effect, my guess is for a short moment, the entire service actually realized why they were really there...

It was so much excitement going on, if you listened with a careful ear anyone with even the smallest reason to be thankful was either praising the Lord or crying out of gratitude. This was indeed a celebration of life. And not just for the dead but the ones who survived. Well I was excited! And I believe for the first time in a long time Sherian was pleased. Girl looked into crowd and knew then her Mother's wish of celebration was granted. Outside of telling Sidney she's her natural Mother, her days of doing what Phyllis Maple wanted was no more. It was time for Sherian to live and do as she pleased without being questioned or threatened by Mother-May-I!

A smile came over her face as she placed her arm around Sidney signaling the director of the funeral they were ready to begin receiving the people on their dead Mother's behalf. Sidney continued to weep even after being seated for a while. Sherian sat tall with her dark shades on and her head held high refusing to become unglued in a church full of strangers who never really knew "The Phyllis Maple" whom they had come to mourn. "Never ever let them see you sweat," is what Miss Phyllis would say... And somehow those words filled Sherian's head.

Well as the people came forth to pay their last respects, so did many cards and overflow of sympathy. It was extremely difficult separating the concern from the outright nosey so after the hugging and shaking of what felt like a hundred hands, Sidney just sat there with both hands glued to the watch rocking back and forth, while Sherian did the honors of what appeared to be at least a hundred more. Dominique and Meagan were among the first to pay their respects and express sympathy. However, just as the line finally began to shorten, a soloist from the praise team belted out the lyrics of "Amazing Grace!"

The atmosphere seemingly stood still at that moment. The few voices heard were muffled and the people instead of moving towards the immediate family, looked as if they were somehow pushed back. The only image that stood out was of a man dressed in ivory of course but with a beautiful crimson flower on his lapel. He too had an antique watch hanging from his front pocket that if set beside Miss Phyllis' watch, it would be an exact replica. I mean for every ruby and rose bud it had, so did the one Sidney held onto. The carvings were identical. And to be quite honest, they were both made and purchased at the same time. One was intended for Sherian but the late Miss Phyllis saw it to be much too expensive for a girl of her age at the time. The other was for the purchaser William Huston... Sidney's Father and Sherian's first love... I suppose it was a token of feelings shared between then. Unfortunately, those thoughts were never expressed. So I guess one could assume this man stood there merely out of guilt. Until now, he was unaware that he and Sherian had created a daughter. Even worse, knowing the man his family intended for him to become, the circumstances wouldn't have changed anything. Success slash power and the normal quote-unquote family was all young William had in mind then and now. So yes guilt brought him to pay his last respects to a servant that knew him all too well.

Sherian was blinded then and since then has had trouble seeing into the heart of a man even today. They say what you don't change, you respectfully pass on — So now as Sherian wishfully reminisces in her mind about what could have been between them, unaware of what lied ahead, William acts just as any other respectable condoler would.

He shook her hand and kissed her on the cheek and as he looked into Sidney's eyes while kissing Sherian, he realized what happened all of those years ago…Sidney had to be his daughter, not Sherian's so called younger sister. Maybe it was the way Sherian suggestively looked into his eyes yet said nothing… or perhaps it's because Sidney's a mirror image of his youngest daughter Jessica.

It's sometimes too much when the truth decides to bluntly appear. What stood in plain sight somehow was colorless. Then all of a sudden, the smallest detail can reveal the missing link, ie. A pair of eyes. A piece of jewelry, etc. Questions form in the mind and usually the answer follows. Human nature would compel you to ponder one's entire existence at funeral. Who are you really? Why am I here? Is it all in vain? And the answers are still unknown. Nevertheless, it overwhelms most and then causes suppressed emotions to take over. All who are there engages and this is considered customary and somewhat healthy. The sad truth is in a few days or possibly a couple of weeks, many forget and life is expected to move on. But does it? I would imagine it changes.

Maybe this is what's causing Sidney's emotions to overload. All she has ever known is Mama and her controlling older sister. Of course Miss Phyllis had siblings and cousins, but Sidney never knew them. Her immediate family consisted of the three of them. Now with Miss Phyllis being instantly vanished out of her life, meaning there is no going back to change anything… She now feels more lost than before.

Sure… she's managed to achieve success from an outward perspective, but within rests a void that has never been understood or fulfilled. Perhaps that's why she continues to sedate herself with "things" hoping that the fast cars, expensive jewelry or choice of men would suffice until its appeal ceases, only to work, leaving her to believe in the deceptions of what drugs have to offer.

Poor Sidney, I guess annoyingly crying outwardly is the only thing she saw fit to do and just like thunder, her cries progressed until finally her voice gave out. So gasping for air, she stood to her feet releasing Miss Phyllis' watch allowing it to fall to the floor and began jumping around uncontrollably. Fortunately, through God's grace, Waverly was next in the receiving line so when she saw Sidney's pain magnify, an invitation was not required for her to step in and comfort her. Sherian, caught off guard as usual shunned William with much disappointment to tend to Sidney. But, just as she reached down to pick up the watch even through the dark shades, with clarity; she saw the identical watch hanging from William's pants pocket. "It can't be," she whispered as she grabbed the watch eagerly trying to prove her sanity. Things were happening so quickly, William walked away unaware that Sherian now had his priceless watch. In her left hand was the one her dear but dead Mother gave Sidney and now in her right hand was the one mistakenly lifted off the only man she ever loved.

Well what felt like time standing still… was actually different parts of the ceremony taking place leading to that long drive to the final resting place. The craziest thing in that is you leave there with the notion it must be something else I can do… But, in spite of it all, that day was picture perfect. The grass was a pretty green. All of the arrangements were placed just so. The minister displayed a reassuring smile and one of the junior choir boys sang while the harpist played as the people exited their cars and gathered close. It was beautiful and almost over. And if there were any doubts in the air pertaining to Sherian and Sidney's ability to go on, they were no more. A sense of peace filtered over imparting pleasant thoughts in saddened hearts. Friends and a few of family members began placing parts of floral arrangements on top of Miss Phyllis' casket in remembrance of gifts given for her to take to eternity. Some of the guests started to leave while others lingered making up conversation just to spend more time. Then all of a sudden, clearly out of the blue, the skies opened up and large drops of rain began to fall so rapidly it literally forced the ceremony to come to an abrupt end. The remaining guests quickly said their good byes and ran for shelter. Dominique and Meagan were among the first to leave. They actually rode together thinking it would be easier since neither of them planned to stay too long. Meagan's husband, Drake had the twins and Dominique's anticipation of her lover's arrival that day kept her on edge all morning. Waverly however, had a different story. Girl could care less about hurrying home. If you recall, she went MIA for almost forty hours.

Upon returning home last evening, unlike her cheating spouse, she offered no explanation what so ever. It's true~ the only call she made that evening which lasted all of sixty seconds was to Meagan knowing how emotional she gets. Girl then took a long hot bath and went to bed reminding Vincent of Miss Phyllis' funeral in the morning. Morning came and she still refused to speak of what had transpired over the last 40 hours. And for the first time ever in all of the years they had been married, Vincent felt a sense of frightening distance from his wife. I would imagine for some individuals looking at one's self can be quite painful sometimes, causing pouring rain to feel like cleansing water. So the fact that it had begun to rain, for Waverly, this symbolized the rinsing away of buried fear leaving a dose of clarity of mind. Unfortunately for Sidney and Sherian, whatever fears they were about to face can't be rinsed away so easily in this shower...

●●●●

"Cher, I can't believe she's really gone..." Sidney whispered with a crackling voice just as Waverly walked up and stood behind them.

Right then Sherian wanted to burst into tears, but she resisted the emotion and moved closer to Sidney in hopes of reassuring her. Sidney was kneeling down beside the casket gently wiping away the raindrops with the end of her gown almost as if she was cleaning silver. It was quite clear that she was oblivious to what was happening around her in that moment. So Waverly just smiled as she walked away saying her good-byes to the late Miss Phyllis. Well, the rain began to come down even harder!

Everyone else was gone excluding the driver in the Rolls Royce who was waiting for them to return to the car. You'd think on any other day, staying longer at the gravesite would have been okay; but not this day. The feeling of wet and cold raindrops was very aggravating to Sherian. More than that, it was hard for Sherian to distinguish the tears on Sidney's face from the rain. Frustrated, Sherian told Sidney to come along, literally pulling her to her feet. Ignoring Sherian, Sidney just cried even harder almost fighting with her to stay longer.

"Sidney! Sidney... it's time for us to go home! There's nothing else we can do here! Mama's dead!"

"Stop saying that! She's just resting! What do you know? But then you think you know every damn thing!"

"That's not true!"

"Yes it is! You're probably relieved that Mama's gone! Now you can really take over!"

Now why did she say that! Sherian drew her hand backwards and slapped Sidney harder than it was raining. Totally taken aback, Sidney screamed ...

"You Bitch!"

"No! Respect me little Girl because *I am* the "bitch" that gave you life! I am your Mother – not Phyllis. She is in fact, *my* Mother and *your* Grandmother!"

Sidney just looked at Sherian with the oddest smirk and whispered; "You have lost your mind; You have gone completely crazy!"

"No, you are my daughter. This shit is crazy!"

Not believing a single word, Sidney replied, "You just don't give up do you? Mama's dead and you have the nerve to disrespect her with these horrible lies! I hope you burn in hell for this big sister..."

Sidney then made a gesture of spitting at Sherian's feet. Too angry to even consider riding back with her older sister as far as she was concerned, Sidney repeatedly shook her head as she walked away hurt by Sherian's words. Oddly enough, I thought Sherian would call out for her but when she remained silent only grabbing up a few of the broken off flowers to take home; I knew she was confused, You see, Sherian always had an explanation for everything except when it had to do with Sidney being her biological daughter and dealing with it. Miss Phyllis called it manipulation to avoid alienation and Sherian always listened to her Mother. So now, as it stands, Miss Phyllis has instructed her to just tell Sidney who she really is – what was to come next was never said...

I once heard someone say, there are two things in this life that can never be controlled... the first being mother nature and second – another person's reactions to what is to be believed... For Sherian, her undecided emotions forced her to wait while Sidney's anger compelled her to simply run for her life. It's true, first Girl was walking through the cemetery with heels knee deep in the moist surface cursing everything she believed in... then before she could get a grasp on what was happening, Girl was barefoot, shoes in hand and running as if she was being chased. It's a wonder that she managed to keep from ruining her gown. And too, I suppose finding one of those AA meetings right now probably isn't on her list of things to do. Mind you, it's raining, she's cold and hungry, her stress level is high and she hasn't had a cigarette since early morning...

So exhausted, she stops near some vacant houses occupied by none other than drug addicts. Sidney was looking for shelter from the cold rain and perhaps a moment of peace to collect her thoughts. Poor Girl wasn't even half way in the entrance before the aroma of the drugs made its way to her nostrils. It's funny; addicts have a way of smelling narcotics in the air just as a former smoker can sniff out a cigarette being smoked from a considerable distance. Maybe she was in the wrong place, but maybe she wasn't after all... Sometimes it's possible to see ourselves in others. Unfortunately for Sidney Sharpe, this was all too much – way to soon...

"This is crazy! I don't have any cigarettes and now this stupid phone won't even pick up a fucking signal!" she screamed just as a young boy walked over to her and asked...

"Hey lady, do you wanna use mine?" After pausing, Sidney thanked him and immediately placed a call to Dominique.

"You not from around here are you?"

Sidney shook her head to indicate "no" as she listened to Dominique's answering machine...

"This is Diamond. I can't come to the phone right now. So you know what to do... so do it..."

Sidney then gave the young boy his phone back and asked, "Shouldn't you be in school right now?"

Laughing, he replied, "No! I'm where I'm supposed to be. I gotta run my store, look out for my customers..."

"Oh, I see... you wouldn't have any cigarettes for sale would you?"

"No way! Those things a kill ya for sure... But, I do have some "China White" now that will keep you going..."

"This is not happening! I need to get out of here!" Sidney uttered just as she pushed her way passed the boy headed toward the door.

The boy, trying to be helpful eagerly grabbed Sidney by her wrist, placed a bag of his so called remedy in her hand and said, "Here... this one's on me! Get yourself together!

You are much too pretty to look sooooo sad…" Poor Sidney, she just looked at him and then at the bag of drugs. Desperately wanting to get out of there she began to run…

●●●●

*M*eanwhile, just a few miles away, Dominique had not so long ago gotten home only to find Hannah soaking in a hot bath full of bubbles. Being the romantic one, Hannah had champagne, fresh strawberries, sushi and Godiva chocolates waiting… Fresh flowers were used as the centerpiece on the cocktail table and scented candles were strategically placed to capture the mood. Dominique was pleasantly surprised to see her Asian lover considering it had been over three months since their last encounter. She and Hannah first met over a year ago on a business trip in Miami. Dominique was researching a case and coincidently interviewed Hannah as a plaintiff's witness. The two bumped heads initially but then literally bumped into each other later that evening in the hotel lobby where they both stayed. The chemistry was undeniable. They were a match made in heaven… What started out as two rooms directly across from one another ended with one being extended for an additional week. You'd think they were both touched – starved by the way they played "connect the dots" all week. Dominique acted like a kid while Hannah was simply in awe of her. Then and now, their love continues to grow just as Dominique's fear of coming out of the closet continues to grow.*

"Hey beautiful!" Dominique said as she entered the bathroom with two glasses of champagne.

Hannah stood to her feet butt ball naked partially covered in bubbles, hair dripping wet and said, "Did you miss me? Tell me you missed me and perhaps I'll let you join me…"

"And if I refuse…" Dominique replied as she gently sat the glasses down. "Well in that case, I'll be forced to come to you Counselor."

The music played softly in the background and as they both stood still hungry for love and awaiting the other's response. The bubbles on Hannah's body began to slide down into the water. Intrigued and totally forgetting her own discomfort of being caught in the rain in her new St. John suite, she slipped out of her heels and began to slowly undress. Hannah smiled as she made her way close enough to lightly kiss Dominique on her bottom lip. Tingles danced at the pit of her belly as she asked her lover,

"What's that for?"

"For all of the times when you touched me where it used to hurt..."

They both giggled as they continued to remove Dominique's damp clothing. Hannah's kisses became more frequent and intense as Dominique's breathing became heavy and deep.

"Do you need a sip of Champagne?" Hannah asked as she reached around from the back of Dominique, handing her a glass.

Taking another deep breath, Dominique whispered, "No...but if you remove your lips from my lower back and sit on the side of the tub, I'll show you exactly what I would like to sip..."

Now that I'm afraid started their, how do you say... romantic flight. It was my first! I mean I have never... They say two heads are better than one, but I'd say two tails are even cuter... These ladies moved from the tub to the toilet and from the toilet to the sink and then somehow ended up in the shower. Maybe it was best that neither had a real penis considering the efforts it would have taken to keep it up! Anyway, just when I thought it was over as I witnessed Dominique coming up for air, she grabbed Hannah by the head with both hands and kissed her wildly for what appeared to be an eternity. Of course Hannah didn't seem to mind; in fact, this somehow escalated things all over again...Dominique turned Hannah around pinning her hands up over her head while pressing her body tightly against Hannah's.

"Now what?" Hannah said trying to break free from Dominique's grip.

Dominique just giggled as she gently bit Hannah on the shoulder, then answered, "Did you remember to bring our little friend?"

"You know I did, I thought you'd never ask."

Next, Hannah quickly shut off the shower as they both existed. Dominique pulled her hair back, slipped on a teddy and then grabbed a bottle of massage oil before entering the bedroom. Contemplating most of their steps, Hannah set at the head of the bed with a bowl of strawberries in one hand and a replica of a man's "you know what" in the other, partially covered by satin sheets.

"Tell you missed me..."

Stubborn Dominique replied, "Haven't we been over this already?"

"Say it!"

"Okay... and if I refuse," Dominique answered with her lips turned upside down.

"Then I'll be forced to screw it out of you..." Hannah said just as she flipped the sheets back to reveal their little friend.

Next, both girls were giggling as if someone was tickling their bellies. I thought they were supposed to be making love. I guess love comes in all forms... And speaking of love, guess who's standing outside of Dominique's front door struggling with the decision to leave or stay...

Dominique's doorbell rang, but she told Hannah to ignore it. She thought that if they ignored it long enough, the visitor would just go away. But no such luck, the bell rang again. By this time, Dominique had already strapped Hannah with their little friend for a real freak session and they were about to begin when the banging on the door began.

Sidney was in deep pain and questioning her sanity for staying sober and was determined to see Dominique. She banged on the door as if her life depended on it (on some level it did). Forcing herself to stop playing house with her lover for a few minutes, Dominique jumped out of bed, closing the bedroom door behind her and ran to the door. She sensed that something was very wrong. At first it was difficult to tell, through the peephole, who was banging relentlessly on the door... But then she heard Sidney's voice calling out for her. She immediately opened the door.

"Sid... what is going on?"

Sidney just stood there like a kid getting caught with both hands in the cookie jaw. She finally felt it was okay to enter once Dominique moved to the side of the door.

"You're soaked! Where have you been?"

"Good observation Counselor."

"Don't move a muscle; my cleaning girl won't be back until Monday..." Dominique said as she went back into the bedroom mistakenly leaving the door half open.

Sidney not listening as usual politely strolled right behind her saying nothing as she tossed her shawl on the chair in the hall and proceeded to pull her gown over her head. Hannah noticed her first and shouted,

"Wait one damn minute... I never agreed to fuck you and who ever this wet hussy is... if this is what you brought me all the way across the country for, well..."

Dominique, to put it mildly was totally embarrassed and knowingly taking a chance, she asked Sidney to wait in the foyer.

"Sid... do you mind!"

Slightly smiling, Hannah added, "So, this is the famous Sidney Sharpe?"

"Pretty much..." Sidney replied removing her gown anyway.

Dominique then snatched the wet dress out of Sidney's hands and literally pushed her out of the room. On her way out, Sidney looked back at Hannah and said with laughter in her voice, "nice dick."

"I can't believe you said that!"

"I can't believe you've got some Asian chic in your bed strapped up ready to fuck you! If anything, I pictured you doing all of the poking..."

Both girls began laughing. Dominique got her wet friend a towel and some dry clothes while Sidney made herself a cup of tea to relax her mind and warm her cold body.

"Here girl! You are without a doubt the craziest friend I have. Tell me, what in God's name has gotten you soaked and angst?" Dominique asked as she sat down beside her friend trying to by-pass her own embarrassment.

"You wouldn't believe me if I told you," Sidney replied placing the bag of drugs on the table.

"So this is what it all boils down to... Your Mother dies and you push the fast forward button to destroy your life?"

"No... this shit isn't even mine! Some little dope dealer gave it to me when I asked him for a smoke. I wasn't buying any drugs! I don't even know why I still have it! Sure, I'd love to get high, but not today. I have to keep my mind clear."

Snatching the drug packet off the table and quickly taking it the kitchen sink to rinse it down the drain, Dominique started fussing at Sidney for all of the times before when she recalled hearing those same words.

"It's not like that this time! I really did get this the way I said..."

"Okay, Okay! So you could have gone home or to one of those meetings. Why here, why me, and for God sake why *now*?"

"Meagan has the twins and Waverly... well..."

"Point taken... So what the fuck is going on?"

Hesitantly, she said, "What I am about to tell you is not only totally unbelievable, it is insane!"

Looking her dearest lifetime friend directly in the eyes, Dominique whispered, "Sid, what ever is going on, most likely has to do with our lives. Trust me; it is not likely to be unbelievable."

"You're funny and always got a damn answer."

"You said it yourself, that's your reason for being here."

Taking a deep breath, Sidney began to share with Dominique what Sherian had shared with her, holding back nothing. She told of how she wished her to hell and of the nasty remark she made about Sherian being relieved about their Mother's death.

"So what did Sherian say after that?" Dominique asked with her eyebrows raised.

Smiling, Sidney replied, "Absolutely nothing... She just slapped the shit out of me."

"Served you right! I would have slapped your ass too if I was there. So then what?" *Dominique added, as she politely checked the time. Sidney then went on reminiscing back to all of the times she could recall Sherian acting like a mother to her rather than a sister. And without saying it, she almost convinced herself of Sherian's tale.*

"Look I'm just rambling on now... I've already over stayed my welcome," Sidney said just as Hannah walked in smoking a cigarette.

Looking over at Dominique, Sidney shouted, "Damn, I've wanted a smoke all this time and you knew she smoked and didn't tell me!"

Dominique simply threw her hands up and said, "I really wasn't thinking about that at the moment..."

Hannah went back into the bedroom to get Sidney a couple of cigarettes. Sidney thanked her and quickly lit one then said her good-byes...

"We'll talk later," Dominique said as she walked Sidney to the door.

"Yeah if not later, then in the morning after our run."

"Are you sure you're up to that?"

Smiling, Sidney answered, "I will be..." Nice meeting you Hannah... and ah... no offense about the dick jokes."

"None taken!"

Sidney then patted Dominique on the behind and whispered, "Pretty girl, but I expected her to look more like us."

"Get out Sidney!"

"What... What did I say... No love..."

"No... No love!" Dominique replied as she shut the door.

●●●●

O n the other side of town, another Mother and daughter issue comes to a head. Meagan has just walked in the house after sitting in her car for almost an hour after talking with her Mother Katherine on the phone.

Katherine called her as soon as she had dropped off Dominique to tell her about the meeting she had set up for Meagan to finally meet her biological mother. Now of course, Meagan wanted to meet her real mother, but the hesitation from going in the house had more to do with her holding the truth from Drake. They say that honest is the best policy... Maybe they should have taken it a step further and stated when it is the best policy... because Meagan is really struggling with this one.

"Hey sweetie, how was the funeral?" Drake asked as he came out from the kitchen, shirt soaked from washing bottles for the twins.

"You're a mess!" Meagan commented as she kissed Drake on the lips.

"I know. Nia and Nyle gave me a fit before naptime so I decided to get some work done with the little time I had available... Why don't you get out of those clothes while I make us some tea?"

"You are such a great husband. But we need to talk..."

"Yeah, I am... But first, I have an even better idea. Would you care to fool around while the twins are napping?"

"Yes... no, Drake. We really need this time to talk. I have something really important that I need to tell you. It's something I haven't been honest with you about..."

"What do you mean there's something you haven't been honest with me about? I'm your husband and we should have no secrets!"

"Drake, I just found out myself after giving birth to the twins. Even when the doctor told us about the blood disorder, I still refused to believe it."

"Believe what baby! Meagan just say what's on your mind!"

"I'm trying!"

Meagan went on to explain that the night the twins were born, Katherine came into her hospital room and claimed she was not her biological mother. She told the story as best she could remember it and still expressed her disbelief. She even told Drake of how she was never going to share this with him in hopes of it being a lie. No such luck...

"This is impossible! Kat is your Mother..."

Looking away only out of shame, Meagan said, "I wish that was true, but Mother has already set a date so that we can meet..."

"What are you going to do?"

"I'm going to meet with her. I need to know for sure!"

Then one of the twins started to cry. Relieved, Meagan quickly ran up the stairs to comfort her baby. Drake yelled..., "What about our conversation?"

Meagan replied, "It's over!"

Maybe some things are best left unsaid. But then what's left to say. Clearly this is between Katherine and Meagan. Who knows, maybe telling Drake will give him a better understanding of her being disconnected right now.

Anyway, several hours passed and evening had come and gone. Daybreak was set to come shortly when Drake awakened to observe his wife quietly hurrying around their bedroom getting herself together for her morning run. He sat up for a kiss and then wished her well.

"I won't be too long," she whispered as she hurried off.

Sidney not being able to sleep for more reasons than one — was already in her car nearly half way to the park. Now Dominique of course, was already there sitting in her car sipping on a bottle of water daydreaming about Hannah. And if you're counting, then that would leave Waverly Corrine left to join the group. Believe it or not, Girl's still sitting in her garage, not contemplating suicide but homicide. The famous Vincent Simmons did not come home last night. And sure Waverly's angry, but more so at herself.

"It's bad enough I have to deal with this old shit! But, your timing as usual is impeccable!" she said to herself as she pulled off, burning rubber nearly almost down her driveway.

I suppose it would have been easier dealing with one issue at a time. But then who says life is fair? I once heard someone say when it rains, it pours." So I'd imagine it's safe to say that these four friends are caught in a storm...

"They're not coming, let's just get started!" Sidney said as she banged on Dominique's truck hood.

Getting out of the car, Dominique merely looked at her as she took another sip of water then politely said,

"Slow down girl, I know there's a lot on your mind... Give them a few more minutes, they'll be here."

"So what do you suppose Waverly's excuse will be this time?"

"Sidney, I have no idea... What I do believe is... she has her reasons..."

"Maybe so, but I'd sure as hell like to hear them... And today! I'm still getting over the fact that she went missing for two days."

"It was one, you're exaggerating as usual."

"I am not!"

"Yes you are… you see, here comes Judge Judy and the white Girl now…"

Pushing Dominique Sidney replied, "Why do you always call her that?"

"Cause she's a girl and she happens to be white."

"I'm telling!" Sidney said smiling…

"Go ahead; you're incapable of holding on to anything anyway…"

The two just continued to giggle. Meagan and Waverly both got out of their cars at the same time and of course greeted each other with a kiss and hug before joining the others. And as they walked toward them, Meagan was still a bit off balanced from the news given to her by Katherine while Waverly on the other hand felt as guilty as some of the criminals she had sentenced and immediately took offense to their giggles…

"What the fuck is so funny?"

Sidney and Dominique just looked at each other and laughed even harder. Meagan also displayed a slight smirk, puzzled by Waverly's remark…

"That's our Judge, always judging!" Dominique added as she began to stretch.

"To hell with you Diamond! I know Sidney told you what happened at that so called salon."

"First of all, no one was talking about you! Second, Sid didn't have much information about the catfight Laila. But since we are all on the subject… How… about it?"

Everyone then focused their attention on Waverly as if she was ready to give this long reasonable speech as to why it was no doubt necessary to beat the piss out of Gina. Instead… Girl simply threw her hands up in the air and shouted…

"I know damn well I'm not the only bitch with shit going on right?"

"You really should stop referring to yourself in that manner," Meagan said shrugging her shoulders.

So for about thirty seconds nothing was said. They all just looked at each other seeing who would be boldest to speak first; in as much as each had a lot on the brain…

"Fuck it! I'll go first..." Sidney said as she walked over to the swing set in the middle of the playground.

The others walked behind her knowing they too had things to share.

"Maybe we should have a moment of silence to reflect upon why we're here," laughed Sidney as she sat down on the swing throwing her legs up in the air starting it to move slowly.

"I really don't think that's appropriate," Meagan replied.

"Hush White Girl! I'm sure what's said here today, won't fall into any categories of appropriate things!"

"Anyway, as I was saying before you so rudely interrupted... You know since my Mother died, Cher has been acting very strangely. At first I figured she was just tripping. But now, I'm not so sure..."

"What do you mean?" Waverly asked...

"Just say it Sid..." Dominique added looking a bit impatient.

"Give her a break Diamond. It's not always easy to just say something that has caused you pain. You work with people every day, so you of all people should know that ...." Meagan replied as she kneeled down beside Sidney causing her swing to stop moving.

Sidney then placed her hands over her face, took a deep breath remembering the principles of being honest from her group and how it has helped others in the past. She began softly,

"Sherian basically said, moments before our Mother was placed in the ground, that she was my Mother. Not Phyllis – not the woman I believed to be my mother, but her..."

"Wow..."

Meagan then added, "Well at least you know who your real Mom is... I don't have a clue..."

"No – wow – is right Waverly. Who in the hell would tell someone some shit like that at their Mother's burial?" Sidney asked disregarding Meagan's comment.

And now confused, Dominique said rather loudly, "Wait – wait – wait – I heard and understood what you said Sid, but what the hell are you talking about Meagan?"

"It's just what I said... After I had the twins, Katherine..."

"So now you're calling your mom Katherine?"

"Well she claims that she's not my Mother anymore, so what am I supposed to call her? Anyway, I had the girls and there stood Mother, Katherine, who ever she is... telling me, her daughter of thirty something years, I'm not hers! I freaked! Who does that? I didn't say anything until now because I could not believe it. Now, I believe it's true and I still don't know who my real Mother is... All I know is she abandoned me in the church (of all places) because of who the hell knows... And now I'm supposed to meet this woman to basically ask her why... I don't know... any day... So when I said, at least you know who your mom is... well at least you know..."

Waverly just looked at all of them and added, "And you guys are looking at me as if fighting some bitch from my past is so crazy... I think not!"

"But you know Sid, after you left yesterday; I started thinking... maybe she's telling you the truth. I mean think about it... You're of age, Sherian has nothing to gain and if anything, she stands to lose the relationship with you. And you have to admit, she has been acting like your Mom more so than a sister for years. You, yourself know how Phyllis Maple was... what she said was law! She may have forbidden Sherian to tell you the truth all this time."

"I hear what you are saying Diamond, but it's still fucked up... And Meagan – I had no idea what you were going through... that's fucked up too!"

"That's for sure, but how about this... it gets crazier..."

Meagan went onto share the doctor's sickle cell diagnosis. And that Nia carried this trait commonly found in African Americans...

"So which one of you is really black? Who passed down the trait?" Waverly asked as she looked at Meagan in eager anticipation of the answer.

A smirk began to form on Dominique's face indicating that her instincts told her that it was indeed Meagan, not Drake because of Meagan's hesitation to answer.

"You're not a white girl after all are you?"

"Be quiet Diamond! That's not funny..." Waverly replied.

"Sure it is... All of this time, I've been calling her "white girl" and her ass is as black as me..."

Sidney simply shook her head as tears rolled down Meagan's face and Waverly's eyes bubbled up as well. Dominique just stood there, looking puzzled as she often does, knowing why Meagan was tearful, but clueless about Waverly's tears...

"Am I missing something? Now I know why the white girl (who's really a black girl) is crying...But what's up with you Waverly? It's not that bad...We both have heard a lot worse..."

Waverly then looked at Dominique and said as her tears began to roll down her face,

"You probably couldn't imagine how it feels since you are always in control."

Taken a back, Dominique instinctively thought back to how she was unable to control her uncle from molesting her, nor could she control her Father from selling her off to his gambling associates. She also thought back to how she was totally unable to control herself from beating her Father to death one night when he arrived home drunk and again wanting to have his way with her... I guess by that time, she too had had enough... So, regretfully, her emotions pushed her out of control. Maybe this is why she has secretly always – always hated men. And yet, she loves Hannah. But thinking back to when she first came to the realization of her attraction to women, Dominique's first instinct to control that emotion, failed miserably...

"Lost for words Counselor?"

Snapping out of her thoughts, she answered, "No I'm just waiting for an answer..."

So taking a deep breath, Waverly said in a very soft voice, "How do I begin..."

But before she could say, Sidney started shaking her head and shouting,

"Oh Lord, I hope not from the beginning... We don't have all damned day! I just want to know how in the hell did you end up in a fight with the owner of the salon in the bathroom, then disappear as if you're some crazy lunatic bitch off the streets with nothing to lose?"

Dominique quickly nudged Sidney as if to say, she most likely has good reasons, while Meagan raised eyebrows and whispered,

"I'd like to know too..."

Waverly rolled her eyes and began to tell the story of how she had worked for Gina and Tony over twenty years ago, while fighting her way through college. She also told them of how her Mom became ill because of her promiscuous lifestyle...

Dominique kindly interrupted, chuckling, "You were a shampoo girl?"

"Let her finish..."

Waverly gave Meagan a nod as if to say thanks and then continued...

"First, let me clearly say that I was uncomfortable with her gestures. But then I just turned them into jokes so I could keep my job...One night when we were all finished and I'm sure I was stressed to the highest degree... I had just found out that my Mother was dying from "Aids" and we really – really needed some money. Gina could see through to my vulnerabilities... That bitch knew she'd worn me down with all of those "what ifs"... So, I finally folded..."

Not wanting to believe her, Sidney said, "What the fuck do you mean you folded?"

"She means that she fucked them for money Sid!" Dominique said without hesitation.

Poor Meagan added, "Oh my God!"

"Come on now... I was only nineteen. Haven't one of you ever made a mistake when you were a kid?"

Dominique smiled and said, "You were a little older than a kid at the time..."

"Fuck you Diamond!"

Meagan then looked Waverly dead in the eyes and said, "I can't say that I understand, but who am I to hold it against you or judge you... You are still my friend and I still love you..."

"Meagan, we all still love her, but you have to admit... This is even crazy for Waverly," Sidney added as she continued to shake her head in disbelief.

Dominique merely turned her lips up and added, "I'll bet you that's not the end of this story... She hasn't told us everything... have you?"

"No, I haven't! I never slept with Tony; he only likes to watch... The shame came from sleeping with Gina all that time..."

"Oh my God!" Meagan yelled again imagining their friend she's known for years from a totally different perspective; upside down with another woman.

Dominique seeing past her girlfriend's expressions of shock and shame, believed Waverly wasn't really ashamed of sleeping with a woman and said with certainty,

"I am sure a part of you liked it!"

"Shut up Dominique!"

"No Sid, we're all friends here. Let her say what's on her mind."

"That's all right, no need to say it because it's obvious. But it's really nothing to be ashamed of," Dominique replied with a touch of sarcasm in her voice.

Now if that isn't the kettle calling it black; you might as well start calling me Romaine instead of Roman...

"Well Dominique, I think we all know what my personal preference is! Now as for yourself... Are you still waiting for Mr. Right or maybe its Miss Right you are really waiting for since you have never even spoken of a significant other?"

Meagan just looked at Waverly shaking her head in disappointment and replied, "That was not nice."

Sidney giggled while thinking to herself, *Oh, but if she only knew.* Then she said, "All right, all right, break it up!"

"There's no need for us to fight amongst ourselves. Our job is to support each other no matter what!"

Frustrated, Waverly whispered, "You're right, this has all been a nightmare. And come to think of it, this shit started when Diamond first told me about those young boys. How are they?"

"Remarkably, they're okay. And I kind of believed from the very beginning there was some truth to the Hernandez' allegations that they were willing participants. But, it really came to light once I heard about Gina and Waverly's run in... I knew there was more. So, what I guess I'm saying is..."

"Forget it, I should have told you guys long ago. You've been my friends my entire adult life. I love you and view you as family. All of you! And, I promise here and now to never allow anything to come between us..."

Next, Meagan started to cry, Sidney smiled as she began to dance and hug her three best friends. Waverly batted her eyes at Dominique, while she returned the gesture thinking, There is no way I'm telling her right now...

●●●●

*M*eanwhile, on the side of town, Vincent is being photographed having some good morning sizzling sex with none other than Miss Paton. You'd think they would have had enough sense to draw the blinds... Who knows. Maybe he wants to get caught. Nevertheless, I'm certain Keith will not hesitate to forward his findings to Waverly. My question is...will she really leave this time? You have to admit, Girl has a lot going on right now. Between getting old... I mean older, your husband lacking penis control, your son secretly hiding in the attic...I mean closet. And topping matters off, having a tainted past coming to the forefront of your life...wow, Girlfriend must feel like she's losing her mind. I don't know about you, but if it was me... Oh – wait a minute, it couldn't be me... Remember, I'm just a fly on the wall... So back to the story...*

"I really do enjoy our times together Paton. Sometimes I wish..."

"What Vincent?" she asked while thinking to herself...*I know damned well this Negro is not going to play me by saying he wished he wasn't married to that bitch he claims to be so unhappy with.*

"I wish we had more time," he replied as he massaged his penis while licking his lips.

"I know that's right!" *Paton added as she went down on her knees to give him, once again what he wanted. So in return he could give her what she wanted – money for the honey...*

Games people play! I believe they even wrote a song about it. Too bad in the real world with open relationships, one's life is not considered a game. Sure – things done in secret can be overlooked as a game and maybe that's the fun of it! But perhaps once the fun is over, in most cases lasting as long as the climax, one returns to his or her public life pretending to be fixed... But it only lasts for another dull moment. Case in point, Waverly and Vincent for several years have managed to build a life together. From the outside looking in, a pretty good life at that! They've raised a son who's an "A" student in college. They've launched two careers that are both successful, they've also built their dream home while maintaining their condo, and are still practically debt free. I think it's safe to say, their life together is hardly considered a game. However, with Waverly snooping around in hopes of catching him with his pants down...she must have considered that to be a game of cat and mouse.

And what about her past... I'm sure she has said more times than not... "They'll never find out!" Secret lives are almost always considered to be a game. And now that it's just about over, her emotions are in overload after parting with her friends. Waverly's decided to cut off all communications with the world. 'Tis true! Girl is "home alone." She even gave Maria, her maid, the afternoon off. So if Keith wanted to get in touch with her – unless he would be willing to take another chance and knock on their door, today would not be a good day...But Keith being the persistent person that he is... calls her anyway!

"Corrine... it's Keith. There's something I need to discuss with you as soon as possible. Call me when you get my message..."

After two days of messages from Keith, Waverly still does not return his calls.

"Hey Corrine... it's me again, Keith... Just calling to see if you received my messages... I hope everything is well with you... Talk to you soon..."

I guess someone's a bit worried. He of all people should know how Waverly, if she so desires, can "get ghost" for a day or two and think nothing of it. Anyway, it's Monday morning and yes, our four friends have already finished their daily run and have returned home. Megan's nursing the twins, while Sidney's at one of those "NA" meetings in hopes of keeping her sanity. Dominique's at work trying to settle her case. And, Waverly's sitting at her desk finally checking her messages, only to find that Keith has been trying to reach her for two days.

"Damn!" she whispered as she immediately called him on his private line. "Pick up… pick up," she repeated just as his answering service came on. Ironically, Grace – Waverly's secretary, was paging her almost at the same time…

"Judge Simmons…"

"Yes Gracie, what's up?" She answered as she ended her call to Keith, unable to leave a message.

"There is a Mr. Keith Sheppard here to see you. He says he has an appointment, but I don't see it on your calendar."

Pleasantly surprised and confused as to what to do first, she hesitated answering… "Gracie, please escort Mr. Sheppard to my office."

Now Grace did as she was instructed, but was concerned to see her boss who's never departed from her schedule for anyone, allow an acquaintance to intrude without warning her first. So Grace did as any nosy secretary would, looked Keith up and down as she escorted him to Waverly's office.

"Mr. Sheppard…" Grace said just before closing the door behind him.

"Keith, I was just trying to call you…"

"Now that's funny; because I've been calling you for two days."

"I know… I needed a couple of days to clear my head. In fact, I just finished listening to the messages a little while ago."

"Well after you see this, you may need a few more days. By the way, you look kind nice in your big fancy office, dressed like royalty."

Waverly knew Keith found something incriminating. His hesitation in disclosing it proved just that… so she stood to her feet, walked over to the mini bar and with her hands trembling, poured two drinks. She then glanced back at Keith, who now was holding an envelope of photographs in his right hand and said,

"Would you care to join me?"

"You know…you really don't have to look at these. You can just take them to your attorney and let him take it from there…"

Shaking her head in shame, having found herself in the same humiliating situation, she simply handed Keith his drink and grabbed the envelope. And before sitting in her favorite chair, she smiled and whispered,

"Well, I guess this is it…"

Seemingly moving in slow motion, she sat down leaning back while nudging her reading glasses in position so that her view could be picture perfect. The corners of her eyes began to water as she viewed the first photograph only showing Vincent and Paton laughing. She looked at the second one showing Vincent completely nude, kissing Paton on her bare back and that's when it became clear to her… she had endured years of blatant infidelity. The third showed Paton giving the good doctor oral sex and the next displayed him retuning the gesture. Having had enough, Waverly threw the photos across the room trying desperately to muffle her angered voice as she nearly screamed in disgust.

"That bastard! I hate him! I hate him! Oh, I feel so damn stupid… Maybe it wouldn't be as bad if I'd done what the fuck I wanted to all of this time. But no! Being a judge makes you more judgmental of your own dumb ass…"

Keith tried to calm her down, but his efforts were useless. So being the gentleman he is and having seen this scene all too many times, he politely sat down and waited patiently while Waverly vented her feelings…

"This is so funny, how all of this was revealed today of all days," *Waverly said as she looked out her window taking in the view of the busy city which usually had the means to calm her… Curious, to say the least, Keith asked,*

"What is so special about today?"

Before she could answer, her cell phone rang a tune signaling her that it was Mr. Infidelity himself… Vincent. Eagerly wanting to answer, if only to tell him where to go, she walked towards her desk saying, "Speaking of Bastards."

"Waverly – don't say anything about the photographs."

Nodding her head in agreement, she whispered just before answering, "You're no fun…Yes!"

"Hey beautiful, that's no way to greet your husband. I know I didn't come home the other night, but I had to work a double. We were very short on staff and there was an emergency so I stayed. I thought I explained that to you… I know you're not still upset about that are you? Come on, today's a very special day for us. Not only does it mark the day we had our son, but it's also your birthday…"

Rolling her eyes… she replied, "I know what today is…"

Starring right at her Keith asked again, "What's special about today?"

"Who's that? Did I catch you at a bad time?"

"No, you didn't catch me at anything. I mean I was just in a meeting with a colleague. Why did you say you called again?" Waverly asked while shaking her head.

"To say Happy Birthday baby. And to confirm our dinner date for tonight. Actually, I've made reservations for four. Our son's bring a date. I think he has something to tell us…"

"Is that all?" she said as she took off her robe.

"Is that all… Oh I get it! You're tripping about turning 40. I'm not too far behind you baby."

"I'm not tripping about turning 40."

"Yes you are. But wait until you see what I have for you. You'll be all too glad that it's your birthday. So until tonight my love…"

"Yeah…tonight."

Well Vincent hung up as he usually did without saying good-bye while Waverly simply looked at Keith and gave him a phony smile.

"So it's your birthday. Wow! Happy Birthday Judge Simmons."

Genuinely smiling this time, she said "So now it's Judge Simmons."

"Well it's not like you ever gave me permission to call you by your first name… Waverly."

"Seems to me that you already know my first name and considering the intimate details of my life you are privy too…"

"Why didn't you just say what your first name was in the beginning? You knew I would find out…"

Shaking her head she said, "I don't know… I didn't know you and I wasn't sure I could trust you with who I really am… Then everything started happening so fast… I guess I never had a chance to properly introduce myself. Besides – you seemed to enjoy calling me Corrine."

So after waiting a few seconds for Waverly to formerly introduce herself, Keith said,

"So who are you really?"

"Who am I really... I have no idea..."

Next, both Keith and Waverly were laughing together for the first time. And that was good. Waverly was able to relax as she collected herself while Keith was just the receiver of a pretty good moment. Its funny how laughter can act as a buffer to one's emotional pain, just as Tylenol can soothe one's physical pain. Unfortunately for both, the lasting effects aren't too long. So as their conversation ended, the relief did as well...

"You know, it's been my pleasure to work with you. Sometimes it's hard for me to tell a client good bye. Especially one as nice as you," Keith explained as he walked towards the door.

Unsure of what to say, Waverly paused, took a deep breath and said in a very soft tone,

"Well I guess this is it... I suppose I have everything I need now..."

"I suppose you do...Good-bye Waverly Corrine."

But then just before he closed he door behind him, Waverly shouted, "Keith!"

Then she quickly went to him, pulled the man back into her office and hugged and kissed him on his cheek.

Keith smiled saying, "You are one special lady. Vincent never deserved you and if you ever need to talk, you know where to find me."

Now if that's not an invitation, I don't know what is... I myself find it agitating that at the most inopportune time in life, you meet the nicest people. Tis true! You both either have totally separate lives or at least one is physically and or emotionally unavailable. Basically not a chance in hell for the two of you to connect. It can only be wishful thinking. That's funny because that's just what Waverly is doing now that Keith is gone and she's left to literally pick up those nasty photos and the resentful pieces of her life. Luckily for her, girlfriends have a way of intervening in one's mess...

"Judge Simmons, you have a call on line one."

"Thanks Gracie," she said as she picked up the last photo off the floor.

And just as she answered, a melody of three came over her speaker singing happy birthday in the worst possible voice. And after singing their part, can you believe they actually wanted Waverly to sing the course that followed... Girl simply laughed and asked,

"Isn't a cake and candles supposed to go along with this..."

Laughing, Sidney added, "And it will my good friend, tonight at Pete's Place."

"Yeah girl...Diamond said we'll really be able to let our hair down because they'll have live entertainment, dinner and dancing! Maybe even some attractive men to look at," Meagan added while being up to her neck in stinky diapers.

Confused Dominique replied, "Meagan Simone, I said maybe Waverly could loosen that ponytail and let her hair down. I have no idea what you're talking about..."

Laughing Sidney added, "Y'all know Girl's interpretation is a bit slow..."

"Whatever! Maybe I'm just dying to get out of this house! Let's go shake our tails!"

"I believe the term is bootie, but nevertheless, I'm supposed to have dinner with Vincent and Victor tonight."

"Today is Vic's birthday also and every year we do this. It's an annual event."

"Awe come on Waverly! Go out with them another night! Your favorite band is playing! I know you could use some time out! Besides, fuck Vincent, you need to get rid of his ass anyway..." Sidney said as she checked her make-up while sitting at the light.

Then there was silence on the line for about ten seconds. Waverly knew she really didn't want to be with her husband that night. Especially in public, being phony at a dinner table for a minimum of two hours. Her thoughts were...

"I'd rather slice him up and serve him to the homeless. Maybe then the good doctor can finally do some good..."

"Look Girl, I've been practicing law most of my life and it has provided me with the ability to truly see a situation for what it is... You and I both know where this is headed. You've done all you can. You owe him absolutely nothing! And when this part is over, you will be a single woman

again. So – what better time to begin than on your birthday…
a new year… a new beginning…"

Waverly questioned it at first…then eagerly said, "You're
right – you're right… Fuck him as Sidney so eloquently said.
It's my turn now to do as I please… But first I need to get
myself together and I need to talk to Victor."

"Whatever you do, don't go home! You know how men
are…If he suspects you're going out without him, he's liable
to try and hurt you," Sidney said with her lips turn down.

"I wish that bastard would give me a reason to hurt him!"

"She's right Waverly! I know half the population in the
system now are in there because of domestic violence. And
I'd hate to have to kill Vincent if he tried to put his hands on
you," Dominique replied chuckling.

Meagan then laughed and said, "The day you commit
murder, is the same day, I'll practice law…"

Dominique simply thought to herself, *Shit if they only
knew…Vincent sure as hell wouldn't be the first…*

"So tonight then ladies… I'll meet you at Pete's and I will
stay away from home."

"Smooches."

"Stomps and Stabbs Sidney Sharpe! And as for you
Meagan and Waverly Corrine… later!"

Meagan smiled as she heard the others hang up and did
the same.

●●●●

*H*ours passed and since Vincent was in route to the
restaurant, he decided to call his son to see if he'd
be on time for their reservation figuring his wife
would be running a little late as usual.

"Hey Dad what's up?" he said as he
looked into the eyes of his lover nervously rehearsing in his
mind what words to convey.

"Hey Vic, did you make it there on time?"

"Yeah, we're here now."

"Your Mother's there with you?"

"No Dad, my friend and I are here waiting for you
and Mother."

"Okay, I should have known she would be running late. Anyway, I'm pretty close so I'll see you in a minute."

"We'll be here!"

"Hey Vic!"

"Yeah Dad," Victor answered with his brows raised.

"I have to admit, I'm a little excited about meeting this girlfriend of yours! Is she cute?"

Victor simply shook his head saying nothing...

"Never mind, I don't even know why I asked that, you're just like your old man... a chip off the old block... so I know she's a knock out... see you in a minute son."

Vincent hung up the phone feeling quite big headed in more ways than one, while Victor just chuckled looking at his cell phone then back at his lover, Jackson.

"What's so funny?" Jackson asked as he toyed with his drink.

Shaking his head smiling... Victor said, "My Dad wanted to know if you were cute."

"Well what do you think?" Jackson asked as he batted his dark ebony eyes looking as if he wore mascara, hair pulled straight back into a smooth ponytail.

"You know I think you are beautiful even though you sometimes go over board on the make-up."

"Well, who ever said beauty is skin deep... they lied! It begins with one's surface!"

"No, you're just crazy. I believe sometimes you have to see past a person's outer being to really appreciate the person's true self."

Turning his lips down, Jackson replied, "That maybe true, but the only thing I'm interested in seeing past right now, is this birthday dinner celebration so that you and I can go somewhere loud and promiscuous and get our freak on... And speaking of birthdays, happy birthday my love..."

Jackson then handed Victor a small jewelry box with a Tiffany label on it. Victor looked at it with wrinkles in his forehead and said, "I don't believe this is not Chanelle! I practically asked for Chanelle!"

So, while Victor was unwrapping his gift, his Father Vincent, was pulling up in his sports car scanning the restaurant front for a familiar face. Well, let's just say, he didn't get it! Instead a rather petite – extremely soft spoken – fresh out of high school – flaming homosexual – eagerly came over to greet him. Opening the door for the good doctor, he said,

"Well good evening Dr... well that's what I says on your tag. How are you on this beautiful evening? I hope you are as fine as you look..."

Vincent just looked at the young man thinking, *If this little (I'd prefer it up my ass) fuck, don't get out of my face right now!!!*

Well, the young guy merely stood there batting his hazel eyes at Vincent then he finally said, "Is there something else you need sir?"

Collecting himself, Vincent answered, "What? Where's Ralph?"

"Well my name is Timothy! I believe they said that Ralph is sick. I'll be parking that big old engine for you tonight sir. Would you like my card so you can call me personally when you are ready to leave?"

Shaking his head no, Vincent thought twice about giving his usual tip. So he place the money back in his pocket, dropping his car key in Timothy's hand to avoid even touch him. Timothy simply poked his lips out and said, "Men!"

Vincent walked away dusting his jacket off thinking, *Fucking Fagots are a disgrace to mankind...*

Well I can't wait to see how the good doctor will respond when he has to place his only son in that category. Now it's one thing to tell a person who you are... but showing them who you are brings along another dynamic to the situation. And poor Vincent with his untimely need to be in the wrong place at the wrong time has just gotten his face kicked in by his only son. As he entered the room, in plain sight sat Victor, cuddled up with a young man that almost looked like a girl. Shocked... Vincent closed his eyes and opened them again to check his vision. Poor guy, that act didn't help matters... All he could imagine then was the valet parker, Timothy, sitting with his son. Angered, he walked over like a "Bat out of Hell."

"Victor!!! What the fuck is going on here? I know this is not what I think it is!!!"

Victor quickly stood to his feet, eyes wide opened, while Jackson hung his head down while placing both manicured hands over his face. Chuckling to himself, he said, "I told you this wouldn't work."

"You damn right this won't work, you're a fucking Fag!!! My Son is a Fag??? This is your girlfriend???"

"Dad! Why don't you sit down... you're making a scene!"

"Don't call me that!"

But Victor was absolutely correct... Practically everyone in the restaurant had stopped what they were doing to observe the heated conversation going on in the exclusive VIP section of the establishment. The staff had already figured out it was indeed Dr. Simmons, a regular, carrying on with his son and what seemed to be his son's lover. As for Vincent, his rage had overcome his awareness of where he was at the moment. It wasn't until the Manager, an associate of his, came over to assist, that he realized his whereabouts....

"Dr. Simmons – is everything alright?"

"Yeah, I wasn't aware that you guys allowed this type of thing to go on in your place of business. My son and I were just about to leave."

The Manager looked surprised seeing that it was the good doctor who was behaving inappropriately. Frozen by his harbored emotions, Victor stood still while starring at his Father with his eyes filling with tears as held onto Jackson's gift. Outraged, Vincent shouted,

"So what... now you are going cry!!! Over this ... over this fucking Boy!!! And what's this?" he said as he grabbed the box out of Victor's hand.

Vincent held up the Chanelle bracelet looking at it with piercing eyes as he read the inscription,

"For my love... Forever Jackson. Oh no...this shit will not happen," he said flinging the bracelet almost two tables away.

Frustrated and hurt, Victor yelled, "What are you doing Dad? This is so unnecessary!! I can't believe this is happening!"

"You can't believe!! I can't believe you're fucking boys!! Or are they fucking you?"

Next, Jackson decided to stand for some strange reason in hopes of saving his pride – I guess... The Manager then attempted to pull

Vincent away from the area, while Victor turned to Jackson acknowledging him as his lover by trying to comfort him in plain sight... Totally out of control now, Dr. Vincent Zachary Simmons pushed the Manager out of the way while turning over the dinner table, basically threatening his son and his son's lover's lives by trying to assault them with his bare hands. Fortunately by this time, someone had enough sense to call the police who were more than happy to escort the good doctor out of the restaurant in hand-cuffs!

Embarrassed would have been an understatement considering Vincent not only had to spend the next 45 minutes on the curb of his favorite restaurant calming himself... He also was seen by another associate and had to witness his son leaving the restaurant hand in hand with his lover for the entire world to see...

"I know it's a bit much Doc, but hey, I see this type of thing daily. It *is* the 21st century... after all."

Vincent looked up at the officers with his brows frowned and said, "Maybe so, but I'm from the old school... and where I'm from – Boys don't fuck boys!"

●●●●

*P**oor Guy... Meanwhile, many miles away in downtown Baltimore, Waverly has just entered the elevator coming from the garage of their condo where Paton also resides and works as a receptionist. Having had to stop at the desk as usual to check on her mail, she took a deep breath and said a silent prayer in her mind. Luckily for her, the doorman was standing post while Paton had taken a ten-minute break. Funny though, I once heard someone say, "When all you have going for you is luck, it's bound to run out." And that's just what happened! When those elevator doors reopened for Waverly to enter, there stood Paton.*

"Bitch," Waverly whispered too caught up in the moment to think before speaking.

Unsure she was speaking to her, Paton said with raised brows, "Excuse me!"

Pretending to be preoccupied with her mail, Waverly replied as she shook her head, "Oh, I was thinking about a stray dog that was following me earlier. In fact, I was just saying, "I hope the Bitch is not pregnant!" *Lost for words, Paton simply looked at Waverly as the elevator doors closed in her face. Well, after only seconds of being in the elevator, literally moments before the doors were to open to the condo, it hit her...*

"This is where he's been bringing her."

She paused for a second then walked into what she thought was her second home mumbling,

"That's quite alright Mr. Man! Very soon... you will no longer invade my space, none of it!"

Girl then politely pulled out her court order which explained that the good doctor, Vincent Zachary Simmons had no more then 72 hours to permanently vacate all known residences owned by him and his wife. Moreover, all marital assets were to be frozen until the court date shown when an appointed Judge would determine basically who will get what. Wow, what a quick turn around... I guess someone's not playing! Maybe she's being a bit extreme, but then who's to say how anyone would respond to such betrayal... I just hope Vincent's in a much better mood mentally when he receives those documents... And Waverly might show some smarts and stay clear away until the time is right... But then sometimes you have to admit... just when you think you've got someone precisely where you want them, a natural yearning kicks in and you ultimately desire to see the look on their face when the "Waste hits the fan." My only advice would be to hold on and anticipate a mess. Because that is just what it literally looks like when that stuff hits the fan...

Anyway, back to "Common Lives"...

The Girls excluding Waverly have arrived at Pete's place. Meagan and Sidney are seated near the stage listening to the band while Dominique's at the bar hiding Hannah and running back and forth pretending to be just getting drinks.

"How long is this going to take? I want to have some fun," Hannah said as she rubbed Dominique on her shoulder.

Giving the bartender a big smile, Dominique leaned over close to Hannah and whispered in her ear, "not long... I promise." *Next, she slid Hannah her second round then carefully took the other three drinks to the table. After sitting them down while moving her hips to the music, Sidney then shouted,*

"Which one is mine?"

"One club soda for you... One Vodka – straight for the "white girl," oh I'm sorry... I'd forgotten... and one glass of champagne for me...

Meagan quickly downed her drink with one gulp and said after blowing out the hot fumes, "So do you think she's going to show? I mean she really didn't sound too enthused about this get together. You know she does have a way of pretending everything is fine when it really isn't."

Sidney and Dominique just looked at each other then back at Meagan and started laughing. Waverly walked up in the middle of their inside joke and as usual smiled displaying those pearly whites and said, "I sure hope like hell you're not laughing about me..."

"No Girl, Meagan was just sitting here getting wasted and wondering if you were going to show up. We were actually laughing at her," Sidney said as she got up to hug Waverly.

"Happy Birthday Stinka, I'm so proud of you... You're getting older, but you don't look old at all."

"Thank you Dominique, although I'm not quite certain if that was a compliment or an insult..."

Giggling, Dominique shouted, "Well would you like a drink?"

"Yeah, that would be nice."

Dominique then danced off to the bar again to get Waverly a drink and to check on Hannah. Waverly sat down after kissing Meagan and said,

"What's up with that Chick?"

Sidney looked back in the direction of Dominique and replied, "I haven't been able to figure that out yet. What I do know is she hasn't sat still since we arrived."

"Maybe there's a cutie at the bar she's not telling us about..."

"Meagan Simone, I must say that your woman's intuition is finally beginning to kick in," Waverly said as she nodded in admiration.

Meagan smiled in agreement while Sidney sat there kind of disconnected to the moment. Waverly noticed and asked, "What's on our mind babe?'

"I was just thinking about my Mother and how she died leaving me with no information to sort through this mess with Cher."

"That's strange because I would have figured her for leaving something to either confirm or deny Sherian's allegations. Listen to me, talking like we're in court."

"What about the Will? Outside of money and her estate, there's bound to be something there explaining what Sherian said."

"You're right Meagan. I'm going to look into that first thing in the morning. I believe I'm due in surgery, but right after, I'm going to see my Mother's attorney."

At that moment, Dominique returned saying, "Did someone mention an attorney?"

"Sidney was just talking about her Mom's attorney and how he might know something related to Sherian's allegations."

"Oh not that again! What are the chances of her lying about that? And if she is, you'll find out soon enough! So how about, if only for tonight, we laugh and dance and maybe have a few drinks. Except Sidney of course! Then, perhaps pick up on our Common Lives at daybreak... What do you say ladies?"

Well Meagan was the first to try a toast with nothing left in her glass to drink. Consequently, she held up her empty glass anyway and shouted,

"Here ye!"

Shaking her head, Sidney said,

"Your drink is gone stupid. Would you like another? Maybe a soda this time?"

"Yeah, maybe I'll get another one."

"That's okay, I'll get it. I've got to go to the bathroom anyway,"

Sidney said as she placed her hand on Dominique's shoulder forcing her to sit this one out.

Dominique just looked at her very strangely hoping she would be able to read her face once she noticed Hannah at the bar. Well Sidney went off to the ladies room first as she said. As she was leaving her bathroom stall, she saw an old acquaintance doing basically what most of her old acquaintances do, "getting high."

"Well if it isn't Dr. Sidney Sharpe! Aren't you looking mighty clean and sober," she said laughing as if there were really something funny.

"Hi Valerie, I can see how you've been doing…"

Taking another hit, she replied, "Actually, pretty well. I'm still at the top of my field…well almost. I've managed to hold on to my good looks, David still loves me, and my son Jackson's a straight "A" student, although he's gay… Can you believe that? Jackson's gay…"

Shaking her head in attempts to block out the drugs spread so neatly on the bathroom counter, Sidney proceeded to freshen her lipstick as she glanced down at the temptation.

"Have some?"

Thinking no, the poor girl said yes and took a line up her nose faster than she could ever recall doing in the past. Valerie laughed and whispered, "That a girl!" *as* Sidney took another before composing herself.

Sniffing hard before exiting, she said, "Thanks, I really needed that…"

Now returning to the club area with the loud music and crowd of people, things seemed to be faster than what they were. Sidney's no stranger to drugs so she did not appear to be high at all. She did however appear to have shaken off the earlier thoughts of her sister claiming to be her Mother and now she was ready to enjoy the night. My guess is Girl never even realized she had just relapsed. Approaching the bar, she noticed Hannah right away…

"Hey, what are you doing all the way over here? You're a part of the family now and supposed to be with us," *she said as she nearly dragged Hannah away from the bar area almost forgetting her own reasons for being there in the first place. So as Hannah picked up her drink, that triggered Sidney's memory and she quickly ordered something for Meagan.*

"Hey bartender, I'll have whatever she's having!"

The two went over to the table. Waverly could see that Sidney was being accompanied by an Asian woman. Meagan was now standing ready to shake her so called bootie, while Dominique sat there nervously hoping that Sidney wouldn't screw things up for her. That's too bad. Maybe she should start hoping for something else...because it looks like she is not going to be able to stop this train from coming...

"Hey, look who I found hiding at the bar... Hannah, I'd like to introduce you to Meagan and Waverly. You already know Diamond."

Well "The White Girl" as they called her continued to dance off beat as some white girls tend to do while nodding her head in acknowledgement of Hannah. Dominique froze out of fear...practically wetting her pants while Waverly stood and politely said,

"Please to meet you Hannah... that's a very nice name. So how do you know Sidney... do you work with her?"

"No, actually we just met..."

"Hannah's *Dominique's* friend if you know what I mean!"

But I don't believe they knew at all what she meant... so Meagan added as she continued to dance her way closer to the band,

"I think what Sidney's saying is she's Diamond's friend and not hers"

Dominique merely coughed basically revealing her discomfort and giving Sidney a signal she was finally able to pick up on. So as a good girlfriend would, she dragged Waverly away saying,

"I believe the two of them would like some time alone."

Well the band was jamming. Meagan, Sidney and Waverly were dancing together as friends sometimes do. Dominique was really trying to play it cool as she attempted to control Hannah's hands from being all over her. No such luck! Meagan, as caught up as she was into the music, somehow noticed their lesbian behavior and shouted,

"Why do you think Diamond's letting Hannah touch her like that?"

And as Waverly turned to see for herself, Hannah kissed Dominique directly on the mouth. Let me just say, it didn't look as if she minded the kiss at all...

"What the hell is going on with those two?"

Sidney continued to shake even harder as she shouted in Waverly's ear,

"I told you that – that was her *girlfriend*, as in "split to split" Get it, our Diamond doesn't prefer the "Dick!"

Waverly immediately stopped dancing and taken in by the view, literally replaying Sidney's comments in her head...said, "Suck my ass!"

Meagan added as she and Sidney continued to dance, "You know I heard that's what those lesbos really do to each other."

Chapter Twelve

Enough is Enough

*N*ow if I could give you a dollar for every time I've heard someone say that, you'd probably be rich. If you could have saved a dollar for every time you've said those same words yourself... well I think you get the point.

Maybe it's easier to explain one's self than to physically take action in response to emotional pain. In any case taking the advice from another, who somehow is not attached to the situation, almost never comes to mind. In most cases, you have to experience it for yourself and be profoundly overwhelmed before stepping out of your comfort zone to do the unthinkable. And still, sometimes your feelings follow you to bed attacking while you sleep, leaving the mind to wander even further out of control. Only to find that once you wake up, you're still in the same sick space with one thing left to say...

"Enough is enough," Waverly whispered totally frustrated with her life.

"He's got to go and today is the day!" *she mumbled to herself as she went into the bathroom to do her morning rituals before going to work.*

Vincent was down in the kitchen throwing away all of the boxes of sweetened cereal and everything he could find with sugar content as he waited for the coffee to finish. He was thinking of Victor and what part if any could he have played in what has happened.

"How could I have not known!" *he said wanting to cry solely out of guilt. The same guilt he felt years ago when he himself was a boy...*

"Be a man Vincent Zachary! Men never cry, only sissy's cry. Are you a sissy or a man? A sissy or a man..." said the voices in his head, reminding him of his painful childhood and his transition to manhood. Snapping out of it, he yelled,

"I'm a Man!"

Waverly over heard him as she came down the steps thinking,

"We'll see..."

Maria was in the lower level doing the laundry with earphones on listening to "Mozart." While Victor decided to allow things to cool down before returning home. He knew his Father would hold nothing back in sharing his homosexuality with his Mom so he decided, with Jackson's help, to leave well enough alone.

Vincent's stress levels were high and climbing... Yet sensing this, Waverly Corrine still convinced herself it would be best to end it all right now. So as she walked into her beautiful kitchen, dry-cleaned robe hanging over her arm which held her briefcase. She couldn't help but notice her soon to be "X" literally throwing away all of their favorite snacks. She thought, this fool is crazy... I can't wait until he puts his own shit into some brown bags.

Clearing her throat, she said, "What a beautiful day for change. Are you reorganizing the cabinets or just tossing the foods you don't like?"

Vincent looked at her, still breathing heavily in and out as he continued to dump the few snacks that were left. Waverly just shook her head as she politely placed the court documents on the table beside his morning paper. Then she sat her things down and proceeded to make herself a cup of coffee. From the corners of his eyes, Vincent could see that whatever she sat there was indeed intended for him. Still ignoring her gesture, he figured he'd deal with what ever it was later. Waverly knowing exactly what she was up against, thought, No, this will not go down like this!

So she said rather rudely just before taking a sip of coffee, "We need to talk."

Vincent chuckled and replied,

"What... about whatever that is you just put on the table? Or about your son fucking boys..."

Closing her eyes, playing back what was just said, Waverly not only spit her coffee across the kitchen floor, she actually choked...

"What!"

"You heard me. Which would you prefer we discuss first – your Honor... Another one of your clever ideas for our future or the fact that our son's a fucking homosexual!"

"Beasely?"

"You see that's your problem right there. All these little baby names you've been calling him all these years. Basically too much sugar in his diet..."

"Now wait a damn minute Vincent, me being a mother to him has nothing to do with whatever you think he is!"

"I don't think shit! I saw it for my self..."

Then at that moment, Vincent decided to pick up the slightly weighted envelope on the table, opening it to see its contents. Waverly's brows rose as she thought maybe it would make her point even clearer if she showed him those horrible photos... So she did. Girl tossed them all right in front of him as if to say... "Gotcha Mother Fucker!"

A silent rage came over him unlike never before. Even to her, it seemed as if he was somehow different. His brows looked as though they had connected while frown lines appeared on his forehead causing deep ridges to form. Looking straight into his eyes, she saw the devil looking back at her. And as he moved closer, a sudden fear washed over Waverly like an ocean as she backed herself up until ultimately, she stood in the corner of their kitchen. He knew this woman who he had been married to for over 20 years, who's usual characteristic of being strong and fearless was now scared. And that he was the cause of the fear in her eyes as he looked her up and down with a big joker grin on his face.

Terrified, she shouted, "Get out of my face Vincent!"

"No, it would appear to me that you want me out of your fucking life!" *Vincent yelled not two seconds before back slapping her as hard as he could. Poor Girl, I would have mailed those papers. The top of her head hit the granite counter top before she fell to the floor. Vincent with is now hardened heart pulled her up by her ponytail with his left hand and knocked the hell out of her with his right fist.*

"Satisfied now! Your Bitch ass want out, you're knocked the fuck out."

Maria stood there in shock. She had come up just in time to witness the last sucker punch. I say that because it was easy to see after the first strike, she was already out of it.

"Clean this shit up!" he said to Maria as he walked pass her bumping her on his way out.

Maria stood still trembling for a few seconds then when she heard the front door slam, shattering the glass as it closed; she burst into tears and ran to Waverly's aid.

"Oh my Lord Mrs. Simmons, what has he done to you?" she cried lifting Waverly's head checking to see exactly where the bleeding was coming from.

Blood was everywhere! On the counter, on Waverly's forehead, dripping from her mouth and so on... Waverly would not open her eyes and Maria was frantic. Finally, she checked to see if Waverly was still breathing and if she had a pulse. Seeing that she was breathing and had a faint pulse, Maria held on to her cross which was around her neck and shouted;

"Bless you God!" She then called 911.

"They're coming Madame, they're coming," *she yelled as she hurried to get some towels to place under Waverly's head. And just as Maria was about to place the last towel under Waverly's head, she started to moan.*

"Where am I," she whispered in a groggy voice, barely able to catch her breath.

"You're here, home, safe with me precious one," *Maria answered as she gently wiped away the blood from Waverly's forehead. Now just like the rest of the Simmons family, Maria had no idea that the telephone lines were being tapped. So when she dialed 911, Heather was listening from the office and immediately called Keith...*

"Hey Big Brother!"

"What's up?"

"Well... I thought you would want to know that your girl's being rushed to the hospital."

"What! Who! Waverly? That mother...!!!! I'm going to kill him... I knew I shouldn't have given her those photographs!"

"Keith – there's no way you could have known she would be foolish enough to actually show them to him... It's not your fault!"

"Yes it is... I knew better! Look, just play the tape back for me..."

Then after only a few seconds, Keith heard everything he needed to hear to draw his own conclusions as to where they might take her and decided to go with his instincts. Angry enough to stomp mud holes in Vincent's head, he immediately checked on his whereabouts over the two way radio...

"Mark..."

"Yeah Man, what's up?"

"Where are you?"

"Well – right now I'm sitting in front of Howard University Hospital. The good Doc has actually gone to work today."

"What about all the commotion going on at the house today... The maid said he busted up the door..."

"Negative on that... I must have been too far away to see it. Dude just pulled off burning rubber like usual when he was leaving the house."

"Alright then Man. Stay on his ass today! Real close! I want to know every move he makes including when he takes a piss!"

"You got it boss."

"Alright Man – I'm out."

●●●●

Just a few cars away, Sidney Sharpe was sitting in her car as well, contemplating whether or not to read a letter written to her by her dead Mother, Miss Phyllis. I would have thought it was kind of convenient to have a Mother leave some final words, but not Sidney... I believe she already knew what was in the letter and that's why she wasn't ready to open it. I guess after returning home late last night and coming to the realization that she had relapsed again, only to find that your dead Mother has basically dropped a letter of explanation in the mail for you... not wanting to deal with it would be reasonable. And now after having a triple espresso at "Star Bucks" she's teary eyed and angry. So she reads...

My Darling Daughter...If this letter has found its way to your tender hands, then I have found my way to Heaven. Know that I have loved you since the day I first held you in my arms. Nothing will ever change that fact. You will always – always be my Sidney. But, I did not give birth to you my darling...Sherian did.

When it happened, she was so very young and society back then was extremely harsh on interracial children... Let me first say that Cher and your Father, young Houston were very much in love. My closed eyes refused to acknowledge it at the time, so I took you from your real Mother with the intent of putting you up for adoption and sending her away to boarding school. Your Father never knew about your *existence my sweet child. So, please don't blame him. All of the decisions were being made by me...*

The watch given to you after my death was originally a gift from your Father to your Mother as a token of his affection and love for her. Through my own selfishness, I never gave it to your Mother. Maybe finally you can help me with that task now that I am gone. If you're wondering who named you, it was me. I took the name from your Mother's favorite doll given to her by your Father. Please don't hate me Sid and please don't blame your Mother... She wanted desperately to tell you many times, but I would not allow her to do it. I was selfish and feared how you would react to this news. I know you must think of me as a coward now, but remember that I love you Sidney and will continue to watch over you always...

Your Mother in Heaven, Phyllis Maple

Now let me just say Sidney's emotional state before reading this "Dear John" letter was precarious at best... The fact that she was even able to get through it was solely God's grace. So, I imagine that even screaming to the top of her lungs would not erase the emotional pain she must be feeling right now. One thing's true – children never asked to be born...and to learn of how you came to be in this world in this way, must be torture! Indeed Sidney's in deep pain. And now after reading what she thought was her Mother's last words, she's in a great deal of it.

"This is so crazy," she whispered as she placed the letter in her purse noticing the Tylenol Extra Strength staring back at her.

This is a fucking joke, she thought as she grabbed her bag dreading the day that lay ahead of her.

You see Sidney was due to be in surgery in less than thirty minutes and beyond the fact that she was still hung over from the drugs consumed the evening before, Girl was unaware that she had loosed the "Monkey on her back." Maybe if she'd known, perhaps she could have sat this one out. Instead, now she's in a room stocked with every known lethal drug to man and only herself to reason with... So as she checked her watch to see how much time she had remaining before surgery... that's when she decided...

"One for Mrs. so and so... and one for me..."

Darn Sidney... she didn't even give herself enough time to come down from the cocaine taken last night. That mixed with whatever she put in the syringe knocked her tiny little body completely out! On any other day, doctors and nurses would have been in and out of that room... Go figure... where's a good doctor when you need one. Now Girl's beeper is going off and they're paging her over the intercom system.

Coincidently, Vincent was not very far from the area where Sidney had passed out... so when he heard the hospital paging Sidney relentlessly over the Intercom, first he thought it was amusing considering her history... Next he immediately imagined himself getting even with his wife by making her best friend look bad on the job. Sidney had been warned before and placed on probation because of her drug problem. Being malice, he thought if he could somehow falsely accuse of her getting high on the job and get her terminated, not only could he get Sidney back for all of the years of her being coy with him, but he would also hurt Waverly in the process...

As he entered the room where Sidney laid helplessly, he immediately thought to himself, Now who's in the wrong place at the wrong time...

"Well will you looky here... Dr. Sharpe!" *He said looking her up and down then checking her vitals just to make sure she wasn't already dead. He picked up the medicine bottle to see exactly what she had consumed.*

"Shame on you Dr. Sharpe... I don't know how on earth your junky ass earned the opportunity to become a doctor in the first place."

Now of course Vincent's mind was moving much faster than he was. In fact, he had already changed his first thoughts and decided to take Sidney home so that he could really screw with Waverly's mind, if you know what I mean... First he thought to himself,

"How in the world am I going to get you out of here without being questioned?"

Then it came to him...

"Yeah, the back stairs leading right to the garage are right behind this room! Perfect!"

Next, he cleaned up her mess, grabbing another bottle of what he assumed to be a sleeping antidote, then preceded to get Sidney upright and disappearing before anyone noticed him. Poor Girl...

Meanwhile at Prince George's Hospital, Waverly Corrine was being hurried down the halls with her maid Maria praying non stop, by her side. Once they got her to the last set of double doors, one of the nurses turned to Maria and said,

"This is as far as you can go!"

Then they disappeared into the operating room. The Emergency Room was crowded and noisy. Maria stood still crying as if she had somehow lost her best friend. And with all of the hustle and bustle, several minutes passed before the same nurse returned noticing Maria standing in the same spot still crying. So after giving her a mild sedative, she placed Maria in a small observation room until she was calm.

"How is the Mrs.?" Maria asked when a doctor came into question her.

"What happened to Judge Simmons? Did an intruder break into their home? The police are there now. They said that glass and blood are everywhere. If you know something, you may want start talking... Assaulting a judge is a very serious crime and is considered a Federal offense. Do you understand what I am saying to you?"

"I don't know anything! I work for the Mrs. I just call 911."

Maria was no fool... Her loyalty to Waverly came first. So getting nowhere, the doctor left the observation and went to the nurse's station to speak with the detectives about his patient. Keith had approached the desk almost at the same time to conveniently listen in on what was being said about Waverly. He then poured on his assertive charm flashing his P.I. badge and easily persuaded one of the nurses on duty to take him back to see Waverly. Poor Girl, it was easy to see she wasn't any good to anyone. Waverly Corrine felt the pain of her injuries and was ashamed to have fallen into the category of a battered woman. A situation she'd seen in her courtroom a thousand times. She was unable to look directly in the eyes of anyone she respected. When the doctors and police attempted to speak with her about what happened to her, her green-gray eyes found the nearest empty space in the room. She stared into that space as if she were catatonic. So by the time Keith entered her room, it was difficult for her to even lift her head. Her eyes were simply filled with water and spilled down the side of her face.

"Waverly... Damn, let me see you. It's not that bad. I won't let him hurt you again, I promise..."

Frightened from the fear of exposure, Waverly shouted, "You can't say anything about how this happened! It's just too much going on. Let them think someone broke into my house! Between my husband and the fight at the Salon, I just can't take anymore! The publicity alone could ruin my career!"

"Okay, okay I understand! But I swear to you, he will not get away with this and will pay for what he's done!" Keith replied looking her directly in the eyes, forcing Girl's head up with his large hands.

Still uneasy, she quickly looked away and said, "Where's Maria? I pray she didn't say anything!"

"No, Maria's cool. They didn't get anything out of her. Maybe I need to get her to work for me," he said with a slight smile on his face.

Smiling, she added, "Don't you make me laugh Keith, it'll hurt my mouth..."

"He's such a coward! I'd like just five minutes alone with him... I'm sorry. What did they say about your head? Are they going to admit you?"

"No... Thank God! I can leave once they're done with my paper work. I just want to go home. I already called Gracie and told her I wasn't feeling well.... And that it'll probably be a couple of days before I return to work."

"Well at least you're half right..."

Puzzled, she looked up at him smiling and asked, "Keith – what do you mean by that?"

"What I mean is – I am not letting you out of my sight."

And with an attempt to return the gesture with her busted lip, Waverly smiled as best she could saying, "Not ever?"

"Ever!"

The two waited for what seemed like an eternity for the doctor to sign Waverly's release papers. Maria had gone a little before that... She waited around out of concern for her "Mrs." She wanted to make sure that she was alright. While waiting, Waverly called her son, leaving him a detailed message to avoid any sought of confusion. But she purposely avoided calling her three best friends in hopes of having one day of recovery to herself.

On the way to his house, Keith stopped by the Deli to get soup and sandwiches for them. But, by the time they arrived at his house, Waverly looked into the bag to see what they were having and said with her brows raised,

"This looks pretty good, but I'm thinking under the circumstances, I'd prefer a glass of wine and a hot bath right now."

Looking at Waverly as if he'd prefer her rather than the sandwich, he nodded in agreement and proceeded to get her a glass of wine. Waverly did not hesitate as she entered Keith's bedroom and made her way to his private bath. So as she ran herself a hot tub of water and undressed, she could hear soft music playing. Looking over to his bed, she couldn't help but visualize herself lying there naked with Keith exploring every inch of her body and eventually entering her private sanctum over and over again. Closing her eyes, all she could do was take a deep breath as he rubbed her hand across her breast. Keith was standing near the doorway watching her through the mirrors. Poor Guy, he'd forgotten just that fast, the glass of wine he'd poured was for Waverly. So instinctively took a swallow of the wine for himself before recalling it was hers.

Damn, he thought to himself walking up behind her unable to keep his hands off from her body.

So there she stood, naked with Keith in front of the mirror hanging on the bathroom door, a man she had been attracted to for a very short time and nothing standing in the way of her attraction to him. He wrapped his arms around her giving her the feeling of a Chanelle blanket in mid spring. His lips were warm and wet and she was disappointed that she was unable to kiss him with her swollen lips. Turning her around slowly, he removed the tie from her ponytail causing her hair to fall softly to her shoulders.

"Are you sure you want to do this?" she asked as the perspiration began to form on her body.

Keith quickly removed his shirt, unbuckled his belt and unzipped his pants with a look of longing and lust his eyes. He replied,

"More than you could possibly know…"

Well, I guess Girl forgot all about getting in the tub. The water just continued to run as they made their way over to the bed. Her desires were fulfilled as he began to ravish her body just as she had imagined a few moments before. As they saying goes, "one and one make two..." But, I'd say Keith and Waverly made love...

●●●●

Chapter Thirteen

All is Fair
in Love and
War

*W*hat does that actually mean? "...fair in love in war" If you looked on the bright side, one could think good follows love and evil is war's companion. However, the dark side suggests anything goes when you're in love so that would include the art of war.

Yet, as many begin on this journey, most people never really anticipate the battle that is destined to be....when your love. Then, they are emotionally consumed when their needs aren't met. Some bow down gracefully, while others get even... I once heard someone say two wrongs don't make a right. Well, that's obvious! But what about when you're doing right and things go wrong anyway? Funny, I heard that — that is just life's process. And oh, how it has a way of just showing up unannounced.

Something like what happened to Dominique. There she was as happy as she could be with her Gay self hiding in the closet and then all of a sudden, she was exposed without warning... Well maybe that was just an embarrassing moment and if that was her only challenge, it would be over. The sad truth is, however, her problems have just begun. If you recall, early in the story, right after Miss Phyllis died, Dominique and Sidney went to see a social worker about Dominique adopting a child. Well that was just her first interview. Now she's in her office pacing across the floor debating with her lover her reasons for not wanting to go to the second interview. Having to watch his boss, Franklin (her assistant) is annoyed by her behavior while he's sitting there trying to complete the settlement agreement their clients and the Hernandez's just signed.

Remember at the beginning, two teenaged boys were found left for dead in the park near the fountain the Media described it as a kidnapping. They also said that the boys were drugged and raped. Dominique through her own investigation believed that they were probably willing participants and were in way over their heads. However, being a responsible attorney, she did as any good lawyer would... She got her clients out of the situation by making her opponents look bad. Therefore, convincing them to settle out of court... The Hernandez's were guilty of having sex with minors and could do without the Media circus that was sure to occur.

So after hanging up the phone with Hannah, Dominique sat at her desk placed her hands over her head laying her head down and started whispering to herself.

"Ready to continue with the work at hand," Franklin said then rudely cleared his throat as he watched Dominique talking to herself. Knowing he was being coy, she raised her head and continued whispering. Franklin then decided to add his own two cents.

"Well if you'd have done what I suggested from the beginning, all of this could have been avoided!"

"If you were completing your paper work over there and not in my business, this conversation would be avoided…"

Franklin simply stared back at Dominique and said,

"Sometimes you're such a moody bitch. This is why I don't do women."

Smiling yet wanting to cry Dominique replied,

"Well I do and she's getting on my nerves with all of this baby shit!"

"Diamond, don't tell me you're having second thoughts about making me your baby's God-daddy…"

"It's Godfather Frankie and yes. I'm just not sure if I can do this."

"But you're not bitch, we're all doing this. Besides I thought I was the only punk in here. Grow some real balls and handle your business!"

Dominique just looked at Franklin and started to laugh. Two seconds later, her laughter turned to tears. She was actually crying.

Concerned he said, "Damn Girl, this is really getting to you. I believe it's time for you to get to the bottom of your reasons for not wanting to do this. See, I told your ass a long time ago when we first met, you need to do some soul searching. You can never fully embrace who you are until you accept your past mistakes."

"Frankie I know the things I've experienced are not who I am, it's just what I've done! I totally get that! It's just that I believe…"

"What Mary? You believe what?"

"I believe some people should not be allowed to have children. They abused them in ways that are horrible. They mistreat them until ultimately the children mistreat themselves. And sometimes I can't help but think if that could have any bearing on who I am…"

At that moment, Franklin stood to his feet, placed both hands on his hips and said with much certainty,

"Well of course it did! That's why you're Dominique Alisa Blake! You're smart, bold, strong and compassionate. Why do you think we love you? The past my dear has a unique way of building God's children, never breaking their spirit. Please... That's just Satan and his army Girl... Why do you think I don't fool with him?"

Scratching her head she said, "I know – you're absolutely correct."

"I know damn well I am! And you need to go back to that crazy shrink or wherever it is you need to go. Look them dead in the eyes with Miss Seszuan right by your side and with both hands in the air; tell them to bring it on!"

"Okay, Okay!"

"Alright-already! Now sign this shit so I can get out of here. I've got my own doing to do!"

So, Dominique signed the papers and Franklin disappeared. After setting there for all of five minutes, she too decided there were some things that need fixing. Girl made two phone calls and off she went. First she stopped by her condo to pick up Hannah then they both took a long drive to up state New Jersey to question and ultimately get answers from Dominique's Aunt Phoebe. Dominique called it a well overdue visit. Hannah, being a college professor knew this Aunt was a direct link to her lover's pain and the reason for Dominique's second thoughts about adopting a child. Well hours passed and by the time they'd finally arrived, Hannah had angst, but Dominique was hesitant...

"Come on now Diamond, we sure as hell didn't come all the way down here for nothing. You and I both know this is where it began. I may not know exactly what happened, but you and this Aunt do! Now I'm going to tell you something and I hope you not only listen, but hear... The fact that you're scared of us being parents has nothing to do with you and I being Gay. Long ago when you were at your lowest point in your life, for whatever reason, you lost hope. It seems that – that is where you've stayed mentally. You basically stop growing. Sure physically and even financially you grew; but, spiritually you went into a stall mode...and you are still there right now. Believe me, when I say facing this will only help – that's what I believe with every fiber of my being…. I am sure it will somehow free you from your past and then we can live…"

Dominique began to cry. Hannah lifted her head and kissed her on the lips. Taking a deep breath she said, "I can do this,"

They went up to the aged house which looked the same way it did all those years ago, smiling at one another and holding hands. Dominique took the first step up the wooden stairs and as always, that step still had a creaking sound. Reassuring her, Hannah stepped up beside her. One would think it was a doorbell because by the time they reached the porch, sixty year old Aunt Phoebe was standing at the door sort of faded out by the locked screen door. Aunt Phoebe always kept the front door open with the screen door locked, something to do with allowing the house to breathe.

So, as she stood there in silence, eyes gleaming from the excitement of seeing her niece whom she hasn't seen or heard from in twenty years, a sense of rest came over her.

"I knew some day you'd be back, Diamond. God sure has been good to you," said the voice from inside the door. Smiling Dominique whispered, "Auntie Phoebe is that really you?"

"Who else would be able to recognize you after all this time you've stayed away?" she said as she opened the door looking both Dominique and Hannah up and down through her reading glasses she kept at the end of her nose.

"I've missed you. I thought about you and this place almost daily; I really missed you."

Laughing she said, "I sure hope you haven't wasted your thoughts on those evil deeds all this time…"

"No Auntie, I haven't only thought about… that!"

Staring at Hannah, Aunt Phoebe she replied, "Look at her lying. You can't lie to me child. Your Auntie knows more than what this here tainted world wishes to give credit for… Who taught you to read and write?"

"You did!"

"And who told you – you could be anything you wanted to be?"

"You did Auntie!"

"Who also told you the eyes are windows to your soul and that I could see you – the real you" she said as she moved out of the way to allow Dominique and Hannah to enter the house.

Shaking her head as she looked back at Hannah, Dominique answered as she held her lover's hand firmly entering her Aunt's house,

"You did Aunt Phoebe! I get the point!"

Watching them she added, "And so do I my dear!"

"What do you mean?"

"I can see that the two of you are soul mates. He has made you hate men! Hasn't he?"

Looking around noticing nothing has changed, Dominique said, "Where is everyone?"

"I'm everyone… the only one left. Your cousin Serena moved away. It'll be ten years soon. She calls every Sunday and comes around twice a year on Mother's day and my Birthday. Last year she gave me this locket with a baby picture of her on it…But enough about Serena. You're here because you're questioning who you really are… right?"

Hannah looked over to Dominique and whispered," I told you… By the way Aunt Phoebe – I'm Hannah."

"Pretty name for a pretty girl! I hope you're nice to my niece. You know I promised her Mother that I'd look out for her. Her Father was a born again "bastard" and got what he deserved! Edward was his name and I knew the first day I laid eyes on him before he married my sister, there was something very wrong with him. I believe that man's father was the devil himself. He abused my younger sister until the day she died then continued with you Diamond."

Now as for Hannah, the conversation was intriguing, but Girl wanted Aunt Phoebe to get to the part that explains what has hindered Dominique so she politely interrupted saying,

"Excuse me Aunt Phoebe, we're here because Dominique and I want to have a baby and she's afraid that she won't be a good Mother."

Confused, she replied "Wouldn't you two need a man for that?"

Shaking her head Dominique explained, "We were going to adopt Auntie. I just thought because of what happened with my Father, I would be classified as unfit to raise a child of my own."

Aunt Phoebe began to laugh. So much so that Hannah giggled also. Dominique, on the other hand, saw nothing amusing about that fact that she had killed her own Father (or so she thought) even if he had sexually, mentally and physically abused her... Puzzled she said, "I don't get it! What's funny?"

"You sure don't child! You actually believe that you killed your Father don't you? You sure as hell didn't kill that bastard! Is that what you've believed all this time? Shit child, you should have come back way before now! I see why you turned to women! I might have too if I thought I'd done something I really didn't do, like murdered my Father."

Hannah sat there looking surprised as she realized what had been weighing on Dominique's heart all this time. Dominique sat there somewhat relieved, but confused and perplexed by her Aunt's comments. She wanted to know who had killed her Father if she hadn't.

"So I really didn't kill my Father, Auntie?"

"Why hell no!"

"But you sent me away and told me to just pretend it never happened. I know I hit him on the back of his head several times and when he fell to the ground, I saw the blood."

"Then you ran to me frightened and I put you on the bus and told you not to look back. I only said that so you'd be able to start over. That Eddie help kill my baby sister and he was working on you! So after you left, I paid him a visit. He liked women and I acted as though I liked him. I was very kind to him if you know what I mean...I nursed his wounds and made him feel real good after the incident with you. So that shit for nothing bastard felt comfortable enough to sleep. While he slept, I cut his throat! Hell, I figured that was the least I could do... considering..."

"Damn!" Hannah said as she placed her hand on her own throat.

"Come to think of it, that was the worse sex I ever had! And to be truthful, I ain't had any since. So I guess we both have been held hostage by that bastard."

"This is incredible; I can't believe I've been torn apart by a lie all these years…"

Just then, Aunt Phoebe left the room. She returned a few minutes later with a small three by five photo of Dominique and her late sister. Giving the picture to Dominique she said,

"Here Alisa, you were about a year old in this photograph. She was a good Mother and you will be also. Go home! Go get your child. Be not afraid… God knows and so does your Auntie. You'll do just fine… I am sure of it!"

Next, Aunt Phoebe embraced Dominique and Hannah. They said their good- byes as Dominique and her lover left Aunt Phoebe's home. As she watched them walk down the steps holding hands, like second nature, she locked that old screen door. Hearing it, Dominique looked back with a smile, glad to finally know the truth. Smiling as well, Hannah said, "I guess we can go get our baby now…"

Nodding her head in agreement, she whispered, "Well, I guess we can…"

●●●●

*W*ow!!! *Guilt is a strong weapon. It's said if you can get a person to believe they're at fault with a mere suggestion, the guilt alone could consume them until ultimately, they destroy themselves. Another individual does not have to be involved for this to happen; the mind itself can convict you. It's true! People come in and out of your personal space daily while on occasion, implanting the notion that something is in fact wrong with whatever it is you're doing. You in turn, sit and ponder the vague suggestion and trip! Later, you reenact the same statement adding your own dysfunctional information there by convincing oneself of its validity… and you continue to trip! Sounds familiar… Even so, you have to admit holding on to unnecessary emotions because they have at one point or another caused you to feel pain, can be self-destructive.*

From Dominique to Waverly…. From Sherian to Sidney and now Katherine; destruction is inevitable when you're running away from self or something you felt directly responsible for…Isn't that what happened with Katherine? She allowed the fear of what could happen, once Meagan knew the truth, kept her from disclosing it at all. Another clear case of unnecessary emotions were derived from her own suggestive thinking. She had already convicted herself mentally. To put it more simply, dysfunctional thinking trips the mind.

Now she is driving home, worn down by her emotions, after leaving the church – the place where she was told to send her daughter to meet her biological Mother. One would think replaying old tapes of what could have been – was enough. She now has new ones to draw conclusions from... and just in case we're moving to fast, let's review... In the beginning, there were Katherine and Theo. Katherine being Meagan's adopted Mom and Theodore being Katherine's late husband, Meagan's adopted Dad. With me so far... good!

Well after years of being unable to have children of their own, on top of countless miscarriages, they decided to adopt. Back then, times were extremely difficult and the adoption process was a very lengthy one for any couple trying to get a healthy white baby. Thus, at the end of their road of frustration, endless praying, and utter desperation, Katherine basically gave up on the idea of being a mother. But, one evening about an hour before service was to begin; Katherine and Theo arrived early in hopes of recovering from their disappointment and asking for forgiveness and the strength to move forward. Little did they know a troubled teenaged girl had not so long ago left her newborn baby behind in one of the pews believing that someone else would be more worthy to care for her. Young Sofia was living in a time when it was not only forbidden to have children out of wedlock, particularly at her age, but it was also forbidden to have a child of mixed race. Being overwhelmed, she ran to the church and left the baby, now known as Meagan behind.

Now when Katherine and Theo arrived, they headed straight for the altar. It wasn't until after kneeling down to give praise and thanks to God for their mere existence, that they heard the soft cries coming from one of the pews. At first Katherine thought she was imagining what she heard until she noticed Theo looking in the direction of the sounds as well. Then she thought, this must be a dream and Theo just happens to be a part of it – until she laid eyes on Meagan for the very first time. Katherine, at that point, believed her prayers had been answered. She didn't hesitate to take and keep Meagan hidden for weeks.

After several weeks, the guilt about taking a child without telling anyone bothered her deeply. So, Katherine returned to the church where she was told by the young priest to rest. He knew that Katherine and Theo had taken the baby and told her that the birth Mother did not want the child and would never return to question the baby's whereabouts. Well that was all Katherine needed to hear. Hard to swallow, but true! Young Sofia stayed away and the child's Father moved away. But then a few years passed and Sofia received word that the young man she had loved and had a baby with, died. Distraught to hear the awful news, Sofia began to feel that there was nothing left in the world to live for so she returned to the church for salvation.

The same young priest, who had become Father Murphy by then, offered her a place in the church to stay where she later found hope for her life. Eventually, after many years of service to the church, young Sofia became a nun. Later through years of loyal service and contrition, she was appointed to the highest position given to a woman in that Parish... "Mother Superior." Now before you go off on the deep end, let me just say... under every robe there's bare skin..."

Now all was well for a long time until the guilt began to manifest itself in Katherine's heart. I believe the seed was planted when Theo died. So years later when Meagan began to have miscarriages, Katherine saw it as a curse. She not only believed it, she began to confess it. This woman had in her mind convicted herself for all of her daughter's mishaps. Consequently, confused and nearly destroyed when Meagan gave birth at the very beginning of our story, Katherine jacked and told her the truth about her birth – the fact that she was not her real Mother. I suppose Meagan would have found out anyway considering she bares the sickle cell trait beneath her milky white skin. Nonetheless, the truth is out and Katherine going to the church before the appointed time.

Maybe it was her need to control things that had her go to the church early so that she could meet Meagan's real Mother first. But, when Katherine realized Meagan's real Mother was Mother Superior, a woman whom she had grown to love and confide in herself from time to time, she nearly passed out. Girl ran straight out of the church hysterical and in tears, headed for home feeling less worthy now than ever before. All she could see was this great woman is Meagan's real Mother and she is was nothing but another liar...

"Where is my faith now Lord?" *she screamed as she pulled up into her driveway never even noticing her daughter sitting on the porch in her favorite swinging chair.*

And as she got out of the car, slamming the door behind, sudden fear came over her when she realized Meagan's car was parked in front of her house. She looked around quickly first hearing the sound of chains that held the swing chair. Then as she walked towards the house wiping her tears with every step, Katherine could see those tight curls hanging from Meagan's head.

"Me-Me!" *she said as she slowly walked toward her.*

A big grin stretched across Meagan's face when she saw Katherine.

Taken by her presence, she asked, "What are you doing here Meagan? You're supposed to be at the church meeting with your real Mother."

Katherine noticed Meagan was dressed especially nice. It's been a while since she'd seen her in non-maternity clothing since she'd had the twins not very long ago.

"How do I look?" Meagan asked as she stood to her feet, slowly turning around in a complete circle.

"You're beautiful Me-Me! You've always been beautiful to me," she answered with a half smile.

Meagan's eyes then began to water as she said, "Well I was thinking if today is going to be the day I meet my real Mother, I should be dressed as nicely as I can for such an important occasion. So… "real Mother," what do you think?"

Realizing what she was gracefully trying to say, Katherine knowing her child, broke down in cried a river of tears. Meagan cried as well. Then they both began to laugh as they entered the home Katherine had raised her in all of those years. And with her soul at peace, Meagan never even mentioned the appointment she was to have at the church. Talk about resolution …

●●●●

*W**ell they say true love casts out all fear. But what happens when there's the fear of losing love? Does it then transform its way to lust? It's said – love gives while lust takes. So I wonder if a person believed they've lost love, could they become revengeful enough to take it from someone else?*

I think so! In fact, I believe that's just what's on Vincent's mind as he's helping Sidney to her apartment. Normally, Sidney would have pulled into the underground garage, but since she was way out of it, Vincent thought he'd be slick and get the management to open the door for him. What he didn't know is that he is being photographed almost every step of the way. So flashing his hospital I.D. and thinking nothing of it, with Sidney looking as if she'd had a procedure herself, the good doctor convinced her management that Sidney was heavily sedated because she's lost it at work in reaction to her Mom's death. Now, Vincent's not only a good doctor, he's also a good manipulator – so I am not surprised by the methods of his madness. In fact, by the time he got her into the apartment, as she was coming to, he actually spoke to her telling Sidney he was somehow helping her avoid being embarrassed at work since he had found her stretched out cold from an overdose. Half true anyway! And his only concern was her safety so that's why he brought her home to put her to bed. Of course he left out the part about joining her...

So as he undressed her down to her naked body, forehead sweating from the anticipation of having his way with her, Sidney's eyes opened wide. Licking his lips, he said,

"It's about time your junkie ass woke up. I thought I'd have to do this all by myself."

Aware of what was really happening now, but under no condition to fight him, Sidney said

"Why are you doing this? It's me, so what... we've had our differences, but... It's me you bastard..."

Taking his pants down with only one thought on his mind, he flipped Sidney over to shut her up and to ride her bareback.

Vincent simply lost his mind. From pulling her hair until some of it was now in his hands to leaving a palm print on her bottom after hitting her repeatedly, Sidney just cried; and the more she cried, the worse things got.

"You won't get away with this shit!" *she screamed just as Vincent hit her again to shut her up then threatened to do the same to her sister Sherian. But when that failed to work, he beat Sidney even more until ultimately choking her until she passed out.*

"Shit – shit – shit!" He shouted after pulling himself off of her.

Sidney's body was bruised badly and locks of her hair were on the bed. Her neck had Vincent's handprints all over it while blood dripped from her rectum and was all over Vincent's penis. This was indeed a royal mess! What started out as lustful revenge has turned into first-degree rape and attempted murder. Panicked, Vincent started pacing the floor and rubbing his chin while dripping semen and blood everywhere.

Looking over at Sidney and then at the circumstances, he thought about the drugs he had stolen from the hospital and got another bright idea.

"I'll give the Bitch another overdose and get the fuck out of dodge."

So that's what he did! And this time – time was not on the good doctor's side. He had already been warned by the police the night before for attacking his son and his son's lover. Earlier that day, shocked by Waverly's throwing the compromising photos in his face, he assaulted her and now this! If ever there was a need for him to run away, now and fast would be the time. Besides, Vincent knew there would be no explaining this away. All the intellect in the world would not help him now.

So taking a deep breath, he calmly filled the syringe with the drugs from the hospital and proceeded to inject Sidney with it. Her body jumped slightly as the Morphine passed through her veins causing her to appear almost lifeless. Shaking his head, he gave her another dose just to be sure she would die. Next, he wiped up the blood and semen from the floor, and then took a shower as if nothing had ever happened. While dressing, he repeatedly reminded himself to remember to get those sheets from Sidney's bed leaving no evidence of the rape. So after pushing her to the floor, he took the sheets from the bed. Poor Girl, Dude had left her there to die. Her pulse was weak and she was losing oxygen rapidly.

Thinking he was clever, he made a special trip to the lower level, placing the sheets in one of the dumpsters. Checking his watch, he then hurried off with Mark on his tail and running on his mind. Vincent's first stop was at his local bank where he withdrew all of the funds he could. He had managed to tuck away almost a quarter of a million dollars in liquid funds. Everything else had been frozen by Waverly since it fell under the umbrella of marital property. When Mark saw him coming out of the bank with what appeared to be a bag full of money, he immediately got suspicious. Taking more photos, *he jotted down the time and continued to tail Vincent. After about twenty minutes had passed and with nothing but Beltway traffic ahead of them, Mark began noticing all the signs pointing them in the direction of the Airport. Remembering never to doubt himself, Mark called his boss.*

Keith and Waverly had just finished making love. She was now in the tub and he was in the kitchen snacking. Hearing his phone ring and knowing that Mark would be checking in periodically, he quickly went back into the bedroom to retrieve it from his pants. Winking at Waverly, he checked the caller I.D. before answering...

"Hey Man what do have for me?" he said as he left the room; thinking it would be best to keep Waverly in the dark.

Chuckling, Mark replied, "I'm not sure of what's going on, but this Nigger's about to jump on a plane and fly the coop."

Furious, Keith said with base in his voice, "Look – whatever you – do not let that Mother-Fucker get on a plane."

"So what do you want me to do? Arrest him!"

"Come on now Man – think! You don't have the authority to do that! Get the airport police to assist you. Follow me?"

"Yeah, I'm following you... but on what grounds."

Keith then thought for a moment and said, "I know – for assaulting a Judge. I can be there shortly with the proof we need. Flash your badge and let them know we've been on this Nigger. And if you have any problems have 'em hit me."

"Cool... I got it!"

At the same time, Waverly's cell phone sounded. Knowing it was Meagan by the ring tone, she slipped out of the tub to answer her phone. Keith had just walked in looking at her, waiting patiently so he could inform her that he would be stepping out for a while. But when she answered the call, immediately her face became flushed and a nervous energy came over her. Dropping the phone to the floor, Waverly Corrine broke down into tears repeating the words,

"I have to go – I have to go! They found her dead! Then the paramedics came... and revived her... Now they are taking her to the hospital!!!!"

Screams followed as Keith stood there puzzled, wondering what in the world has happened. Well grabbing Waverly was out of the question because Girl was fumbling around looking for her clothes and trying to get out of there as fast as she could.

"Wait–stop–calm down!!! I'll take you wherever you want to go!" he said as he finally was able to grab a hold of her.

Waverly was sniffling as she began taking deep breaths, still looking around for her blouse. And when she finally saw it, she noticed it had bloodstains on it from her encounter with Vincent. Being a gentleman, Keith politely took the blouse from her and tossed it on the bed then went over to his chest drawer and got her one of his sweatshirts.

"Thank you Keith," she whispered as she watched him dress, thinking to herself, *Whoever did this to Sidney will pay... I will personally see to it that they burn in hell*

So, I guess it's safe to assume, Vincent's plan of hurting his wife has come to pass...

●●●●

*M*eanwhile, over at University Hospital, Meagan has just arrived. Since she'd already called Dominique and Waverly, she quickly located Sherian in hopes of finding out exactly what happened. It didn't take her very long. In less than five minutes, she noticed Sherian at the end of the corridor with her face pressed up against the glass, just like Sidney was when her Mother died. Trying to be strong, she hurried down the hall, calling her name, holding back her tears...

"Cher... Sherian..."

Turning around to face Meagan with a desperate look of fear, she too burst into tears. The two embraced each other as Sherian cried while Meagan held her tightly, rocking her back and forth. A few minutes passed then one of the doctor's came out to speak with them. Noticing him first, Meagan said,

"So tell us how bad is it?"

"Is she a fighter?" asked the doctor.

Sherian replied by saying "If that's all it will take then we've got a good chance. That's all she's ever done..."

"Well that's all we have then. She's pretty much stable and if she makes it through the night, She'll have a better chance. Unfortunately though, the next twenty-four hours or so will be critical...I know this is hard for you. It's hard on us as well, we've grown to love Dr. Sharpe too."

"So – are you saying she may not make it? She can't die – she's my daughter. The last time we were together, we fought and I hit her... I never got the chance to apologize... And I never got the chance to tell her how much I love her.... She just can't die – not now!"

Looking at the doctor, eyes watering as fast as her heart was racing, Meagan whispered, "There has to be something you can do. Maybe it's something you haven't thought of yet. Go on back in there – you can save her!"

Empathizing with their feelings and knowing there was nothing else he could do at this time, he made a deal with them...

"I'll tell you what... If I promise to do everything I can to bring her out of this, will you two stop crying?"

"Yes, of course we will," Meagan responded.

Wow! Things weren't looking to good. Sidney was near death. Dominique was burning up the highway to get to the hospital while Sherian and Meagan were practically numb sitting there waiting for time itself to pass. Waverly has just arrived not knowing what to expect. If you ask me, "Common Lives" has become a common mess. And bursting in the door, looking as if she'd just ran a marathon; Waverly came running down the corridor like a ghost was on her trail.

"Where is she...where is she!" she said nearly out of breath.

Looking up at her friend, Meagan answered,

"She's in there, but they're not letting anyone in right now."

"Who found her? How the fuck did this happen?"

Standing to her feet with her arms wrapped around herself, Sherian answered,

"I found my baby and no one knows what really happened. No one but my baby and she's in a coma, fighting for her life."

At that moment, Dominique came rushing down the hall as well. But unlike her friends, crying out of control, this chick looked like she wanted to kill someone. As she got closer, you could see that Hannah had come with her. It was easy to see terror in Dominique's eyes so

Waverly immediately hugged her in an attempt to calm her down. It's crazy, she almost sounded like she was speaking in tongues. Sherian just shook her head and tried to explain, what she knew, to her daughter's three best friends.

"I guess you guys already know what happened at my Mother's burial... I wasn't trying to hurt her; I just wanted her to know the truth about us. Sidney said some really mean and hurtful things and I hit her... I know I overreacted... Before that moment, I have never raised my hand to that Girl. I swear to you. I wanted to apologize for hitting her so I called her house. I called her work number and her cell phone... I don't know how many times... Sidney would not answer the phone... I mean, I know she's pretty stubborn; she is my daughter after all... So I got in my car and drove to her house. I knew something was wrong the moment I arrived. It just felt kind of eerie. When I got to her apartment door, it wasn't even closed entirely. It was as if who ever was there had just left. I called out for Sidney and didn't receive an answer..."

At that moment, Sherian started crying again. Her emotions spilled over to Meagan and she began crying as well. Waverly and Dominique just looked at each other as if they were able to read each other's mind. Frustrated, Dominique shouted,

"So what was all this about her dying and being revived? Couldn't she have some sort of brain damage and shit!"

"Like I said when I got there, she was out of it. The sight of her blew my mind. There she was all balled up, completely nude on her bedroom floor. The only thing I could think to do was call 911!"

"What do you mean she was naked? Meagan said she overdosed!"

"No, my baby might have taken too many drugs, but someone raped and sodomized her first. Sidney was beaten really badly. There were bruises all over her body."

"No – No – No!"

"Come on Diamond, she's going to be alright. We will get through this."

●●●●

*S*peaking of getting through things... I wonder what the good doctor's contemplating now that he is sporting new jewelry – handcuffs! Boyfriend must have thought he was home free, standing in line waiting to board the plane. Believe it or not, he actually claimed mistaken identity after all he's done. I suppose with I.D. reflecting he was the good doctor, a bag full of money and a one way ticket to Paris, even from up here things just didn't add up. Funny thing about it, the thing that caused him to flee, is not what he's been arrested for. And I'll bet knowing that, gives him a false sense of hope.

So after being read his rights, the good doctor was placed in the back seat of a marked car and escorted back to the city for due process. I guess he'll be catching another flight...

Well as night fell, the girls being equally exhausted wanted to stay at the hospital in hopes that Sidney would wake up soon. They somehow persuaded Meagan to go home and at least check on her babies and promise to call promptly if anything changed. Swearing to nap there herself, Dominique sent Hannah home, while Sherian sat by Sidney's bedside wanting to be the first to look into her eyes. Waverly found her way to the hospital cafeteria, seeking caffeine to fuel her tired body. She was still searching her mind for the reasons that everything was suddenly upside down in their lives in just a matter of days. So while thinking back over the years, knowing she herself held a shameful secret, she couldn't help but think, *Maybe if I'd done something different in choosing to face my past years ago, when Sidney needed me most, I would have been there for her and not stopped at the gate with my own selfish needs... What am I saying? How could all this possibly be connected? I must be losing my mind*

Little did she know... things were indeed connected! Waverly's inability to see things as they were prohibited her from seeing the people she loved most... as they were..... Their true self. Think about it! Girl being ashamed of what she did all those years ago forced her to stay in an uncommitted marriage for the sake of appearances. Her clouded vision of herself forfeited what was in plain sight – her son! Now maybe we can say, Vincent was just being vengeful and using Sidney as his torch, but aren't they connected? Her direct link to his wife made her a great target. What's worse, in all of this, Waverly's guilt holds truth. The only thing left now is for Keith to reveal it. And *with the clock ticking until the good doctor's arraignment in the morning, although it may not be necessary for Waverly to physically press charges against her husband, Keith Sheppard knows it sure as hell would give them the upper hand. And believing it could possibly take an earthquake to move Waverly, Keith and Mark are together now developing the latest photographs of Vincent's day, hoping they will reveal something they can use. They have no idea they're holding the missing link.*

"I hope you're right! Maybe once she sees these pictures of him with this other "Bitch" she'll have enough sense to press charges" Mark chuckled as he handed Keith the photos.

"Hope so man. Catch you later…"

Well hours passed and just before daylight was to break, Sidney Sharpe opened her eyes coughing and moaning like she had something caught in her throat. Sherian had fallen asleep with her head resting on Sidney's arm, while Waverly and Dominique sat in the windowsill watching the monitors and trading horror stories for most of the morning. At first they thought she was dreaming again, considering the monitors didn't indicate a change. But then, Waverly noticed her lips quivering as if she was trying to say something. Before you could bat your eyelids twice, Waverly was tapping Dominique on the leg saying,

"I believe she's waking up! I believe she's awake!"

They both went over to the bed like two teens in trouble to witness the miracle of life. Sherian's head rose slightly as she too could feel Sidney's other hand caressing her head. Sidney merely looked at all of them one at a time with an assurance, sort of smiling to let them know she was alright. One would think her first words would be, what's going on or how did I get here? But not Sidney, I believe she already knew, so Girl's first words were,

"Where's Meagan – is she alright?"

"Where's Meagan? Of course she's alright," Sherian said softly, standing to her feet.

"You had us going for a while there… I almost thought we were going to lose you," Dominique said as she rubbed Sidney's leg.

"Yeah Girl, she's right. I made a promise to myself to see to it that who ever did this to you will most definitely burn in hell!"

And at that moment, hearing those words come from Waverly's mouth caused Sidney to replay her last moments with Vincent in her mind. Sweat beads covered her forehead as the painful thought entered her mind, Would her best friend be able to forgive her?

"I'm still here by the Grace of God. I should have died. Waverly, I am so – so sorry. I was only trying to feel better. That's why I took the drugs; I wasn't trying to kill myself."

Waverly just smiled, looking over at Sherian then back at Sidney and said,

"There's no need to apologize. We're just glad you're here. We know you didn't do this to yourself and as soon as you tell just who it was, he will regret it!"

"He sure as hell will!" Dominique added as she walked over to the corner placing a call to Meagan.

Next, Sidney's eyes filled with water and just as she whispered the name "Vincent," *Waverly's eyes watered as well.*

Sherian not making the connection began discussing options to ensure Sidney's health was going to be the priority.

"You know, they say in cases like this when you are raped, we have to be concerned about venereal diseases and a possibility of impregnation. In fact, the Doctor wanted to give you something to abort any possible fetus, but knowing your history, I wouldn't allow it. Not without you knowing…"

Confused, Waverly looked over at Sherian shouting!

"You would allow it! Are you even hearing what the hell she just said?"

Noticing something really wrong, Dominique quickly hung up on Meagan to intervene.

"Wait – wait – wait a minute now! Can we all calm down a moment? What's all the fussing for? Someone is a little sick here!" she said pointing her head in Sidney's direction.

Now by that time Sidney had set up in the bed in an attempt to explain herself…

"Waverly, you have to believe me when I tell you; I was alone in the hospital when I took those drugs! They must have knocked me out because I remember waking up in my bed with Vincent standing over me."

Shaking her head not wanting to believe that her best friend could have slept with her husband she said,

"None of this is making any sense... Why would Vincent do those horrible things to you? I know he can be a bastard, but to brutally beat, rape and sodomize you? And, there were way more drugs in your system than you could have consumed on your own. If what you're saying is true..."

"What do you mean IF? Are you saying you don't believe me? How in the world can you believe that good-for-nothing-only interested in wetting your ass soon to be ex-husband of yours – over me! You and I go back just as far as you and his sorry ass goes! Besides, even as I sit here ashamed and humiliated by that Mother-Fucker, you somehow married, lying to you never crossed my mind! Can you say the same for him? He's always lied! Look at you, still covering for him! This is so fucking sad...And why are you looking like that?" Sidney said as she pulled Waverly's hair away from her face.

Dominique simply shook her head whispering, "Here we go again... Look Sid, you winding up here was only the icing on the cake. The last twenty-four hours have been a rollercoaster ride for all of us. Waverly's looking a bit beaten up because she has been... And by the same "Dick" that put you in here. See... That's why I prefer women! They're so much nicer to look at and they don't go around sticking their body parts in places they don't belong..."

And before she realized what she had said or who was listening, Dominique looked around stopping at Sidney then, added, "Well some of them anyway."

Shaking her head, Sidney replied, "You just cannot stop yourself can you? I'm laying here "tow-up from the floor-up" and you're still cracking jokes. Why don't all of you just go home and give me some time to myself."

Agreeing, Sherian added, "Maybe that's not a bad idea. My baby could use some rest."

"Not just them Cher – you too! I know what you're trying to do. I got the letter from Mama and I believe you Cher, but I'm just not ready to deal with that right now. I just don't need all of this..."

"Oh, I see! You're just fine! Who do you think found you? I came looking for you to make things right! I had no idea I'd find you half dead... Girl..."

"Okay – okay, let's all settle down. Sidney, Sherian has every right to be here. She's your Mother like it or not! Waverly and I are your friends. We wanted to be here and if you now need time to yourself, we will respect that. But, nothing will change. This incestuous shit will still be right here until we all look it directly in the face and fight it together. Waverly's no fool, she'll come to accept what has happened and once we find Vincent's sorry ass, we'll relocate a few of his body parts. So that only brings things full circle right back to you. I agree that you need time to think about your plans. Plans to change your life once and for all for the better... Whether we are in your life or not, isn't the issue. You must get balance within yourself. Back and forth with those drugs has got to stop or you're going to die... There! I've said all I can say. I just hope once this is all over; we can all take an early vacation... We damn sure need it," Dominique said.

Well after all that, Sherian politely left the room while Sidney laid down turning her back to them all, hurt and angry. Waverly stood there visualizing her husband of twenty years, forcing himself on her unstable otherwise happy-go-lucky friend. Poor Girl instantly became ill and ran out of the room to collect herself.

"So after all these years, this is the best we can do? All for one and one for all... What happened to support one another no matter what? You know yesterday, I visited my Aunt and believe it or not, it took me twenty years to get up the courage to face her. Well, long story short, what I thought happened between us never happened at all. We lost all that time, which cannot be replaced, because of a lie. I sure as hell hope the same thing doesn't happen to us."

And equally stubborn, Dominique went back to the windowsill, sat down and propped both feet up and waited. Sherian must have spoken to the Doctor on her way out the door because he and three other technicians accompanied by two policemen in uniform were on their way down the hall to see Sidney. And as they all disappeared into Sidney's room – one by one, Waverly hung her head partly in resentment, but mostly in shame. Girl was in tears and if things couldn't get any worse, her cell phone rang with a ring tone that indicated her son was calling. Pulling it out of her pocket, she remembered Vincent yelling, "Victor's fucking boys or boys are fucking Victor." *Whichever was the case, he implied that Victor was a homosexual.*

"Hey Beasely... Before you get into why you called, can you just tell me what happened between you and your Dad? Are you really... Are you sleeping with boys?"

"He told you huh?"

"Just answer the damned question! No lies, it's me son... your Mother."

"Yes, I am a homosexual Mother, but I'm still Victor. Dad just zapped out! He didn't even try to understand. I'm a man and I happen to be a Gay man!"

"But you never came to us..."

"I was trying to tell you the other night when we were supposed to have dinner, but you never showed up."

"I guess everyone has something hidden somewhere. Are you alright?"

"Yes, I'm fine. I spoke to Maria, are you alright?"

"Yeah, I'll be fine. But one day soon when things settle down, we're going to talk – okay?"

Smiling he answered, "I can't wait!"

Returning the gesture, Waverly said, "I'll bet you can't. I love you."

"I love you too Mother..."

A comforting moment to ease the tension... Being preoccupied by her phone call, Waverly never noticed Meagan walking up behind her...

"That sure sounds interesting."

Startled, Waverly replied, "Girl that was Beasley... He's going through something too... no let me rephrase that...He's a homosexual and I'm going to have to work on some acceptance in that area. You know, at least I can try and understand him."

Taking Waverly by the hand, walking her over to the glass window which allowed them to see into Sidney's room, she leaned her head on Waverly's shoulder and said, "See our Girlfriend over there… Besides the fact that the staff who is taking care of her are also her colleagues and I have no idea what all those people are saying to her… Sid may be the youngest, but even in the mist of her storm, she's still standing stronger than any one of us. Now I don't know about you, but I sure as hell don't know any perfect people. Maybe there was a part she played in winding up here, but who's to say… She was not in her right frame of mind. Losing someone you thought was your Mother, only to learn that your older sister is actually your Mom… I'm not sure what I would have done. Before my Dad died, he would always say, "Walk a mile in my shoes before sentencing me." Today, I can say I fully understand that comment. So when you say things like your son's a homosexual and you're going to try to understand him… Acceptance is the only key to loving him. Understanding comes when you too have walked in his shoes…"

"Still friends?"

"Until the end."

"So what do you say we go in there and work this mess out…"

Pausing, Waverly replied, "Yeah…sure…You go ahead in first, give me a few minutes and I'll be right behind you."

So giving Meagan half smile, Waverly turned away just as her cell phone rang again signaling her that it was an urgent call. Checking the caller I.D. first, she saw it was Keith Sheppard and immediately answered.

"Hi…"

"Hey, are you still at the hospital?"

"Yes, I am and I have great news… Sidney's out of the coma."

"That's great. I'm happy to hear that. However, there's something I need to talk to you about and unfortunately, it's about your husband."

"So talk…"

"Well, it's kind of touchy, so I'd prefer to discuss this face to face. I'm on my way through the doors right now… Can you take a minute?"

"I suppose I can…"

Now besides not wanting to be informed of anymore wrong doing by her husband of twenty years, coming to terms with the fact that she once loved him made matters much worse. It was difficult to hear the underlying truth about her husband. But, I believe Mr. Sheppard knew more than he was taking credit for and could feel Waverly's pain... So with gentle hands, Keith disclosed the new photos of Vincent and Sidney. He had no idea that this was the Girlfriend Waverly was in the Hospital to see. Attempting to hold back her tears, Waverly stood tall as she received confirmation of Sidney's story.

"I feel like such a fool..."

Keith went on to say how the good doctor had been taken into custody and the arraignment would be at noon that day. As for Waverly Corrine, battling the truth about her twisted life was the only thing left for her to do. They say when the pain of remaining the same is greater than change, the act of change takes on a new form. I believe that's just what Girl did when she took those undisputed photos from Keith to give them to the police as proof of her husband act of raping her best friend. Now maybe the pictures alone wouldn't convict Vincent, but Waverly knew they'd at least prove he was indeed the last one with her...

"You've been such a great help through all of this... I guess I'd really need to say – thank you."

Smiling, Keith replied, "You already have..."

Returning the gesture she added, "Well how about if I want to say it again?"

"Sounds like a plan to me..."

"Then I'll call you later..."

"Can't wait..."

And after kissing him right on the lips, slightly placing her tongue in his mouth, she whispered, "Good-bye Mr. Sheppard..."

"Good-bye Waverly Corrine..."

While walking away, resisting the urge to look back, she couldn't help but thank God for all of those crazy years with her soon to be ex-husband. For if it had not been for that, how could she have ever met Keith Sheppard. It's said, if you look really hard, you can find the blessing in the worse situation. I just hope for these four girls, the worse is over and they too can find the blessing in all of it.

Chapter
Fourteen

Still Friends?

*A*s *Waverly entered Sidney's Hospital room, she couldn't help but notice the up beat spirit hovering in the air. Meagan and Dominique were sitting in the windowsill smiling as if the joke was on her, while Sidney was setting up in the bed, talking on the phone like she was chatting with a long lost friend.*

"So what's going on?" she asked with her brows raised, looking at Meagan and Dominique.

Just then, Sidney hung up the phone, smiling from ear to ear shouting, "I did it! I did it! And I have to admit, it does feel better."

So again Waverly asked, "What in the world is going on? Am I in the wrong room?"

"Of course you're not in the wrong room silly. But I believe Sid has something she wants to tell you..."

"Why thank you Meagan... First of all, that was Cher on the phone and although I won't be calling her Mother anytime soon, we're going to work things out!"

"That's wonderful news Sidney. I don't think I could live if Victor chose not to forgive me, if I'd done something terrible to him and believe me; I've done some things..."

Interrupting Dominique said, "Will you let the Girl finish Judge Judy!"

"Anyhow, I've decided that no matter how long it might take or what emotions we may go through, I'll be here when you're ready. I also know I had no control over what happened between me and your husband. All I can say is that I'm sorry for the pain it has caused you. He used me to hurt you... It is the only thing that makes sense. Dominique told me what happened to you. I was just in the wrong place at the wrong time."

Waverly then started to cry...

"You know... I was just thanking God for allowing something good to come out of all those years of marriage. And now for you to tell me you're sorry for *my* pain... It blows my mind. I know it wasn't your fault Sid. In fact, I have proof right here that he was the one who entered your apartment with you. But I didn't need it. I believed you the moment you said Vincent. The coward in me just didn't want to believe that I have been married to an animal all these years and didn't have a clue... Can you ever forgive me? Will you please forgive me for showing any doubt?"

And interrupting again Dominique shouted,

"Of course she forgives your crazy-ass! Now let's have group hug and plan a much needed early vacation!"

"Hell yes, I'm all for that! Please forgive me but... I just have to add that the thought of you sleeping with Dr. Vincent Zachary Simmons – my goodness; that's just too nasty for words."

"Well Meagan Simone, if you swear to never say it again, I'll promise to stay away from Drake..."

"You got yourself a deal sister!"

"So where do you suppose we should all go once I get the hell up out of here?"

"I really don't give a shit as long as Hannah can come!"

"Oh fuck, here we go again! Let's just get it right before we leave... If we have to double up again, I'm not sleeping with you guys! I'm not into Asian or Black women!" shouted Waverly.

Looking around, knowing she had been cornered once again by her witty friend, Dominique replied, "We know... you like Spanish flies!!!"

Now that was not funny...

The End